Under a Veiled Moon

Also available by Karen Odden

The Inspector Corravan Mysteries
Down a Dark River

A Trace of Deceit
A Dangerous Duet
A Lady in the Smoke

UNDER
A
VEILED MOON

AN INSPECTOR CORRAVAN MYSTERY

───◆◆◆───

Karen Odden

CROOKED
LANE

NEW YORK

Copyright © 2022 by Karen Odden

All rights reserved.

Published in the United States by Crooked Lane Books, an imprint of The Quick Brown Fox & Company LLC.

Crooked Lane Books and its logo are trademarks of The Quick Brown Fox & Company LLC.

Library of Congress Catalog-in-Publication data available upon request.

ISBN (hardcover): 978-1-63910-119-1
ISBN (ebook): 978-1-63910-120-7

Cover design by Melanie Sun

Printed in the United States.

www.crookedlanebooks.com

Crooked Lane Books
34 West 27th St., 10th Floor
New York, NY 10001

First Edition: October 2022

10 9 8 7 6 5 4 3 2 1

To George, Julia, and Kyle, always,
and to kind and encouraging teachers,
wherever we may find them

We are as clouds that veil the midnight moon;
How restlessly they speed, and gleam, and quiver,
Streaking the darkness radiantly!—yet soon
Night closes round, and they are lost for ever:
—Percy Bysshe Shelley, "Mutability" (1816)

"Youth is a blunder; manhood a struggle; old age a regret."
—Benjamin Disraeli, *Coningsby* (1844)

"Then rose from stream to sky a wild farewell,
Then shrieked the timid, and stood still the brave."

THE LOSS
OF THE
PRINCESS ALICE

SALOON STEAMER in the THAMES, Sept. 3rd, 1878.

AN AUTHENTIC NARRATIVE by a SURVIVOR, not hitherto published.

HEARTRENDING DETAILS—FACTS NOT MADE PUBLIC—NOBLE EFFORTS TO SAVE LIFE—ROBBING THE DEAD—PARTICULARS AS TO LOST, SAVED, AND MISSING—PLAN OF THE LOCALITY.

SKETCHES BY AN EYE WITNESS.

BEAUTIFUL POEM, specially written on the event,
NOW FIRST PUBLISHED.

MEMORIAL FOR ALL TIME OF THIS FEARFUL CALAMITY.

WHOLESALE OF J. F. NASH, 26, FLEET STREET, E.C.

Select Character List

Wapping River Police

Michael Corravan, acting superintendent
Charlie Dower, scribe
Sergeant Andrews
Sergeant Lipp
Sergeant Trent

Scotland Yard

C. E. Howard Vincent, director of Scotland Yard
Gordon Stiles, Scotland Yard inspector and Corravan's former
    partner
Sergeant Hammond

Princess Alice

Captain William Grinstead
Frederick Boncy, chief steward
Constable Briscoe, passenger
John Eyres, helmsman
Ned Wilkins, crew member

Bywell Castle

Captain Thomas Harrison
Henry John Belding, mate
Peter Dimelow, engineer
John Conway, helmsman/river pilot
George Purcell, stoker

Other Characters

Ma Doyle, Corravan's adoptive mother in Whitechapel
Colin Doyle, Ma Doyle's son
Elsie Doyle, Ma Doyle's daughter (Colin's twin)
Belinda Gale, novelist and playwright
Harry Lish, Ma Doyle's nephew who lives with Corravan
Tom Flynn, newspaperman at the *Falcon*

Winthrop Rotherly, commissioner of Wrecks
Edgar Quartermain, head of the Parliamentary Commission,
  Rotherly's superior
Mr. Wood, surveyor of Moorings
Lord Baynes-Hill, MP and barrister
Archibald Houghton, MP and manufacturer
Quentin Atwell, author and doctor
Seamus O'Hagan, former boxing hall owner in Whitechapel
James McCabe, head of the Cobbwallers
Finn Riley, member of the Cobbwallers
Timothy Luby, head of the Irish Republican Brotherhood

CHAPTER 1

London
September 1878

We all carry pieces of our past with us. Sometimes they're shiny and worthy as new half crowns in our pockets. Sometimes they're bits of lint or scraps of paper shredded beyond use. Plenty of my memories carry a stab of regret or a burn of shame with them, and honestly, there are times when I wonder how we all bloody well live with the fool things we've done.

I've made a fair number of mistakes since I first donned a Metropolitan Police uniform in Lambeth, over twelve years ago now. Investigating murders and missing people isn't a task for those who aren't willing to go down the wrong alley three or four times before finding the proper one. But those errors are a result of making a poor guess based on limited knowledge, and while they may cause a few sleepless nights, they can be set aside.

The mistakes that feel less forgivable are those that hurt someone you love. Worse still is when you discover your error only years later. Often, there's nothing to be done. Too much time has passed to make amends. And those mistakes—ach, it's bloody difficult to forgive yourself when you should've known better, should've known to pick your head up and cast about to see what might happen as a result of your actions. Perhaps there's no easy way to learn that lesson, other than failing to do it once and discovering later just what it cost.

Sometimes, during the evenings we're together, my Belinda reads aloud from whatever book is occupying her at the moment.

One night she related a Greek myth about a man whose wife was killed by a snakebite. By virtue of his music, he weaseled his way into the underworld and convinced the king of Hades to release her. The king had one condition, however, of the rescue: neither the man nor his wife could look backward as they were leaving. And what did the fool do? He turned back to be sure his wife was still with him. He couldn't help himself, poor bloke. So the mouth of hell opened up, and she vanished forever.

But perhaps we can't always help what we do in a moment of crushing fear.

When I was nineteen, scared out of my wits and fleeing Whitechapel with only a bag of clothes and a small pouch of coins Ma Doyle thrust into my hand, I didn't look back. Unlike the man in the myth, I should have, though.

Perhaps then hell would not have opened up around me thirteen years later.

★　★　★

On the first day of September, I woke to pale autumn sunlight and a feeling of well-being. It didn't happen often, and it took a few moments to recall the cause. I lay still, listening to the Sunday quiet of my house, to a lone costermonger's wheels creaking and rumbling over the cobbles outside, and the bells from St. Barnabas's tolling from the next street over. I no longer attended church, but I did believe in God—a reasonable and just God, although sometimes the world twisted justice around, like a boat line hitched badly around a metal cleat so it emerged from the knot in a direction you didn't expect.

As I stared at the ceiling, I collected my thoughts with some satisfaction. I'd been acting superintendent at Wapping River Police for three months now, and we'd just resolved a case involving smugglers who'd been bribing Custom House men to underweight the scales, to avoid paying proper taxes. It had occupied my every breath for the past four weeks, and now I felt a sense of relief, like a weighted yoke off the back of my neck, as I always did when an important case ended. The newspapers had even printed something good about the police yesterday as a result. God knows we needed it. Sometimes I still cringed at the memories of the corruption trial last autumn, with mobs cursing us plainclothes men for being frauds and cheats, and newspaper headlines proclaiming how London would be better off if we were all at the bottom of the Thames. But with the river murders of last April resolved and this smuggling case concluded, it seemed the police were slowly earning back public trust. Of course, the stories published about our successes were full of inaccuracies, and by omitting any reference to the tiresome inquiries, the endless walking, and the misleading clues, they were nowhere near the whole truth, but at least they painted the police in a satisfactory light.

The door to Harry's bedroom, next to mine, opened and closed, and as I heard the boy start down the stairs, I slid out of bed. The coals in my bedroom stove had burnt to ash, and the room was cool, with a dampness that lingered after a rainy August.

Standing at the window in my nightshirt, I looked across the way at the two-story red-brick terraced houses, built cheek by jowl, mirror images of those on my side of the street. The sunlight, golden as a well-baked loaf of bread, inched down from the roofline and struck the upper windows, flashing a shine that made me squint. It was a pleasure to think I had no plan for the day but to visit the Doyles for Sunday tea. What with the smugglers and my new responsibilities at Wapping, it had been over a month since I'd seen Ma, Elsie, and Colin—longer than I liked.

From downstairs came the sound of our kettle shrieking.

Harry would be preparing tea for himself and coffee for me. My brew was a holdover from the tastes of the previous century, I knew, but I couldn't abide weak liquids in the morning. I'd taught Harry how to make my coffee properly after he said he'd do whatever necessary to keep me from growling at him.

Harry Lish had come to live with me here in Soho six months ago, after his father died, his mother having passed away years before. Harry was Ma Doyle's nephew, but as she'd told me when he arrived at her house in Whitechapel, he didn't belong there. His speech was too well schooled and his manners more Mayfair than Merseyside. Although barely sixteen, Harry was determined to study medicine, and I'd found a place for him at St. Anne's Hospital with my friend James Everett, a physician and surgeon who supervised the ward for brain injuries and mental disorders. Harry was leaving the next day to spend a fortnight or so observing in an Edinburgh hospital, a special opportunity arranged by James, who found in Harry an eager and intuitive student.

I pulled on my shirt and a pair of trousers with the special side pocket for my truncheon, a vestige of my days in uniform. It being Sunday, I was off duty, but the Doyles lived in the heart of Whitechapel, and there was no point in being foolhardy. I splashed water on my face and ran a comb through my hair before stowing my truncheon and heading down the stairs.

"Good morning, Mickey," Harry said as I entered the kitchen.

"Morning." I accepted the cup he pushed across the table. The pocketbook he always took to the hospital lay beside his saucer. "Are you not coming with me to the Doyles's?"

He winced an apology. "I would, but there's a special procedure."

"On a Sunday?"

He nodded, his brown eyes keen. "Dr. Everett is performing a craniotomy on a woman with blood on the brain."

The coffee suddenly tasted sour. But far be it from me to dampen his scientific ardor.

"You'll only be watching, I assume?" I asked.

Regret flickered over his features. "Observing from the balcony." Then he brightened. "Richard will be assisting, though."

Richard was a second-year medical student at University College here in London, who worked at the hospital and had taken Harry under his wing.

"How did it happen?" I asked. "Blood on the brain?"

"She fell off a ladder," he replied. "If Dr. Everett doesn't operate, the blood will continue to press on the internal parts and organs." He touched his fingertips to the side of his head. "She's already having secondary symptoms—seizures, confusion, and the like."

"Ah. What time is it? The operation?"

He upended his cup to drink the last of the tea. "Ten o'clock, but I want to be there for the anesthesia."

"Of course." *What could be more entertaining?* I thought as I raised my own cup to hide my smile.

He reached for his coat. "Besides, I doubt Aunt Mary will expect me. I saw them on Tuesday. My aunt and Elsie, I should say," he amended as he thrust his arm into a sleeve. "Colin was out somewhere . . . as usual."

In his voice was an undertone—hurt, strained, subdued—that could have served as a signal of something amiss. But it was one of those moments when you must be paying proper attention to take it in, when you must be standing quite still. And we weren't. Harry was dashing up the stairs, calling over his shoulder, "Wait for me—I'll be right down," and I was rummaging on the table amid some newspapers for my pocketbook—where was the bloody thing?—and the warning went unheeded.

I swallowed down the last of my coffee. Harry did well by me, leaving no grounds in the bottom, meticulous in a way that boded well for his success in a profession that demanded precision. With my pocketbook found, I shrugged into my coat, and when Harry reappeared on the stairs, his boots sounding quick on the treads, I waved him outside and locked the front door. We walked to the corner, where we bid farewell and separated. I watched him, hatless, his lanky boyish frame hurrying along, not wanting to miss the thrills to be found in the medical amphitheater.

I found myself grinning as I turned away, for I liked the lad, and we'd come to understand each other. Belinda says that in our both being orphans and clever, as well as in some of our less desirable traits such as our prickly aversion to owing anyone anything, we're more alike than I'm willing to admit. There's part of me that agrees with her, though Harry and I have our differences. Sometimes I wonder where I'd be if I'd had Harry's book learning or someone overseeing my education and guiding my professional progress the way James does for Harry. Oh, my real mother had taught me to read before I lost her, and working at Ma Doyle's store had made me quick at my sums. But every so often Harry would let slip a phrase in French or Latin, or he'd mention some curious bit of history, much the way James or my former partner Stiles does, not to show off his learning but just because it floats around in his brain. And I'd think about how we can't be more than our past permits us.

Then again, my advancement within the Metropolitan Police has been my own doing. There's some satisfaction in that too.

CHAPTER 2

It was a fine day for a walk, and I headed to my favorite pub—the only one within a mile of my house that served a satisfying wedge of shepherd's pie in a proper crust. It was where I usually spent part of my Sunday, with the papers, and I knew the Doyles wouldn't expect me before two or three at the earliest.

My favorite table was occupied by two men, but I chose another near the window where a newspaper was lying, its ruffled pages evidence of it having already been read at least once. I flipped it over to find the *Times* masthead and the bold headline "Sittingbourne Disaster," with a drawing below it of a railway train with the engine, tender, and two cars tipped over on their sides and the usual chaos of people and their belongings flung from carriages.

I let out a groan.

Sittingbourne was fifty miles east of London, on the south side of the Thames, not far from where the river let out to the North Sea. I scanned the article, but there weren't many facts provided other than it had happened the previous night, August 31, on the London, Chatham and Dover line, when an express train bringing trippers back from Sheerness and elsewhere had run off the rails. It seemed to be the result of either eroded ground or a rotted railway tie that destabilized the iron rail above it—the same problem that had caused the disaster at Morpeth last March, as well as half a dozen other accidents that had occurred around England in the past few years. Early reports indicated three dead and sixty-two injured, with numbers expected to increase. The article closed with the usual gloomy declarations about how, until railways are held to a standard of safety by Parliament, accidents such as this would continue to plague travelers.

I stood and went to another table, where I found a second paper whose account included the additional facts that, for some unknown reason, the railway train had been on the ancillary line instead of the primary line, approximately one hundred yards from the station; and five passengers, not three, had been killed. This version also included, on an inside page, lurid descriptions and illustrations of mangled bodies and children's toys strewn among the broken carriages.

Those poor families, I thought. *What a wretched ending to a pleasant excursion.*

As I refolded the paper, worry nicked at my nerves. Belinda would be traveling home from Edinburgh by train in a few days. She'd been visiting her cousin for a month, which was the longest I'd gone without seeing her these three years since a burglary had first brought me to her home. The thought of her in a railway disaster carved a cold, hollow space in my chest.

But even as I imagined it, I dismissed my worry as nonsensi-cal. Belinda had made this trip dozens of times, and the line from Edinburgh was one of the newest and safest. Besides, the newspaper's pessimism notwithstanding, parliament *had* mandated new safety devices and procedures. No doubt this Sittingbourne disaster would require yet another Parliamentary Commission, and the Railways Inspection Department would be saddled with the task of providing weeks of testimony and filing endless reports. I didn't envy them.

After finishing my pie, I took my time reading the remainder of the papers, then rose, shrugged into my coat, and left the pub, strolling east until I crossed Leman Street into Whitechapel. Many of the narrow, pocked streets were without signs, but I'd grown up among these crooked alleys, with buildings whose upper floors overhung the unpaved passages and oddly shaped courtyards, and I tacked left and right, left and right, until I reached the street with Ma Doyle's shop. It always opened at one o'clock on Sundays, after Roman mass, and as I anticipated, there was the usual bustle around the door.

What I didn't expect were the wooden planks that covered one of the windows.

Alarm pinched at the top of my spine and spread across my shoulders.

Burglary wasn't uncommon in Whitechapel, but we'd never been the target. Usually it happened to businesses that foolishly kept wares in the front window overnight, or those whose owners were unpopular or had some sort of falling-out with the Cobbwallers, the Irish gang from Seven Dials that had extended its reach east and now ran gambling, extortion, and the like here. I couldn't imagine any of these were true in Ma's case. She was known to be a good neighbor, free with a cup o' tea and sympathy. As for James McCabe's Cobbwaller gang, Ma was too astute to fall on the wrong side of them.

Stepping close to one of the two remaining windows, I observed the shop's interior. Everything seemed as usual: a dozen people, still in their church clothes, chattering and laughing while choosing their candles and tea and sundries, and Ma's friend's son, Eaman Casey, behind the counter, wrapping up a parcel in brown paper. I'd only met him twice, but he seemed a decent bloke of about twenty-three, smart and sensible. From a peculiar quality in the air when Elsie was present, I gathered Eaman was sweet on her, though I'd yet to discern her feelings. I watched as he counted out coins, liking that he took the time to talk with one of Ma's oldest friends, bending his head attentively as she replied.

A set of indoor stairs led directly from the shop's storeroom to the living quarters above, but rather than make my way through the crowd, I went around back to the outdoor stairs. The bottom swaybacked step was newly loose, shifting under my boot, but the rest of the treads were firmly in place, though they creaked all the way up, just as when I lived here. I knocked twice and inserted my key in the lock.

Even as I did so, I heard the twins, Colin and Elsie, their voices raised as they talked over each other—Elsie with a sharp edge of frustration, Colin growling in reply. *Odd,* I thought as I pushed open the door. Since they were children, they'd baited each other and teased, but I'd never known them to quarrel.

Colin sat in a kitchen chair tilted backward, the heel of one heavy boot hooked over the rung. He glared up at Elsie, who stood across the table, her hand clutching a faded towel at her hip, her chin set in a way I recognized.

"Hullo," I said. "What's the matter?"

Both heads swiveled to me, and in unison, they muttered, "Nothing."

They could have still been five, caught spooning the jam out of the jar Ma hid behind the flour tin. Except that under the stubble of his whiskers, there was a puffiness along Colin's cheek that appeared to be the remnants of a bruise.

Colin *thunked* the front legs of the chair onto the floor and pushed away from the table. "I got somethin' to do." He took his coat off the rack—not his old faded one, I noticed, but a new one—and stalked out the door, pulling it closed behind him.

I raised my eyebrows and turned to Elsie. She grimaced. "He's just bein' an eejit, like most men." Her voice lacked its usual good humor; she was genuinely angry.

Jaysus, I thought. *What's happened?*

But I'd give Elsie a moment. "Where's Ma?"

"Went down to the shop for some tea." She stepped to the sideboard and moved the kettle to the top of the stove. The handle caught her sleeve, pulling it back far enough that I caught sight of a white bandage.

"Did you hurt your wrist?"

She tugged the sleeve down. "Ach, I just fell on the stairs. Clumsy of me."

The broken window and Colin's abrupt departure had been enough to alert me to something amiss. Even without those signs, though, I wouldn't have believed her. I knew the shape a lie took in her voice.

"No, you didn't," I said.

Her back was to me, and she spoke over her shoulder. "It's nothing, Mickey."

I approached and took her left elbow gently in mine to turn her. "Let me see."

Reluctantly, she let me unwrap the flannel. Diagonal across her wrist was a bruise such as a truncheon or a pipe might leave, purple and yellowing at the edges.

I looked up. "Who did this?" My voice was hoarse.

Her eyes, blue as mine, stared back. "Mickey, don't look like that. It was dark, and I doubt he did it on purpose."

"Jaysus, Elsie." I let go of her, so she could rewrap it. *"Who?"*

"I don't know! I was walking home from Mary's house on Wednesday night, and before I knew it, twenty lads were around me, fightin' and brawlin', and I jumped out of the way, but one of them hit my wrist, and I fell."

"What were you doing walking alone after dark? Where was Colin?"

She gave a disparaging "pfft." "As if I'd know. Some nights he doesn't come home until late. Or not at all."

Harry's words came back to me: *"Out . . . as usual."*

I cast my mind back to my own recent visits. Colin had often been absent, partly because he'd been working on the construction of the new embankment, but that had ended in July. So where was he spending his time now? And where had he earned the money for his new coat?

We both heard Ma's footsteps on the inside stairs.

"Don't tell Ma," Elsie said hurriedly, her voice low. The bandage was completely hidden by her sleeve. "She has enough to worry about. Swear, Mickey."

Even as I promised, I wondered what else was worrying Ma. But as the door at the top of the inner stairs opened, I had my smile ready.

Ma emerged, carrying a packet of tea from the shop. "Ah, Mickey! I'm glad ye came." Her face shone with genuine warmth, and she smoothed her coppery hair back from her temple. Her eyes flicked around the room, landing on Elsie. "Colin left?" The brightness in her expression dimmed.

"Just now," Elsie replied. Their gazes held, and with the unfailing instinct that develops in anyone who grew up trying to perceive trouble before it struck, I sensed meaning in that silent exchange. But before I could decipher it, Elsie shrugged, and Ma turned to me, her hazel eyes appraising.

"You look less wraithy than usual." She reached up to pat my cheek approvingly. "Elsie, fetch the preserves. I'll put the water on."

"I'll do it, Ma." I went to the stove, tonged in a few lumps of coal from the scuttle and shut the metal door with a clang. As Elsie sliced the bread, I filled the kettle and Ma took down three cups and saucers from the shelf.

The tension I sensed amid my family derived from something drifting in the deep current, not bobbing along the surface, driven by a single day's wind and sun. Something had changed. I wanted to know what it was, and I began with the obvious.

"What happened to the shop window?" I asked.

"Ach," Ma replied as she ferried plates, knives, cups, and the board with the sliced bread to the table. "It was broken last week. The glazier's comin' tomorrow to fix it."

I drew a chair out from the table, and as I sat, one leg jiggled under my weight. I shifted my position gingerly, wary of it collapsing altogether, and felt a momentary annoyance with Colin. He knew how to fix a bloody chair. I'd taught him myself. Ma shouldn't even have to ask.

Elsie brought the teapot and poured for each of us. "Sorry, do you have the wobbler?"

"It's no matter," I said. "I can fix it later."

"Oh nae. Colin'll do it," Ma said as she settled herself in the chair opposite. "He's been meanin' to, only he's been busy."

Elsie's mouth tightened with doubt as she set the teapot on the trivet and took her seat, but I knew better than to ask about Colin. Ma never discussed one twin in front of the other.

"When was the window broken? What time of day?" I asked.

"Tuesday night, late," Elsie replied. "We heard the smashes and shouts from our beds. We both stayed awake the rest of the night, watching in case they torched it, but they just left."

This had me sitting bolt upright in my chair. "Why didn't you send for me?"

"Ach," Ma said. "No one was hurt, and you've plenty on your shoulders already."

Elsie opened her mouth and shut it again. If it were up to her, I'd have been told. But Ma didn't like to make a fuss.

"But why our shop?" I asked.

"It wasn't only ours," Elsie corrected me. "Next morning, we found there were four others, not to mention the man who was killed."

Word travels fast within Whitechapel, but it hadn't made it to Wapping. Then again, I'd spent all my time of late at the Custom House and Records Office upriver, and crime here was the province of H Division.

"Was it anyone we know?"

Elsie shook her head. "*I* didn't. Name of Sean Doone."

I'd heard the name Doone all my life, but I didn't know this man. "Where were the other shops?"

"Along Wickly Street," Elsie said. "On the way to Boyd."

No wonder I hadn't seen them on my way here. Wickly began at the next corner, running to the south and east, and I had come from the other direction. But the shops on Wickly were all owned by Irish. The thought brought a fresh wave of unease. "Have the police been?"

Elsie replied, "Well, o' course, but no one'll talk to them."

Ma brushed some stray breadcrumbs from the table onto her palm and dropped them onto her saucer. "They stole some candles and sugar. Nothin' even worth mentionin'. It's over and done." Her lips pursed, and Elsie and I both took the hint. Ma didn't want to discuss it further; she wanted us to enjoy our tea.

"Aye," Elsie agreed as she spread jam on her bread. "The costliest thing was the window, smashed to pieces, a bloody bother to sweep up." Her mouth twitched slyly. "Should've had a starglazer, wouldn't 'a been so messy."

I recognized the gibe about my former thieving days for what it was, and I played along, grinning and flapping my napkin halfheartedly in Elsie's direction. "I saw Eaman at the counter just now. Is he doing well?" I asked, sly in my turn.

Elsie's cheeks pinked, and she shot me a glare.

"Eaman is doin' very well," Ma said with the good-humored air of halting a squabble before it began. "He manages the shop and our stock very capably without me havin' to say a word, and folks like him."

Elsie peered at us over the rim of her cup. "'Cause he lets them natter on! He listened to Mrs. Connelly for twenty minutes the other day, talking about her bird."

Ma gave a rap of rebuke on the table. "Mind you, that canary is all she has to talk to, now that her daughter's married and gone." She stirred in a lump of sugar. "Eaman's just bein' kind."

"I know," Elsie replied. "And all the old biddies like it."

I raised an eyebrow. "And you?"

"Ah, hush," she said as she rose to refill the teapot from the kettle on the stove.

I happened to glance at Ma, and to my surprise she wasn't smiling at our bit of chaffing. She was watching Elsie, and whatever Ma was thinking deepened the vertical lines between her brows. A quick glance at Elsie's hands, usually so deft, fumbling with the handle of the kettle, and I knew I'd stumbled into what rivermen call a "muddy eddy." I sensed Ma didn't mind the thought of Eaman and Elsie together. But could this have something to do with why Colin and Elsie had been fighting? Did Colin not approve of Eaman? Or of Elsie marrying and leaving home? But Ma was no Mrs. Connelly. She wouldn't be left talking to a bird.

Ma broke the silence cheerfully: "We saw Harry for tea on Tuesday. Did he tell you? He was all in a dither about a man who fell from a railway carriage and broke his skull open. That boy does love his work at the hospital."

"Rather too much." Elsie returned to the table and set the teapot on a doubled towel. "He likes to tell us how scrambled the brains looked, while we're eating."

I chuckled. "James is sending him to Edinburgh to observe surgery for a fortnight and to a sanatorium in Surrey afterward. He says Harry's a natural talent, wants to send him up to the Royal College in Edinburgh in a year. Says he'll pay the tuition."

Ma's eyebrows rose. "He's taken quite an interest. I'm ever so grateful."

"He hasn't any sons of his own, has he?" Elsie asked before she popped the last bit of bread with jam into her mouth.

"No," I said. I watched Elsie out of the corner of my eye as I sipped. Blue eyes, delicate features, thick braids of auburn hair coiled around her head, to keep them out of her face. She was nineteen and pretty, verging on beautiful. Plenty of young women her age were married by now. Did she truly fancy Eaman, or was there someone else? The detective in me couldn't help but wonder, even if these people were my family. Then again, as Belinda says, family members can be the most inscrutable of all.

"Elsie, love," Ma said, her voice easy, "seein' as you've finished your tea, would you run down and spell Eaman for a bit?"

Elsie glanced at the clock, which showed half past three, and rose agreeably. "Of course, Ma." As she headed for the door in the hallway, Ma watched her, smiling with a wistful fondness.

The door closed behind Elsie, and I asked, "Is it serious then, between Eaman and Elsie?"

"Ach, it's hard to say. For what it's worth, I like him for her. He's a good bloke." She grimaced, her eyebrows aloft. "Not like the rest of the lot." Her tone suggested there were dozens.

"How many are there?" I asked, half in jest.

She waved a hand. "Paddy Coughlin, Finn Riley, Angus McKay, Marcus McBride—you might remember the oldest McBride? John was your age. Married now himself, to Mary Wallace."

I nodded.

"Half of the lads hereabouts are Cobbwallers," she continued disparagingly, "and the rest are young fools with nary a thought in their heads but for cards and drinking their wages." She adjusted her cup on the saucer. "If I had to guess, I'd say Eaman'd be her choice. Only he's a considerin' sort. Not that he doesn't love her—I think he does—but he's not one to give pain to either of them by jumping in without proper thought."

"What's worrying you, then?" I asked. "Is it Colin?" As she hesitated, a sudden clatter followed by angry shouts rose from the street, and her gaze shifted to the window above the sink. The voices faded, and when it seemed no further noise was forthcoming, I asked, "Or is it the shops and the dead man?"

She sighed. "The Chapel has changed, Mickey."

"How?"

"There's alwus been some ill feeling toward us in London, of course, but not here. Even with the few folks who weren't Irish, we all got by together. Now, we've folks coming in from Russia and Poland and—" She waved her hand toward the window. "Goodness knows, I don't blame 'em for coming. They wouldn't be flocking to us if they could make a living where they come from, but I can't imagine they're finding it easy here either."

"There's not enough work?" I asked.

"Nae." She winced. "Not to mention those bloody handbills and advertisements. Seems they're everywhere these past few months, even more than before."

I knew which ones she meant. The ones that offered positions, but with "NINA" at the top: *No Irish need apply*. "Is that why Colin's angry?"

"Plenty of 'em feel the same, Mickey. There's day work at the docks, same as always, but he's not getting more'n a day or two a week now."

I felt a prick of relief. This at least was something I could fix. "I could find him something elsewhere."

"I was plannin' to ask ye," she admitted. "And perhaps you could remind him how you were able to make a fresh start in a different part o' London."

"Do you think he'd move?"

"I don't know, Mickey. But every year he seems . . ." She looked down at her rough, reddened hands, one on either side of the saucer with the empty cup. "Less happy. Ever since Pat died."

At Pat's name, the breath stuck in my lungs, and I had to ease it out. "I know Colin took it hard."

Her eyes still lowered, Ma nodded. She rarely mentioned either of her dead sons, Francis or Pat. I never knew Francis, the eldest, for I'd been taken in by the Doyles after he died, but Pat was my age, close as a brother, and we'd lived together, worked as a pair on the docks, and watched each other's backs. He'd been killed in a stupid, senseless knife fight two years after I left Whitechapel.

With a sigh, she met my gaze and I saw her grief, an old, sorry ache that mirrored mine.

I swallowed. "If Colin's not being hired for dock work, what is he doing, now that the embankment is built?"

"He doesn't talk to me much."

"Does he talk to Elsie?"

"No more'n he can help." She gave a wry look. "But she's harder to shake off."

I could believe that. "I'll speak to him," I said. "When I arrived, he and Elsie were arguing, and he stalked out. Didn't seem like he had much interest in seeing me."

Her face fell at that, and I could have kicked myself for saying so. Silently, she pushed back from the table and carried the tea things to the sideboard, where she capped the jam and rewrapped the remaining bread in brown paper. Then she opened the cupboard to retrieve her wooden sewing box and a blue skirt that was probably Elsie's, along with some socks and a pair of Colin's trousers. She resumed her seat at the table, spread the skirt across her lap with the hem uppermost, threaded her needle, tied a knot, and pieced together two edges of a rip. "Now, let's have a proper visit," she said with a smile.

Longing to undo my blunder, I steered the conversation toward Harry and his successful apprenticeship at the hospital, and for the next hour or two, our conversation rambled from news about Ma's friends to the parishioners and priests at St. Patrick's and my own work, which always furnished plenty of amusing and peculiar stories. Ma laughed to the point of tears at my description of a raid on a brothel by the Yard the previous week, when three men tore out of the back door in the only clothes they managed to snatch up—the prostitutes' skirts, hoisted up around their middles.

"Bless you, Mickey," she said, dabbing at her eyes with the edge of her apron. Then she settled the last mended sock on the pile and rose to put the sewing box away. "You always could tell a story."

"You taught me," I replied.

She waved off the praise with a deprecating smile, but we both knew it was the truth.

My own mum read to me from books, but not the Irish tales Ma told as we'd all gather on her bed at night—Elsie, Colin, Pat, and I. Ma had a knack for sending words spinning in the air like coins, shining enough to make us forget that we might not have eaten quite as much as we wished for supper. Her voice sank low for the giant warriors Cuchulain and Fionn mac Cumhaill and lilted for the fairies who tormented Johnny Friel. It was only later that I realized those stories sprung inside me a small, secret pride in being Irish. In one of my favorite tales, the giant Fionn mac Cumhaill strode across mountains, dragging his enormous club, to kill a lesser giant, Cuchulain, at his house. Cuchulain's clever wife, Una, told her husband to climb into the baby's bed, so when Fionn mac Cumhaill arrived and Una asked him to do her the favor of checking on the baby, Fionn backed out of the house straightaway, assuming a fully grown Cuchulain would naturally be ten times the baby's size.

The Irish characters were powerful and clever—and foolish sometimes too, but Ma's stories were always brilliant, hewing to a taut line, suspenseful and surprising by turns. Belinda said once that my listening to Ma's stories was a fine apprenticeship for writing the final reports for my cases, and perhaps she was right. Except that for me, events weren't presented from the beginning the way Ma told them—or the way Belinda wrote her novels, for that matter. My investigations usually began somewhere in the middle, with pieces plopping in helter-skelter, like heavy raindrops around a boat in the river.

A fog-heavy dusk had fallen, and by the darkened window, I dried the cups as Ma washed them.

"How is your Mrs. Gale?" she asked.

The Doyles knew about Belinda, though they hadn't met her yet. Indeed, as a result of Belinda's promise to her mistrustful and protective father on his deathbed, we'd been very discreet for nearly three years. It had only been last spring during the river murders, which had necessitated Belinda being protected by the Yard, that we'd revealed our attachment to our closest friends.

"She's in Edinburgh," I said. "Due home in a few days. Her cousin fell and broke her ankle, so Belinda went to help."

"That's kind." Then she frowned, as if a sudden thought troubled her. "Is she comin' home by train, then?"

I nodded. "I don't like the thought either, after yesterday."

"Ah, I'm sartin she'll be fine. Accidents aren't near so common as they once were." She peered up at me. "I do hope we'll meet her soon."

"You will," I promised as I replaced the last dish on the shelf.

She took the towel from me and smiled. "It's getting late."

"I'm going." I took up my coat, kissed Ma on the cheek, promised to talk to Colin soon, and left.

As I reached the bottom step, a shadow emerged from the alley, and I felt someone approach from behind. My right hand was on my truncheon even before I turned.

Two hands came up in a gesture of surrender. "It's just me." Colin's voice picked over the syllables in a way that told me he was two or three drinks along, but not so far gone that he didn't care that it showed. His boots scuffed the dirt as he came near, and he lowered his hands and thrust them into his coat pockets. The night breeze, ripe with the scent of smoke and meat from the nearby butchery, blew Colin's brown curls off his forehead.

He must've been lurking in that alley, waiting for me. All that Ma said, all her worry, made me temper my voice. "Why'd you run off, Col?" I asked. "I'd have liked a proper visit with you."

"Ach." His shoulders twitched as if avoiding a weight. "Elsie's always harping at me like a bloody shrew." His voice slurred over the last word. "But I stayed 'cause of a message I have for ye."

My guess was Elsie wasn't shrewish so much as she was worried, same as Ma, but she had a different way of showing it. Smelling the whiskey on Colin's breath and observing the surly set to his jaw, I was beginning to understand their concern.

I shifted my feet to maneuver him into a position where the light from the window of the nearby pub would fall on his face. I hadn't been looking at him closely enough of late. My strongest memories were of him as a young boy of six or so, slender and light-haired, his eyes sparkling with interest as I taught him how to whittle a whistle or tie a stopper knot that wouldn't slip.

Colin's eyes were as brilliantly blue now as they'd been then, just like his older brother Pat's, although Pat had never looked at me so warily. "Don't bark at me, all right?" Colin asked.

I replied evenly, "Am I likely to?"

He pulled a face.

"All right, I won't," I promised. "What sort of message?"

"It's from O'Hagan."

I stared. *O'Hagan.*

Those three syllables were all it took to bring me back to thirteen years ago, when I'd been one of O'Hagan's regular boxers, in a bare-knuckles hall underground, no more than a sweaty pen at the bottom of a ladder, where the dirt wasn't thick enough to absorb all the blood and cheap rotgut whiskey that fell. I'd boxed for O'Hagan until the night he'd asked me to throw a match, and I'd done something bloody stupid that ended with me fleeing Whitechapel, sleeping rough until I found my feet.

"Why'd he send you, instead of coming to me himself?" I let him see my disgust at O'Hagan's cowardice.

Colin glanced back toward the house. "He knows you used to live with us. Mebbe he thought you'd listen if I was the one asking." He sniffed. "Instead of payin' him no mind like you well might."

I frowned. O'Hagan and I had declared a truce of sorts years ago. I had never come after him for keeping illegal boxing halls and a fleet of bookmakers, and in return, I'd been able to move about Whitechapel unmolested. I certainly harbored no affection for O'Hagan, but I wondered why Colin assumed I'd ignore him. However, it wasn't worth asking, with Colin in this state.

"He just wants to meet you," Colin said. "To talk."

Guesses about why ran through my head with the speed of a fast current, but I asked merely, "About what?"

Colin's eyes veered away, and he shrugged. "Might have something to do with the Cobbwallers."

The muscles across my upper back tightened.

O'Hagan belonged to the Cobbwallers now? I suppose it shouldn't have surprised me that James McCabe's gang was running boxing halls as well as everything else. But like all London gang leaders, McCabe demanded absolute loyalty and discretion from his members. I couldn't imagine a circumstance that would cause O'Hagan to discuss anything about the Cobbwallers with me, a policeman.

"Go on," I said.

"Two Cobbwaller men are dead." Colin peered at me aslant. "Murdered."

My stomach lurched. In the wake of the Clerkenwell bombing, police had sought out and killed Cobbwallers. That was a decade ago, but it was a black mark in our history, and no doubt O'Hagan and McCabe remembered it. "Are they blaming police?"

"Dunno."

His evasive look sparked hot fear along my nerves. "Colin, you're not mixed up with the Cobbwallers, are you?"

There was the briefest pause before he drew his head back as if in surprise and shook it dismissively. "Nae."

That hesitation made me long to press him further, but it was almost as if I felt Belinda's hand, gentle on my sleeve, counseling patience. There would be time to ask again when Colin was sober.

Besides, if I did as Colin asked, he might confide in me more readily.

"All right." I stepped forward and put my arm around his shoulder, tugged him close for a second. "Tell O'Hagan I'll meet him."

As I released him, his eyes betrayed a flash of relief. "Wants you to come tomorrow night."

Come where? I wondered. Not to the Doyles's, certainly. And not his old boxing hall either. The police had closed it down not long after I stopped working there.

I cocked my head. "Where do I find him?"

"Goose and Gander," Colin said.

A pub near the docks where O'Hagan first found me, I thought with a flare of annoyance. With anyone else, I'd have given them the benefit of the doubt, but I knew O'Hagan. He wanted to remind me who'd held the cards when I was eighteen.

"I'll see him tomorrow," I said. "But in case I miss him, tell him to send a message to me at Wapping. He can just name a place and time. Doesn't need to sign it. I'll know."

"A'right." He nodded a goodbye and took a step backward.

I resisted the impulse to lay a hand on his arm to keep him from leaving, but I couldn't help asking, "Are you all right, Colin?"

"Aye, fine," he said, and flashed a grin that reflected some of his old openness with me. Then he turned away.

"Good night," I called, fighting down the impulse to detain him again, wishing to hell he was sober, so I could talk to him, ask if he might let me find him work.

"Night," he threw over his shoulder.

I watched him stride away. He'd been a lively child, impulsive and mouthy and at times reckless of his own safety. Sometimes I'd catch him imitating Pat and me, in the way we'd carry ourselves, or wear our caps or hold a knife. It annoyed Pat to no end, and he'd shoo Colin off, but I didn't mind. When I was one of the youngest members of Simms's thieving gang, I'd watch the older boys swaggering and try it for myself later as I walked down a quiet street alone. So I'd give Colin a wink, and he'd give me a roguish smile back.

There wasn't much sign of that boy anymore. Then again, he was nearly twenty, same as I was when I left the Chapel.

Darkness swallowed up his figure, and I turned away, wondering if part of the reason Colin had been on edge earlier with Elsie was because he had a message to deliver, and he wasn't wrong in assuming I wouldn't be happy to hear it. But why was Elsie angry? Surely he hadn't told *her* about O'Hagan's message. Was she nagging him about his drinking? But I hadn't smelled it on him until just now.

What worried me still more was how Colin had glanced away when I asked why O'Hagan asked him to deliver the message, and he'd seemed a shade too surprised when I asked if he was mixed up with the Cobbwallers. If he was lying—and two Cobbwallers were already dead—

Just how close were O'Hagan and his ilk brushing up against these people I loved?

The thought put a thick knot in the soft place underneath my ribs.

CHAPTER 3

Wapping Police Station stood on the north bank of the Thames, six miles east of my former division, Scotland Yard. When Wapping was built near the end of the previous century, at the behest of a local magistrate who wanted to halt the looting of West Indies ships anchored near the London Pools, the main entrance to the three-story brick building faced Wapping High Street. But perhaps even then it was the back entrance on the river, with a dock that could hold multiple boats, that mattered most.

I climbed out of the cab at the front door, but as I did most mornings, I cut down the narrow alley between the station and the warehouse next door. The flagstones held small puddles from last night's rain. Three-quarters of the way along, I reached the stone slab that topped the stairs leading down to the Thames's muddy shore. I descended half a dozen steps, taking care not to slip on the green muck, and as I emerged from between the two buildings, the breeze flapped the bottom of my coat. The air stank of the river's oily brine and the ammoniac lye from the wool manufactory downstream. At the bottom of the stairs, I headed east along the shore and then out to the pier, a long wood-planked arm extending over the water. Four of our galleys bobbed in the waves, ready to deploy, their lines coiled neatly beside metal cleats.

My boots gave muted thumps on the sodden boards, which were soft from years of drenching. Back when I worked at Wapping in uniform, before my time at the Yard, it had been my superintendent Mr. Blair's habit to spend a quarter of an hour here, just to get the feel of the river for the day. Blair was corrupt and recently ousted, leading to my temporary appointment, but the morning vigil was one of his better habits, one I'd adopted for my own. I planted my boots a few feet from the pier's end and surveyed downstream to Tunnel Pier, then across the river to Lambeth and Southwark, with the wharves and stairs rising from the murky brown margin, and finally upstream to Custom House. Even this early the boats were massing near it.

Growing up on the Thames, my very pulse became attuned to its waves, my days to its ebb and flood tides. Mud-larking along its banks as a child and working the docks and a lighter boat as a young man, I have been beside, in, on, amid, and—once, frighteningly—under its waters. I've seen the river when the waves flare brightly off the sterns of steamers and when the water is leached of all color in the dead of winter. This fine September morning, flashes of sun glinted on the hulls of sturdy tugboats, masted ships, pleasure steamers, small lighters, and enormous coal ships—all different lengths and widths and tonnages, moving at various speeds, carrying passengers and parcels, the spice and silks, the metalworks and mail that make our modern life what it is. The newspapers said that England's economy was depressed, but you wouldn't bloody know it from where I stood.

An enormous collier barreled its way down the middle of the river, its hull draping a fifty-foot shadow over the water, its white-crested wake rocking some of the smaller boats. One of the waves met the prow of a barge twenty yards offshore, heading downriver, which gave a shrill whistle of warning to a second, smaller barge coming upstream and steering to starboard to avoid it. The men on each vessel flung obscene gestures as they passed.

I turned to walk back up the pier and was met halfway by Sergeant Lipp.

"Begging your pardon, Corravan . . . sir," he said, tacking the last word on belatedly.

I pretended not to notice. He'd known me for four years in uniform, and I wasn't used to my new rank either. "What is it, Lipp?"

He jerked his head in the direction of the south shore. "A dead body, over at East Lane Stairs."

In Southwark. A borough as crime infested as any on this side of the river.

"Murder or accident?" I asked.

"Couldn't say." He hesitated. "Who'd you like to send?"

"I'll go," I replied. I had nothing particularly pressing for the morning. Besides, my old superintendent had never been one to sit behind his desk for deaths on the river—and that was another habit of his that I'd taken for my own.

"Yes, sir," he replied. "Take one of the boats?"

I nodded. "I'll bring Charlie Dower along. If the dead man has no identification, I'll want him to do a sketch on the spot. No use dragging the corpse here, only to travel back over again to find someone who recognizes him." I pulled open the back door, and Lipp followed me inside. "Find a constable, and you come too."

★   ★   ★

In recent years, there had been talk of purchasing motorized crafts for our division, but for now we still relied solely on galleys—twenty-seven-foot, clinker-built open rowboats with three thwarts for oarsmen—the same as the River Police division had used since opening in 1798. After retrieving the necessary oars, we made our way to the pier and launched one of the boats.

Charlie Dower had been a clerk at Wapping for nearly two decades. A short man with a cheerful countenance, he had exceptionally legible handwriting and a talent for sketching. Charlie, Lipp, and the constable took up the oars, and I steered with rudder strings from the stern, carefully navigating upstream across the morning traffic.

"Crowd already gathered," Charlie said as we approached the shore. It looked to be largely dockworkers and rivermen, but I saw a few bonnets and heard the chirping, excited voices of children. I stepped out of the boat and stood on the bottom stair with Charlie and Lipp, leaving the constable to secure the line around the metal cleat and remain with the boat.

"Make way for the police," I said. And when no one moved, I repeated the sentence at a bellow.

At nearly six feet in height, I was taller than most of those who'd gathered, and although people grumbled, and one man hissed, they drew out of the way as I climbed. Lipp and Charlie followed in my wake until we reached the body. My heart sank at the sight of the man, who lay sprawled partially on his side across the second, third, and fourth steps from the top. He was perhaps forty years of age, respectably dressed, decent trousers and boots, a faint indentation in the brown hair at the back of his head where his hat had rested. Often a hat was useful to us, for it had the name of a haberdasher or even the name of the wearer inside. I glanced around. "Was he wearing a hat?"

There was a general muttering, from which I gathered that the hat had been removed and was probably already being pawned.

With a sigh, I bent over the body and began my inspection from the top. There were only traces of blood on the filthy gray stone beneath the head wound, which could indicate he had been killed elsewhere and thrown down the stairs to conceal where it had happened; but then again, he could have slipped and tumbled, and the blood could have been washed away by the night's rain. The smell of gin rose from him, strong enough to overpower the stench of the river.

"Sir," Lipp said, and gestured to the man's left hand. The two middle fingers had been crushed at some point, a traditional punishment for a gambler who hadn't paid his debts.

I observed both hands. No rings. I reached into his various pockets. Some loose coins, two pins, a few scraps of paper, two receipts too sodden to be legible. I left them where they were. With no proof of identity, our first task would be to discover where he'd been seen last.

A drunken sot and a gambler, I thought. I'd have two different kinds of establishments to visit, both with patrons who weren't the sort to talk to me voluntarily.

"Charlie, sketch his face," I said. "I'll take it around, see if anyone recognizes the man. Send a copy to the Yard, as they'll likely hear about a missing person before we will. And then, Lipp, you and the constable take the body to the morgue. Ask for Oakes and tell him I'll be by tomorrow morning."

"Yes, sir."

Charlie already had his pencil and sketchbook out. Within ten minutes, he had an accurate likeness, minus the gash near his temple. He tore out the page and gave it to me. "Good man," I said, rolling it carefully and putting it inside my pocket as Charlie began to compose a second.

Lipp went to the boat and retrieved the two-poled canvas stretcher we used for removing victims from a scene. After Charlie finished, I helped shift the dead man onto the canvas, and Lipp and the constable took up the two poles, bearing their load carefully down to the galley.

★   ★   ★

I spent the afternoon going from pub to pub and into the occasional gambling hall, fanning my way out from those establishments closest to the water to those farther away. At last, I stopped, my logic being that if he was drunk, he couldn't have walked any great distance, and it would be a struggle for even two men to carry him for long.

This sort of work might feel tedious to some, but I never minded. My persistence usually yielded results. However, thirteen establishments later, no one had seen him, not the barkeeps nor the patrons nor the prostitutes.

What the devil?

I eyed the sketch critically. Charlie had provided a good portrait. *Who was this man no one had seen?* I wondered, as I pushed open the door to one last pub.

After receiving the same regretful looks and shakes of the head as elsewhere, I ordered a bowl of beef stew and some ale, and took up a newspaper, the *Standard*, from a nearby table. Below the fold was a notice about the previous night's violence in Whitechapel, with three injured and a shop damaged by fire. *Another shop,* I thought uneasily. The article concluded by making a conventional observation about the "natural belligerence of Irishmen" that made me scowl as I spooned up the last bit of stew. As I left the pub, the bells from the church on Jamaica Road chimed five.

It was time to return to Wapping. It hadn't slipped my mind that I was supposed to meet O'Hagan, and I wanted to have time to write up my notes beforehand.

Still, on the way back to the river, I made quick stops into a chophouse, a cigar shop, and a chemist, showing the sketch with no success. It seemed increasingly likely the man was from another part of town altogether, and the corpse had been brought here and dumped to conceal the circumstances of his death. I could only hope that someone had made inquiries about him at the Yard. It always depressed my spirits to imagine no one noticing a man's absence.

Standing on the stairs where he had been found, my gaze slid out to the river. The sun had dropped over the darkening water, but no matter that it was the end of the natural day; dozens of vessels still hurried along as if hell-bent, their prows spearing relentlessly toward their destinations.

Depending on when he'd been killed, the man could have been rowed here with the current, from either upstream or downstream. He could even have been rowed over from Whitechapel. It would be odd if his murder was somehow connected with the violence across the way. But I'd seen stranger coincidences.

CHAPTER 4

Having finished writing my daily report, I left Wapping, walking past the London Docks to Sloane Street, where the Goose and Gander stood at the corner of Hackford. The sight of it brought back the afternoons Pat Doyle and I would come here, our spirits buoyed by the shillings in our pockets from working on the docks. We steered clear of most public houses—like the English Pearl, a few doors down, or the Drum and Thistle—but we two Irish stevedores found a welcome here, in this low-ceilinged room with a pair of rusted swords and a Celtic Cross over the mantle. Joining in on the bawdy choruses after a few pints made Pat and me feel like men—Irish men—and, for a while, as if we belonged. I'm not proud to admit it, but I liked it when someone who wasn't Irish was scowled out of the place.

Life was hard on the docks. The dockmaster, named Smithson, always hired Pat and me as a pair because he knew that together we could accomplish four times what any other single man could. It didn't keep Smithson from treating us the worst, though. If there was a swan-necked cart with a wheel that wasn't working properly, that would be ours for the day. If we took time to fix the wheel, our wages would be docked. Sometimes we didn't get a cart at all and had to haul the goods on our backs. If a bag of tea burst because it was roughly handled or at the bottom of a heavy pile, we'd be blamed. Pat and I kept to ourselves, mostly, though after a time we banded with a few older Irishmen who were hired regularly. We did our work, held our heads down, stayed out of people's way. Still, most days Smithson would shout at us for being feckin' Irish eejits, which worried me because Pat was quick to throw down whatever bag he was toting in order to free up his fists, and I'd have to remind him that we needed the money more than we wanted Smithson to pay for his spite. I hated it too. But we had no choice but to stay and take it.

It was the docks that taught me what being Irish meant because growing up in my part of the Chapel, Irish was all I knew. Like hundreds of others during the famine years, my parents sailed from Dublin to Liverpool, making portions of that city along the Mersey River more Irish than English. My father was a silver-smith, and a skilled one, but there wasn't enough work for all the silversmiths who had landed in Liverpool, so he and my mum came down to the Irish part of Whitechapel. With anti-Irish feel-ing running high, shops elsewhere in London wouldn't hire a man with black hair and blue eyes named Corravan, with an accent straight out of County Armagh. My mum never told me so, but my father did what many Irishmen had to do—plied their trade sideways. He became a counterfeiter, making two-bit coins in a cellar somewhere, with fumes that clung to him when he came through our door at night. He died when I was three years old, too young to remember him well, but old enough that the odor of suet and oil and the bitter tang of cyanide had rooted itself in my brain. During one of my earliest cases in Lambeth, I walked into a house and recognized the smell straightaway, like I knew the smell of tea or hops or onions. That's when I realized how my father had put bread on our table.

The rancor against the Irish grates at me sometimes. Not to say we don't deserve some of it. Four years ago, two Irishmen in Lambeth threw firebombs into one of Barnardo's English orphan-ages, to protest that Parliament had just prohibited the Irish from setting up orphanages for our own. The next morning, the corpses of twenty-six children were laid out on the street and on the front page of every newspaper in London. For weeks after, shame hacked at my insides. I could barely meet anyone's eye.

But we Irish don't all deserve to be tarred with the same brush, and it's hard to bear the ugly opinions printed in the papers. Now-adays, I stop reading if I catch a hint of hatred in the first lines, but there was a time when I would read the articles and letters from "concerned citizens" and "true Englishmen" because I wanted to know the worst that could be said of us. That was before I realized that words could be infinitely malicious. There was no worst; there was only more. I still remember the conclusion of one letter because it seemed so preposterous: "The Irish are the dregs in the barrel, the lowest of the low. They kill their fathers, rape their sisters, and eat their children, stuffing their maws with blood and potatoes indifferently, like wild beasts."

Well, that wasn't true of any of the Irish I knew. Indeed, as I laid my hand on the doorknob of the Goose and Gander, I was reasonably certain that inside I'd find Irish folks sitting, eating normal food, and playing cards.

I pushed open the wooden door, greeted the barmaid, and asked if O'Hagan had been in. She shook her head. "Not yet. He usually comes around eight."

I ordered a pint and found a table in the corner where our conversation could be private but from where I could watch the doorway without turning my head. Half an hour later, the knob turned, and I could have predicted it was O'Hagan entering, just by the stealthy way the door moved into the room.

Seamus O'Hagan appeared much as I remembered. A little bulkier in the chest and waist, and his face was fleshier, though he was a large man and carried the weight well. He still had the same flinty, dark eyes that flicked about habitually in search of weakness or want. I hadn't recognized that tendency on the day he'd come to the docks, hunting for new hands for his boxing club. I'd only felt flattered that he'd chosen me, eejit that I was.

O'Hagan gave me a smirk of recognition like he would've given me years ago. But today I was no eighteen-year-old desperate for money. I didn't need anything from him, though I did have a question I'd rather have answered than not.

O'Hagan went to the bar, bought a pint, and came to the table. Glass in hand, he stood looking down at me. "Corravan."

"O'Hagan." I gestured toward the seat opposite. I'd been nursing my pint, wanting to keep a clear head, so mine was only half gone.

He sat and assessed me before he spoke: "You look a'right."

I nodded.

"At Wapping?"

"For now." I took a sip. "Colin said you have a message for me. I haven't much time. I've somewhere to be."

He shifted his bulk in the chair, which creaked underneath him. "You heard about the killings in Whitechapel? One in Boyd Street, one on Folgate."

Boyd was the next cross street over from the Doyles's shop, so this might be the dead man Elsie had mentioned. Folgate was farther away. I recalled the article I'd read that afternoon about the shop damaged by fire, but it hadn't mentioned anyone dead or the name of the street. "Not really."

At a chorus of laughter, his eyes darted to another table before returning to me. "They're our men."

"Cobbwaller men," I said.

A jerk upward of his chin confirmed my guess. "Stiles is investigatin' one of 'em. Not sure if the Yard knows about the other."

I'd anticipated that O'Hagan might admit he was part of McCabe's gang, but I wasn't prepared to hear him speak the name of my former partner.

My surprise pleased O'Hagan. A small ugly smile pulled at one side of his mouth. "Wot, you think I don't know who he is?"

I rested a forearm on the table and leaned over it. "So you're an errand boy for McCabe. What does he want?"

The humor went out of his face. "Wants to see you. Has something to say about 'em."

Jaysus, I thought. Did McCabe imagine himself so far beyond the reach of the law that he had nothing to fear from meeting me? And what's so extraordinary about two deaths? Fights among gangs erupted periodically. McCabe knew it as well as anyone.

I snorted. "McCabe's helping the police now?" O'Hagan's lips clamped together, and he remained silent. "Who does he think is doing it?"

"Dunno."

I drained my glass and set it down. "Why doesn't he come to Wapping, like any other citizen?"

He sneered at me. "Don't pretend to be stupider than you are. Wants me to bring you."

"Like I said, I can't tell him much. I haven't been at the Yard or spoken to Stiles in weeks."

His lips pursed in disbelief.

"Tell me," I said, steering the subject in a different direction. "Where does Colin fit in?"

One thick dark eyebrow rose.

"Why did you ask him to bring the message?" I asked. "What's he to you?"

His eyes were flat, giving away nothing. "McCabe told me to get the message to you. I knew you lived with the Doyles, back when. Thought it was the easiest way."

I gave him a look that told him I assumed he was lying, and I didn't much care. But my brain was jumping from point to point.

If Colin was mixed up with the Cobbwallers, I'd never get it out of O'Hagan, not if he thought McCabe didn't want me to know. But McCabe? He might tell me the truth.

So I'd see him. But I needed to talk to Stiles first. Because while I had no intention of serving as McCabe's instrument of revenge against whoever was killing his men—or whatever it was McCabe wanted from me—I didn't want to misstep with McCabe, speak out of turn. Stiles would keep me from kicking stones hidden under the water.

"All right," I said to O'Hagan. "But I'm not meeting him in some back alley where I get killed for whatever I don't know or because I tell him something he doesn't like."

O'Hagan's eyes rose to the ceiling, and he gave a bark of laughter. "He ain't going to kill a Yard man for that." He tipped his glass upside down to drain it and *thunked* it onto the table. "Let's go."

"Not tonight," I said. "Tomorrow."

His eyes narrowed. "He wants to see you now."

"Like I said before, I have somewhere to be."

His face screwed up in frustration. He didn't relish having to bring my refusal back to McCabe. He spat out, "Tomorrow, then."

"I'll be here," I said.

If McCabe did have any thoughts of killing me, he wouldn't now, knowing I'd had the chance to tell someone we were meeting.

CHAPTER 5

It had been sunny in the morning, but now it was pouring rain, and I'd left my umbrella at home. As I hurried along toward Stiles's house, I hunched my shoulders in a vain attempt to keep the rain from running down the back of my neck.

When I was at the Yard, it had been Gordon Stiles who would remember to hand me an umbrella from the metal stand. It wasn't the only reason I missed my former partner. We had worked together at the Yard for the better part of a year, and he'd helped me solve the river murders. Calm and amiable, with some of the public school polish I lacked, Stiles had a way with people, and although he was nearly a decade younger than I, there was no one I'd rather have beside me in a crisis. Not to mention that I could trust him to be discreet.

I rapped on his front door and heard him call, "Who is it?"

"Corravan."

The door opened, and Stiles's face, looking up at me, showed a warm smile tinged with surprise. His fair hair glowed in the light coming from his parlor behind him, and he wore a white shirt loosened at the collar and rolled at the cuffs. In his right hand was a glass that held a prudent half inch of amber spirits. "For God's sake, what brings you out on a night like this? Come in, come in! Hang your coat, and I'll fetch you a towel."

I undid the buttons, eased out of the damp wool, and hung it on the rack. I slid the truncheon from my side pocket and laid it on the bench. I'd only been here once before, back when Stiles was recuperating from pneumonia in June. It had struck me at the time that Stiles lived quite well. Unlike my rooms, which were merely serviceable, his held comforts. A good mirror, pleasing lamps, a thick rug under my feet.

I glanced down at my mud-caked boots, lowered myself onto the bench, and undid them. By the time I had them off, Stiles had returned with a towel for my hands and hair. I entered the front room, where a fire burned cheerfully on the hearth, and sank into a chair opposite the one Stiles had occupied before my arrival. The table beside it held an open book and a plate with the remains of his supper. Some sort of pie, by the looks of it.

Stiles returned to the parlor. "I'm afraid I don't have any of your usual brew, but I've put on water for tea." He sat. "What brings you?"

"I've just come from Whitechapel, where I had a pint," I said, and added pointedly, "with O'Hagan, my old boxing hall owner, who apparently now works for McCabe." I shrugged. "Perhaps he always did. I don't know."

His expression grew thoughtful. "So he's a Cobbwaller." Stiles sat back and folded his hands. Only then did I realize he'd left his glass of spirits in the other room. I avoided spirits, given how they affected me, and Stiles was nothing if not tactful.

"What did O'Hagan want?" he asked.

"He says McCabe wants to talk to me about two of his men being murdered. That you're looking into one of them." I paused. "He spoke of you by name."

Stiles stared. "That's disconcerting. It's not even my case."

"It isn't?"

He shook his head. "It's Winn's. I've been in Sussex the last two weeks."

"Ah—the stolen jewelry." I'd heard about the burglary from Director Vincent.

"We caught the thief and the fence. Managed to retrieve most of it."

"Good." I shifted in my chair. "Has Winn talked to you about the murders?"

"Some. When I saw him yesterday, he didn't mention a second man, but he's investigating the murder of a man named O'Farrell. It happened Friday night."

"Who was he?"

"Young bloke, nineteen or twenty. He collected money for McCabe from gambling halls, fences, and the like."

Likely O'Hagan's second dead man, I thought.

Stiles winced. "He was shot."

I grunted in surprise. Usually gangs fought with knives. They were easier to obtain, cheaper, quieter, and much less likely to draw attention from the police. "Where was he found?"

"In Folgate Street, behind one of McCabe's pawn shops," he replied. "A constable came across his body facedown near a dustbin. It was laid out plainly for anyone to see, the bullet hole in the back of his head. A message of sorts, I'd say."

A low whistle came from the kitchen, and Stiles rose, returning a few moments later with two cups of tea. He'd left his own black but put milk in mine. I took a sip and lifted my cup in thanks.

Stiles set his cup on the table nearby, rested an elbow on the arm of the chair, and rubbed his forefinger over his mouth. "Who is the second man?"

"Sean Doone. Actually, he was killed first, the Tuesday before, on Boyd Street, but I don't know if he was shot," I said. "Five shops nearby were burglarized that night as well. One of them was the Doyles's."

Stiles's eyes widened. "Oh lord, Corravan. I hadn't heard."

"Less than a mile from Folgate. I'm surprised Winn hadn't connected the two."

"I am too. He's been working in the Chapel for the past month. I'll certainly mention it tomorrow." He sipped at his tea. "When are you seeing McCabe?"

"Tomorrow evening, which is why I'm here. I thought it was your case, and I didn't want to go in blind. But it might be a chance for me to find out information for the Yard. It's not everyone who can meet with the man."

"Hardly," Stiles replied with a short laugh. "Er—are you acquainted?"

"No. And I'll likely be hooded before I'm brought to him, so I won't be able to find him again."

Stiles frowned. "Then you should have someone watching."

"If he wants me to do something for him, he won't want me dead," I said, a shade more confidently than I felt. "Why has Winn been a month in the Chapel?"

"More violence and looting than usual." Stiles paused. "Fights in the street, burglaries of houses, sometimes with guns. It's happening nearly every night now."

The skin prickled along the back of my neck. "That's new," I said. "Any notion why?"

He rose and tonged a few more coals onto the fire. "There might be a new gang encroaching on McCabe's business."

The warmth from the fire was thawing me out, and I sank deeper into the cushions. "So McCabe is fighting back, and they killed O'Farrell and perhaps Doone in retaliation. But who is this other gang?"

Stiles lifted a shoulder and let it drop. "At the end of July, one Russian murdered another in Cobb Street."

"Only a few streets from Folgate," I said. "You think they could be by the same hand?"

"We-e-ell." He drew out the word doubtfully. "Both were shot close range with pistols, but in the case of the Russians, it was two bullets, and they entered here." He tapped his hand over his heart. "Not the head." His expression sobered. "However, we do know guns are making their way into London illicitly. Only by sheerest luck the Yard found a crate with thirty pistols last week. We don't know their intended destination, but given what Winn has told me, I'm concerned it's Whitechapel."

"Thirty pistols?" That was an enormous number of guns to set loose anywhere. "How did you find them?"

"They were hidden under a layer of gin bottles. A train from Birmingham offloaded it at Liverpool Station, where it was supposed to be retrieved by a Mr. Morgan, probably an alias. Luckily for us, we found the crate first—and only because the crate came apart at the side seam somehow, and some of the bottles broke. We found the guns when we lifted them out."

"Did Mr. Morgan ever appear to claim it?"

He gave a look. "No, and the bill of lading had a false address—although the notes used to pay for them were authentic Bank of England."

"Hmm."

"McCabe might know something," Stiles said, "and he might tell you, assuming the guns aren't coming to him—which it sounds like they're not if they're being used to kill his men."

I sipped the last of the tea and set the cup and saucer on the table.

"I'll give you whatever he tells me." I stood and nodded toward the open book on the table. "What are you reading?"

"*The Prime Minister.*" He grinned sheepishly. "Anthony Trollope's latest installment."

"Belinda likes his books."

"Plenty of politics and society intrigue, where it's safer, on the page." He rose, but I waved him back into his chair.

"Stay by the fire," I said. "I'll see myself out."

"Take one of my umbrellas," he called.

And so, thanks to Stiles's kindness, I arrived home, fifteen minutes later, less drenched than I would have been.

Chapter 6

At the morgue the next morning, I waited for the medical man, a surgeon named Oakes, who was occupied with another dead body but wouldn't be long. After half an hour, he called me in to view the man we'd found on the stairs. The room was cold, and the corpse lay on a scarred, stained wooden table. He was still dressed in his undergarments and shirt, though his coat and trousers had been removed and set aside on a nearby chair.

"God's sake, Corravan," Oakes grunted. "Did you pull him out of a bloody distillery?"

"I know. He reeks." I came around to the side of the table so I could stand opposite Oakes, near the man's head. "I found him facedown on the East Lane Stairs, south side of the river, just west of Glendinning's Wharf. You saw his hand?"

He nodded. "An old injury. You're thinking he might've owed money?"

"Perhaps."

He peered at the man's head, took a damp bit of flannel, and wiped the skin thoroughly clean. "Was his head on the edge of the stair? Because there's bruising here on the cheek." He turned the man's head and pointed. I could see the faint graying of the skin. "Can't say for certain," he continued. "It could've been from falling, but he also could've been hit with something."

"If you had to take a guess?"

He sniffed. "Are the East Lane Stairs in good repair?"

"Not five years old."

"Well, this was caused by something round, not a sharp edge."

"What time was he killed?"

Oakes moved the man's arm. "Around midnight, I'd say. No later than two."

No reasonable person would take a carriage into that part of Southwark at that hour, so it's likely he was killed west of the steps and rowed downstream with the ebb current. "What about his hands? Any sign he tried to break his fall?"

"No signs of that. O' course if he was drunk, he wouldn't have had time to get them up. Wouldn't've been thinking quickly enough. But I'm not sure he was as drunk as all that." He turned and picked up the coat, putting it to his nose. "Ech." He dropped the coat back onto the chair. "His *clothes* reek of gin, but . . ." His voice faded as he peered closely at the end of the man's nose, going so far as to crouch and look up into the nostrils. "No swelling or burst vessels in there or on his cheeks." He moved the undershirt, pressing his hands on different spots across the bare abdomen. "There are no signs of him being a habitual drunkard, and in a man this age, they'd begin to appear. No sign his liver is enlarged, or his pancreas. No bloating, and his muscles have a fine tone." He fished an instrument from his pocket, pried open the man's mouth, and peered inside, letting the mouth close as he stepped back. "No bleeding in the esophagus. Indeed, if I had to guess, I'd say there was more gin on his clothes than in his blood."

I wasn't wholly surprised that this might be a murder disguised as an accident. But why not simply throw the body in the Thames? Why go to the trouble of putting it on the stairs?

"Anything still of value on him?" I asked.

"A ring. I found it inside the lining of the coat. My guess is it slipped through the hole in his pocket, and he might not even have known it was there. It's still shiny, and there's no indentation on any of his fingers, which makes me think it's new, or perhaps he rarely wore it. Might not even be his, I suppose, though it appears the proper size." He went to a cabinet and took it from a small tray, dropping it into my cupped hand. It was a plain gold band, not terribly heavy but certainly worth stealing. I peered inside for engraving but found none. The man was likely married or widowed. Why wouldn't he have been wearing it? And why hadn't it been taken? Any thief worth his salt would have found it, patting down the hem and lining.

A thought occurred to me, and I picked up the dead man's coat to inspect the right cuff. It was frayed; the coat appeared to be several years old. "Do you think he was right-handed or left?"

"Left, I'd say," Oates replied. "From the muscles in his palm."

I turned the left cuff inside out, and there it was—a fold of fabric that formed a discreet pocket the size of a playing card. A snort of satisfaction escaped me.

"What's that for?" Oates asked.

"An ace," I replied as I replaced the coat in the pile. "Let me know what else you find. We'll need his name before he can be buried."

"I know, I know," he grumbled. "Help me turn him before you go."

Together we flipped the body onto his front. Oates lifted the shirt away from his back and pointed. There was a bruise the width of a truncheon across his right shoulder, near the neck.

I'd send a message to the Yard to let them know it wasn't just a dead body, but likely a murdered one.

★ ★ ★

At Wapping, Sergeant Trent nodded a greeting. "A visitor, sir. Gave his name as Mr. Flynn." He added dubiously, "Of the *Falcon*. He arrived 'bout half past ten and told me he'd wait for you, so I put 'im in the first room."

I understood the sergeant's mistrust of newspapermen, but the thought of a visit from Tom made me smile. I hadn't seen him in months, for he'd been traveling most of the summer, following Disraeli and the Marquess of Salisbury to Berlin for the signing of the treaty that divided up the spoils of the Russo-Turkey War.

Like the Yard, Wapping had three rooms for interviewing or holding people as we prepared charges. The doors were closed except for the first, which stood ajar. I peered in and saw Tom, in profile, standing in the weak sunlight at the window, staring out at the river. He was a short, sturdy man with a round head, a nose that turned up at the end, and olive-green eyes that I knew were keenly perceptive, often challenging. His hands were dropped into the pockets of his coat, which hung long on him. Bold as brass and damned clever, with a keen recall of everything from the exact wording of political speeches to financial figures, Tom worked early and late, didn't print stories before he knew the facts, and had helped me on more than one occasion. Over the years, I'd come to owe him. And trust him too, I suppose. I'd give him information when I could, and he didn't abuse me when I couldn't. He reported on all sorts of matters for the *Falcon*, but his chief concern was Parliament, politics, and—lately—foreign policy. He had the trust of at least a few MPs from all different factions—the Tories and Whigs, the back-benchers and the cabinet, the men who'd served for decades and the young ones who hadn't even made their maiden speeches yet. What's more, he understood their politics, which often seemed a muddle to me, with parties that spliced and reformed, like when the Whigs and the Peelites banded together to form the Liberal party. Some issues made for strange bedfellows, as Tom would say.

"Tom."

He turned, and his eyes lit as he gave his usual one-sided grin. "Corravan."

"How was Berlin?"

"Quarrelsome." He grimaced. "And hot as Hades."

I hung my own coat on one of the hooks on the wall, then held out my hand for his frayed specimen. He peeled it off and tossed it to me, but not without removing his pocketbook and pencil.

"What brings you?" I asked.

"Gloating, in part," Tom said. "I told you Director Vincent would send you over here once Blair was dismissed."

I snorted. "Aren't you the clever one."

We settled into chairs, and I studied him. Tom could wear a bland face and make it look natural. But he wasn't bothering to hide his concern today.

"What is it?" I asked.

He tipped his chin up toward the door behind me. "Do you mind?"

I gestured for him to please himself. He pushed the door shut and resumed his seat. "We've been hearing reports of rising violence in Whitechapel. It's not usually my concern, I know, but it has implications for Parliament."

I remained silent. Three times in the span of as many days, I was hearing this story about violence in Whitechapel. Neither Ma Doyle nor Stiles nor Tom were ones to raise alarms needlessly;

there was something behind their concern. I wouldn't relate any specifics of what Stiles told me, but I could tell Tom this much:

"I know there were two shootings last week, and several shops have been looted—including the Doyles's. When I asked Ma about it, she said the Chapel is changing, a lot of new people coming in. The Yard is wondering if there's some fighting among new and old gangs. Anything more you can tell me?"

"We have a source that says the Irish may be causing it." Tom paused. "McCabe and the Cobbwallers, I mean."

Except that it's McCabe's men who are being killed, I thought. *And he wouldn't cause violence without a good reason, knowing it would bring the attention of the police. He has too much to lose.*

"You look skeptical," he said.

I sat back. "Do you think he's starting it, or responding? Why would he be lashing out?"

"Couldn't say." Tom's voice was sober. "They're a bloody vicious bunch, Corravan, and canny. They spread just enough terror to keep anyone from bearing witness against them."

"Oh, I know."

"Do you know why McCabe would be doing this now? Do you have any experience of him, any insight into how he thinks?"

I'll have more after tonight, I thought, but I said only, "I grew up in Whitechapel, not Seven Dials. He didn't move into the Chapel until after I left, and I've never laid eyes on him, so far as I know."

"Likely he stays out of the way of inspectors," he said wryly.

"He runs pawnshops, gambling, counterfeiting." I turned my hand over. "Usually he keeps matters in hand, and so long as it doesn't imperil everyday Londoners, we generally don't interfere."

"That's why you're surprised he'd be starting trouble," Tom finished. "Hmph." His eyes narrowed in a way that told me he was piecing together a story.

"What does this have to do with Parliament?" I asked.

A long pause. "Not to be shared," he said. "With anyone."

I nodded my promise.

He rested his elbows on his knees, leaned in, and lowered his voice. "For the past five months, there's a group of moderate MPs who've been meeting privately, trying to find a way toward restoring Irish Home Rule."

A bark of derision escaped me. Eighty years ago, when the Act of Union dissolved Irish Parliament, Irish MPs began coming to London to serve. But as they were always a minority, Irish concerns were largely neglected, which resulted in decades of anti-Irish harassment and heartless policies. Occasionally, the idea of home rule would resurface because a few MPs recognized that giving Irish MPs the power to govern Irish affairs would diminish resentment and violence here in England. But the majority of MPs believed the Irish were a lawless rabble that needed a "firm hand," so the proposal always drowned amid protests. In the past decade, the Irish Republican Brotherhood had used occasional bombs and threats to pressure Parliament into reestablishing home rule, but thus far the violence seemed only to solidify British resolve against allowing it.

I shook my head. "It'll never amount to anything."

But Tom didn't echo my skepticism. His eyes were earnest. Sober. Hopeful, even. "I know people think it's impossible." Tom raised a hand. "But it's different this time. There are mutterings about Gladstone coming back in the next year or so. Home rule couldn't happen under Disraeli, of course. He abhors the Irish."

"Beyond the usual Conservative suspicion?"

"Yah. He wrote it in a letter to the *Times*." Tom raised his truncated forefinger and adopted a lofty tone: "'The Irish hate our order, our civilization, our enterprising industry, our pure religion. This wild, reckless, indolent, uncertain, and superstitious race have no sympathy with the English character.'" He waved his hand. "He went on about Irish clannishness and their coarse natures."

"He wrote that as prime minister?" I asked in disbelief.

"No, before. And he used a pseudonym."

"Jaysus."

"Not one for understatement, is he?" Tom's brow furrowed. "There are plenty of MPs who don't like the Irish—"

"They like the money from the Irish factories and fields well enough," I retorted.

"Well, yes," Tom admitted. "But the industrialists especially don't like the sound of the Molly Maguires in America."

I knew of the secret society that had begun in Liverpool in the 1830s, but I hadn't heard of them overseas.

Tom must have seen my confusion. "They immigrated to Pennsylvania coal country in the '50s. After two mines caved in, they formed unions to strike for better conditions and fair wages. Twenty of them were hanged last year for rioting." He paused. "The English have dozens of factories in Ireland."

"So Irish Home Rule could bring about laws requiring higher wages and safety measures."

He pursed his lips. "Costly."

"Well, that rules out the MPs who are industrialists and manufacturers," I said. "In addition to the MPs who simply hate the Irish, of course. So who's left in these talks? A few on the fringe?"

"No," he corrected me. "MPs from both sides."

"Conservatives and Liberals?" I asked, astonished. "What Conservative is going to be in favor of Irish Home Rule?"

Tom's eyebrows rose. "You'd be surprised. They won't admit it publicly, of course. Don't want to alienate their constituents. But there *are* a few—mostly because they're tired of fighting about the 'popish lot.'" His voice flattened. "But no, I meant both Irish and English. Not just ordinary MPs—cabinet members as well."

The most powerful MPs in the land.

I blew out an exhale. "Anyone you can tell me?"

"John Bright, for one."

"President of the Board of Trade? You can't mean it."

He nodded. "Lord Granville and Lord Baynes-Hill are two others—powerful men, leaders in their party. And five Irish moderates."

"That's still nowhere near enough MPs to pass a bill," I said.

"No, but there could be, once Disraeli is out," Tom replied. "Providing an agreement could be drawn up and presented. Half the trouble is most people assume they could never reach one."

"But even if Gladstone is PM for a few years, Disraeli will be back—or so they say."

"Perhaps." Tom shrugged. "But there's talk of passing the conservative torch to Lord Chancellor Cairns, or even the MP Archibald Houghton. Both are wealthy manufacturers, to be sure, but neither seems to have Disraeli's aversion to the Irish—although I doubt they'd approve of these meetings."

I frowned. "You say they're secret, but they can't *stay* secret if they're to accomplish anything."

Tom spread his hands. "The group is testing the waters quietly and finding a good amount of support." He paused before adding, "So long as home rule only pertains to Irish domestic concerns, not imperial ones."

"Naturally," I said drily.

"Well, what do you expect?" Tom asked, letting his impatience show. "There are plenty who remember Clerkenwell in '67. And Mayfair Theatre was only five years ago."

I felt a pinch of shame, recalling the afternoon when three bombs went off during a performance, and two of the queen's daughters were nearly killed amid dozens who died. "Those bombs were set by the Irish Republican Brotherhood," I replied. "Not your average Irishmen—or even Cobbwallers, Tom."

"Yes, well." His mouth tightened. "People in London tend to forget the distinctions when dozens of people are dying and injured in their streets."

"So with the increasing Irish violence in Whitechapel—whether it's the Brotherhood or Cobbwallers—people are afraid, and sympathy for home rule erodes."

Tom rubbed his hand over his mouth. "You think the Cobbwallers and the Brotherhood might be acting together?"

I grunted skeptically.

"I know this strikes close to the bone for you. But—"

"Viciousness strikes close to the bone for me—whether it's Irish or English."

Tom gave me a look. "Most people would say Irish *is* English."

"Not if you grew up in my part of Whitechapel."

He grimaced. "Understood."

"I'll see what I can uncover for you," I said. "I can't imagine McCabe starting trouble unprovoked, and the IRB always claims their violence, which hasn't happened. It might just be the natural consequence of too many people living in too small a space and scrapping for necessities."

Tom slapped his hands onto the arms of the chair and stood. "Let me know what you hear."

I handed Tom his coat, and he put on his battered hat and bid me goodbye.

After he left, I thought about the meeting I'd be having with McCabe. I wondered what he'd have to say about the escalating violence. I was glad I'd talked not only to Stiles but also to Tom Flynn beforehand. More than once his insights had been exactly what I needed to hear, and just in the nick of time.

I sat down in the chair behind my desk, realizing for the dozenth time that Superintendent Blair was shorter than I. I needed to replace this chair, which perched me up too high. Then again, I was still only acting superintendent. I could bear to hunch over my desk for a while yet.

After several hours spent reviewing notes, I stepped out to find some supper, to fortify myself for the task of composing the weekly report for the Yard director, Mr. Vincent. Back at my desk, I was nearly finished when I heard a knock at my door and glanced up. The clock on my wall showed a quarter past eight.

"Yes," I called.

The door swung open, and Sergeant Trent was standing on the threshold, his jowly face red, his expression distressed. "There's been an accident, sir. Two ships crashed."

I laid down my pen. "Where?"

"Just beyond Gallions Reach. One of them is the *Princess Alice*."

A groan escaped me. The *Princess Alice* was one of a small fleet of pleasure steamers that made daily excursions of about forty-five miles down and back up the Thames, leaving Swan Pier near Tower Bridge in the morning; arriving mid-afternoon at Sheerness, where the river reached the North Sea; and returning to Swan Pier by moonlight. For only two shillings, passengers could hop on and off any of the steamers, to spend parts of their day at the famous Rosherville Gardens or the music hall at Gravesend.

"How bad is it?" I asked as I reached for my coat.

"She's sunk, sir."

CHAPTER 7

"Sunk?" I managed. "What the devil ran into her?"

"A collier. Not sure which one."

"Damn," I said as I pulled on my coat. The *Princess Alice* had a wood hull and probably weighed less than two hundred tons, compared to a steel-hulled collier, which was likely eight or nine hundred tons, especially if loaded with coal. It would be like a runaway railway engine striking a hansom cab. The steamer would have gone under in a matter of minutes.

"Weather was fair today," the sergeant said grimly. "Like as not, it was a full boat."

I could picture the open wooden decks, fore and aft of the paddle box, with hundreds of men, women, and children milling about by lantern-light, lounging against the rails, singing along to the cheerful music from the boat's small orchestra.

As I did up the buttons, another thought halted my hands: we would have no idea who the passengers were. There was never a manifest on those pleasure steamers. Another oath flew out of my mouth.

"Come with me," I said, and Sergeant Trent nodded. I went to a cupboard where we kept supplies, hoisted a parcel of blankets tied with string, and handed it to the sergeant. I took another parcel for myself and retrieved two bullseye lanterns from their hooks, then told Sergeant Trent to fetch us a cab. We went out to Wapping High Street, and he hurried to the corner, withdrew the metal police rattle from the pocket over his heart, and shook it vigorously.

★   ★   ★

Gallions Reach was a seven-mile ride east of Wapping Station. Once we passed the East India Docks, the streets were blessedly clear, and the driver urged his horses. Out this far, there were no churches to toll the hours, but with a glance up at the moon's position among the clouds, I estimated it was not long after ten o'clock as we drew close. We could smell the pungent ammonia and sulfur, byproducts from the Beckton Gasworks, even before we saw the lights on their retort houses and towers. From ahead, we heard the cries and shouts of a gathered crowd on the margin of the river. There were already at least a dozen carriages and carts abandoned along the road, and as people dashed in front of us, not heeding the danger, our horse let out a high-pitched neigh, and the cab halted.

"I daren't go any farther," the driver called down to us. "Afraid I'll hit someone!"

Sergeant Trent and I clambered out with our blankets and lanterns, and I paid the driver. The stink of the river assailed us, and the sergeant grunted his disgust. With Erith, the processing plant for London's sewage nearby, this was a swampy, stench-filled stretch of water at the best of times, but tonight it smelled particularly vile.

By the light of other people's lamps and lanterns, we made our way along a wall of stone five feet tall that served as a bulwark against the river when it flooded. Jostled by desperate people running past, we reached a break in the wall and halted to take in the scene. A cloud veiled the moon, and I could see little more than flares and flickers from lights and lanterns and shadows moving through the murk of darkness. At last, the cloud shifted, so I could discern shapes out on the river. Among a dozen smaller boats and ships, the collier was a black hulk looming against the lesser darkness of the sky. Three small boats, each with a lamp of some kind at the bow, appeared to be making their way to shore.

But there wasn't a remnant of the *Princess Alice* to be seen. The passengers all would have slid into the water, the sudden sharp cold a knife twisting in their lungs.

"Your lantern, sergeant," I said tersely and lit my own, stepping forward and raising it high, illuminating the riverbank close to me. A man sprawled in the mud, a gash on his forehead spilling blood down the side of his face. Two men, dead, their eyes open and mouths slack. A child facedown in the water. A man stumbling past, clutching his arm, which hung at an unnatural angle from his shoulder, calling, "Louisa," in a hoarse voice. A woman keening and rocking a silent child, a daughter whose dark hair fell lank across her back.

Around me echoed the voices of men and women, recently arrived, scrambling across the pebbles, frantically calling out the names of friends and relations—

Charlotte, Charlotte Ambrose—Anthony—William—Henry Blight—Louisa—Mary—Elizabeth—

My heart thudded thickly in my chest.

"Mother of God," muttered the sergeant beside me, his voice rough.

Close by us, another man, with his arm around a woman's waist, attempted to help her reach higher ground, but her skirts hampered her so badly she sank back onto the shore, crying, "Never *mind* about me! Go! Please, James! Go! Go look for Samuel!" Unwillingly, he let go of her and stumbled off into the darkness, leaving her, crumpled and sobbing, on the rough stones.

I took a blanket from the stack, bent, and put it around her. "Let me help you."

Her hands grasped my shoulders, and her face was twisted with desperation. Gasping through chattering teeth, she begged me, "Find Samuel for me! Just find him! Please—please, just help my husband find my boy!"

Tears burned at the corners of my eyes. "We'll find everyone we can, mum," I promised her.

I stood and met the sergeant's eyes. We both knew the ebb current moved fast at this time of night. The survivors and their kin would never locate each other, stranded as they were along this long, dark shoreline.

As I stood, a gust of evening wind sent the cold straight through my thick overcoat, and I wasn't even wet. "We need to get these people out of this wind, or they'll die of exposure."

The sergeant nodded. "Other side of the wall would be better."

"Or the closed carriages," I replied. "But we'll need to find something we can use as a stretcher."

"I'll pass 'round the blankets for now, sir," Sergeant Trent said as he hefted my parcel along with his own. Though I couldn't see the sergeant's face, I heard the shock in his voice. He'd served at Wapping for two decades, long enough to see the filth and even death that the river carried every day, but this scene was something else altogether. It was worse than a railway disaster. In that, at least the passengers had a chance to extricate themselves and crawl to safety. And if this narrow section of shoreline was anything to go by, not dozens but hundreds of people had drowned.

The sergeant moved off with his burden, and I helped the woman to the wall before returning to the shore. Two of the small boats had been dragged onto the stones, and I watched as two men lifted a woman out. I saw three other bodies in the lighter, but none of them moved. Sergeant Trent was already at the woman's side, wrapping her in a blanket and directing the men to take her out of the wind.

I scanned the beach again, and this time I found a uniformed man. I strode toward him. "I'm with the River Police. Are you with the gasworks?"

"Aye! And I saw it happen! I'm the night watchman, just there." His thumb pointed backward, over his shoulder

I could make out the tower's dim outline on a small rise near the river's edge. "What the devil happened?"

"'Twas the bloody *Bywell Castle*," he said indignantly. "Came flying down the river and smashed her up."

"Have any crew from the *Princess Alice* come ashore?"

"No sign o' the crew, but there's a constable was on it." His expression was grim.

"With his family?" I asked.

He nodded. "Seems they might've drowned. His wife and son."

The knot in my stomach twisted. "Where is he?"

"Rowed to the other side to look for 'em." He jerked his head toward the south shore and the Plumsted Marshes of Woolwich. "Some boats came from over there."

I stifled a groan. We'd have bodies along the south shore too.

"Most boats nearby tried to help," he continued. "The damned *Bywell* realized what they done, threw out some lines, put lifeboats out. *Duke of Teck* steamed by 'round half past eight and took some survivors back to Swan's."

The *Duke* was another of the pleasure steamers, in the same fleet as the *Princess Alice*. I was grateful they'd come by, of course, but as I considered the hodgepodge of boats that had offered aid, it was becoming clear that both dead bodies and survivors would be spread out all along the river, not just downstream from the accident but on both shores and anywhere boats saw fit to leave them. Helping friends and relations find each other was beyond our abilities at this point. The important thing was to move people out of the cold, transfer the injured to hospitals, and keep an eye out for someone who could utter a coherent and reasonably unbiased sentence about how the devil something like this could have happened.

"Sir!" Sergeant Trent approached, waving his hand over his head.

Another boat drew up to shore, and the watchman stepped forward to help. I reached the sergeant. "What is it?"

He gestured toward the young man at his side. "He's from the gasworks."

The man wore a fine coat and a silk top hat new enough to reflect the light as he lofted his lantern into the air between us. "My name is Brantlinger. We can offer you two sheds, where people can take shelter."

"Thank you," I said. "Two sheds, you say?"

"They usually house our railway carriages, but we've removed them to make room." He gave a glance around and added apologetically, "They're not heated, but they're better than this."

"'Specially as it's likely to rain," Sergeant Trent added.

Screams burst out anew, and the three of us pivoted as one, our eyes peering toward the shoreline. Two rivermen had drawn a boat up onto the pebbles. Inside were three slack-boned corpses, and a woman bent over the gunwale, clutching one of the dead by the shoulders, as his head lolled. She unleashed a long, incoherent cry that fell into a wordless keening.

The sergeant's face screwed up in sympathy; the gasworks man stared in horror.

"Brantlinger." He didn't hear me. "Brantlinger!"

His gaze jerked to meet mine. His face was stricken.

"We need to put survivors in one shed and bodies in the other," I said. "Survivors need blankets and hot food and tea. Take care of them first. Then we'll collect the rest."

His body convulsed once, and then again, as if he'd been struck a blow. "Of course," he managed. "I'll do everything I can."

Under a moon that slipped in and out of the clouds, Sergeant Trent and I spent the next few hours helping people into wagons that ferried them to the gasworks yard. To my relief the sheds, less than half a mile distant, were cavernous, dry, and even reasonably warm. The smaller shed provided plenty of room on the platforms on either side of the tracks. Groups of people in sodden clothes, with mud streaked across their faces and hands, huddled together, draped in rough blankets, some weeping and others talking in low, urgent tones.

At some point, we received reinforcements from the Wrecks Commission, who would be responsible for managing the aftermath of the disaster. Commissioner Rotherly didn't come himself, but one of his deputies oversaw thirty fresh men who took over the transport of victims. The corpses we placed on stretchers, and rivermen carried them to the larger shed, on my orders placing women and children on one side of the rails and men on the other. As the moon descended, I heard a rumble of thunder to the east, and I prayed it wouldn't rain until we had everyone—the survivors and the dead—inside one building or another. At last, Sergeant Trent and I climbed wearily into a cab. He dropped me at Wapping and continued home. It was nearly four o'clock in the morning, and I found a young man sitting up but asleep on one of the benches near the entryway, a folded paper between his loose fingers.

"Said the message was important," the desk sergeant said. "Wouldn't leave it."

I put my hand on the boy's shoulder and shook him gently. "Wake up."

Blearily he looked up. "Be ye Corr'van?"

I nodded.

"Got a message," he said, fumbling to hand it to me.

"You could've left it," I said.

He shook his head vehemently. "Wouldn't get paid unless I brung an answer."

I opened the paper and read: *Where are you? O.H.*
O'Hagan.

"Damn." The word slipped out before I thought.

"Ye fergot?" the boy asked with a smirk.

I didn't bother to answer. "Take this back to him." I turned the paper over, picked up a pencil from the nearest desk, and scrawled my reply: *Princess Alice steamer hit by collier at Gallions Reach. Hundreds dead. Need 2 days. Will see you Friday.*

McCabe might not like the delay, but there was no help for it.

The other message I wrote was to the Yard director, Mr. Vincent, to be delivered to his home immediately. I explained that he needn't bother going to Gallions Reach, as there was nothing more to do tonight. We'd need daylight to dredge the river, to begin the work of recovering the bodies from the muck at the bottom of the Thames.

CHAPTER 8

I stopped home for three hours of sleep and two cups of coffee, to prepare for the long day ahead before returning to Wapping. While the commissioner of Wrecks would be responsible for raising the *Princess Alice* and determining the cause of the accident, Director Vincent would want my impressions from the night before and would ask Wapping to give what assistance we could. Knowing the director as I did, I guessed he would be at the division early this morning, and I wanted to be there when he arrived.

But as I crossed the main room, I saw Vincent standing inside my office, his lean frame silhouetted against the window that overlooked the Thames.

Director Vincent was exactly my age, thirty-one. The second son of a baronet and a former correspondent for the *Daily Mail*, he had a public school education and a fastidious code of ethics that the Parliament Committee had depended on to refurbish the Yard's credibility after last autumn's scandal. I had not always appreciated him, nor he me. During one particularly unpleasant half hour, he had compared me to a rabid bear barreling through the woods. But during the case of the river murders, we'd found a wedge of common ground. Now, we trusted each other—at least enough that he chose me to fill the role of acting superintendent.

As I crossed the threshold, Vincent turned. His expensive hat was in his pale hands, held at his waist, and his voice held both sympathy and regret. "You must have had a hellish night."

"It was over by the time I arrived," I said as I removed my coat. "The *Princess* was sunk, and there was nothing we could do but hand out blankets and ferry people to shelter. If it wasn't for fishermen and lightermen and their boats, we'd have lost even more. And the commissioner of Wrecks sent some men," I added. I had reasons to dislike and mistrust Commissioner Rotherly, but I gave credit where it was due. "Beckton Gasworks gave us two dry railway sheds. Thank God they did, or people would have died of exposure."

"It renews one's faith, doesn't it?" Vincent asked. "People rallying round."

"I'm guessing a lot of Londoners know people on the *Princess*. The problem is we don't know their names."

"I understand." Vincent put his hat on top of a stack of papers on the desk, unbuttoned his overcoat, hung it on the rack, and took a seat. He wore a fashionable coat and trousers of fine gray wool, tailored to his lean, lithe form, with a white, starched, stand-up collar above a silk tie.

"Do you have any sense of how it happened?" he asked as we faced each other across my desk.

I shook my head. I wasn't going to repeat the watchman's allegations that it was the *Bywell Castle*'s fault for speeding down the river. Too often, civilians blamed a larger ship regardless of the circumstances. "Nothing beyond what I wrote in my message."

Vincent tipped his head. "Thank you for sending it as soon as you were able."

Despite myself, I felt one side of my mouth crook, and in his eyes, I found an answering flicker. One of Vincent's early gripes with me was that I did not communicate with him "in a timely fashion." As Ma Doyle would say, Vincent didn't need to have his fingers in the pie, but he wanted to know when it was being taken out of the oven, and I'd learned to do things differently.

"Two Yard men had family members on board the *Princess Alice*," Vincent said unhappily. "One, a nephew; the other, a son-in-law."

"Did they survive?"

Pain deepened the furrows in his brow. "The son-in-law is still missing. The nephew is almost certainly drowned. He was only seven years old and didn't know how to swim."

That was true of most Londoners, young and old alike. The Thames wasn't a place one swam voluntarily. I knew how, but only because when I was sixteen, I'd been thrown into the river, a rope around my waist, to learn. As the dockmaster said, he might rescue the cargo, but he wasn't bloody jumping in to save me when I fell off a lighter.

"And the women in their skirts," Vincent added.

"They're a heavy weight," I agreed. "Nearly impossible to swim in."

Vincent rested his elbows on the chair arms and templed his fingers, peering at me over them. "Do we have an estimate regarding how many souls were lost?"

"Upward of five hundred. The evening ebb current was probably three or four knots, so the bodies will be spread out along both shores."

He stilled. "Good lord. So many on board."

"It was a perfect day for an outing," I said regretfully.

"We've been inundated at the Yard, of course. People who can't locate their family members and friends are clamoring to file cases of missing persons."

"It would help if the bodies from the south shore could be brought over so people don't have to travel back and forth."

Vincent frowned in perplexity. "I assumed that was being done. You said all the bodies were being transferred to the gasworks sheds."

I shook my head. "You can't move an unidentified corpse from one county to another. It's an old law, not generally known."

"I can't imagine it's germane very often, but it's certainly a hindrance here. I'll see if we can suspend that temporarily." Vincent crossed one limb in its pressed trouser leg over the other. "I know that the Wrecks commissioner usually oversees these matters, but I'm assigning you to oversee the investigation, reporting to me." I stiffened, but Vincent appeared not to notice. "You'll need to coordinate with Rotherly, of course. He'll be handling the practical matters of raising the *Princess Alice*, retrieving bodies, and helping the families identify and claim them. But the Home Office and I are tasking you with discovering how this happened."

That was going to irritate Rotherly to no end. He didn't like me any more than I liked him, and he would perceive this unusual step as an affront and a threat to his authority.

"May I ask why?" I asked.

"I'm concerned this may have some correspondence with the Sittingbourne disaster."

That caught me up short.

I hadn't made the connection, but like the *Princess Alice* disaster, the railway accident had taken the lives of average Londoners, both wealthy and working class, traveling for pleasure to the sea and back.

"I see," I said, leaning back into my chair. "You think they're related? That . . . they're not accidents?"

His face was nearly expressionless, but I knew him well enough to understand this meant he was deeply concerned. "There was exploded dynamite found underneath one of the railway cars," he replied. "It seems the dynamite was used to destabilize the track. Men only discovered it yesterday, as they finished sifting through the wreckage. As such, the investigation falls under the province of the Home Office and the Yard rather than the railway investigators and the Board of Trade."

"Dynamite," I echoed hollowly. Vincent knew, as I did, that the only people in England who could reliably obtain dynamite were members of the Irish Republican Brotherhood. They were supplied by the Fenians, the arm of the Brotherhood in America, where the situation was very different. There, the Brothers were free to raise funds openly and speak out for the cause of Irish freedom, and after the Civil War ended, they recruited thousands of Irish veterans who had military training and access to arms and explosives. Indeed, the Brotherhood's use of dynamite was so established that no other group of malcontents would use it lest it be misinterpreted.

My stomach coiled tight as a rope around a winch at the idea that the Irish might be behind Sittingbourne and the horrifying scene I'd witnessed last night. "Has the Brotherhood claimed responsibility for it?"

"No." Vincent's fair brow knitted. "But, Corravan, you recall the Brotherhood's bombings in Edinburgh eighteen months ago."

I winced. "Four of them within a fortnight."

"The prelude to them was several months of violence in Cowgate," Vincent said.

The poor Irish part of Edinburgh. Like Whitechapel here.

I shifted uneasily in my chair. "So you're drawing a connection to the looting and murders in the Chapel and the Sittingbourne crash and possibly the *Princess Alice*?"

"You have to admit they follow a similar pattern," Vincent replied. "Stiles seems to think that the Whitechapel violence has to do with the Cobbwaller gang, not the IRB. However, given that these are all violent acts with the effect of stirring up fear in London, we have to acknowledge the possibility that the Cobbwallers and the IRB might be acting together."

I fell silent, turning this over in my mind. I doubted that the Cobbwallers would be calling attention to themselves this way. And the mercenary Cobbwallers and the political Brotherhood might both be Irish, but I didn't think it likely they'd be acting together. However, it wasn't impossible; I didn't know enough to speculate. "I'll keep it in mind," I said slowly. "But so far as I remember, no one was killed in the Edinburgh bombings. They were in empty shops and a church. Only a few people were even injured. The purpose seemed to be for Luby to show what he could do. The Sittingbourne and the *Princess Alice*—well, this is a wholly different scale of destruction."

"I know." He sighed. "But there's the dynamite at Sittingbourne. And as you may remember, in the aftermath of Edinburgh, Timothy Luby issued a statement that he would no longer rely on words to convey his message. 'Only deeds,' he said. That could be interpreted any number of ways."

So this disaster on the river might be the second of a series, I thought. *And Luby might not say a word until he was finished with the rest.*

"You understand the gravity," Vincent said.

I choked down the sudden thickness in my throat. "God, yes."

We were silent for a moment.

"Do you have any idea where Luby is?" I asked.

"No," he said. "We're looking. Edinburgh and Manchester divisions are keeping their eye out as well, but he knows how to keep his head down."

"Aside from the timing, which I agree is suspicious, is there any proof that the Brotherhood caused the *Princess Alice*?" I asked.

"Not yet." Vincent ran his hand absently along the front of his waistcoat. "And we won't know for some time if dynamite was on board the *Princess*. I've asked the Wrecks Commission to postpone raising the ship, to prioritize retrieving the bodies. It's the only humane thing to do." I nodded, and he continued. "I want you to oversee the work of compiling the lists of the survivors and the dead. If this was an attack, I wonder whether particular passengers were the targets." The difficulty of that must have registered on my face, for he added, "I know there were hundreds. I left a message at the Yard for Stiles to come here straightaway. A temporary reposting. I thought you might appreciate his assistance."

Relief eased the tightness in my chest. "Stiles can compile the lists. You can direct people looking for family members here."

"I would keep those lists private," Vincent cautioned. "Once a survivor's identity is certain, we can publish it in the papers, which will aid families in finding their relations. But keep the list of the dead for your own use, at least for the time being. Some of the corpses may be difficult to identify, and we don't want to make an error."

"Of course," I said. "If Stiles begins that task, I can get on with discovering how this happened." My mind was already making a short list of people I should attempt to speak to: the two captains, certainly. But also first mates, stewards, and pilots for each of the ships, if they came through it alive. If not, I'd need to seek out some of the surviving passengers and witnesses from the shore.

"Very well." Vincent took a breath that flared his nostrils, and with the air of someone resolving to cope with the matter at hand, he continued, "The captain of the *Bywell Castle* was waiting for me at the Yard this morning. He's utterly distraught, of course. I settled him in one of your interview rooms."

That was one fewer man I'd have to find. "Would you like to be present?"

Vincent shook his head. "He already spoke with me—albeit in a rather incoherent fashion—in the cab on the way here. And I must make my own reports to the Parliamentary Review Commission this morning. They're already asking for details of this, as well as of Sittingbourne. And I must explain why I have asked you to take the lead. There shall no doubt be some picayune grumbling, which I shall do my best to allay." As Vincent stood, I rose as well, passing him his coat from the rack. At the door, he paused. "Do keep me informed. Frequent reports, please. Daily, if possible."

"Yes, sir," I replied. "What is the captain's name?"

"Harrison. Thomas Harrison."

"And have you heard about the captain of the *Princess Alice*? Is he alive?"

"No news as yet, which worries me." He placed his hat on his head. "His name was Grinstead. I fear he went down with his ship."

"By God, I hope not," I said. Aside from hoping the man survived, it was always best to have the captain's account.

Vincent nodded before turning away.

As I resumed my seat at my desk, watching Vincent approach the front door, it swung open, and Stiles entered, paused to exchange a greeting with the director, and came toward my office.

"Corravan," he said as he reached the threshold. His expression was somber. "Dreadful business."

"I'm bloody glad you're here," I said.

"From what I gather, it'll take weeks to untangle this debacle." Stiles undid the buttons on his coat. "Vincent said you have a possible murder as well. An unidentified man."

The disaster had swept the man from the East Lane Stairs out of my mind. "Yes, I do. But for today, we need to focus on the *Princess Alice* and put procedures in place for gathering the names of the survivors and the dead."

"Of course," he said in his usual agreeable way. "What can you tell me about the crash?"

I recounted everything I'd seen the previous night and the substance of what Vincent had told me, concluding, "I'll talk to the captain of the *Bywell Castle* and ask Andrews to find me the captain of the *Princess Alice*, if he's alive. The first mate or chief steward, if he's not. I hope one of them made it."

Stiles grimaced. "No doubt it'll be a muddle, with witnesses from the two ships. Conflicting accounts and all that."

"It was all confusion last night in the dark," I said. "I'll send everyone I can spare this morning to help the commissioner of Wrecks with the recovery of corpses. Beckton Gasworks offered us the use of two sheds, one for survivors, and one partitioned in half, so the corpses could be separated into men and women, to minimize searching. The next step is to begin compiling passenger lists. I'd like you to take that on. We can release the names of survivors to the newspapers. The list of the dead we'll keep for ourselves for now."

Stiles's eyebrows rose in agreement. "God forbid we misidentify someone. It's only going to become more difficult as the bodies decompose in the water—or out of it."

"I know." I paused. "Vincent told me the Yard has been overrun with people asking about missing relations." My mind jumped to the dead man on the stairs. "Speaking of which, did anyone come to the Yard, looking for a missing man yesterday?"

As usual, Stiles followed my train of thought. He shook his head. "Two missing women this week, but no men. How certain are you that he was murdered?"

"He's better dressed than most drunkards and has a cheating pocket in his left sleeve."

"Ah. A gambler, then."

"And not a single person within half a mile remembers seeing him. Oakes thinks his head might have been struck with something round, not the edge of the step, and there's a bruise on his back." I found the sketch among my papers. "Here's his likeness for you to use."

"Thank you. I left the Yard's copy there, in case someone came looking." He pocketed it carefully. "Is the body still at the morgue?"

"So far as I know. They're going to be busy."

"Yes, of course." His face sobered.

A rumble of conversation in the outer room made me glance at the clock. Half past eight. All the men would be present, and they'd be prepared for a difficult day.

"Put advertisements in all the major papers, asking crew members of both ships to come forward to give statements," I said. "It'll save time hunting them down."

Stiles nodded.

"And let Captain Harrington know I'll be with him shortly. He's in the first room. I don't like to make him wait, but I want to assign the men their duties. I'll speak with him afterward."

"Of course. But—er, I believe his name is Harrison, according to the papers."

"Ah." I scrubbed my hand over my head to rouse my brain. "Yes, right."

I gathered all the men together before our large map and showed them precisely where the disaster had happened, describing what had been done thus far. Pulling only Sergeants Trent and Andrews aside, I sent everyone else out with orders to assist however they could in the task of retrieving bodies, identifying them, and getting the names to Stiles. All fifteen of them nodded to a man, despite the grim prospect and the rain that was beginning to pelt our windows.

As the room emptied, I asked Trent to remain at the front desk to make a record of inquiries by family members and to tell any witnesses I'd be with them as soon as I could. I turned to Andrews. "Can you find me the captain of the *Princess Alice*? Man named Grinstead. Vincent says he may have gone down with his ship, so if you can't find him, find the first mate, the steward, or the pilot."

"Yes, sir."

And now, at last, it was time to speak with Captain Harrison.

CHAPTER 9

In the kitchen, I made tea, one cup for each of us because the interview rooms were always cold in the morning. Opening the door, I found the captain seated in a chair, with his crossed forearms on the table, his head bowed so his forehead rested on them. As I closed the door behind me, he looked up. He saw the cups first and then his gaze shifted to my face. A man perhaps two decades older than I, about fifty years of age, the captain had a round visage with blue eyes and lines about his mouth that suggested general good humor, although at the moment, he wore a weary, stricken expression. His dark woolen coat smelled of the river. If I had to guess, he'd spent most of the night doing what he could to assist and probably hadn't slept.

I put the tea in front of him. "I'm Inspector Corravan, acting superintendent here at Wapping."

"Captain Harrison of the *Bywell Castle*." His right hand came toward the cup, slowly, and grasped the body of it, as if needing the heat. The crisp, unfrayed state of his collar and cuffs suggested some affluence, but he had a boatman's hands—thickened with muscle between the thumb and first finger, reddened from the weather, with blue veins along the back and a whitish scar at the first knuckle on his finger. I had a similar scar myself from a bad pinch caused by wrapping a line too fast around a cleat. A mistake he probably hadn't made in years.

"I'm cold down to my marrow." He took a sip. "Thank you."

"I'm sorry for the wait."

As I settled into my chair, he said, "Mr. Vincent says you know the river better'n most."

"I grew up working on it," I replied. "Stevedore, then lighter-man. Four years here at Wapping Station. Five at the Yard before returning here."

His eyes narrowed, as if recalling something he'd heard or read about the events that led to my transfer, and that topic had no place here. "Captain Harrison, could you tell me everything you remember from last night?" I tipped my head toward the door. "The director had to leave, to make his reports. I want to hear it from you directly."

"Yes, yes, of course." He licked his lips, then ran a rough hand over them to remove the spittle. "We were steaming downstream, three-quarters of the way along Gallions Reach, heading north-east, close by Tripcock Point."

"How fast?" I interjected.

"Five knots," he replied. "Perhaps six."

Not overly fast, considering the current, I thought. *If he's telling the truth.*

"It was dark," he continued, "and we could see the lights of Beckton Gasworks on the north shore off to the port side. There were a few colliers lined up to offload, taking up a good part of the river, so we maneuvered away, taking up a place toward the south shore of the river. It's deep enough there." He paused for my assent, which I gave readily. "And then the *Princess Alice* emerged from behind the point. I was at the rail, not far from my lookout man. When I saw her coming up Barking Reach showing her masthead and port lights, I assumed she would proceed on to the north shore, and we steered to come closer to the south shore, by Tripcock Point."

With an uneasy feeling, I guessed what might have happened.

The international rule was that two steamships should pass each other port side to port side. But as navigation on the Thames was overseen by several different organizations, the laws were errati-cally enforced, especially when local customs contradicted them. When the ebb tide was strong and the north shore was busy with large ships, it was customary and often more practical for a small boat going upstream to punch the tide and stay close to shore where the current wasn't so fierce, leaving the open water toward the middle free for the larger craft, which needed more room and depth to maneuver anyway. Seeing as how the *Princess* made stops along the south shore on her return voyage, she probably punched the tide at half a dozen spots on the way. My guess was the evening ebb tide would have been flowing at three or four knots, an advantage to the *Bywell Castle* on its trip downriver, but a substantial current for the *Princess* to battle going upstream. Swan's Pier was still some ways west of Gallions Reach, but once the *Princess* had passed the gasworks, with all the collier traffic, she'd look for a break in the traffic and cross to reach the north side.

"And you didn't see the green starboard light?" I asked.

"Not at first. But then, I could swear she turned and steered straight toward us. 'Twas the strangest thing!" He shook his head, as if still bewildered by it. "As soon as I realized what she was about, I stopped the engines and reversed them, full speed." He blew out a soft breath. "But she doesn't stop on a shilling."

"I know," I assured him. "The *Bywell* probably weighs at least eight hundred tons."

"Nine hundred," he replied. "Without her load of coal."

I nodded. "And then? Do you remember the moment of collision?"

"Every second," he replied fervently. "As our prow moved forward, I heard shouts from below. Someone on the *Princess* hollered, 'Ease her! Where are you coming to?' But we kept advancing—" He stopped abruptly and rubbed a hand over his face, tugging at his skin. At last, he dropped his hand and resumed. "First the *Princess Alice* vanished—I couldn't see her beneath our prow—and then I felt the smash and heard wood crunching and grinding and cracking . . . and the screams." His voice grew hoarse, and he looked down at his cup.

"What happened afterward?"

He didn't answer at first, just kept his head down.

Finally, I said, "Captain?"

He drew a ragged breath and met my gaze, his eyes glassy with tears that he dashed away roughly with the heel of his hand. "I ordered the crew to do what they could. They're all experienced rivermen, hardly needed me to tell them. They sent over lines for people to climb up, lifebuoys, our boats, planks, ladders—anything we could think of—and the mate kept the whistle on, full blast, to call other boats to their aid."

I opened my pocketbook and pencil, and based on the captain's account and what I'd seen and heard for myself, I drew a sketch of the river, with the point on the south shore and the approximate placement of the two ships at the moment of collision. I pushed it toward him. "Is this an accurate rendering?"

He studied it and placed a thick forefinger along the *Princess*'s starboard side. "Yes. We struck here, in front of the paddle box."

With most of the tea in him, his color looked somewhat better. I asked, "Could we start a bit earlier? What happened yesterday? Where were you moored? Was there anything odd about the schedule?"

He frowned and drew a folded handkerchief from his pocket. "I can't see what difference that makes."

My suspicions roused by his reluctance, I didn't reply, just waited.

He dabbed his handkerchief to his nose before answering. "We've been held up at Millwell for the past week, in dry dock for painting. The dock was crowded, and what with this and that, by the time we left, we were three hours delayed." A flicker of annoyance crossed his face, and I understood. Too long of a delay and he'd miss the evening ebb current.

"Where are you headed?" I asked.

"Newcastle, to pick up a cargo of coal, and then onto Alexandria, in Egypt."

"You're based in Tyne, then?"

He nodded. "My usual route is Newcastle to Egypt." Perhaps he saw my face change as I realized he didn't usually navigate the river, for he added hastily, "I brought a Thames pilot onboard, although I am under no obligation to do so by law. Man named Conway. John Conway."

Worry darted along my nerves. With that name, he was likely Irish. But I didn't ask. I didn't want the captain to speculate why it might be relevant. No doubt I'd meet Conway soon and see for myself. "Anyone else new on board?" I asked.

He rewrapped both hands on the cup, as if trying to absorb the last bits of warmth. "Nearly everyone. I had paid off my regular crew, planning to take on a new one when I reached Newcastle.

Aside from Belding, my mate, the men on board were runners, but I've used several of them before, and they're good men, as you probably know."

"Yes, I do." Runners, being London men who opted for shorter trips so as not to be away from their families for long periods, tended to be steady, experienced, and sober.

"What is Belding's full name?"

"Henry John Belding," he replied and gave the man's address in Lambeth, which I noted in my book.

"And this Conway," I said. "What can you tell me about him?"

"A quiet sort. Seemed capable. Took the wheel like he knew what he was about."

That eased my worry about Conway somewhat. "Were you sounding your whistle as you came downstream?"

"Every half mile, as is customary that time of night."

So the Princess *should have heard the collier coming,* I thought.

"Is there anything else you can remember? Anything remarkable?"

The captain shook his head despondently, his eyes on mine. "I remember all of it, too well. The screams. The children. Their shrieks coming from the darkness below." His voice dropped. "And then the silence."

★　★　★

I escorted the captain to a carriage, and then, back in my office, I took a fresh page of paper and wrote out my notes, with reference to my sketch indicating the boats' positions. For now, I omitted my impression that the captain's account might not be complete, but he was genuinely distraught and had not intentionally steered his ship into the steamer. I'd nearly finished when Trent appeared at my door. "The captain of the *Princess Alice,* Mr. Grinstead, is drowned, sir."

"Andrews found him already?"

Trent shook his head. "His chief steward, Frederick Boncy, is here, and he identified his body this morning. He's been with the *Princess Alice* for four years and is prepared to give an account. Should I put 'im in one of the interview rooms, sir?"

"No. I'll see him in here. Those rooms feel even colder than usual today." I paused. "Trent, let me know if John Conway appears. He was the pilot for the *Castle.*"

"Yes, sir." Trent returned a moment later with Mr. Boncy, a tall man with thinning brown hair and a wretched expression on his face.

"I'm sorry for this tragedy," I said.

Mr. Boncy sat in a chair, his hat in his hands, his red-rimmed eyes fixed on mine. "He could swim."

"Beg pardon?"

"The captain could swim!" he said impatiently. "But he wouldn't have spared himself. Last I saw, he was helping a poor woman and her son, and . . ." His voice faded, and his eyes veered off, seeming to fix on a point in midair. I've done that myself. Held the image in my mind and stared at it, trying to comprehend how it might've been different.

"Could you tell me your impressions?" I asked. "From the beginning."

Mr. Boncy inhaled, then blew out. "When we rounded Tripcock—"

"No, earlier," I interrupted. "From Sheerness. Begin there."

"Sheerness," he repeated.

"Yes."

He gathered his thoughts. "Well . . . we left at a quarter past four, same as always," he said. "We had more passengers than usual, what with people not wanting to take the train—"

"Because of the railway crash at Sittingbourne," I inserted.

"Yes. So we had new passengers with luggage coming on board, folks who'd spent a holiday at the resort and were return-ing to London. One of them was a police constable. Man named Briscoe, I think it was. I'd met him on the journey down, the previous week."

"A constable, you say?" I repeated, wondering if this was the same constable who'd taken a boat to look for his wife and son on the south shore. I drew out yet another blank page to make a note. At the top, I wrote, "Mr. Boncy" and the date. "Do you know what division he's in?"

He considered. "Finsbury, I think. G Division."

"Thank you. Go on."

"We had a short delay as we passed the region near Blyth Sands, as there was a large powder barge we had to steer around. We reached Gravesend at just before six," Boncy continued, "and Hopgood, the regular helmsman, stopped ashore. His friend John

Eyres took his place. Nothing unusual there, and Eyres is a good man. He often takes the *Duke of Teck* or *Duke of Cambridge*—two of the *Princess*'s sister ships—upstream. We continued on to North-fleet, where we picked up more passengers."

Northfleet was home to the Rosherville Pleasure Gardens, with an archery lawn, a lake with ducks, cliff walks, a bear pit, a theater, and a promenade with a view of Tilbury Fort.

"Then we passed the Tilbury Docks, the marshes, and the warehouses."

I nodded in understanding. "You reached Erith."

His face wrinkled in disgust. "Rounded the curve into Half-way Reach and came on Crossness Pumping Station. It looks like a palace, but there's a foul stench in the river when the wind's blow-ing from the south like it was."

"I know."

"And then we came up Tripcock," he said with a sigh. "I watched a tug straight ahead of us, pulling a barge so fast it was lifting out of the water."

"Really? I hadn't heard about the barge."

"Oh, it was there," he replied. "In fact, after the accident, the tug was one of the first boats to make its way toward us to help."

"And you were on deck?"

He nodded. "Mind you, I'd have been below except one of the passengers stopped me to ask what that infernal smell was. Then I heard shouts, and the hull was looming over us before we could do aught about it."

"I heard that the *Princess Alice* seemed to change direction. Starboarded first, then ported."

He frowned and leaned forward. "Look here, the *Bywell Castle* was moving faster than it should've, given the time of night. The evening ebb current is strong, and it was dark. Most boats com-ing downriver watch their speed, so they don't take boats coming upstream by surprise."

"Yes."

"There was a moon, but with the clouds, it wasn't a steady light. We heard the *Bywell Castle*'s whistle, o' course, but we assumed it was coming down the middle of the river like the big ships usually do."

"Was the *Princess* hugging the shore?" I asked. "Punching the tide?"

He appeared disconcerted that I knew about that maneuver. "Well, yes," he admitted. "It keeps us out o' the way o' the colliers lined up for the gasworks. There's always half a dozen of 'em either at anchor or making their way down river at that time of night."

"Officially, it's against the rules for navigation," I said, though I could anticipate his answer.

"It's the custom," he retorted. "Besides, it wouldn't 'a mattered. We could 'a been steering to the north shore, and we'd still 'a been hit, only on our port side instead. There was no maneuvering away from that ship in time. She's too big and was moving too fast."

"What do you remember of the moment the *Bywell Castle* struck your ship?"

"Prow hit straight into the starboard side, just 'a front o' the paddle box. Made a grinding, shrieking sound, and the wood deck popped away from the frame. Cut the ship." His hands came up to demonstrate. "Back part tipped to the stern and sank, and the front part pitched straight down into the river, throwing passengers off as it went. Most of 'em couldn't swim."

"You?"

A half-ashamed, half-defiant look. "I swam to the *Bywell Castle*, grabbed a hawser, climbed one of the lines, and pulled myself onboard." He shook his head in disgust. "The captain of the *Bywell Castle* was reversing his engines, trying to back away, but I hollered at him to stop. He'd cut people to pieces. He told me he'd drift to shore, and I told him better that than add to the dead."

That jibed with what Captain Harrison had said—that he'd put the engines into reverse—although he claimed to have done it before the collision and didn't mention he'd stopped them at the urging of Mr. Boncy. Was that a purposeful misdirection, or just the natural result of memory being sheared to pieces at a moment of peril?

"Then I helped unload one of their lifeboats into the water," Boncy continued. "Got right back onto the river, hauled four people aboard 'afore they could drown."

"Good man," I said mildly. "Tell me about Mr. Eyres. Where was he?"

His chin came up. "At the helm, where 'e should 'a been. Don't you be faultin' him."

"Do you know if he's alive?"

"I dunno. I didn't see what happened to him."

"Ah." I took out a sheet of paper and a pen, pushing it toward him. "Could you write down the names of your crew?"

He wrote for a minute, then pushed the list, about a dozen names, back toward me. "I put a check mark beside the ones I'd guess are dead."

"Why?"

"Couldn't swim."

That took out fully half the list. But he was betting on Eyres being alive.

"Where can we reach you if we have other questions?" I asked.

He provided his address, and I opened the door to usher him out.

Trent was standing there. He stepped aside and waited until Boncy was out of earshot before he said, "Beg pardon, but we found P. C. Briscoe, from the *Princess*. I put him in the first room." He hesitated. "Lost his wife, sir, though he saved his son."

A groan escaped me, and he nodded gloomily in agreement.

Relieved though I was to have a second account to compare with Boncy's, I dreaded facing the man's grief and forcing him to relive the event. But there was nothing to be done. I entered the room, bearing a cup of tea, and placed it on the table in front of the constable. The room was slightly less frigid than it had been earlier. The man was a few years younger than I, perhaps twenty-seven or twenty-eight, with a round face, a thatch of brown hair, and a rather oversized mustache. His brown eyes were bloodshot, and his right hand clutched at a handkerchief.

"Constable."

"Sir."

"I'm very sorry about your wife."

His expression tightened with resentment. "I had to cross the river three times, looking for her. The bodies are scattered everywhere."

I nodded in understanding. "We're trying to bring them all together in one place, but—"

"I know the law," he broke in, his eyes flashing. "But it seems you could make a bloody exception. Christ, it's merely common sense!"

"We're looking into suspending it," I said evenly. "Where did you board the ship, Constable?"

My emphasis on his title recalled him to himself somewhat, and the anger faded from his face, leaving it slack. "At Sheerness," he replied dully. "We'd spent a few days with my sister and her family."

"From what I gather, the trip was uneventful until the boat neared Tripcock Point."

"I'd say so," he said.

"What is the first odd thing you remember?"

"We heard a whistle, a deep one, that seemed closer than it should be," he said. "I looked around, but I couldn't see any-thing. We hadn't come far enough along Tripcock Point yet to see upriver. It's a blind curve."

"Yes, it is," I replied.

"My wife and son and I were aft, and I didn't think anything more of the whistle because I was trying to make sure Tommy didn't climb over the rail. He's only four years old," he explained, and I nodded. "Then I felt the boat turn to port, sharpish. My wife, Sally, felt it too. She looked at me, surprised, like."

"And then you saw the collier?"

"We'd passed the point, and you couldn't miss it!" His eye-brows rose. "Someone shouted to stop, but within seconds, we were in the hull's shadow, and then the hull itself was above our heads." His head was tipped back, and he stared up toward the ceiling, as if watching it all over again. "We could all see there was no help for it. I put my boy under my arm, and Sally and I ran toward the boxes where the life buoys were kept. One of the crew was handing them around, and I managed to put one around my boy, but you can imagine the people grabbing for them. I told my wife to hold onto me with both hands. I knew she couldn't swim, but I can. I thought I could get us to shore." His voice broke, and tears shone at the corners of his eyes.

"What happened?"

"The smash threw us—threw us off our feet," he replied. "The boat just broke apart, the wooden pieces buckling and ripping." He shook his head, his expression stunned. "It was so cold, it made my lungs stop. I couldn't draw a breath."

I knew that feeling.

He put his hands over his face, and his voice sank. "There were people everywhere, bumping us and grabbing for anything that wasn't sinking. We came back up to the surface, and I could hear the collier engines, and the water was cold, but I could still feel Sally's hands. Then something flew at us—a timber bursting out of its frame, I suppose. I felt it hit Sally, though it missed me and my boy. She let go, and she was gone."

The current would take a person swiftly downstream. "You got your boy to shore?" I asked.

His hands fell away, revealing hooded eyes dull with grief. "I know it's what Sally would've wanted—that Tommy lived rather than her. But he hasn't stopped crying."

I imagined neither of them would for a long time. I closed my pocketbook. "I'm sorry." I swallowed. "Did you find her?"

His chest caved with the sigh. "No. They're still dredging the river."

"We won't stop until everyone is found."

"The hell of it is we nearly missed the boat at Sheerness," he said bleakly. "Tommy dropped one of his toys, and we ran back for it. I was angry with him—stupidly because the *Duke* runs only forty-five minutes behind. We could have waited. Perhaps it was God's way of trying to save us, and we didn't listen." He leaned over the table, his gaze intent. "Do you know which boat was in the wrong? It was the collier, wasn't it?"

I understood his feeling, wanting to find a single cause, a place to lay the blame. But the truth rising to the surface seemed to be that both ships were at fault. It wasn't a story that would sit well with some.

I said only, "It's a terrible tragedy. I'm glad you saved your son. So many children died."

"I should consider myself lucky," he said bitterly.

I hadn't meant that. But there was no point in speaking. I'd felt loss like his before, a loss that shredded all reason, a loss that tore language from its meaning, so that nothing anyone said made a whit of difference.

CHAPTER 10

The next morning, I stopped in at Wapping to review Stiles's two lists of survivors and of deceased, the latter much longer than the former, and to read a two-page, detailed report from the Wrecks Commission—drafted by a man named Turner and signed by Rotherly—regarding the mechanical details of retrieving bodies and dredging the shallow parts of the Thames. They were making better progress than expected, I noted with relief. I asked Sergeant Trent to have the Wrecks report copied for Vincent, added two pages of notes summarizing my own discoveries, and ordered it taken by messenger to the Yard. I was glad my reports weren't going to Rotherly, who was not going to be pleased that both boats had broken rules. Enforcement of proper navigation laws fell partly under the Wrecks Commission, which meant some blame for the disaster might be placed at his door.

That done, I went to the Lambeth address provided by Captain Harrison for the mate Henry Belding, one of the few permanent crewmen who had been aboard the *Bywell Castle*. On entering a small boardinghouse, I found Mr. Belding in a frayed armchair in a dingy parlor, the window adorned with only one half of a pair of curtains, and the hanging mirror askew and black at the corners. Mr. Belding held open one of London's hundreds of newspapers, so as to read an inside page, and I could see the bold headline below the *Observer's* masthead: "Speeding Collier Causes Deadly Disaster on Thames." Over the top of the paper, I could see the man's scowl, his brown eyebrows meeting over the bridge of his nose.

I understood his annoyance. Newspapers were the bane of my existence during a case like this. Some would print stories that were half-truths or even outright lies that misled the public and stirred up ill feeling and panic like a whirlpool. Other papers seemed to take a malicious glee in recording just how quickly the Yard and Wapping fell in the public's estimation. But the sight of Belding reading reminded me that I ought to at least be glancing over the larger daily papers. Now and then, one offered a nugget of truth that assisted our investigation.

I crossed the parlor threshold, introduced myself, and explained that the captain had given me this address. With a grunt, he folded the newspaper and set it aside, and so that I might face him, I drew a chair a few feet closer. This revealed a brown spot on the carpet. I tried not to think of what might have caused it.

"I'd like to gather your impressions of the accident," I said.

Mr. Belding shook his head, his eyes angry. "Papers're sayin' it's our fault for going too fast, but it's just people wantin' to throw blame somewhere, whether it's true or not, so long as it ain't at them. It's bloody nonsense."

"I don't believe the papers," I replied. "Indeed, I haven't read them."

He gazed at me narrowly. "Well, you spoke wi' the captain. He's an honest man. I'll have naught more to add."

"It's our procedure," I said, "to gather accounts from as many people as we can, to form a clear picture. Could you tell me what happened, beginning with Millwall Docks? It seems you had a hard time leaving."

"Aye, we did. Damned unlucky! If we hadn't hit that bloody barge, we'd not ha' been delayed, and none of this would've happened."

What barge? I wondered.

He saw my surprise and thrust out his lower lip. "Ah, shouldn't 'a mentioned it. Naught to do with the accident."

"Which happened hours later and in a different part of the river," I allowed. "But I'd like to hear, all the same."

He rubbed his hands over his thighs. "Nothin' to tell. We cleared the outer dock, and a barge drifted across our path. It was their fault, and the *Castle* warn't damaged, so after a time, we were allowed to go."

A barge, being smaller and easier to maneuver, should have given way to the larger ship, it's true. But the captain's failure to mention it made me uneasy.

"How many other accidents have happened involving the *Bywell Castle* in, say, recent years?" I asked.

"None." His chin jutted forward. "That's what's so bloody strange! The captain's one of the best I know. I've seen him dock the ship with two feet to spare at Alexandria. He's careful. He's got an interest, y'see."

"In the *Bywell Castle*?"

He nodded. "Owns part of it."

"Is the barge why you were delayed coming downstream?"

"Aye, but first we had to wait for a pilot. The first didn't come, so the captain had to hire another."

"John Conway?"

"Dunno his name."

"You had a lookout?" I asked casually. The captain had mentioned one, but I wanted to be sure. The *Bywell Castle* would need one because the ship's forecastle was raised, so the helmsman's view was obstructed.

Belding appeared offended that I even asked. "O' course. Man named Hardy."

"A runner?" I asked.

"A good one."

"And the captain? Where was he?"

"Standin' at the rail, as was proper."

"And the pilot was at the wheel, to take his orders." I waited for his nod before I added, "Could you describe him for me?"

"Flamin' red hair, blue eyes. About my height, forty or so years old." My expression must have changed, for Belding looked askance. "Why d'you look like that? Aye, he's Irish, but I wouldn't hold it against him, so long as he knew his business. And neither would the captain! B'sides, why're you asking all these questions about *our* crew? We weren't in the wrong. We had a right to be where we were, and we *weren't* going too fast." He glanced over at the newspaper in disgust. "'Twas the *Princess* wasn't where she was supposed to be."

"There were good men on the *Princess*," I said. "Did you know the captain drowned, helping his passengers?"

My reminder had its intended effect. His face became doleful. "I'd heard. It's all a bloody shame." He studied his hands, heavy in his lap, before he squinted back up at me. "I went to the gasworks and helped shift bodies yesterday."

"That was good of you."

"Well, the bodies're beginning to stink." He grimaced. "Some have nary any clothes. It ain't proper for women to see 'em so. The Wrecks is thinking o' putting the belongings in boxes, letting folks identify the dead from their jewelry and such."

A clever idea, I thought. I'd never seen that done before, but we'd never had a disaster of this size.

The remainder of Mr. Belding's account accorded with that of the captain, but as I headed back to Wapping, I reflected on the one important difference. Perhaps Captain Harrison truly didn't think the barge incident was relevant; after all, it had nothing to do with the later accident except insofar as it caused a delay that put the *Bywell Castle* in one of the half-dozen tricky places on the river where there was a greater possibility it would hit the *Princess Alice.* He might even have forgotten the lesser incident in the face of the greater.

What would have been the usual time for the Bywell Castle *to pass Tripcock Point?* I wondered. They were running behind schedule because of two separate delays. Frederick Boncy had blamed the *Bywell Castle,* saying they'd been moving faster than usual. Had they been hurrying so as not to miss the evening ebb tide out to the North Sea? I would press the captain about his speed. I had other questions for him now, as well.

As for the pilot of the *Bywell Castle* being Irish—well, it certainly didn't mean he was a member of the Brotherhood. But I wanted to hear from John Conway, soon.

★ ★ ★

Back at Wapping, my first question for Sergeant Trent was about Conway. He shook his head. "No sign o' him, but you've two others who've been waiting a good bit. Mr. Eyres is in the first witness room, and Mr. Rotherly is in your office." He paused. "Mr. Eyres has been here nigh two hours."

I was tempted to see Mr. Eyres first, but I knew Rotherly would take it as an affront and whine to his superior, Quartermain. I thanked the sergeant and entered my office, bracing myself.

Winthrop Rotherly was a lanky man, bird-chested, with a head that he held forward of his neck, and narrow-set gray eyes. He had been a member of the Parliamentary Review Committee evaluating the Yard after the corruption scandal, and using it as an opportunity to forward his political ambitions, Rotherly had parroted every utterance of Chairman Quartermain, claiming that he too was in favor of shutting down the Yard and eliminating plain-clothes men from the other divisions. My interview had lasted an excruciating two hours, during which Rotherly had expressed how hopeless it was to expect men like me, who had been raised in "certain areas of London and without proper schooling," to operate with civility and what he called "aptitude." I had taken some pleasure in pretending not to know the meaning of the word.

"Corravan. At last." Rotherly's tone suggested that he assumed I'd slept late, dallied over a pleasant breakfast, and strolled to Wapping. But he inclined his head as if to prove that he, at least, knew how to be civil and was determined to shame me into behaving decently.

"Mr. Rotherly." I unbuttoned my coat and removed it. Sheer contrariness caused me to take my time hanging my coat properly on a hanger instead of slinging it over a prong on the rack like I usually did.

"Are you ready to make your report?" he asked.

I took a seat and folded my hands. "No. Not by any means."

He remained standing, staring down at me. "Corravan, the Parliamentary Committee has a right to know what happened and who is to blame, in a punctual fashion."

Poor Rotherly, I thought as I gazed up at him. *This time you're the one serving as the whipping boy for a Parliamentary Commission. How do you like it?*

He drew a folded paper from his coat and passed it across the desk. "I received this message this morning."

I opened it and read: *"The Irishman Conway at the helm of the Bywell Castle is dangerous. Look into his past associations."* It was signed merely *"A concerned citizen."*

Damn, I thought. *Is that a reference to the IRB?*

"You know that anonymous allegations can't be used as evidence," I said. "The Yard receives dozens of these messages every year. Most are proven to be completely misleading."

"But you will look into him."

"We're looking into everything," I replied curtly. "And everyone."

He clasped his hands behind him. "I have made my own inquiries."

Of course he had.

"The fact is, if the *Bywell Castle* had ported her helm, she'd have gone clear," he declared. "There was nothing in her way to the north!"

I could have said several things in response—not least of which was that there were, in fact, several colliers to the north, anchored and waiting near the gasworks. But I didn't want to lay down any of my cards. I merely fixed an expression of resigned patience on my face.

"Dragging this on is only going to compound problems—not only for the Wrecks Commission but for the entire city," Rotherly continued, his nostrils flaring. "People need to be reassured that travel on the Thames is safe again. And do you have any idea how this has disrupted traffic? It has slowed everything from Blackwall Reach to Battersea!"

"I'm sure it has."

"It's a serious detriment to tradesmen, who are trying to move their goods onto the docks—not to mention London shopkeepers and people who depend on those deliveries." He flung his open left hand in an easterly direction. "There are over one hundred and seventy ships bottlenecked between here and Sheerness, with goods that will spoil and lose their value if they can't be offloaded. Thousands of pounds' worth!"

And you report to the Board of Trade, I thought. No doubt the owners of those ships and goods companies were making their displeasure known. It was common knowledge that they poured money into the coffers of political aspirants. This shipping tangle wouldn't help Rotherly become elected to the House of Commons.

"And then there's the matter of safety," he said. "With all the congestion, captains lose the ability to move and maneuver, which causes still more accidents."

Captains navigated obstacles every day, but I held my peace.

There was a long silence, and at last his thin veneer of civility vanished. "Don't think I don't understand what you're doing, Corravan," he said sourly. "It's *base* and *unprofessional*. You're taking your revenge against me for what was a legitimate inquiry into corruption at the Yard."

"And you're rushing me because the delay is inconvenient for your Parliamentary ambitions," I shot back.

His lips thinned. "As if you have no ambitions yourself! You're delaying your report, manufacturing complications, all so you can seem important and prove your worthiness for this post, Corravan—a post you don't deserve."

A hot wave of anger rose. "I don't need to prove my worth."

"You do if you want to stay superintendent," he retorted. "You may be Vincent's choice, but even he can't stand up to the entire Commission if you make a muddle of this, and trust me, I can have everyone against you at a moment's notice!" He swept his hand in an arc, as if the committee were in the room with us. "I'm not the only one who will assume you're reluctant to blame this pilot because he's Irish."

"Captain Harrison gave the orders," I replied between gritted teeth. "And he said nothing about Conway disobeying them, so if there were any mistakes made, they weren't the fault of the Irish pilot."

"And if the Captain's memory is confused or incomplete?"

I flinched inwardly, given my own suspicions about that, but I wouldn't be bullied into making Conway my chief suspect.

"I refuse to issue a report full of falsehoods. We'd *all* look like fools," I said. Then I dug my upper and lower teeth into my tongue to keep it silent.

"Well, of course we want the truth," he scoffed. Then his demeanor altered, in the manner of a boat tacking in the other direction. His hand came out, as if to suggest a truce, and his tone was conciliatory. "Even if you're not wholly satisfied, can't you at least name the more likely responsible party? Share some recondite scraps of evidence you've found? We can release them to the papers, and that would satisfy people that you're at least doing *something*."

"We need to speak with everyone involved before making conclusions," I said with a glance toward the door. "Indeed, I have someone from the *Princess*'s crew waiting to be interviewed."

He drew himself up so that his head was set back in its proper place above his spine, and his nostrils flared with his exhale. "Well, far be it from me to keep you from your duty. But if I discover you have shaded your report one iota, out of some misbegotten desire to protect this Irishman, I will have you charged with obstruction." He placed his hat on his head, picked up his ivory-topped cane, and stalked out, closing the door behind him.

A fortunate thing, as what I hissed under my breath was better not heard by the men in the main room.

It was, as Rotherly would have said, base and unprofessional.

*   *   *

I found Mr. Eyres, the substitute helmsman from the *Princess Alice*, pacing as he waited for me. It was still cold in that witness room, so I asked him to follow me back to my office. The man, of medium height and slender, with short light-brown curls, looked disconsolate. He sank into the chair and rested his elbows on his knees, his gaze on the hat he held between his hands.

I thanked him for coming, which caused him to look up. His eyes were bloodshot, as if he hadn't slept.

"When did you come on board?" I asked.

"At Gravesend." Eyres's voice was heavy with regret. "My half brother, Creed, and I, both."

"Which of you was at the helm?"

"I was. He was assisting."

"And what was your heading as you approached Gallions Reach?" I asked.

"Captain gave me orders to stay on the south shore once I cleared the Point."

"To punch the tide."

He assented.

"So you were steering north until then."

"Yes," he said. "But as we cleared it, I saw the *Bywell Castle* coming toward us, and I realized we needed to keep straight on, or we wouldn't clear the collier. Only I felt the wheel pull to port."

"As if you'd hit bottom? Or as if the tide pulled you?"

"Neither." His head shake was quick, definite. "Like there was something wrong with the rudder."

I sat back. *A mechanical problem?*

"I know it sounds like I'm—I'm lying to cover my own mistake, but that's what happened!" he said stubbornly.

"There can be malfunctions," I acknowledged. And this turn to port jibed with what Constable Briscoe had said. "And then?"

Eyres put his hands up as if they were on the wheel and spun them clockwise. "I turned the wheel back, like so, but by then, the *Bywell Castle* was upon us, and it was too late. Even if the rudder had been working, we couldn't have avoided them."

"So you didn't give the wheel a port stroke?"

He leaned forward, his eyes glaring. "I tell you, I didn't! Not even half a one. There was something wrong with the rudder!"

"Meaning no offense, but had you or Creed been drinking?"

His spine stiffened. "Only a pint of ale with some pie before we came on board. My mind was clear."

"All right." I folded my hands. "What happened after that?"

"I was shouting for Creed to get the lifebuoys to the passengers and unload the lifeboats, to move people away from the paddle box because it seemed the *Bywell* would strike there. And by God, it did." He swallowed hard, remembering. "But there were too many passengers. There was nowhere for them to go, and the metal prow chopped us like we was no more than a raft. The deck cracked under my feet and began to tilt, with people falling everywhere and screaming bloody murder. And then . . ." A frown came over his face.

"What?"

"The oddest thing," he said. "Do you believe in spirits, Mr. Corravan?"

"No," I admitted.

"Well, I do," he said, his voice steady. "It was just before the *Bywell* hit us. I was at the wheel, but looking up, so I saw her coming toward us. And you'd think I wouldn't be attendin' to anything else, but 'twas like a spirit was warning me that someone was coming up from behind, meaning me harm."

I didn't believe in spirits, but I could believe he'd perceived something. In my experience, at the moments when my life is in danger, every sense is twice as sharp.

"Seconds after we were hit," he continued, "someone grabbed me from behind."

"Trying to save himself, at your expense?"

"No." His expression was dismissive, irritated. "He took me by the throat. How was choking *me* going to help *him*? No, he wanted to throw me down. I had hold of the wheel, which kept me steady as the boat lurched, but when I took a hand off to push him away, he dragged me away from the wheel, and threw me toward the water. I slid in."

"You can swim?"

"Oh, aye. Was born upriver in a little town near Slough," he said. "We all swam."

"And did you notice anything at all about him?"

He hesitated. "About my size, I'd say. Fair hair. Near white in the moonlight, almost like a ghost."

I nodded, filing that away. "Where did you come ashore?"

"Edge of the marsh, on the south bank."

"Is there anything else you can tell me?"

Eyres shook his head glumly. "I don't believe this accident was my fault, but—" He groaned, and his eyes sought the ceiling. "I wish to God I hadn't been on that boat." He met my gaze. "I can't sleep. I wake thinking I'm hearing boat whistles, and I know I've shouted out, by the dry feeling in my throat."

"I understand."

"I don't—I don't want to think on this anymore."

"Of course." I stood, signaling I wouldn't press him further. "Thank you."

He rose with a sigh of relief and shuffled to the front door.

After watching him leave, I went to the desk where Stiles had temporarily established himself. Several pages lay before him, written in his clear, slanted hand. "Are those the survivors or the dead?" I asked.

Stiles looked up. "The dead, in order of us finding them. I gave Sergeant Trent a ledger for all the passengers, and he's inscribing them alphabetically by surname as they come forward or are found, along with the date; and for the dead, the date the body is claimed." He grimaced. "Neither the ledgers nor the newspapers are complete, I'm afraid. There have been some mistakes in the papers."

"Well, we'll do our best."

Stiles's eyes darted toward the doorway through which Mr. Eyres had departed. "Did he have anything to add?"

I reviewed what I'd learned thus far, including the two separate reasons the *Bywell Castle* was delayed.

As I concluded, Stiles looked thoughtful. "So you're missing a river pilot."

"The original pilot of the *Bywell Castle*, yes," I said, puzzled that out of the entire account, this detail caught his attention.

He explained, "I just wonder if it might be the dead man from the East Lane Stairs."

I drew a chair close to the side of his desk and sat.

"I went to the morgue this morning," Stiles said. "Oakes gave me a magnifying glass, so I could see the man's hands more closely. He has some small scars." Stiles's right forefinger traced an arc over the first knuckle of his left and into the curve of the palm, between the thumb and forefinger. "One of them is a bit like yours, only on his left hand. And I remembered what you told me once about lightermen getting tattoos of anchors, here." He ran his fingertips under the hair at the nape of his neck.

"That's right," I said, although I didn't remember telling him so. I had one myself; so did Pat. We'd been tattooed the same day, at a shop near Spitalfields Market. "Good that you found it."

"The man's hair concealed it. He might have begun as a lighterman, but given his clothes, I'd say he's at least a helmsman now—or was before he died," he amended.

"Speaking of clothes," I said, "they reeked of gin. Does Oakes still think he wasn't a sot?"

He nodded. "Someone probably spilled gin on him, to make his murder look like a drunken accident."

"But if it was a murder, why'd they go to the trouble of putting him on the stairs?" I asked. "Why not dump him in the Thames?"

"To serve as a message to other gamblers?" Stiles guessed. "But then we're back to the question of why make his death appear an accident with the gin."

I wasn't going to try to sort that muddle. "What matters is this man was likely killed on Monday—presumably because he owed someone money, or he was caught cheating at cards. So if he was the pilot originally hired, it explains why Captain Harrison needed to hire Conway at the last minute."

Which meant Conway wasn't even supposed to be on the Bywell Castle. The thought gave me a glimmer of satisfaction.

"The captain would recognize the pilot," Stiles said. "If he hired him before."

I agreed.

"I know it's only one man when we have dozens to identify—" he began.

"It's important," I interrupted. "No doubt he has family who are worried too."

Stiles tapped his written pages into a neat stack and laid them aside. "Where can I find the captain? I can show him the sketch before I visit the family."

I gave him the captain's temporary address at the boarding-house nearby, and Stiles plucked his coat from the rack and left.

★ ★ ★

I spent the remaining work hours recording the notes from my interviews. I wanted to leave Wapping at a reasonable hour so I could see Belinda, who had promised to return from Edinburgh on the afternoon train.

I finished the last sentence, blotted it, and was bundling into my coat when Charlie Dower knocked on my door, his face heavy with concern. "Sir, do you have minute to look at summat?"

His right hand held a newspaper, and my stomach sank. We were approaching forty-eight hours since the disaster, and it was my experience that this was when, in the absence of facts, the initial shock had abated and, in its wake, the rumors took hold. Newspapermen needed to sell their papers, and human nature being what it is, Londoners wanted a story, even if it was false.

Wordlessly I put out my hand, even as his eyebrows rose in warning that I wasn't going to like what I found.

I read the headline under the *Sentinel* masthead: "Drunk Irishman Steers the *Bywell Castle*!"

A curse escaped under my breath. But I read on:

As the Wapping Police division investigates the cause of the horrifying "Princess Alice" disaster, certain distressing facts have come to light. According to the stoker on the collier "Bywell Castle," at the time of the collision, the crew of the "Bywell Castle" had all been drunk, and the Irish helmsman was the drunkest of them all.

Shortly after the collision, the stoker, Mr. George Purcell, along with three other crewmembers, climbed onboard the cutter lowered from the "Bywell Castle." They hoped to rescue several dozen out of the water, for the boat was intended to carry thirty. But by the time they reached that part of the river, only five remained alive. They took them aboard, along with four dead bodies, and steered downriver. On reaching Erith, Mr. Purcell voiced his accusations of drunkenness to a police constable, who also took down the names and addresses of the survivors. This paper has confirmed the PC's report of Purcell's account.

"Damn everything," I muttered. I knew how some would interpret that ambiguous final line. But by this account, the newspaperman never spoke with anyone on the *Bywell Castle* except for Purcell—not the captain nor the mate, Belding, nor Conway himself, none of whom were named. It was only one man's story, but it could cause no end of trouble because whenever the Irish were blamed for something, a wave of violence and crime followed.

Jaysus, what a tangle this was.

Charlie gave a soft cough. "It ain't going to help matters, is it?"

"No, Charlie, it's not," I said gruffly, and handed the paper back to him. "Good night."

"Night."

I finished up the last button on my coat and closed my office door behind me. There was no point talking to someone like Purcell. I'd seen his type before, noisy men who said stupid things even louder if they thought people were listening. But it seemed increasingly important I speak with Conway. Rebuking myself for not asking Stiles earlier to prioritize finding the man, I stopped at his desk, scribbled a note asking whether he'd discovered any mention of Conway, and placed it where he'd see it in the morning.

As I reached the front door, the desk sergeant handed me a written message. "It's just come, sir."

It was a note from Vincent, in his perfect penmanship: *I will attend you at Wapping at ten o'clock in the morning.*

I knew Vincent well enough to understand his intent with this message. He hated to be pounced on unexpectedly, so to his mind, this was a courtesy as well as a way to ensure I would be present when he arrived. I, on the other hand, would almost rather not have known he was coming. Given Purcell's story, Vincent's suspicions of Brotherhood involvement, and my Irishness, this was likely to be an uncomfortable conversation.

CHAPTER 11

A lit lamp hung from a heavy iron hook to the side of Belinda's back door.

Beckoning me.

Despite all my worry, my heart lifted as I turned the key in the lock and pulled the door open to find a second lamp inside, illuminating the hallway.

There is nothing like knowing someone longs to see you, I thought, *to banish the wretched images of the last two days.*

From the staircase at the end of the hall came the swift click of her heels. Visible first were her black, polished shoes, then her pale green skirts, and then all of her appeared, one hand holding a lamp, one hand on the banister. The thought came to me unbidden: light and balance. A sculptor couldn't have represented her character more accurately than she unconsciously did at that moment.

A warm smile spread over her face. "Michael!"

Four strides and I was at the bottom of the stairway. She stood several steps above, and I looked up at her, taking her in. Her dark hair was down around her shoulders, and her hazel eyes were bright and shining in the light of the lamp. As she gazed at me, a shadow fell over them, and her smile dimmed. "Darling, this must have been an awful few days for you."

I climbed until we were eye to eye, and I could take her lovely face between my hands. Just looking at her made something in my chest break open, allowed me to breathe deeper than I had since she'd left. Her hand came off the banister and her arm slid along my shoulder, as I kissed her to make up for the month she'd been away. My hands were in her hair, her lips parted under mine, and I couldn't say how long we stood there, the entire world collapsed down to those two steps. At last she drew away, her breath coming in small gasps. "It's cold," she murmured. "Shall we—take the stairs?"

"Take me anywhere you like," I said hoarsely, but she heard the laughing note underneath and chuckled softly in reply.

She led me up two flights, setting the lamp on a table in the upper hallway. We didn't need a light to find our way to her bed.

★   ★   ★

We lay amid the rumpled sheets, each propped on an elbow. By the lamp she'd lit, we could see each other. She'd offered to fetch cups of the coffee she always had ground especially for me, but I'd refused and wound a long shining brown lock of her hair around my forefinger to keep her here because I wanted to hear her talk, to take in her voice, to hear about her time away.

"It was somewhat of an odd visit," she confessed. "We three— Catherine and Margaret and I—were all close as children, and we remained so until Margaret moved up to Edinburgh. But it seems over the past few years, whenever I see her, she's . . ." She hesitated.

"What?"

"Out of sorts," she replied. "Oh, I know the fall broke her ankle, and she's in pain, so I can understand her being irritable on that account. But it isn't just that. She's agitated and anxious and . . . quite unhappy, in good part because of her son, Edgar."

I recalled her telling me at some point that Edgar was either attending Oxford or would be attending next year.

"What's wrong with him?"

"He's spoilt," she said frankly. "We've all known it for years, but Margaret has begun to see it too, and she knows it's partly her doing." She plucked the bedclothes and smoothed them. "I can't blame her, really. After she lost the first two babies, I think she was . . . almost too grateful for Edgar. She indulged him in everything, and as children do, he's become selfish as a result. Oh"—she gave a small shrug—"he has manners, which he takes out when it suits him, and he's as clever as his father, Philip, was. But Edgar is often disrespectful and even . . . cruel with Margaret. I don't think he would've dared if Philip were still alive." Her eyes were full of regret for her cousin. "She didn't *intend* to spoil him, of course, but now it's too late. He doesn't listen to her, or even talk to her much."

The phrase, a near echo of Ma's, made my thoughts slide toward Colin.

"What's the matter?" she asked.

I shook my head. "Nothing. Is Edgar at university yet?"

"He will be shortly. And that's another problem. He doesn't have what Harry has—a genuine interest in study and a willingness to work." She sighed. "Margaret fears he'll become one of those dissolute young men who gamble and visit opium dens until dawn."

I hadn't considered how lucky I was that Harry wasn't the sort I had to threaten or cajole. If anything, as James once said, Harry was too much in earnest.

"How was your visit otherwise?" I asked.

Her face cleared. "Oh, very pleasant. Edinburgh has its troubles, of course, but the castle and the views are just wonderful, and I walked out of doors every day. There were the usual dinner parties and concerts in the parlor, and Catherine came for a week, which perked us all up. We drove out into the country several times, with Margaret in a wheeled chair, and Catherine and Margaret would paint while I read or wrote. I think we all felt a bit as if we were children in Hertfordshire again." She gave a small laugh, a laugh I loved, and I felt myself smile along with her. But after a moment, the humor slipped away from her face. "Now, tell me about the *Princess Alice*," she said.

There was a time when I would have held back, when I would have wanted to hide that I was uncertain and fumbling and frustrated, and the case was just a muddle, typical of the early stages. But Belinda had seen me at my most unsettled and dejected, and, in the case of the river murders this past spring, particularly, her insights had helped turn the case toward a resolution. She listened attentively, with her usual nods of understanding, as I related everything that had happened since Tuesday night, concluding, "I'm feeling a certain urgency to hurry and fix blame because Rotherly—the Wrecks commissioner—is impatient. He doesn't like displeasing the Parliamentary Committee."

She frowned, as if trying to recall him. "Was he the one on the committee who—"

I nodded. "He told me I was holding back the report to make myself look important and protecting the pilot on the *Bywell Castle* because he's Irish."

"Oh, for goodness's sake."

"Parliament wants a resolution, but I suspect that it'll be more complicated than they want. On the one hand, the *Princess Alice* was breaking the official nautical laws, though many smaller ships punch the tide there. On the other, I suspect the *Bywell Castle* was going faster than it should have, especially for that time of night. And then there's also the dubious possibility that the *Bywell Castle* crew was drunk and one or both pilots were inept. Nothing is certain yet, but I have a feeling the accident is the result of several causes."

"The committee would prefer a single place to fix the blame," Belinda said, "so they could prevent it from happening again—although that usually works better in theory than practice."

I nodded. "And meanwhile, in the absence of a clear answer, the newspapers are making hay, inventing stories that only cause problems and interfere with what people truly remember."

"Well, you're adept at assembling a better story, Michael." She dimpled. "I've seen you do it once or twice."

"Easy for you to say," I grumbled. "You're allowed to make things up."

She laughed, then sobered. "I saw the newspaper account about everyone drinking on the *Bywell Castle*."

"A complete invention. They certainly didn't confirm it with the pilot. Unless there's something I don't know, Conway hasn't even been found yet." I shifted and shoved the pillow out of the way. "It rankles that the paper didn't even question it. They just threw it into the headline. By the captain's account, Conway was sober and responsible. The captain's exact words to me were 'He knew what he was about.'"

She grimaced. "It's unfortunate, but at least it was only the *Sentinel*, not one of the larger papers. Do you know where to find this man Purcell?"

"The captain probably knows, but I'm not going to bother because I think he's spouting nonsense. The captain certainly didn't seem the sort to be soused—and as I said, he has a financial interest in the *Bywell Castle*."

"Calling attention to the pilot being Irish seems irresponsible on the part of the paper," she said, "given the effect it could produce."

"I'm sure that's going to be Vincent's first comment tomorrow, followed by 'Can you pretend you're not Irish?'"

"Oh, Michael, do you think so? I'd guess he doesn't want you to pretend, but he probably wants to be sure you can be impartial." Gently she unwound her hair from my finger and lay back on her pillow, one hand tucked behind her head, revealing the soft pale flesh of the inside of her upper arm, and I couldn't resist running a fingertip along its curve. "If only so he can assure skeptics like Rotherly that he's spoken to you about it."

"I know." I rolled onto my back. The moldings above, where the ceiling met the wall, took on a different appearance than in the day. In the flickering glow of the lamplight, the carved edges cast shadows that took shape, slipped away, reappeared. At the corners were elaborate cornices with flowers and leaves that seemed to wrinkle and shift. "It's not as if all Irish folks are out to drown six hundred innocent souls—or to belong to a gang, for that matter. Most of them are just trying to feed themselves and their families, for God's sake."

She propped herself on her side to face me again. "No one thinks it's all Irish people. It's only a minority who belong to the Cobbwallers or the Brotherhood." When I didn't reply, she continued, "What's worrying you, Michael?"

"I don't know." My shoulders squirmed. "I just hope Vincent doesn't think I would wrongfully protect an Irish pilot."

"He knows better," Belinda replied, her voice practical. "You work hard enough that I daresay he sees you as an inspector first, an Irishman second."

My eyes flicked to her face. "It's not the only reason I work hard."

She heard the tight note in my voice. "Of course not." She sat up and drew the bedclothes up over her knees, wrapping her arms around them. "But people are concerned about Irish violence. It was a frequent topic of conversation in Edinburgh."

"Given the bombs in Edinburgh last year, I imagine it would be." I paused. "Any conversations in particular?"

"Last week, Lord Baynes-Hill and his wife Frances came to dinner. I've met them several times, and Frances and Catherine are intimate friends."

Lord Baynes-Hill, I thought, my pulse quickening. *Tom had named him as one of the leaders of the secret talks.*

"Why do you look like that?" she asked.

"I recognize his name," I said. "What did he say?"

She gave me a searching look, as if she sensed there was more I could reveal, but let it go. "He says the Edinburgh branch of the IRB calls themselves the Green League. Did you know?"

I shook my head.

Belinda continued. "Lord Baynes-Hill explained—very cogently, I thought—that he believes the Mayfair Theatre bombing in 1875 taught the Brotherhood something important—that nothing was to be gained from individual acts of violence, even if they threaten the lives of the royal family. The Brotherhood needed to demonstrate that they could manage a *series* of events effectually, which is why they bombed four places, one right after another. It certainly accomplished its objective, to raise awareness of the Irish question."

"I know."

"Now Lord Baynes-Hill is afraid it's only a matter of time before they attempt the same sort of sequence here in London. He feels that the sooner we move toward home rule for the Irish, the better, but he worries it can't happen until Gladstone returns."

I groaned aloud, and my eyes sought the ceiling with its elaborate carved medallion, from which hung the chandelier.

"Why, Michael." Her voice held both surprise and concern. "Do you think the Brotherhood could be involved in the *Princess Alice*? Do you think it could be the beginning of a sequence here?"

I bit my tongue to keep from telling her that it could be the second incident—or even the third, if one counted both the railway crash and the violence in Whitechapel.

Or was I taking a coincidence in timing too far?

Perhaps I was, but Lord Baynes-Hill was correct to say the Brotherhood's plans and methods were evolving. Whereas the Clerkenwell bombing had been a series of bumbling mistakes, with the IRB putting the dynamite in the wrong place and failing to break through the prison wall, the Mayfair Theatre bombing had been almost perfectly executed—four separate dynamite bombs, one at each corner of the theater. Although one of them failed, three of them went off within a minute, causing a stampede to the doors, ending with hundreds injured and forty dead. There was no doubt that over the years, the IRB had become more adept in its acts of terror, more calculated in making its plans and putting the pieces into place.

Into my mind came the thought of the murdered pilot on the stairs—followed by a thought that put a sick feeling in my gut.

What if I have it wrong? What if his death didn't incidentally cause Conway to be on the Bywell Castle? *What if the pilot was killed in order to put an Irish man—an IRB man—at the helm?*

"What is it?" Belinda asked. "You've gone white as the sheet."

My eyes met her worried gaze, and I tried to reel my thoughts back from where they were heading. I didn't want to see conspiracy where there was only coincidence. Still . . .

She shifted so she could face me straight on. "You've already considered it might be the Brotherhood, haven't you?"

I swallowed hard. "Aside from Conway—the pilot on the *Bywell*—being Irish, there's no evidence of it. And I'm not willing to assume Conway is a member of the Brotherhood—or that he caused this—without talking to him." I let out a sigh. "I bloody wish he'd come forward."

Belinda remained silent.

"And perhaps the newspaper is right, and he *was* drunk. He'd stay sober if he were involved in a plot, would he?"

"It's likely," she said. "Besides, Luby hasn't said a word about the *Princess*."

"That's true." I shoved down my worries that Luby was using only deeds for now, that words would come when he finished.

"I know you hate the idea of the Irish being involved." She pleated the trimmed edge of the bedclothes between her fingers. "But in the past, if the Brotherhood *did* cause the *Princess Alice* disaster, they'd have claimed it—otherwise there would be no point. It makes me wonder, what if there is another group that would want to bring about a maritime disaster like this? A company that wants to take over steamship travel, perhaps? Or was there a group of people on board who might have been a target?" I shrugged by way of reply. "And," she added, "perhaps the *Princess Alice* isn't part of a series of attacks at all. It might truly have been an accident, the result of several small mistakes, as you say, but anti-Irish sentiment is causing people to make up stories about it."

I'd seen rumors like this catch and spread before. "And the longer it takes for me to find the truth, the more the rumors grow."

"Because people are frightened and desperate to understand what happened, Michael. It's the most fatal disaster in London in years," she said, as if I needed reminding. "Not even the largest railway disaster or mining disaster killed this number of people— and so many of them women and children. It's drawn the attention of the entire country."

She's right, I thought. And God knows, there were plenty of people who despised and resented us Irish, who'd be willing to believe the worst. "It's an easy story to sell in the papers," I said shortly. "Even if it's a lie."

"You'll find the truth," she replied. "It may take time, but you always do."

Not always, I thought, *and not always in time to prevent further trouble,* but I didn't say so. She was trying to be kind. There was no reason to snap at her.

Belinda leaned close, then settled on my chest. She ran her fingers through my hair, got them caught in a tangle, and smiled as she gently combed it out. "You haven't forgotten your promise about Saturday, have you?"

"Your soirée? No, of course not." This would be the first time I would be attending her weekly gathering, the first night she would be introducing me to her friends. We had laughingly owned that we were both a bit anxious about it, but it seemed the proper time, and her return from Scotland provided a good reason for a larger party, which would mean less attention focused on me. "My new coat and trousers are hanging in my room."

She touched her forefinger to my chin. "Thank you."

And though I closed my eyes and let myself be swept into her kiss, and later into sleep, the possibility of rumors expanding and dispersing over London like one of our infamous miasmas, fostering rage and fear like a disease, stained my dreams with dread.

CHAPTER 12

The next morning before I headed to Wapping, I went to Beckton Gasworks, to see for myself how the Wrecks Commission was managing identification of the bodies.

As I drew close to the two railway sheds, the stench of decomposing flesh reached my nose, and I groped hastily for my handkerchief. *Best to get the worst of it over with,* I thought, and entered the one for the corpses. On the bare floor lay bodies side by side, in four neat rows perhaps forty deep, with men on one side of the iron tracks and women on the other. Here and there, a blank space on the floor showed where a body had been removed. There was only one Wrecks man, halfway down the men's side, standing near a woman bent over a body, both hands raised to her mouth, stifling a cry.

My stomach tightening, I turned away and walked into the other building, where I found Sergeant Trent between a Wrecks man in uniform and a gray-haired man whose white collar and black coat identified him as a priest. No longer were there men and women in sodden clothes, wrapped in blankets, sobbing and clutching each other's hands. Instead, the cavernous space was strangely silent. On one side of the railway tracks stood long tables with small lidless cardboard boxes, rather like miniature open coffins, placed side by side. Several pairs and trios of people moved along the row, poring over the boxes, taking up one and then another with shaking hands.

I caught Sergeant Trent's eye, and he left his position against the wall and made his way toward me.

Meanwhile, I picked up one of the boxes from the nearest table, tipping it so I could see the various items inside as they shifted and tumbled. Some coins, a pin, three matching bone buttons, probably taken from a coat, and a simple, wide silver ring large enough for a man's finger. So little to signify a life. Yet there were gaps in the rows of boxes. Some had been claimed by people who had known the dead intimately enough that they were able to identify a corpse from as little as this.

"Morning, sir," Sergeant Trent said.

I replaced the box in the row. "A good idea," I said, my voice husky. "Rather than trying to identify the bodies."

"'Twas Mr. Stiles wot suggested it to the Deputy," he replied.

"Ah," I said. I shouldn't have been surprised. Trust Stiles to find a less agonizing way for people to claim their dead friends and relations.

"We've collected jewelry and buttons, eyeglasses, pocket watches, snuff boxes, and such," he explained. "The number on the box matches a tag around the dead person's wrist. It's easier than seeing the bodies. As you can guess, most of 'em aren't looking much the same as when they was alive."

"It's been days," I agreed. "They're decomposing."

"And it saves folks the trip, crossing the river." He grimaced. "We're allowed to bring these bits over, but not the bodies themselves."

"I know," I said, understanding his frustration. "Vincent was going to try—"

A shriek came from one of the young women. "It's Tom's!" Her voice broke. "Tom's ring." With trembling fingers, she examined the object in her palm, then she clenched her fist around it before turning and burying her head in an older woman's shoulder, her entire body heaving, her cries like those of a small animal caught in a trap. The other woman's face was pinched and gray. His mother?

I stifled a groan. *What a bloody wretched business.*

The Wrecks man picked up the box and guided the two women to a separate table with two chairs. The younger one sat opposite him as his thick fingers removed the remaining items and laid them on the table. The older woman looked on blankly, her face slack, all signs of emotion gone.

As I left, I heard another cry of pain as a man identified the items in a different box.

If some monsters had caused this disaster, this ugly sprawl of death, would they have done so if they could have stood in my shoes, here in this building, and seen the suffering it brought? And could they still be so heartless as to cause more?

And if it was an accident, then the sensational rumors were a desecration of these people's grief, a mockery of their most sincere feelings.

CHAPTER 13

At Wapping, I found a note on my desk, addressed to me in Stiles's hand. Hastily, I unfolded it to find a few lines:

Captain Harrison says our dead man is the river pilot he usually requests for the Bywell Castle, *Mr. William Schmidt. As Schmidt's parents live abroad, and his wife is deceased, I have asked Mr. Schmidt's father-in-law Mr. Benjamin Davis to identify the body at the morgue. He is engaged today, but I'll escort him there tomorrow. He has never heard that W. S. gambled or drank to excess. But he wasn't dismayed to hear of his death. I gather there was no love lost between them. I'll discover what I can. —S.*

And then a postscript:

Regrets, I have not come across John Conway yet, alive or dead. I will pursue.

I refolded the note and walked toward my office, thinking about Schmidt.

It certainly wasn't unusual for a man to keep his gambling and drinking from his father-in-law. But if those vices weren't the cause of ill will between Schmidt and his relations, I wondered what was. I found myself hoping Stiles would uncover yet another plausible motive for his murder. It would make me feel better to know that Schmidt had been murdered for reasons having to do with his own personal failings and not in order to bring John Conway on board the *Princess Alice*.

But where the devil was John Conway? Why had he still not come forward?

As I reached my office, the building's front door swung open, with the hinges screeching in protest, and closed with a slam that shook the windows. I spun around to see Captain Harrison coming straight toward me, carrying a newspaper coiled tightly in his left hand like a truncheon. His bearing was still dignified, but his color was high, and his eyes wide and bright with indignation. In his wake was another man, younger and slighter of build, who held his hat in his hands and cast his gaze about curiously, as if he'd never been in a police division before.

"Mr. Corravan, have you seen this?" As the captain reached me, he unfurled the paper. My heart sank as I glimpsed the masthead. It wasn't the *Sentinel*. It was the *Beacon*, a newspaper that prided itself on its lurid stories. I'd had several bitter quarrels with Fishel, one of their more sensational writers, who had published accounts that nearly wrecked my cases.

"Drunken Irishman at the Helm!" proclaimed the headline.

I stifled a groan. "I saw something similar in the *Sentinel* last night." I waved him and his companion into my office, where the captain stood with his carriage upright, and the young man remained deferentially behind. I wondered if he was a river pilot; he had an intelligent face and an air of competence.

"Mr. Corravan, I understand you have a great deal to resolve, but this slander must be publicly corrected!" The captain's cheeks flushed. "George Purcell is a liar! I've brought an engineer who can corroborate my account."

Ah, an engineer, I thought. *Yes, that fit with his demeanor.*

I turned to him. "Your name?"

"Dimelow, sir," he said. "Peter Dimelow."

"How long have you worked on the Thames?"

"Nearly fifteen years," he said. "I know George Purcell. When he came on board that day, he *was* rather the worse for drink"—a quick, apologetic glance at the captain, which led me to believe he'd already been chastised by his superior for allowing it—"but as he is a fireman, it was my opinion he could manage his duties, as they were purely mechanical."

"What do you say to his claims that everyone was drunk?"

Mr. Dimelow shook his head. "A fabrication to cover up his own shameful weakness. I've made several voyages with Captain Harrison and have never seen him even faintly intoxicated. And the other officers were sober as well." I took note of the hat held at his side. A hat held by the fingertips could betray a tremor, pointing to inner turmoil or doubt. His bowler was motionless. "Purcell is—frankly—a blustering fool, although under normal circumstances that matters not a whit. He's shoveling coal."

"But it wasn't normal circumstances," the captain interjected. "It was the worst possible."

"Begging your pardon, Mr. Corravan," Dimelow continued, "but I'd say he was likely plied with drink and urged to make his story as sensational as he could. I heard he was still drunk the next morning."

"If you consider it logically, Purcell's account is wholly improbable," the captain added earnestly. "How could so many efforts toward rescue have been made if everyone was drunk? And this bit about how the Irish are more prone to drunkenness is absurd! I've worked with plenty of Irish who are steady and sober as anyone."

"Some men speak to newspapers to feel important." I undid my coat and hung it on the rack. "I wouldn't worry. People like Purcell don't tend to make credible witnesses in court, where it matters—usually because the paper has paid them a fee—or, as you suggest, purchased their drinks."

Mr. Dimelow looked relieved and the captain somewhat mollified.

"I have a few questions I'd like to ask you, though, privately, Captain Harrison." I didn't want him feeling as though he had to maintain and defend his previous answers in front of Mr. Dimelow. The captain nodded to the engineer, who nodded back respectfully and left the room, closing the door behind him. I settled in my chair and gestured for the captain to sit opposite.

"Thank you for helping to identify Mr. Schmidt," I began. "Mr. Stiles has spoken with the man's family."

The captain slumped in his chair. "Wretched business, on top of everything else. He was a good pilot."

"And what sort of man was he?"

He considered a moment. "I'll admit he was not particularly amiable, but he did make three journeys with us, with no trouble at all." He shrugged. "It's difficult for Prussians just now because of the war. But I don't believe in holding anyone's nationality against him."

"He was from Prussia?"

"Born there. His father was a helmsman on the Rhine, so it's in his blood. He came here when he was seventeen and began as a lighterman."

"Did he ever mention how his fingers were injured?" I asked.

"He told me they were smashed between two boats as a young man." His mouth twitched. "He never made that mistake again."

So Mr. Schmidt's crushed fingers might not be due to unpaid debts. But he also could have been lying to the captain, who didn't seem the sort to approve of a gambling habit.

"Had you ever seen him drunk?" I asked.

"Never." He leaned forward. "I permit myself one cup of ale at lunchtime, no more, and I advocate the same for all my men." His right hand cut a horizontal line in the air. "If I'd known Purcell was in that state—well, I wouldn't have let him on my ship, my engineer's opinion notwithstanding."

"And can you tell me anything about Schmidt's personal life? His late wife or her family?"

"I'm afraid not," he said.

I leaned my elbows on the desk and folded my hands. "You didn't mention the collision you had with the barge as you left Millwall."

He looked momentarily nonplussed. "Well, it was hardly relevant to the *Princess Alice*, and it wasn't a collision. I'd have called it a bump, and the barge admitted they were at fault. They steered into our path. I had a few papers to sign, and we were allowed to proceed." He rubbed thoughtfully at his chin. "I served on an investigative board for the docks for one year. If there is one thing I understand, it's that you must keep your gaze focused on the task at hand. Introducing extraneous information is unhelpful."

A fair point. "I understand you are a part owner in the *Bywell Castle*."

"I own one-sixty-fourth of it."

"Were you rushing downstream so as not to lose the ebb tide?"

He tapped a forefinger gently against the chair arm. "Mr. Corravan, we couldn't make up all the time we'd lost, so I didn't try.

If we could catch some of the tide, so be it. But safety is more important than speed. One cannot sacrifice the one for the other. It rarely pays."

"Tell me about Mr. Conway, the river pilot you took on. How did that come about?"

"Well, I sent the usual message to Mr. Schmidt three days before, hiring him for the journey, requesting that he meet me at the ship at nine in the morning. When it was half past nine, I decided something must have detained him. Fortunately, Mr. Conway was available."

"How did you find him?"

"He was at the dockmaster's office, picking up his wages for another journey he'd made. It was fortuitous, as he was able to take Schmidt's place."

Fortuitous or orchestrated? I wondered, my earlier suspicion flaring. "Was he the only pilot available?"

"Well, he was the only one at the office, sitting on a bench," the captain said. "There was some confusion about the amount he was owed, so Conway had to wait to speak with the clerk. I must say, he was quite good-natured about it. Not everyone would be."

Or was he finding a reason to linger because he was waiting to be asked to join the Bywell? The flare of suspicion burned brighter.

"What else can you tell me about Mr. Conway?" I asked.

The captain's eyebrows rose. "Why, nothing. I'd only just met the man. The dockmaster vouched for him and showed me his record of twenty years and over four hundred voyages up and down the Thames. That was enough for me."

"He followed your orders?" I asked.

"To the letter."

"Any signs of intoxication?"

"Absolutely not!"

"And did you see him after the collision?"

He hesitated. "It was dark and there was a great deal of confusion. Immediately after the collision, I went aft to help unload the lifeboats. He may have followed me once the ship stopped. I don't recall seeing him, though."

"We haven't been able to locate Mr. Conway," I explained. "He hasn't come forward. Do you have any idea why?"

"None at all," he said, with some surprise. "Given these head-lines, I'd imagine he'd want to clear his name. But I have his address. It was his first time with us, so I planned to enter it into our log." He withdrew a somewhat battered black pocketbook from inside his coat and paged through it. From where I sat, I could see the tidy entries in a neat hand. "Locks Mews, number three," he read aloud, and I made a note of it, hoping it truly was Conway's address.

"I'll pay him a visit." I glanced at the clock; it was nearly ten. I thanked him, walked him and Mr. Dimelow to the front door, swung it open, and saw them into a cab. As they rolled away, another rolled up, and Vincent disembarked. "Good morning, Corravan."

"Good morning, sir." I led him back to my office.

Vincent closed my door with the quietest click and adjusted the chair that the captain had vacated, so its back stood perfectly parallel with the desk, before he sat. "I caught a glimpse of Captain Harrison leaving. Was he here to discuss the reports in the newspapers?"

"Both he and his engineer say Purcell is a drunken sot." I spread my hands. "The captain insists that he wasn't intoxicated, nor was his crew. I have no reason to doubt him, sir."

Vincent's head tipped questioningly. "And Mr. Conway? The Irish pilot?"

I stiffened at Vincent's use of the word "Irish" despite myself. "The captain says that Mr. Conway was at the wheel and obeyed orders. He saw no signs he was drunk."

Vincent lowered his chin and fixed his eyes on mine. "I'd like to know whether you believe the fact that he is Irish is salient, given Sittingbourne and the Whitechapel murders."

I didn't like the way this was tending. "I wouldn't assume so," I replied at last. "Are you giving any credence to the anonymous letter Rotherly received?"

"No. We both know how little those can be relied on." Vincent leaned in, just an inch, although with him, the smaller the gesture, the stronger the feeling behind it. "But Corravan, I must ask—less for myself than for anyone who might inquire." He waited for my nod. "Can you hold your biases in abeyance for this investigation?"

I willed my voice to remain mild, without a note of defensive-ness. "I hate the thought that an Irishman or an Irish group might have caused this." I paused, recalling that horrifying night on the Thames and the wretchedness I'd just witnessed at the gasworks shed. "But it's not the Irish I know, sir. I've no trouble holding whoever did this to account. It's nothing short of murder of innocent people if it was a planned sabotage."

Vincent was silent for a moment. "What do you know of this man Timothy Luby? Is he a madman, as some say?"

The question surprised me, and I considered for a moment how to answer it.

"No," I said, the syllable dragging long. "I don't think he's a madman." Vincent seemed to be waiting for me to continue, and I recalled some of what I had read of Luby's speeches, which were printed in their entirety in the Irish papers. "I don't agree with his methods, but I think he's been pushed to his limits."

His eyebrows rose. "Go on."

"When the potatoes failed, one million Irish died in five years, from starvation and dysentery and famine fever because England wouldn't send them grain." I stopped to let him weigh that fact.

"They sold it overseas instead," he replied soberly.

I nodded. "To Luby, Irish misery over the past century has been the product of our leaders' policy of accommodation, relinquishment, and spinelessness, which results in yet more poverty and violence."

Vincent leaned back with a sigh. "I'm ashamed that some of Ireland's tragedy derives from mismanagement by men from some of our most prominent English families." He shook his head dispiritedly. "But I cannot countenance terror being unleashed on the people of London."

"No, sir."

Vincent templed his fingertips and touched them gently to his mouth. "Thus far, Mr. Luby has not made a public statement concerning the *Princess Alice* disaster. My fear is he is keeping silent until he's finished, so as to make his demands that much more compelling. If Sittingbourne was first, and the *Princess Alice* second, what will be the third?"

I eased sideways in my chair, "It's still possible that the *Princess Alice* was a tragic accident. We haven't found dynamite yet—"

"They didn't need it," Vincent interrupted. "With Conway at the helm, the *Bywell Castle* became their device."

"But the captain said it was only chance that Conway was at the dockmaster's office that day, picking up his pay from another journey. Until I speak to Conway, I won't assume he's a member of the Brotherhood—or, frankly, anything about him."

"Conway surely knows we'd want to question him," Vincent said. "You must admit, the fact that he hasn't come forward makes him appear guilty."

"He could be in hospital or with his family, recovering, and they haven't thought to notify the papers."

Vincent let me see his skepticism. "How could he have been injured on the collier? From what I gather, the collision barely rocked it."

"But he may have been injured in the aftermath—unloading the lifeboats perhaps. We've no notion of most of what happened that night." Vincent's expression seemed to concede that was true. "Either way," I added, "I will find him soon, I swear."

He rose from the chair. "Good luck."

"Thank you, sir."

* * *

Conway's house, number three in Locks Mews, was small, well kept, and in a short street with only four other houses. I rapped on the door, to no avail. I went around back, peering into a window. The place looked as though no one had been home for days.

Returning to the front door, I looked left and right. There was no one about.

Vincent would never approve of what I was about to do. I certainly couldn't include anything I found here in my reports.

I slipped my case of picks out of my pocket, chose two of the proper size and shape, and opened the door, letting myself in. By the dim light through the windows, I searched the place, finding no evidence of a wallet, money, or anything of value, aside from some clothes, that would suggest he was ever coming back.

Damn. This does suggest a guilty flight, I thought.

Until I caught sight of the shelf by his bed. On it, in a leather frame, was a portrait of a young woman. Beside it lay a gold ring and a lock of brown hair tied in a faded ribbon. I picked up the ring and studied it. Much too small to be a man's. If I had to guess, this had belonged to his late wife.

If—God forbid—Belinda had died, I'd never have left those keepsakes behind if I were planning to be gone for any significant amount of time.

I picked up the portrait. She was pretty, with brown hair and a pleasant face. The glass was without dust, as if he tended it regularly.

I was willing to bet Conway's participation in the disaster wasn't premeditated or intentional, for he hadn't planned to leave. If he wasn't dead, he was in hospital or in hiding. But how *could* he have been injured on the *Bywell Castle*? And if he was in hiding, why? Who was he afraid of?

CHAPTER 14

I hadn't forgotten that I was to meet McCabe, head of the Cobbwallers, on Friday night, but what with one thing and another, I didn't leave Wapping until nearly half past seven. I was still dressed in plainclothes, but I took the precaution of concealing my truncheon in the special pocket of my trousers, covering it with my large coat.

O'Hagan had asked to meet at the Waterman Pub, and I arrived at just past eight o'clock. He was already seated near the hearth, with two men who eyed me and stiffened as I approached the table. One muttered out of the corner of his mouth; O'Hagan's right hand rose an inch above the table and resettled, and the two men sat back in a way that made me think of dogs heeling at the command of their master.

I glanced around the pleasant room. I'd been here several times, and I knew there was a back room that would be private enough for a conversation, but I didn't remove my hat. McCabe wouldn't be here. This would be merely a stopping point, for he would want to be certain I had no one accompanying me.

My coat still buttoned, I stood at the table, showing no impatience, knowing O'Hagan would enjoy that sign of nerves, the same way he used to enjoy seeing his boxers' restless feet and hands before sending them into the ring. With deliberate slowness, O'Hagan finished his pint and rose, and I followed him out the back door, with the two other men behind. Their shadows came alongside me and vanished in the lights from windows above. We cut through one lane, a mews, a courtyard, another mews, all of which I recognized, and at last we halted at an unnamed crossroads that stank of rancid fish.

Wordlessly, O'Hagan put one open palm toward me. I undid my coat and withdrew the truncheon from its pocket. Then I bent and slid the knife from my boot. I handed both to O'Hagan, who passed them to the shorter of the two men before he ran his hands over my person.

"For God's sake," I muttered. When O'Hagan finished, I held out my hand in return, and with a short bark of laughter, he withdrew a black hood from his pocket. As I hoped, he left me my hat with the reinforced brim, so I wasn't entirely without a weapon. I pulled the coarse cloth over my head, adjusting it so the seam didn't cut across my face and I could breathe, and kept my hat in my right hand. The cloth smelled of cheap tobacco, no doubt from a previous wearer. I could see bits of light through it.

O'Hagan's footsteps fell away, and the two men each took one of my arms, presumably so I wouldn't trip, and walked me forward.

We started down Bett's Alley, no more than a narrow passage, really. About thirty paces on, we turned right and then left, walked forward and back, then took enough turns that I stopped counting and started to gather what information I could. I felt the dirt under my feet give way to cobbles and back to dirt. I smelled burnt bread and the piss of cats, stenches that the dustman left behind, even if he carted out the waste. Then came a waft of an acrid, metallic smell that would be easy to identify again, as the men's steps slowed. Merely from the feel of the hands on my arms, I could tell the men were tense, watchful, looking about. We stood silently, waiting for God knows what. A signal, perhaps, that it was safe to advance.

A keen anticipation quickened my pulse. It might seem peculiar that I, as a senior inspector at Scotland Yard, had never met one of the most infamous figures in the London underworld, but our paths had never crossed until now. No doubt McCabe took some effort to keep himself out of the way of the police, so we didn't know much about him, but I brought the few facts to mind.

James McCabe was brought up in Seven Dials by his grandfather, a notorious thief-taker with a network of pawn shops and receiving houses where stolen goods could be sold or returned to their rightful owners for a fee. I'd never heard much about his father but after his grandfather's death, young James, shrewd and determined, expanded his modest empire of pawnshops, low-rent boarding houses, gaming houses, opium dens, boxing halls, and counterfeiting establishments. But never brothels. It was a peculiarity of McCabe's; rumor had it that his mother was a prostitute, and he'd never wanted anything to do with that business. During the past decade, McCabe had extended his reach into Clerkenwell, St. Luke's, Spitalfields, and Whitechapel, but he tended to keep his crime orderly. People understood his rules, and so long as they played by them, he didn't change them arbitrarily. When they didn't, his revenge had been swift and uncompromising—a snitch's house burned to the ground, a thief's hand cut off, an informer stabbed and left for dead in an alley with his mouth full of feathers. Unlike some leaders of the underworld, including Murphy in Southwark and Shelton in Lambeth, McCabe didn't vent his fury in rash actions but tended to calculate his movements. To my mind, that made him a more dangerous man.

At a low whistle from somewhere ahead, both men tightened their grip on my arms, and we advanced, my feet moving unsteadily down a short slope of small loose stones. The man on my left rapped twice on wood and then pushed open a door that swung away from us with a low creak. I was shoved across the threshold, and the air collapsed behind me as the door closed. I reached up and tugged off the hood.

McCabe stood behind a table, his shirtsleeves rolled, his heavy hands resting on the top rail of a wooden chair. He was probably ten or fifteen years older than I, forty or forty-five, and perhaps a few inches shorter. But there was a bulk to his shoulders that made me think of filled sandbags. His eyes were as Irish blue as my own, looking at me from under hooded lids. His complexion was pale, almost fine, as if he didn't spend much time outdoors, but his hands were broad and weathered. He turned one of them over, revealing a scarred palm, and gestured for me to sit in the chair opposite.

In these situations, when I have no idea what someone knows, or what someone assumes I know, I stay quiet. I let him study me for as long as he liked, and at last his left eye twitched and crinkled, and I saw what might have passed for the beginnings of a smile.

"What can I do for you, Mr. McCabe?" I asked, at last.

He chuckled softly. "You're mighty p'lite. They teach you that at the Yard?"

"No reason not to be polite. We're just two men talking."

He gave a throaty sniff, folded his hands at his waist, and sat back, all the humor wiped from his face. "O'Hagan told me about you."

"I expect he knows a good bit."

There was a short silence.

"Do you know, I began as a star-glazer myself," he said conversationally, but the words scraped at me like a razor against a strop. How did O'Hagan know that piece of information, that I'd been a star-glazer? It was years before I'd met him. I'd been barely thirteen. I was one of a hundred boys who worked under a brutal man named Simms. Then again, London's underworld was a web of connections. It wasn't unlikely Simms knew O'Hagan. More important to me was the reason McCabe laid down this shard of knowledge. He wanted to demonstrate his long reach—both into Whitechapel, where I'd been a thief, and into my past.

McCabe pushed back from the table, deliberately, as if to reassure me he meant no harm. He paced slowly back and forth before the hearth. Though his step was firm and as noiseless as a cat's, he walked with a slight imbalance that spoke of an old injury. A man less sure of his power might have tried to hide the infirmity, but McCabe didn't. At last he turned to face me. "Beggin' your pardon if I keep you."

I spread my hands. "I have time."

"Do you know where I come from?" he asked.

"Seven Dials, or so I've heard."

A grimace. "Ach, ye know as well as I, it don't matter the name of the place."

I spread my hands again, to let him know I was listening.

"My grandda was a thief-taker. Did you know that?"

I allowed I did.

"Back in the day o' the Bow Street Runners, he used to snap up thieves and let 'em go for ransom." His mouth twisted. "He saw the possibilities of havin' thieves in his pocket and police in his pay, receivers and fences and pawnbrokers, all working together. Taught me plenty 'afore he died."

"What about your father?" I asked.

He returned to his chair, his bulk creaking it. "A jockey. He was thrown from a horse. Died before I knew him to speak of. Like yours."

Again, I felt surprised by McCabe's knowledge about me. Had I ever mentioned my father's death to O'Hagan? Perhaps. More likely, knowing I was living with the Doyles, he'd guessed I'd been orphaned.

McCabe set his forearms on the table and rubbed the palm of one hand absently over the knuckles of the other. I sensed him feeling his way forward, as if down a dark alley, careful of his steps and willing to take his time. "You're not at the Yard anymore?"

"No. I'm at Wapping, at least for now. They needed a temporary superintendent."

His mouth twitched, which told me he knew about Blair's disgrace.

"There was a shooting a while ago here in the Chapel, by a Russian," he said. "You know about it?"

"I heard."

"They're moving here, you know. Russians, Poles. Men from places I never heard of."

Was McCabe blaming his two dead men on the Russians and Poles? I wondered.

"You want a name?" he asked.

"I imagine you'll tell me if you want me to know."

"Dead man is Jovanovich. Man who killed him is Belsky." He pursed his lips. "Not so tall as you, and thinner. Black hair, brown eyes, about your age." He touched his cheek. "A scar here, and a big chin."

"Do you think he's killing your men?"

"No." He drew out the syllable. "Just want you to pass it along to your friends at the Yard. If Belsky's causing trouble, I don't want the blame landing on me."

"All right," I said. "I'll pass it along."

He glanced away and then back. "What does the Yard say about my three men?"

So there had been another murder since Monday night, I thought. "O'Hagan told me there were two. Not that I've heard anything about them."

His eyes narrowed in disbelief. "Not a word?"

"I haven't been at the Yard for three months," I replied. "There are twenty men there, each with at least thirty cases on their desks. Why would I know about these murders? Not to mention I've been bloody busy of late. So if you have something you want to know, you need to explain yourself."

One shoulder raised and lowered as if to concede my point. "Three shot dead in the past fortnight. Is the Yard doing it?"

I didn't pretend to be affronted. "I know you're thinking of Clerkenwell. But there's a new man at the helm—Director Vincent—and he's a stickler for laws. He'd never condone Yard men killing anyone. He'd arrest them himself."

A skeptical smile formed around his mouth and vanished.

"Even if he weren't the upstanding sort," I added, "he can't afford another scandal."

This was a logic McCabe understood.

He deliberated for a moment before he said, "I've a man who told me he saw Yard men kill one of 'em."

An eyewitness? I wondered, feeling a stab of dismay. *And more than one Yard man?* I sat back, wanting to anchor my spine against the wooden back of the chair.

He tipped his chin up so he could look at me down his nose. "So you think it's Russians, trying to shake me out of my place?"

His tone told me this was a test to see if I'd jump at the chance to push his suspicion away from the Yard. I wasn't about to tell him that Stiles was already looking at the Russians. I shook my head. "I'm not going to make guesses that might steer you false."

McCabe gave a nod, as if I'd satisfied him. "The man who told me the Yard men were to blame—well, I might have reason to doubt 'im."

"One of yours?" I asked.

He gave a noncommittal sound, but his eyes held a bitterness that made curiosity flare along my nerves. Had this man once been one of McCabe's but was no longer? Did this mean a rupture in the Cobbwaller gang—perhaps one of the younger members breaking away?

"What's his name?" I took care to flatten my expression, so he would see no reaction, no matter what he said.

"Finn Riley." His eyes never left mine, but I didn't have to feign indifference. The name was vaguely familiar, but there were plenty of Rileys in Whitechapel.

"O'Hagan says the first two men were found in Boyd Street and Folgate," I said. "What about the third?"

"Deal Street."

I wasn't supposed to know their names. "Who are they?"

He hesitated, weighed the cost of telling me, then shrugged. "Sean Doone, Tom O'Farrell." He cleared his throat, as if that second name was harder to say than the first. "Ian Dwyer."

I didn't know him, either. "When was Dwyer?"

"Two days ago."

"How were they killed, specifically? How many shots?"

"One, in the back of the head. All three of them." He frowned. "I'll tell you another thing. There's reports of guns coming into Whitechapel. By the dozens."

The skin around my eyes tightened.

"Thought that might int'rest ye." He planted his heavy elbows on the table. "They ain't for me. More guns means trouble for both of us."

"Yes, it does. Any idea how they're coming in?"

"Couldn't say," he said.

"I'll pass that along," I said.

"That's right, Mickey." His voice held a note of scorn for what to him seemed no action at all. "You pass it along."

This was the third time he'd dropped a piece of information that suggested he knew plenty about me. This one made me more uneasy than the others, for some reason. Perhaps because Mickey was a name I'd left behind in Whitechapel, when I'd run for my life.

McCabe's eyelids were half lowered, but his gaze was unwavering, and he turned over his palm for the third time. It called to mind the old Irish tales Ma Doyle used to tell; the giants were always beaten on the third try. McCabe jerked his chin upward. This was my signal to depart, so I rose and knocked on the door. When a man opened it, I put the hood back over my head.

A key scraped in the lock behind me, and once we were back out in the cold, the men walked me about a third of a mile in silence, taking a series of turns. At last, the hood was yanked off, my truncheon and knife silently returned, and the two men melted away into the shadows.

I stowed my possessions in their usual places and stared up at the roofline. Above it was a silvering quarter-moon, tipped so far it reminded me of a metal pan on one side of a dockyard scale, until a cloud slid over it, dimming it to nothing.

The thought that the Yard was being blamed for the murders worried me, and I hoped I'd convinced McCabe that Riley was wrong. If I hadn't, and the Cobbwallers retaliated, the Yard would clamp down, starting a cycle of revenge killings and arrests like the one between the police and Murphy's gang in Southwark four years ago.

But there was something else McCabe said that nagged at me, sparking a feeling of danger close by.

I retraced the last few moments of my conversation with McCabe and found it. McCabe had called me "Mickey."

O'Hagan called me "Corravan," same as the men on the docks did. "Mickey" was what the Doyles called me. It's what Colin called me, as soon as he could speak plainly, after he got over the funny sound he'd make at the back of his throat because he couldn't say his "k's" properly.

My heartbeats slowed to thick, hard thumps driving into my ribs.

"Mickey" was McCabe's way of telling me that he knew Colin. That he had Colin close enough to learn that from him. Which meant Colin felt more loyalty to McCabe than to me.

I didn't want to think about how that hurt.

I needed to find Colin.

I needed to know how deep he had waded into these waters.

CHAPTER 15

The Waterman was busier than it had been two hours ago. O'Hagan sat at a different table, with three men, playing cards. I caught his eye and tipped my head toward my shoulder, to ask him to come speak to me. At first, I thought he'd refuse, but after a moment, he rose, leaving his pint on the table, and sauntered to where I stood.

"Where's Colin?" I asked.

"Dunno." He rubbed his reddened nose with the back of his hand. "You talk to McCabe?"

I nodded.

His eyebrows lifted, and he looked at me questioningly.

"If McCabe wants you to know about it, he'll tell you," I said, my voice flat. "Where's Colin?"

"I'm not his keeper," he retorted. "Mebbe he don't want you to find him."

"He's my family. I'm responsible."

"He's nigh twenty years old!"

"Tell me where he is, or I'll tell McCabe our deal is off."

He crossed his arms and glowered at me. "Try Pinton's. There's a game."

A chill ran down my back, but I nodded and left. Pinton's was a pub with a tough gambling hall upstairs. They had cheats who would lure players in by letting them win for half a dozen games before they took everything back, and then some. I knew several men who'd had to borrow from the moneylenders on Chipwell Street after a few nights at Pinton's. What the devil was Colin doing there?

I entered the pub and headed toward the back stairs. At the bottom, two burly men stood like watchdogs, nursing their pints. One of them saw me approaching and took a step, preparing to ward me off.

My hands in the pockets of my overcoat, I stopped a few feet from him. "I don't need to go up. I just need to talk to Colin Doyle." I let my eyes flick from one to the other, registering their faces. "He's not in any trouble. I used to live with his family. Name's Mickey Corravan."

"I'll see if he's here," one said, and handed his pint to his friend.

A few minutes later, the man returned with Colin in tow. By unspoken consent, Colin and I stepped over to a quiet corner of the room.

"You talked to O'Hagan?" Colin asked, his voice easy, as if it barely mattered.

"I did." Shouts erupted at a nearby table, but not for worlds would I have taken my eyes off Colin just then. "Turns out it was McCabe who wanted to see me. We had an interesting conversation just now."

His expression remained neutral, but I saw a shadow of something—guilt, perhaps, or worry—appear fleetingly in his eyes.

I leaned close. "How deep are you in with him?"

He scowled. "Who said I was?"

"He knew I used to be a star-glazer."

Colin grimaced. "O'Hagan probably told—"

"He called me Mickey," I interrupted. And when Colin's face changed—God, his remorse made him look like a boy for the briefest moment—I added more gently, "And he did it in a way that let me know he'd heard it from you."

His eyes darted sideways, and I sensed a growing interest in our conversation from the two men guarding the staircase. I put a hand on his shoulder. "Let's go outside."

We stood together a few feet from the door, where there was no window. The chilling wind parted his curls, revealing the paleness of his scalp underneath.

"Now, what are you doing for him?" I asked.

His head still down, he shuffled side to side, then fell back against the brick wall.

"Jaysus," I said, exasperated. "Just tell me. I'm not going to shout at you, stupid as you're being."

His chin came up, and any sign of shame or guilt was gone. His eyes glinted in the light coming from a window across the way, and he burst out, "What right do *you* have to shout at *me*? What right do you have to tell me anything?"

"For God's sake, Col, you're the closest thing I have to a brother," I flashed back.

He turned to stare down the street.

"Ach," I groaned, softening my voice. "What are you thinking? Getting mixed up with the likes of them?"

"That's rich, coming from you. You boxed for 'em for nigh a year."

A snort escaped me. "Since when do you do something bloody stupid just because I did it?"

A look of uncertainty passed over his face, followed by indignation. "So when you do it to earn money, it's fine, but when little Colin does it, it's not?"

"But you don't need to—"

"Well, someone had to after you left," he snarled.

All I could do at first was stare. It had been the work of years to load that much bitterness into his voice, and that, more than the words he spoke, got through to me like a hand slammed against my chest. Clearly, he had a reason for resentment that he'd been holding close, and I took a step backward, to give him space to throw it down on the ground between us.

"What do you mean?" I asked quietly.

"When you left, you took money—money we needed. Didn't you think about that?"

"Two pounds, twelve, which I paid back within a year!"

"I don't mean *that!*" He grimaced. "I mean the wages from your boxing and working on the docks! When you left, don't you remember? The roof was leaking, and Sean and Paddy Byrne came to fix it? They finished, and we didn't have the money to pay them. They mocked me for months 'til it was paid." He swallowed hard, as if the shame still choked him. "B'sides which, Ma had laid out money for new stock and couldn't pay that either. She had to borrow money from a man in Chipwell Street, at interest. You know how that is. Took us years to dig our way out."

Ma had never given a hint about any of this. Ever. Of course she wouldn't. She'd never want to saddle me with that guilt.

I forced out the words: "I didn't know."

"How could you?" he shot back. "You left without a backward glance! We could'a all gone to hell, so far as you were concerned."

The cold running along my bones had nothing to do with the damp night air gusting around us. "That's not true," I managed. "God, that's not true. I thought of home every single bloody night! How could you say that?"

He shrugged, his face full of mistrust. "Not what it seemed to us."

I had a sudden sick feeling, the breath sucked out of me as if I'd been punched just below my ribs. But I'd think about that later. Right now, I had to find a way to convince Colin he had alternatives—and that I could help him find them. "Regardless of what I did, working for men like O'Hagan and McCabe is a mistake, Colin."

He pushed himself away from the wall. "I'm getting back to my game."

"Wait." I made one more attempt. "What does he have you doing? Collecting money?"

"What does it matter?"

"I don't want you to end up dead."

His jaw hardened. "Like Pat, you mean?"

Pat. Briefly my eyes closed as I sent a silent apology to Pat that I had taken my eye off Colin long enough for this to happen.

"Finally feeling guilty about that, are you?" he asked. "I can see you do."

"About his death?" My voice rose. "Jaysus, Colin. You can't blame me for that! I wasn't here—I hadn't been here for years!"

"Damn right you weren't!" he exploded. "And if you hadn't left, Pat would still be alive. He'd never have got mixed up with those men!"

"I didn't make that choice for him!"

"Yes, you did! You left him no choice! You know how the docks work. You can't be alone!"

"There were other Irish there!" I fired back. "And what good would I have done him, staying and dying in some godforsaken Chapel alley?"

Colin shook his head in disbelief. "O'Hagan wouldn't 'a killed you. Says he would've given you a chance to explain."

"That's what he told you, is it? And you believe him?"

"Yah."

"Well, I believed Ma," I snapped. "She came to the dock that day, told me O'Hagan thought I'd ratted him out to the police, and I had to run. So I did."

Colin's mouth screwed up in an ugly line. "All worked out for you, didn't it?" he asked, as if that was all that mattered to me. He took another step toward the door.

I put an arm out to stop him. "Colin, I can get you away from McCabe and Whitechapel. You can still undo this. Hate me if you want, but don't be so proud you can't admit you made a mistake and change direction."

He evaded my reach and kept walking. "Stop worrying about me," he threw over his shoulder. It was less an attempt at reassurance than a command. He didn't want my help in any way.

"Wait. Just—"

He didn't even turn his head. The door opened, and voices and shouts of laughter became clear for an instant. Then it closed behind him, and the sounds vanished, and I was alone.

Stunned, I stood for a moment, holding that last image of him, his profile silhouetted by the light coming from the pub window, his dark curls tumbling over his forehead, the sturdy bulk of his shoulders and chest.

My stomach in a snarled knot, I turned away.

All the way home, I found myself pausing at corners, using shop windows as mirrors, checking over my shoulder because I felt someone trailing me. The feeling didn't leave until I reached my own door. Even then, I scanned the empty street as I inserted the key in the lock and entered my house.

It seemed I hadn't been followed.

Perhaps it was just the feeling that my past was slipping up behind me in the dark, coming close enough to remind me that it's always there.

CHAPTER 16

I woke with a feeling of dread sitting heavy as a sack of grain on my chest. I'd felt this before, plenty of times, although usually it was because of a case.

In a foul humor, I came out of my house and raised a hand to hire a cab. The driver slowed—but as he looked at me, he shook his head and drove on. What the devil was that about? My scowl deepening, I walked to Wingate Street, where there was always a long line of cabs looking for fares. A newspaper boy stood nearby, shoving a baked roll into his mouth, and I offered a coin for one of the papers under his arm. I climbed into a cab, unfolded the *Standard*, and read the headline.

"Irish Brotherhood Man at 'Bywell Castle' Helm! More Attacks Anticipated!"

The jouncing of the cab over the cobbles made it impossible to read the smaller type, and I shouted to the driver to stop. He didn't hear me—until I roared at him, "Damn it, stop the cab!" He halted, and I scanned the three paragraphs, snatching up the salient sentences:

Mr. Timothy Luby has maintained a stalwart silence about Irish Republican Brotherhood activities. However, an anonymous missive delivered to this newspaper's offices has suggested that the IRB used Edinburgh in March 1877 as a proving ground for London.

John Conway, the pilot of the "Bywell Castle," is a member of the IRB. His name appears repeatedly in the IRB ledgers of attendees at their meetings.

And the final line: "As we have seen, where the Irish Republican Brotherhood has acted once, it will act again and again, with no remorse."

I felt the blood drain from my face and a tingling begin in my arms.

"Drive on," I shouted.

"Aye, guv'nor," came the gruff voice from above, and the wheels turned again.

I strongly doubted that Luby had been reached and had refused to comment on the attacks. More likely, he hadn't been found at all. I also discounted this new "anonymous missive" with its alarming suggestion and the final line, which was pure fearmongering. But what riveted me was the comment about John Conway.

There is certainly more than one John Conway in London, I thought. But how had the newspaperman discovered his name? Surely Captain Harrison wouldn't have talked. Had Purcell?

A groan escaped me. There was no getting around the fact that Conway hadn't come forward. Much as I hated the idea, one plausible explanation *was* that Conway was IRB, and he was in hiding because he was guilty of sending hundreds of innocent people to their deaths.

I closed my eyes to recall Conway's flat. Tidy and lonely, with that tender memory of his wife enshrined on the shelf.

Then again, perhaps the woman wasn't his wife. Or perhaps she was his wife, but she had died, and her death had embittered him to the point of well-disguised madness. Perhaps she'd been killed in a way that made Conway bitter against the English, or Londoners in particular. Or he might avidly believe in the IRB's goals of home rule.

There was no point in these guesses. I simply had to find the man.

★ ★ ★

I spent all of Saturday morning searching for Conway among dead bodies, first at the gasworks and then, across the river, at the

Carstairs Works, where they had been placed in a long, window-less shed that stank of rotting flesh. Combing through the corpses was a wretched, nasty business, but I was desperate to find Conway, and I needed first to ascertain he wasn't dead. The one piece of luck was that I could look for his flaming red hair. I found two people with hair of that color: one, a woman, and the other, a child no more than eight years old. The Wrecks Commission was nearly finished bringing bodies out of the river, having dredged both banks constantly for four days. As I finished my inspection, I felt reasonably certain Conway had survived.

Next, hospitals. There were dozens throughout London, but I began with those on the south shore because they were nearest. St. Bart's was only half a mile from the Carstairs Works, and while they hadn't received anyone matching Conway's description, they did provide the names of eight other hospitals on the south shore where survivors had been brought. None of the eight had anyone matching his description in their wards; nor since Tuesday night had they admitted and released anyone matching his description.

The sun was falling, and the shadows had swallowed up the streets by the time I decided to stop. It had been a long, wearying day, but as I left the last hospital, I knew I couldn't go home without seeing Ma. I needed to talk to her about Colin, to learn what she knew, and to see if together we might find a way to convince Colin to let me extricate him from McCabe's clutches. All day, as I trudged from place to place, I had replayed Colin's words and expressions, turning our exchange this way and that, trying to see my departure from Whitechapel through Colin's eyes, and wondering what had happened between the time I left Whitechapel—when Colin was a cheerful, roguish boy—and now. It wasn't as if I hadn't seen him over the years. Had I really been so oblivious to his growing bitterness?

I climbed the steps to the Doyles's door, knocked, and—when I didn't hear an answer—put my key in the lock, turning the handle as I did so. I pushed—but something was blocking the door.

"Ma? Elsie?" I called, my voice sharp. "Are you all right?"

"I'm comin', Mickey," Elsie replied, and after a moment the weight against the door shifted, and I heard the scrape of an object along the floor.

I entered and gestured to the chair. "What's that for?"

She shrugged. "I'm here alone. Wanted to be safe."

I looked at her, puzzled. "Any reason you wouldn't be?"

"Just being careful."

I removed my coat and hung it over the chair by the door. "Where's Ma?"

"Visiting with Mrs. McKibben." Elsie bent to add coal to the stove.

First Conway, then Ma, I thought. *This is not my day for finding people where I want them.*

"A cuppa?" Elsie asked over her shoulder. "We don't have any of that mucky stuff you drink."

"Tea's fine," I said with smile. "You know it is."

She flashed a grin and reached for the kettle. Her hands moved capably to freshen the tea in the pot and arrange the cups, but I sensed her studying me out of the corner of her eye. Meanwhile, I reconsidered my disappointment at Ma not being home. Elsie was observant and practical, like Ma. But in the way of twins, she probably knew more about Colin. Ma herself had admitted that Colin talked to Elsie more.

I drew out a chair, realized the wobbly leg was still unrepaired, and pushed it back, choosing a different one instead. "Elsie, I saw Colin last night."

"Oh?" She relocked the door before sitting down across from me.

"I found him at Pinton's," I said.

Her cheerful countenance sobered.

"How much time is he spending there?" I asked.

A vertical worry line like Ma's formed between her brows. "I couldn't say where he spends his time, Mickey. He's not home, barely ever, not even to sleep. But Pinton's." She sighed. "I feared he was gambling. He gave Ma money last month, and . . . well . . ."

I took her meaning. It was more than he should have had.

Except that no one ever came out ahead at Pinton's in the end. No matter how clever Colin was, Pinton's wasn't a reliable source of income. And if he was merely collecting for McCabe, he couldn't be making much. So where was Colin getting the money? Fear ran like a knife tip along my spine.

Dear God, let Colin not be skimming from McCabe. That's a death sentence.

I kept my voice easy. "Ma said he's only working a day or two a week at the docks. Because other men are taking his place."

She scoffed. "He's not even working that much."

"He isn't?" *If Colin couldn't find dock work, this might be why he got mixed up with O'Hagan and McCabe in the first place,* I thought.

"Ma doesn't know, but none of the docks will hire him anymore."

"Fighting?" I guessed.

She nodded. "He cut somebody. The man had to go to hospital."

I remembered the bruise I'd glimpsed on Colin's cheek the day I'd come for tea. "Was that why you two were quarreling on Sunday, before I arrived? You looked like you were giving him a talking-to."

"Nae." The kettle began its low whistle, and she rose, using a doubled towel over the handle so she could pour water into the pot, to let the tea steep. "He was telling me what to do, and I wasn't having it."

"What to do about what?" I asked.

"He was sayin' how I ought to be taking up with a friend of his instead of Eaman. But I'd never. He's a nasty mug."

"And besides, you're fond of Eaman, aren't you? And he's fond of you?"

She nodded, and her face softened in a way that told me plenty.

"But Colin doesn't like him," I added.

Her eyes flashed. "Says Eaman's dull as a post, but he's not. I told Colin he could use a bit of dull himself, if it meant decent and trustworthy."

I could imagine how Colin would take that.

She poured the tea into our cups. "Colin just always wants to be in the thick of things, wants to feel important."

"I know." Even as the words slipped out, I realized they were true. Not surprisingly, Elsie could name what Colin wanted most.

Elsie added milk to my cup and pushed it on its saucer over to me. I took a sip; it was strong, the way I like it. She leaned back in her chair and put the side of her thumb into her mouth to nibble. That gesture told me she had plenty more she could say. I had only to wait. As I set the cup back into the saucer, it gave a muted clink, an echo from the hundreds of times I'd sat at this table. The ghost of Pat hovered near my right shoulder, laughing and scraping a chair back so he could lower his lanky frame into it.

"When you left, Pat took it hard." Her words broke the silence, and I looked over to find her eyes steady on mine. "But Colin took it worse."

"Worse?" I echoed dubiously. "But he was so young."

She looked at me in astonishment. "Ye can't mean that!"

Bewildered, I remained silent, and she threw up her hands, just like Ma did when she was overcome by disbelief. "He bloody *worshipped* you. Jaysus, Mickey. How could ye not see it?"

I stared, nonplussed.

"He used to pretend his name was a shortened version of yours. Colin and Corravan," she said, turning over her left hand and then her right, like two sides of a scale. "He'd watch you whittle a bit o' wood, and afterward Ma would have to hide all the knives, or he'd be slicing his fingers to ribbons. If you came home with a bandage on your hand after boxing, he'd want his hand wrapped too. Do you honestly not remember?" Her eyes were wide with amazement. "I was nobbut small myself, and I remember it clear as glass."

I shook my head, as if to clear it after a blow. Scraping back from the table, I stepped to the window. The cold came through the pane, and I drew some deep breaths to clear the hot pinch in my lungs. I shut my eyes, and like a distant, muted bell from a boat offshore, I could hear Colin's young voice, prideful. "See, Mickey? I lost a button on my shirt too." And my absent reply: "We both need to be more careful, oughtn't we? Poor Elsie has to sew 'em back on."

My eyes opened, and I surveyed the jagged roofline across the way. "Didn't Ma tell him why I left?"

From behind came a genuine, rueful laugh. "Of course not! Colin couldn't keep a secret to save himself. He'd natter on to anybody who'd listen, tell people where Ma hid the daily receipts if she didn't keep watch."

Even as she said it, I recalled Colin's bright, open air, the way he'd confide in people, talk to strangers on the street. At the time, I'd put it down to his natural friendliness, but perhaps it had also been a way to make himself feel bigger than his britches. "I remember."

"We couldn't have O'Hagan hearin' anything about Ma and me helpin' you leave," she continued. "He'd assume we knew where you went. So Colin pestered Ma all evenin', and finally she told him you were tired of workin' at the docks, and she didn't know where you'd gone, but no doubt we'd hear from you once you were settled."

I turned to face her. "What did he say?"

She looked sorry, and as if she'd rather not tell me, but I kept my eyes fixed on her until she said softly, "Nothin'. Didn't say a word. But I heard him crying in his bed . . . more than once."

So we'd both been miserable those first few nights.

My mind jumped forward to the day I'd seen Colin again. O'Hagan had discovered I hadn't been the one to steer the police toward his boxing club, and he'd put out that it was safe for me to return. I'd come here straightaway and been greeted heartily at the door by Pat, Elsie, and Ma. Colin had remained in a chair by the fireplace, whittling a whistle or some such. From my pocket, I'd pulled out a police watchman's rattle that I thought he'd like. He'd accepted it, given it a shake, and thanked me before returning to his whittling. I'd ruffled his hair, thinking he was preoccupied. But perhaps it was only the feigned indifference that followed being hurt.

This memory was displaced by a more recent one—Colin's peculiar comment that I'd likely pay O'Hagan no mind.

Colin hadn't been speaking of O'Hagan.

Colin had been telling me, in his own roundabout way, that I hadn't been paying attention to *him*. And it was true. But did he mean when he was a child? Or now, all these years later?

I returned to the table and took up my cup again. The tea was lukewarm but sweeter than the taste in my mouth. "What did *you* know about my leaving?"

"Well, that's a different matter." She replaced her cup in its saucer. "I was here the day it happened. Ma and I were at the shop, behind the counter, and Mrs. Murphy came in, bustling like she does with her news."

Into my mind came the image of a heavyset woman with auburn hair curled tight to her head. I nodded.

"She says to Ma, 'Mary, O'Hagan's place was raided last night, and his men are looking for Mickey.'" As she spoke, Elsie rolled a tie of her apron between her thumb and forefinger until it made a tight, tidy coil. "Ma knew what those words meant, even if I didn't, though I knew it was something bad from the way Ma looked of a sudden—pale and scared. But you know Ma. She made up her mind quick enough. Asked Mrs. Murphy to mind the shop, reached into the till, took the money out, and stood there for a minute like she wished it was more."

A lump rose in my throat, and I had to swallow twice before I could speak. "It was enough. More than enough."

"Then she grabbed my hand and hustled me upstairs, telling me to fetch your things and put them in the brown sack that was under her bed. I gathered all your clothes from the hooks and folded them fast and neat as I could. I remember thinking it was good it was a Monday because they were clean from the Saturday wash. I took your knife from behind the trunk and put that in too, near the bottom, and meantime, Ma wrapped some food in a cloth, and that went in on top."

The scene took shape in my mind: Ma's swift hands cutting cheese and bread with the long knife, calling to Elsie to hurry, for goodness's sake.

"I asked Ma if you were going to be all right, and she stopped, right there"—she nodded toward the end of the table—"and put her hand to her stomach like she was going to be sick. 'God'll watch over him,' she said, 'but we're going to help him along.'" A wry smile put a dimple in her cheek. "I'm not sure if 'twas God or you she was helping, but that's when she realized all I was seeing and how I needed to be told *something* because if she didn't tell me, I might ask someone else.

"So she asked if I remembered you mentioning O'Hagan, and I said yes, and she told me he wanted you to do something wrong, and you wouldn't do it, which made him angry, so you had to go away. It wasn't the whole truth, of course, but it was enough."

Her eyes were sober. "I knew you boxed for O'Hagan, so I thought you were friends, but she said, 'O'Hagan's no friend to anyone. He's a snake.' And the look on her face told me he'd kill you if he found you."

She took a deep breath. "Then she held me by the shoulders, looked me straight on, and said you wouldn't *want* to leave us, but you'd have to, at least for a while, and we couldn't be sad or cross with you. And we mustn't tell anyone that we heard about the raid, or that we'd helped you leave, especially not Colin." Her eyes flicked to a cupboard beside the stove. "Then she found a pair of Father's shoes, saying you were the only one with feet big enough, and you might as well take them."

I could picture the shoes. Brown, with good thick soles. At the time, I had wondered where they came from on short notice. I hadn't thought of them in years, as they were long worn to shreds, holes in the bottom first, and then the seams ripping as I outgrew them.

"She gave me money she couldn't spare," I said.

"Aye, including seven pence saved from my piecework," Elsie said, one eyebrow arching. "You can thank me now."

She meant it lightly, but the burning at the back of my eyes made me take up the pot and add more hot water from the kettle so she wouldn't see my sudden, stinging tears. From behind me came her voice, repentant. "I'm only making a jest, Mickey. I was glad to do it, 'specially when Ma said it might make a real difference to you. Made me proud I could help."

Yes, Ma was always good that way, letting you know that she saw you'd done your part, making you feel like your contribution meant something.

"Then she left me in the store with Mrs. Murphy and went to find you at the docks," Elsie concluded.

I returned the kettle to the stove and brought the full teapot back to the table. "I was a fool. I had no idea what it cost all of you when I left. I'm damned sorry, Elsie. I truly am."

"Nae," she protested. "It wasn't your fault. You were just doing what Ma told you." Her mouth pursed in regret. "Ma said when she found you at the dock, you looked scared. She always felt sorry about that, wishing she could'a broke it to you easier. But p'rhaps making you afraid was proper, if it made you go far enough to be safe."

"You said Pat and Colin took my leaving hard," I said. "What about you, afterward?"

She swallowed a sip of her tea. "Ach, I'm a girl, so I didn't need you in the same way. And so far as my sums and reading, you'd brought me along far enough I could teach myself."

"You always were the cleverest of us."

She grinned. "'Tisn't what you said when you were trying to teach me my multiples. But no matter, I learned them in the end."

I winced. "I wasn't as patient as I should've been."

Her head tipped and she looked at me in a way Belinda does sometimes. A way that makes me think women are the repositories for most of the kind understanding in this world. "You were as patient as you knew how, Mickey. It was enough."

I nodded my thanks and glanced around the room. "Did O'Hagan ever come looking for me back then? Here?"

"Not that I know of," she said, as if the idea startled her. "Ma never told me, if he did."

"Hmph."

"He should'a realized from the first that you never would have ratted him out."

"Not that I didn't want to," I replied. "But Ma told me that's how I'd end up dead. And he wasn't worth it. Wasn't family and wasn't a friend."

"It's true." Elsie poured more tea, and wisps of steam took shape and dispersed over our cups.

"Ma told Pat why I left, didn't she?" I asked.

"She did. And he came around, after a time."

"Came around," I echoed. Pat had never let on he was angry with me for leaving, only that he was glad I was still alive. I could still see the bright expression on his face and feel his arm thrown around my shoulders.

"He thought you should've stayed here." She sighed. "You know Pat. He was dead certain the two of you could've fought back, fixed things with O'Hagan."

Yes, that was Pat, always ready to lead with his fists.

Elsie shook her head. "Ma told Pat he was bein' a bloody eejit. And once you wrote that you were fine, he stopped talking foolishness. 'Course, the day the letter came, Ma had to keep him from running straightaway to Lambeth."

I stared down at my hands. Big, ugly hands, with scars and a few knuckles that hurt when it rained. Pat's hands had been smaller, leaner than mine, but quicker. He'd brace a wheel with his left foot, sling a sack from his right shoulder onto a wooden cart, and fasten it on with a Carrick bend knot in less time than it took to tell it.

"Mickey," she said tentatively.

I looked up.

"Why *did* you go to Lambeth?" she asked.

Her expression told me that despite what she knew, she still wondered if I'd wanted to go, if I'd had a plan, an intention.

"It's where my feet were when I stopped running," I replied. "It was as far as I got."

The sky outside was black, and in the light from the lamp, her eyes were large and sparkling and curious. It seemed that in the absence of information from me, guesses—mostly incorrect—had filled in the space, like water seeping into a dug hole. And there was no reason I couldn't give an account of what had happened. It was long ago, and the memory didn't chafe me anymore.

"I didn't stop running for two days," I said. "I knew O'Hagan had people all over Whitechapel and Seven Dials, so I headed across the river. I slept in the basement of a warehouse with the rats one night and decided I'd better find some work quick. My food was gone, and I didn't want to spend any of the money if I could help it, not knowing how things might get worse, how I might need it to travel farther away. I could've jumped on a train out of London, but . . ."

"This was what you knew," she said.

"I didn't want to go too far from all of you," I corrected her. "So, the next morning, I started walking."

"'Course you did."

I leaned back in my chair. "Why do you say that?"

"That's what you always did when you were troubled." She grinned at my surprise. "Ma said it helped ease your mind, and even if she was in bed with us, I could tell by her breathing she stayed awake 'til you came home."

"There's not much you didn't notice, is there?"

"I was young. I hadn't much else to occupy me." She divided the last of the tea between our cups. "How did you find work with the police?"

"I walked a mile or so and came upon the division at Lambeth. I saw a young man in uniform, and"—I hesitated—"well, he looked like me."

"Irish?"

"No, but about my size, built like a boxer. So I went inside, asked in my most polite voice if they were looking for new policemen, and the sergeant brought me to Mr. Gordon, the superintendent. We talked, and he asked if I was fleeing trouble."

"Did you tell him?"

I gave a short laugh, remembering. "At first, no, but when I started falling over my words, he put up a hand. 'Why don't you try again, lad.'"

Elsie chuckled.

"I almost stuck to my lie," I admitted. "Thank God I didn't. Not that I told him everything, but I said I'd been bare-knuckles boxing, and I'd quit because the owner wanted me to throw a match, and when I didn't do it, he was angry with me, so I thought it best to find something new. I left off the bit about O'Hagan thinking I was a rat and wanting to kill me."

Her eyes were round. "What happened then?"

"He asked if I could read and cipher, and I showed him I could. He had me write up a short version of a newspaper article. Had me box with a sergeant named Landry, to be sure I could handle myself. That's all." A snort escaped me. "I was lucky it was Super-intendent Gordon rather than Chief Inspector Moss. Moss hated the Irish, would have thrown me out on my ear, but Gordon never gave a sign he held my race against me. They found me a uniform and I started. Used Ma's money to rent a room until I earned my first pay."

"You never told me any of that," she said.

"You never asked."

We sat in silence until I broached the question I'd brought with me: "How deep is Colin? With McCabe, I mean?"

Her entire body stilled. "McCabe? I don't think he is. Colin's collecting money from betting houses for O'Hagan." She grimaced. "He was a bear about admitting it."

"Elsie," I said, keeping my voice gentle, "O'Hagan passed a message to Colin, asking me to meet him. But James McCabe was the one who really wanted to meet me, and he wouldn't have asked O'Hagan to pass the message without knowing something of Colin."

Her expression paled. "You saw McCabe?"

"Last night."

She sank back into her chair, and my heart ached at the unhappiness on her face.

She swallowed. "What—what did McCabe want with you?"

"To tell me about his men being killed here in the Chapel. Wanted to know if the Yard had anything to do with it, which we don't."

"Did McCabe mention Colin?"

"Never spoke his name," I replied truthfully.

That brought a measure of relief to her face. "Well, I can understand McCabe asking questions. Four dead in a fortnight."

"Four?" I asked. "He told me three."

One eyebrow rose. "Another was found in St. Mary's Gardens this mornin', with a bullet in his head, same as the others. I heard from Mrs. McGarry, and then I read it in the paper. One of the four was a relation of McCabe's. His nephew."

So it was personal, I thought. *Which of the four?*

"Do you still have the paper?" I asked.

"Sorry, no. I used it to light the fire."

"What else did it say?"

"Well, it said Irish were fighting Irish," she said, her expression dubious. "But seein' as these are McCabe's men, I'd say it was unlikely. No one would dare go up against McCabe." She set her elbow on the table and rested her chin in her hand. "Would they?"

Irish against Irish? Ordinarily, I'd say no—but yes, if someone in his gang had splintered off.

"Hmph," I said. "Which paper?"

"The *Observer,*" she said.

The Observer *again.*

Church bells struck from St. Botolph's, reminding me of the hour. Belinda's Saturday evening soirées began promptly at eight o'clock, and I wanted to see her beforehand. I rose and plucked my coat from the chair Elsie had used to brace the door.

"What's the real reason the door was jammed?" I asked. "Have O'Hagan's men been coming here? Or someone else?" A look flickered over her face that made my voice sharpen. "Elsie? Who was here? When?"

"On Wednesday night," she admitted. "It was just the once, and I don't know if they were O'Hagan's. They didn't say."

"How many?"

"Three."

"Jaysus." The word came out in a hiss. "Did they threaten you?"

She shook her head hurriedly—too hurriedly. "One of 'em had a gun here." She touched her waist. "But he never took it out. They just wanted to know where Colin was."

Another gun in Whitechapel. Fear ran along my nerves, down to my hands, making them tingle.

"How did they get in?" I asked. "Wasn't the door locked?"

"I'd just come from the market, with my hands full. They followed me up."

Cold razored down my spine. "Elsie—"

"I know, I know," she broke in. "But it never used to be like that! It was still *day*, for goodness's sake—half past three in the afternoon!"

Well, Ma said things were changing.

A heavy breath escaped me. Not for the first time I wished I could convince the Doyles to come live near me, or anywhere else. But Ma always refused with the same reply: their livelihood, their store, their church, and their friends were all here.

"You should have told me," I said.

"And what would you have done? 'Twas the day after the *Princess Alice*! And they meant me no harm."

Not that time, I thought. My eyes flicked down to Elsie's wrist and back up. "Ma doesn't know, does she?"

"No." Her chin lifted. "And don't tell. It'll do no good."

"I won't—but only if you swear to tell me if it happens again," I said. "And take the shop stairs."

"I have been, ever since."

I pulled on my coat. "Tell Ma I stopped in, would you? I'm working out what I can do to help Colin."

And given what you've just told me, getting Colin away might be good for all of you, I added to myself.

"O' course." She handed me my hat. "Be safe home, Mickey."

I rested my hand on the doorknob. She stood close by, ready to lock it behind me and to brace the chair again. I put my arm around her shoulders. "I'm glad you were here." I kissed the top of her head. "For God's sake, be careful."

She nodded against my chest, and I left. Not three steps down, I heard the chair scrape back into place.

I hated that she had to do that.

CHAPTER 17

My work, particularly at the Yard, brought me into contact with people from all swaths of society, and as crime doesn't keep to calling hours, I was perhaps surprisingly well informed about matters of proper dress for morning, afternoon, and evening in the better houses. When Belinda had first broached the idea of me attending one of her soirées, I took myself to Savile Row and put myself in the hands of a capable tailor, vowing that I would not balk or even flinch at the price. I succeeded in the main, although the man's mouth twitched at my expression when he showed me the bill.

At home, I washed, dressed, and took a cab to Belgravia, recalling an evening several months ago when I'd stood alone in the shadow of one of the mature plane trees in the gated crescent opposite Belinda's house. She and I had argued terribly the night before, and in a miserable state of mind, I had watched as one carriage after another rolled to a stop before her stairs and discharged its elegantly attired passengers. At least a dozen times, the front door opened, allowing the strains of music from a string quartet to float out into the night. And each time it closed, muting the sound, I had the aching sense of something precious being taken away.

Tonight, however, I wouldn't be standing in the shadows. I would attend. But I wasn't sure how long I would stay. This business with Colin was too troubling for me to be decent company. Elsie's explanation had filled in the sketch that Colin's few choice phrases had provided. Now that I understood, I wanted to speak to Colin again. Perhaps this time, I could do better.

I was early, but I knocked, and the door was opened by Belinda's footman, Collins. He bowed as if he'd seen me every day of his life, and took my coat and hat. "I'll tell Mrs. Gale you are here."

From the dining room came Belinda's voice, low and agreeable:

"I'm sorry, Stevenson, I should have mentioned it sooner. Mr. Wells rearranged his trip to Manchester in order to come tonight, and I'd like to seat him next to Miss Goddard—no, on her left. He doesn't care for Mrs. Wallace."

"Very well, mum. And where should I put Mr. Brownlee?"

"Next to Mrs. Franks, please. They're distant relations. Neither will take offense."

Collins stepped inside the dining room, and I heard a soft sound of surprise from Belinda. In a moment she appeared in the doorway, one hand on the wooden frame. She wore a silk gown the color of moss, and her dark hair was down around her shoulders in soft, rich coils. Her pleased smile faded to an expression of concern. With quick steps, she came toward me, her eyes searching mine. "Michael, what's the matter?"

Mindful of Collins, I said nothing. She drew me by the hand into her study, closing the door behind us. The room was silent except for the ticking in the corner that came from a tall, severely carved clock that had belonged to her father. She gave it a quick glance.

"I know I'm early—" I began.

"Don't be silly." She came close and ran her fingertips along the cloth on my shoulder, then let her hand drop. "You look magnificent," she said with a quiet smile that I forced myself to return. "But what's happened? Is it the *Princess Alice*?"

"Colin's in with O'Hagan and McCabe." I paused. "And what's more, I think he blames me for driving him to it."

Her eyes widened. "What?"

I gave her a concise version of my conversations with Colin and Elsie.

Her immediate indignation and loyalty slayed me. "It's not fair to blame you for anything that occurred in the aftermath of you leaving. Of *course* you regret that you hurt Colin—and Pat too—but you had no choice! Colin should be able to see that now, even if he couldn't then."

I took her right hand in both of mine. It was warm. I ran my finger over the callous on her third finger, the result of scribbling with her pen.

"What are you going to do?" she asked.

"Colin can get out. Or rather," I corrected myself, "I can get him out. It's not too late to undo this."

A shade of uncertainty crossed her face. "What will you have to give McCabe?"

"I won't give him much," I replied. "Nothing that will hinder anyone's investigation at the Yard. Hell, it might even help. But I have to do something."

She bit her lower lip, held it with her upper teeth.

"I just didn't think, Bel. I was so stunned that day Ma came to the docks that I did what she said and ran without looking back. But it was never my intention to . . ." My voice faded at the expression on her face.

"Goodness, of course not. You of *all* people," she said, more fervently than seemed warranted.

Mystified, I asked, "What do you mean?"

"Michael," she said, as if I should know.

My eyebrows rose. "Bel?"

"You left without a word of explanation," she replied. "You vanished."

"Because Ma Doyle told me to run."

She put her other hand on top of mine. Her voice was gentle. "What I mean is, it's rather like what your mother did to you."

My breath, my heart—everything stilled.

Belinda's face was stricken. "Oh, Michael, I'm sorry. I thought . . . the way you told me . . ." Her voice trailed off. "That's what I thought you meant. You'd never do it on purpose to anyone else."

With my heart thudding unsteadily inside my ribs, I pulled my hands from hers and stood motionless. I hadn't thought of those days in some time, but now they came at me with the bulk and relentlessness of an express train.

For days, I'd run through the streets, and when I glimpsed a woman who looked like Mum, I ran faster, only to find every time that it wasn't her. Each day whittled down my hope that she would return, like a sharp blade shaving at a spindly stick of kindling. At night, bereft and unmoored, I'd take refuge in one of the hundreds of wretched little nooks in Whitechapel alleys, or in a doorway or one of the old church priest holes where Roman clergy hid from persecution during Queen Elizabeth's reign, crouching motionless for hours, often until dusk. Sometimes I was found; other times I was not. On the occasions when my mother's friends fed and sheltered me, I accepted it thoughtlessly, as children do. Until the night I reached for a second piece of bread, and Mrs. Tell's mouth tightened. I snatched my empty hand back as if I'd touched a hot stove.

The next day I stole a loaf of bread and brought it back to Mrs. Tell and her four children, and that night at supper, I swallowed down my questions about why my mother had left. I swallowed down my fear that I'd been dull and difficult and too great a burden, and my worry that she was lying dead or hurting somewhere. I swallowed down the wish that I didn't have to lie or steal to earn a place at a table. I sank my longing and uncertainty deep inside me and weighted it down with one-sixth of a loaf of bread.

"Michael?"

As I raised my head to look at Belinda, I sensed movement out of the corner of my eye, and I spun to see who had intruded on us.

It took me a moment to realize it was my reflection in the tall gilt-edged mirror on the wall. I hardly recognized myself, in this evening coat and white shirt and waistcoat, with the glint of buttons at my chest, standing between two brocade chairs on a crimson patterned Turkey carpet.

I'd come a long way from that boy in Whitechapel.

"Colin losing you, and you losing your mother aren't quite the same," Belinda said.

"He'd already lost his father and his older brother," I replied, my voice heavy. "There is only so much loss we can take. He was just a child."

Her brow furrowed.

"That's why he talked to me the way he did." My hands felt like weights at my sides. "God knows I never meant to hurt him. But at least I can fix this. McCabe told me what he wants from me; I'll simply make it an exchange instead of a favor."

"An exchange for what?"

"Why, for letting Colin go," I replied in surprise.

She looked skeptical. "If Colin wants to be let go."

"He can't be that much of a fool. I'll find him decent work, a position, set him up somewhere far away from here, give him a fresh start." I drew a deep breath and blew it out. "I know. I'm playing Perseus, the mighty, invulnerable rescuer, again."

She gave a smile that told me she too recalled that old conversation of ours. "Colin is no Andromeda chained to her rock."

"But he *is* chained to McCabe—who never lets people go once they've worked for him." Her expression altered, and I added, "He can't. They know too much."

"Oh, I'm sure," she replied.

"So I have to help—particularly as I can do it without too much trouble or risk." A pause. "I couldn't live with myself if I didn't and something happened. He's Ma's last boy."

"What if he is too ashamed to let you help him?"

I started. "Ashamed?"

"If he feels your disdain."

"It's not disdain! It's worry." I ran my hands through my hair. "He's one of the few people on this earth I love."

"Does he know that?"

"For God's sake, Belinda! How can he not? And there's nothing shameful about changing your mind!"

"But he may think there is," Belinda replied.

"So it's better to double a bad bet?" I asked. "For God's sake, all the gambling he's doing, he should understand how stupid *that* is."

"*I* know that," she said in a tone that reminded me I was arguing with the wrong person. "But, Michael, right now you sound disdainful. Contemptuous, even," she added, her voice carrying a warning. "Shame is hard to bear, especially if Colin secretly suspects he's in the wrong. If you speak this way to Colin, he's going to ignore you."

"Then I'll make McCabe kick him out," I said stubbornly.

"Michael." She glanced at the door. From beyond it came the sound of a growing number of voices, laughing and talking.

"You should go," I said. "Or rather, I need to go."

Her lips parted. "But Michael—" she began, dismayed.

"Bel, I meant to stay. Truly, I did," I said. "But—"

"It's only a few hours."

How could I explain my fear that every second I let Colin continue down this path made pulling him away from it harder?

Her face fell, and I hated myself for disappointing her. "I'm sorry," I muttered.

She sighed. "I understand. Of course you must find Colin." She bit her lip. "However, you should stay for a few moments. I asked Lord Baynes-Hill tonight especially for you."

"Lord Baynes-Hill," I repeated.

"I'd intended to tell you when you arrived." She adjusted the necklace at her throat. "He and his wife should be here any minute, and I think a meeting could benefit both of you."

She was right. A quarter of an hour's discussion with the leader of the home rule talks could be crucial.

She added, "I'd imagined the two of you having a more sociable exchange at first, but I daresay he'll understand you jumping straight to the matter at hand. He wants the same thing that you want, after all—a stop to the violence."

"Yes. Yes, of course." I paused. "Thank you."

She nodded.

I stepped forward and took her hand. "Bel, next time I'll stay. I promise."

"Don't promise," she said, withdrawing her hand. "Not until this is over."

I deserved that, I thought unhappily. "All right."

The foyer sounded full of visitors greeting each other.

"I'll send Lord Baynes-Hill in when he arrives." She stepped to the door but paused with her hand on the knob. "When you talk to Colin, try to remember that you've made mistakes too. Perhaps then he'll see there's no shame in acknowledging it rather than . . . doubling his bet, as you say." Our eyes held for a long minute. She winced. "And be careful, would you? With McCabe. He's killed people, Michael. He's dangerous."

I nodded. "I know."

★   ★   ★

It's not unusual for me to turn over in my mind advice that Belinda gives me and realize she has a fair point.

In the ten minutes before Lord Baynes-Hill appeared, I paced about the quiet room, weighing all that Belinda had said. I let myself recall times when my shame had overcome my better judgment, when I'd stubbornly taken a second wrong step into the mud rather than own that I was wrong, out of fear that someone would mock me for my mistake. How could I convey to Colin that it was the mark of a man to admit when he'd taken a false step, to pull his boot back from the mud and settle it on the firm path, never mind what anyone else thought?

The study door swung open to reveal Lord Baynes-Hill, a man of about forty-five, narrow of face and shoulder, with a receding hairline, alert eyes, and a pleasant smile.

"Mr. Corravan," he said with a bow of his head.

"Lord Baynes-Hill," I replied. There was an awkward silence as we studied each other. "I know this is peculiar."

He waved a hand. "It isn't the strangest meeting I've had over the years, to be sure. Mrs. Gale said you wanted to speak to me on a matter of some importance."

"Did she tell you who I am?"

"Nothing other than a friend."

"I'm a senior inspector at the Yard, currently acting superintendent at Wapping."

"Ah," he replied, sobering. "You're coping with the *Princess Alice* disaster."

"Yes." I considered how to begin. "Lord Baynes-Hill, I know you are concerned about Irish violence, and there are private discussions being held with respect to Irish Home Rule."

He drew himself up. "Where did you hear that?"

I understood what he meant. "Not from Mrs. Gale. Someone else I trust."

"Nothing remains secret in this city," he said, shaking his head resignedly.

I said, "If the IRB is shown to have caused the *Princess Alice* disaster, it will affect the outcome."

His right foot slid backward, and he rocked back on it. "You do get right to the heart of the matter, don't you?"

I hesitated and then said what I had admitted several days ago to Belinda. "Because I'm worried. Home rule could change everything, and I hate to see the possibility go up in smoke."

His expression softened. "I'm worried too. I'll admit, the rumors have already made some of our group reluctant." Clasping his hands behind his back, he took several paces to the right and then pivoted. "The difficulty is there will be an election soon."

"And MPs who are sympathetic to home rule won't get reelected if people believe the Irish are behind the disaster," I added.

"Which is why we've been taking pains to keep these talks quiet. I don't want them to be politically detrimental to anyone."

"I understand," I said. "But I'm in a position to know the facts about the accident, and the newspapers are not. For instance, I have discovered no proof that the crew of the *Bywell Castle* were drunk, or that the pilot is a Brotherhood man."

Lord Baynes-Hill cocked his head. "The newspapers said his name was in their ledger—although I have wondered if they aren't circulating sensational rumors, to sell more papers." He met my gaze. "Dare I ask, is your skepticism because you are Irish?"

"I'm skeptical because the pilot hasn't even been found yet," I replied. "The captain of the *Bywell* spoke well of him, and Mr. Conway has a record of twenty years of piloting boats responsibly up and down the Thames."

His expression became thoughtful. "Do you think it truly was an accident?"

"I don't know," I admitted. "But I'm not willing to blame anyone, including Conway or the IRB, until we know more."

He nodded in acknowledgment.

"So I would ask you—"

"To hold our judgment in abeyance," he finished. "To wait before we abandon our efforts."

"And don't believe everything you read."

"I will bear that in mind. Thank you." The ends of his mouth curved. "Would you do me the favor of coming to see me—promptly, if you please—when you know more? Given the delicacy of our endeavor, sometimes a seemingly insignificant piece of information can change the outcome of one of our discussions."

"I will try," I promised.

He bowed his head in thanks. "And now shall we return to the party?"

"I can't stay. I have something to attend to," I said.

"Ah. Well, good night. A pleasure to make your acquaintance."
He extended his hand, and I took it. "Truly."

"And yours."

He left and closed the door behind him. I sensed he had England's best interests at heart; he seemed capable, reasonable, and willing to consider what I told him. Put simply, I liked him. I might have anticipated I would; Belinda wasn't the sort to suffer fools as friends. It relieved my worry some to think this was one of the men steering our country.

CHAPTER 18

I went home, changed my clothes, and stepped back out into the street.

Now, where to find McCabe?

My first thought was to find O'Hagan, so I started for the Waterman, hoping he'd be at the pub playing cards.

But on my way there, as I crossed Milford Street, only one street away from Bett's Alley, where the two men had put the hood over my head, my pace slowed, and I wondered if I could retrace my steps.

I made my way to the corner where I'd been hooded and stood with my eyes closed, remembering. Opening them, I walked forward thirty paces or so, turned right, and then left. From there, I let the smells lead me. At last, prowling along the alleys near the metallic scent, I found the door with the sloped entrance and pushed it open. Unlike last time, the room was full, with every table occupied. A few people glanced my way, but without interest, and I approached the barkeep. "I'm looking for James McCabe," I said. "He asked me to be in touch with information, and I have some."

His eyebrows rose. "Your name?"

"Corravan." Then as an afterthought, I added, "Tell him Mickey Corravan." If I was correct about why McCabe had let that name drop, he would understand what I meant giving it now. "Meanwhile, I'll have a pint," I said, and pulled one of the stools to where I could perch comfortably.

Ten minutes later, one of the men who'd brought me here last time appeared at my elbow.

"Come wi' me."

I laid a coin on the bar, nodded my thanks, and followed the man to a back door. A lantern halfway up a flight of stairs shed enough light to climb by. At the top was another door, and he knocked three times. From inside, I heard a metal bolt scrape, and the door swung open.

It might have once been a bedroom at the inn, but now it held only a table set for cards, half a dozen chairs, and lamps. McCabe sat in one of the chairs, his eyes narrowed. "You shouldn't ha' come."

I cast my eyes at the three other men. "We need to speak privately."

At a small, irritable tip of McCabe's head, the three men left, closing the door behind them. I heard another door open, and I wondered if they were merely going into the room on the other side of the wall, but there was nothing I could do about that. I'd speak softly.

I unbuttoned my coat and sat down, resting my elbows on my knees. "Was the man found shot near St. Mary's Gardens one of yours? A fourth?"

He gave one slow nod, and in his eyes was a coolness that arrested me like an anchor jerking a boat to a stop. Something had happened between last night and tonight. I'd lost some goodwill, and I had no idea what I'd done. But perhaps there was an easy way to get it back.

I'd lay down a low card from my hand.

I took a breath and blew it out. "The Yard isn't killing your men. But I spoke with a man I trust, and he admits they're seeing more guns in Whitechapel these past two months. Seems pistols are coming in from one of the Birmingham makers."

"I told you."

"The Yard seized a case of guns in gin crates being held at a railway station." I paused. "Were they intended for you?"

Slowly, he licked his lips, folded them inward. "I'd hardly admit it, would I? But no."

"So who's buying and distributing them?"

His eyes were blank. "No idea."

I was losing his interest—and losing my opportunity. I'd rather have him angry with me than indifferent. "What do you make of the newspaper saying that Irish are fighting Irish? Do you think it's true?"

He shrugged.

It was time to play my last card. "Did you have anything to do with the *Princess Alice* disaster?"

That caught him up, as I anticipated it would. His eyes sparked and he let out his breath in a scornful hiss. "It's a disgrace you're even asking. I've a friend whose sister and niece were on that steamer. We don't kill women and children for no reason. What good would it do us?"

It might sound peculiar that I believed the man. But I did. "Do you think it's IRB?"

"Mebbe." His eyes narrowed. "Seems odd Timmy wouldn't'a said so, if it was. He wouldn't waste it."

So you know him well enough to call him Timmy and say that, I thought, tucking that piece of information away.

"Fair point." I sat back. "Now I need to talk to you about Colin Doyle."

His eyebrows rose.

"You need to let him go."

A long minute passed, during which I sensed McCabe making a series of calculations. Then he lifted his chin, peering at me down his nose. "I don't let people out."

"You can make an exception. Colin's no fool. He'll keep quiet if he knows he dies otherwise."

An expression of craftiness came over his face. "You're asking for a lot. What has he done for you, to deserve such loyalty?"

I formulated a reply he'd understand. "I owe Ma Doyle," I said. "He's her last son, and I'd do anything for her. And whatever else you may be, McCabe, you understand loyalty. You're more potato than rot."

His lips curved oddly, as if he were trying to hold a smile in the back of his mouth. "What makes you think Colin wants to get out? He earns a living wi' me."

"He might not at the moment," I admitted, "but you're going to help me convince him he does." I leaned over the table, keeping my voice low. "And if anything happens to Colin afterward, I will tear your organization apart. So long as he's alive and safe, I will help you find out who's killing your men, without giving you up to the Yard. But if anything happens to him—by your hand or anyone else's—I will make you pay."

There was a long moment. At last, his mouth twitched. "All right. I'll let Colin go, and I won't touch him."

Despite my best effort, I couldn't conceal my surprise at how easily he agreed. I replayed his words in my mind to parse them.

"And he isn't to be touched by any of your men," I added cautiously.

"Aye." The humor faded from his face, and he backhanded the air to forestall further appeals. Still, I felt wary, until it came to me that for McCabe, with hundreds of men to call on, losing a single man collecting money wasn't much. With relief, I realized that Colin couldn't be in too deep with McCabe if he was willing to let him go without a fight.

"But you'll do something for me in return," McCabe said.

Naturally, I thought.

"You let me know if it's Finn Riley killing my men." He tapped the table with his thumbs. Three taps.

"He splintered off? You're certain?"

There was a sudden dangerous glint in his eyes.

"Is he a fool?" I asked. "He must know the risk he's running, challenging you."

"He's only doing it because someone's backing him," he replied.

"Giving him guns," I said.

"And money," he said. "I'd give a lot to know who."

As would I.

"All right." I nodded. "Which one was your nephew? O'Farrell?"

He flinched. "My cousin. Papers got it wrong." His chest expanded with a deep breath. "But yes, O'Farrell. You're a clever one."

"You want me to be," I said. "Don't you?"

He turned over a palm in acknowledgment.

In the distance, I heard church bells chiming the hour.

He stood. "It's time for you to go, Mr. Corravan. I've somewhere to be."

So did I.

CHAPTER 19

I left McCabe with my thoughts like the chop of waves during a storm. I had acquired a few important pieces of information and wormed a promise from McCabe not to hurt Colin, but everything else about the meeting unsettled me.

Yesterday we'd reached something like a gentleman's agreement, an understanding, even something like a cautious, temporary alliance. But tonight he'd acted as though he distrusted me all over again. Or perhaps he simply had other matters on his mind.

As I walked, I took apart our exchange second by second, word by word. McCabe had seemed angry about something beyond Finn's defection. Had Finn taken others with him? Or had someone else taken Finn?

Good God, could it be Colin, forming his own gang?

Even as the thought came into my mind, I dismissed it. Colin didn't have the power for that, the reach, the experience. It had to be Finn.

I recalled the twitch McCabe gave when I said that he had to let Colin out. Had that been impatience, or a sign that he found the demand vaguely humorous? Or a sign of nonchalance?

I couldn't dispel the sense that McCabe had acquiesced too easily. But why?

My next thought halted my feet:

Because Colin had already left.

That had to be it.

If McCabe's gang had fractured, and Finn had split away—and Colin had gone with him . . .

My fear and fury formed a riptide inside my chest. *Damn everything. Damn everything ten times over.*

The only place I could think of finding Colin was Pinton's. I turned north and ran.

Outside the gambling house, I took a moment to recover my breath before I pulled open the door. I crossed the floor to where two men again guarded the staircase, and the one I recognized put out a hand.

"He's not here tonight."

"Is he really not here, or did he tell you not to call him down for me?"

"He's not here, guv'nor."

The man was lying. The sly spark in his eyes—the joke he was having with himself over tricking me—gave it away. But I didn't care; he'd told me what I needed to know. I left the place and took up a spot in the shadows around the corner, grateful that the clouds scuttling across the sky were dropping no rain.

By the time Colin emerged from the doorway and started down the street, silhouetted against the weak light from windows and the odd gas lamp, I'd spent two hours mulling over the argument we were going to have, and I was angry and frustrated enough that I wanted to grab him right there. But instead, I tailed him for a few streets, watching for anyone following either of us, and then I chased him down soundlessly and pushed him into a wall.

He bounced back from it, his left fist coming up in a swift undercut aimed at my chin, and it was only by pure reflex that I dodged it and backed him against the bricks, one of my hands on each of his shoulders, pinning his arms.

"What the hell are you doing, Colin? Did you leave the Cobbwallers? Did you actually betray McCabe?"

He glared up at me and let go a string of curses, which I interrupted.

"Shut your head!" I growled at him and gazed straight into his face. Our breaths were coming fast, and as he wrenched his shoulders in protest, I heard a muted *thunk* of something heavy striking the wall behind. His expression flattened, and quick as lightning,

I ran my hand down his side to his waist and felt the unyielding metal of a gun.

For a moment we both froze. "Colin." It came out hoarsely. "Where'd you get it?"

He merely stared up at me.

"McCabe says a group has splintered off," I said, "and my guess is you went with it."

His eyes were dark with anger. "What the hell does it matter to you? Jaysus, Mickey, leave me alone!"

In those words, I heard an admission I'd guessed correctly. When I'd seen McCabe tonight, he'd known Colin had left. He'd been laughing up his sleeve at me trying to get Colin out. Well, so be it. That wasn't what mattered.

"I *can't* leave you alone, damn it," I retorted. "I am not going to let you being young and bloody stupid take you from Ma." The mention of her seemed to give him pause. "Now, I'm going to take your gun and step away, but I swear to you, if you run instead of talking to me, I will drag you down to Wapping, throw you in a room, and make up charges if I have to, to keep you there and safe."

"All right!" he growled, and another curse came from between his gritted teeth.

Slowly I eased my left hand inside his coat and withdrew the gun, stowing it in my pocket as I removed my right hand from his shoulder and backed away.

I wanted to confirm it had been Finn Riley who'd taken Colin away from McCabe. But even more I wanted to explain. I needed to clear the misunderstanding that lay between Colin and me if I had any chance of him listening or answering any of my questions.

I began slowly. "Col, when I left Whitechapel, I was running for my life. But you're right. I didn't think about what I left behind. I wasn't thinking about how it would affect you or Ma or Pat or Elsie. But I thought about you all every day, how much I was missing all of you. I was so bloody miserable. And afraid. More than anything, afraid of . . . of starving, of being killed in my sleep before I found a place to live. Of never being able to come back." My voice caught, and I coughed to clear it.

His face screwed up in disbelief.

"But it doesn't mean I didn't *care* what my leaving did to you. I just had no idea of it." The words came out in a rush. "When you're young, you—you don't think that way, and I was younger than you are now, Colin. I had no idea what I was leaving behind me. If I'd given it any thought, I'd have said I was leaving Whitechapel and taking my mess away from all of you. That's as far as I could think at the time. But it was wrong of me. I can see that now."

He sniffed and turned his head to stare down the street.

I continued. "I know you weren't told why I left, not right away, and you had a lot of time to think I'd just gone off and forgotten about you. But I came back as soon as O'Hagan admitted he'd made a mistake. As soon as it was safe." Still, Colin was silent, and I felt compelled to fill the silence, somehow. "Surely that has to count for something. And I'm here now, trying to keep you from making a mistake that at some point you won't be able to come back from. Some mistakes you can't undo if they go on for too long." I slowed my words. "But this one, you still can. It's not too late." I paused. "Let me help you, Colin. Please."

He glared up at me. "You can't just throw me against a wall and tell me what I'm going to do."

"Fair enough," I granted, and put up my two hands. "I'm sorry I threw you against the wall."

He snorted. "You and Pat always left me behind, sitting on the steps with Elsie. But I'm not a bloody child anymore!"

Was this where some of his resentment began? Suddenly, sharply, into my mind came the image of Colin and Elsie on the steps, her with a doll and Colin with a set of marbles he'd lined up in a row. And Pat and I stepping carefully around them, on our way somewhere.

"You're right," I said. "You're not a child anymore. Which is why what you do now—and who you do it with—matters. It'll affect the rest of your life. I talked to McCabe. He says he'll let you go. And I can get you far enough away from whoever it is you're with now."

His face was incredulous, his tone injured. "You say you know I'm not a child anymore, but you're still treatin' me like I have no say! Who are *you* to talk to McCabe about me and—and *plan* what the two of you are going to do for me, without asking me the first thing about it?"

"Colin—"

"I'm not just grown. I've things I'm doing! People respect me. You just don't know!"

I clenched my teeth. "Fair enough. You're grown. Then act like it. Have some integrity. Don't change sides from one gang to another." He opened his mouth to protest, but I raised my voice and kept on. "Don't lie to people, telling Ma you can't work on the dock because there are too many Russians and Poles taking the jobs when it's really because you're picking fights and sending people to hospital. And don't tell other people to lie for you, saying you're not upstairs gambling when you are!"

He raked his fingers through his hair in frustration. "You're one to talk about integrity! You're Whitechapel Irish, Mickey. Remember? And you're puttin' on police airs, acting like you're better'n all of us, taking up with some hoity-toity woman in the West End—"

"Leave her out of this, Colin. I mean it."

He heard the razored edge in my voice and knew he'd gone too far. But he gave another snort. "Oh, yes, sir."

I felt a flare of anger and impatience with this boy.

"Who split off?" I asked. I wanted him to say it. "Who are you working for now? Tell me, Colin."

Years ago, Colin would have done anything Pat or I had bid him. Now he merely shook his head, his resistance as solid as the wall at his back.

"Is it Finn Riley?" I asked.

Colin stiffened, and his chin came up. "Did Elsie say so? Jaysus, she can't keep quiet."

Instantly I looked away to conceal my thoughts. *Elsie? What the devil did she have to do with this?* My mind leapt to Elsie's account of her quarrel with Colin. *Was Finn Riley the "friend" Colin had been pressing her to take up with?* After a second, I met his gaze again. "It wasn't Elsie."

"It's not what you think," he burst out, then clamped his mouth shut.

I remained silent, waiting for whatever Colin would say next, hoping like hell it would help me understand what was happening inside his head.

"Why'd you leave McCabe?" I asked.

His eyes slid away from me, and he shrugged. "All I was doing was fetching money from one place to another. Anybody can do that."

Was that what was behind this? Wanting to feel important? Perhaps that's how Finn Riley had pulled him away. I imagined Finn Riley being a few years older, confident, arrogant, so sure he could take on McCabe. Someone like that plucking Colin out of the crowd around McCabe *would* make him feel chosen and special.

"What did Finn promise you?" I asked.

"I get a third of everything."

A third? That meant Finn Riley had a partner.

"Think on it," I said. "Finn Riley's partner isn't going to want to give up any of his share. He'll find a way to make Riley doubt you."

Colin's chin came up. "Nah. Finn trusts me."

"Why?"

He merely looked at me.

Worry spiked again inside me as I wondered what Colin would've had to do to earn Finn Riley's trust so quickly, but I pushed that aside.

I studied his heavy, stubborn jaw, his eyes bright and belligerent. *It's Pat all over again,* I thought. Pat, who thought he could take on the world, so long as he had me, his loyal friend, with him. Only Colin wasn't choosing his loyal friend wisely.

"Colin, please let me get you out." My voice was low, insistent. I heard the pleading note and saw his look of impatience, but I kept on. "Finn Riley won't find you. Neither will McCabe. I have friends in Lambeth or even farther, if you want."

He shook his head, so his dark curls shifted. "I know what I'm doing, Mickey. You'll see." His voice was confident, taut, full of certainty. Even excitement.

It made me think of the day he'd come home with a trinket he'd bought for Ma, his eyes bright, swearing it was silver. I didn't have the heart to tell him it was plate.

The moon slid out from behind a cloud, and for a long moment, in its light, we could each see the other clearly. The anger was gone from his face, replaced by a stolid patience, as if he was resigned to standing there for as long as it took for me to be done. My own anger faded, replaced by a stabbing, sick regret that I couldn't change his mind, that I'd let him drift far enough away from me that I'd lost all influence. That I couldn't make him see what he was doing.

At last, I said the only thing I could think of: "Just be careful, all right?"

He gave a laugh that sounded almost genuine, bemused, even indulgent. "I'm fine, I tell you. Go on, Mickey. Go be a policeman." He pushed himself away from the wall, both hands low, the palms open, as if to assure me he meant no harm. He just wanted to walk away.

And he did, turning his back on me.

The last I saw of him, he was rounding a corner, leaving the street empty, except for me.

I remained there for a long moment, the weight of my worry like a thick pall dragging at my shoulders.

I hoped to hell Colin was right. He seemed so certain that Finn Riley trusted him that I nearly believed him. God knows, I wanted to. Perhaps Colin *was* close enough to Finn Riley to be protected from the jealousies and backstabbing that happened because power shifted in new gangs as easily as the tide.

But what did this have to do with Elsie? Why would Colin think she'd have mentioned Finn Riley?

Out of nowhere came the memory of Ma Doyle saying some of the lads were sweet on Elsie. I closed my eyes, putting myself back in the Doyles's kitchen, and I could hear the tone of Ma's voice, but I couldn't recall for certain if she'd said Finn Riley's name. But she might have.

I opened my eyes to the dimly lit street. Was that a card Colin believed he held up his sleeve? But what would happen when it became clear to Finn that Elsie preferred Eaman? Then again, perhaps Finn already knew, and it didn't matter because he really *did* value Colin.

A gas lamp flickered unevenly, and I headed toward home, the gun an off-balance drag in my pocket.

Clearly there was no point in arguing with Colin further. If he had once worshipped me, he certainly didn't now.

At least I'd done what I could to make him safe from McCabe, who knew I could make good on my threat.

Perhaps Colin was right. It was time for me to go be a policeman.

CHAPTER 20

I lay in bed, listening to rain slapping at the windowpane, and realized it had only been a week since I'd woken with a sense of well-being, looking forward to Sunday tea with the Doyles. The house was silent, and I felt Harry's absence keenly. Perhaps it was because Colin felt suddenly lost to me, but I missed Harry, missed his quirks and insights and even his talk about books. I thought back to several months ago, the day he'd been outraged over Tennyson poaching the French story of Elaine of Astolat for "The Lady of Shalott." The boy had a sense of fair play. I admired that about him, among other traits.

Pushing aside the bedclothes, I rose and looked outside. Last night the clouds had been blown across the sky, but now they were stagnant and gray. I stared through the rain at the houses opposite. The entire street was built on borrowed land, for this part of Soho had been developed only after parts of the Fleet River had been covered over to make way for railway tracks. Part of me loved the thought of the Fleet running, hidden, under the city, a silent stepbrother to the Thames. Across the way, a woman came out of a house, closing the black door, her umbrella at the ready, and carrying an empty sack. She was probably on her way to the shops.

I turned away with a sigh. It was time for me to leave too. The gun I'd taken from Colin was still on my washstand, and I emptied the chamber of the bullet and held the gun in my palm, studying it for a moment. A nice Webley with a black handle. I knew how to handle a pistol, of course, but I was glad my daily life didn't require one. I slid the firearm under my mattress and put the bullet inside a drawer. I dressed, made my solitary cup of coffee, and opened the door. The rain drove me back inside to pull my umbrella from its stand.

As I crossed into Whitechapel, I smelled wood smoke to the north, and though it drew me away from Wapping, I followed the odor until I came upon a crossroads, where a burned building smoldered on the northeast corner, its charred wooden walls smashed and tumbled into the street. On either side were shops whose windows had been broken. A small crowd had gathered. Some people watched while others helped shopkeepers hammer planks over the windows to keep the rain from coming in.

"When did this happen?" I asked a bystander.

"Two o'clock or thereabouts," he replied, and turned his head to spit. "Must'a been a dozen or so. All in black hoods and caps, bold as brass. Came through with torches, threw 'em at Paddy's." He gestured toward the shops. "Them's lucky, just had windas broke."

"Anyone hurt?" I asked, dreading the answer.

"One dead. Two in 'ospital."

With a heavy heart, I turned and walked south. Under the butcher's awning, a boy hawked papers, and I handed him a coin without asking which it was. I found a cab with a poor horse, miserable in the rain. *Bloody hell*, I thought. *We're all miserable today.*

I settled in the cab, opened the paper—the ink blurring some with the wet—and read the headline, in large bold type:

"Irish Republican Brotherhood to Blame for Sittingbourne & Princess Alice Disasters! More Attacks to Come! Wapping Official Warns Terrified Londoners to Stay Home!"

I stared so long at the headline that my eyes went dry. Then I blinked them, hard, and checked the masthead. It wasn't the *Beacon* or the *Sentinel*, from whom I'd expect an inflammatory headline like this, but last night's edition of the *Evening Star.*

With a horrible sense of foreboding, I peered at the type and read:

One of the worst railway accidents of recent years happened on Saturday afternoon at Sittingbourne, within a hundred yards of the station. A tremendous smash, the shock of which was felt the whole length of the train, resulted in shattered carriages being pitched down the embankment. Hundreds of passengers were seen in every direction, bleeding from their wounds, and the shrieking and sobbing of injured women and children were pitiable to hear.

The inquest initially revealed that a metal rail had become disengaged from the underlying wooden ties. But it has now become clear that a small charge of dynamite exploded, destabilizing the rails as the train ran over them. Furthermore, the under-guard of the goods train, an Irishman named Mr. P. McPherson, had shunted trucks onto the main track, thereby requiring the railway train to divert to the second track, where the dynamite was laid. Remnants of the sunburst flag of the Irish Republican Brotherhood were found at the scene. Subsequent to the accident, Mr. McPherson has vanished, and this paper is investigating his connections to the IRB.

Now we have learned that the "Princess Alice" disaster was similarly caused by the actions of a single man—the pilot of the "Bywell Castle," an Irishman named Mr. John Conway, a last-minute substitute. It has been confirmed that his name appears on rosters of attendance kept by the Irish Republican Brotherhood. The man who was supposed to have piloted the ship, Mr. W. Schmidt, was murdered the night before the "Bywell Castle" left its berth in Millwell, with the result that Mr. Conway was brought on board.

We all recall the chaos and misery caused by the IRB in the Clerkenwell Prison disaster and the Mayfair Theatre bombing, with hundreds of Londoners and members of our royal family injured. Are these incidents at Sittingbourne and on the Thames merely the first two in another onslaught against innocent Londoners? An official at

Wapping Division counsels frightened Londoners to stay home to avoid the possibility of peril!

As usual, the newspaper had omitted some important facts and exaggerated others. For one thing, some trucks at Sittingbourne *had* been shunted onto the main line, but that wasn't unusual, and the under-guard was right to direct the train onto the second line.

But this was the first I'd heard that the under-guard was Irish. And this phrase, "investigating his connections to the IRB"—did that mean he *had* connections to the IRB or that they were merely guessing he did? And who had notified the papers of that?

I flung the pages down on the seat beside me and planted my elbows on my knees, clutching my hair and thinking hard.

The only people who could know more about the accident than we did were those who caused it.

But was it the IRB or someone else?

And what was this drivel about a Wapping official? Thank God they hadn't put my name anywhere in the article—but people would likely assume the "Wapping Official" was me. A groan escaped me, and I willed the cab to hurry.

If Stiles hadn't found John Conway, I wouldn't sleep again until I did.

As the cab drew up to Wapping, I saw a cab pulling away and thought, *I'll put money on Vincent being here already.*

I entered and greeted the desk sergeant.

"Morning, sir." His eyebrows rose as he tipped his head backward, toward my office.

"Vincent?" I asked, barely waiting for his nod.

He held out a folded paper. "Also a message, sir. From Mr. Stiles."

I opened Stiles's note as I walked through the main room. It was dated the previous evening:

> *John Conway in hospital. St. Theresa's in Turbin Street. He was sleeping, sedated tonight when I found him. Internal injuries, but doctor thinks he will live.*
> *—S.*

I refolded it with a sigh that came from the depths of my lungs and—not for the first time—felt profoundly grateful for Stiles's thoroughness. St. Theresa's was a very small hospital, usually devoted to women and infants.

As I reached my office, I halted at the threshold. Vincent stood by the window that faced the Thames, as he often did in his own office at the Yard. My windows were dirtier; I doubted he could see anything much out of them.

"Director Vincent," I said.

He turned. "Ah, Corravan. Are the men on the river?"

I nodded. "Still helping to raise the bodies and identify them."

His eyes slid down to my side, where my hand held the paper. "Which one is that?"

"The *Evening Star*."

"It's in the *Standard* and the *Times* as well." His eyes told me he was angry, but the constraint in his manner told me that he knew—as I did—that there was nothing we could do about what the newspapers printed. We merely needed to get on with our work, quickly.

I dropped the folded paper onto my desk and undid my coat buttons.

"That flag is a complete fabrication," Vincent said. "We never found one." He fidgeted with the edge of his waistcoat. "Just to satisfy my curiosity—what is the significance of the sunburst to the IRB? Ireland is hardly a land dominated by the sun."

It seemed an oddly idle question, but I answered. "It's a reference to the Fianna of Irish myth—brave warriors who performed all sorts of heroic feats. They referred to themselves as *Gal Gréine* or *Scal Ghréine*. It means 'sunburst.'"

"Ah," he said absently. After a moment, he added, "The *Standard* said Mr. Luby will be making a statement."

Despite knowing it was a possibility, my spirits sank. "Claiming these are the actions of the IRB?"

"That was intimated."

Intimated, but not stated outright, I thought. *Still, it was a thin thread to hang hope on.*

"Corravan, I must ask you . . . about another matter." Vincent appeared uncomfortable but determined, and belatedly I understood he'd been stalling.

Warily, I nodded.

"Why are you meeting with James McCabe?"

I drew back in surprise. "You're having me followed?"

A look of disappointment came over his face. He'd been hoping I would deny it. "Not I," he replied.

"Rotherly?"

He sighed. "Quartermain. Without my knowledge. But he's the chairman, and the Yard is still under review, so he's not obligated to notify me."

Quartermain was my old nemesis from the Parliamentary Review Commission. But my guess was Rotherly, that toady, was behind this. Neither of them had wanted me to be appointed acting superintendent at Wapping, but Vincent had insisted. After our recent exchange, Rotherly no doubt wanted to make sure I was denied the permanent position. My meeting with McCabe would furnish the ammunition he needed.

"Last night, he sent a message saying you'd met for nearly half an hour and demanded to know why." Vincent folded his hands together, settling them at his waist. "Quartermain's motivations aside, I have to admit, I'd like to know myself."

"It has nothing to do with the *Princess Alice*," I said. "It's a personal matter."

"At the moment, *everything* has to do with the *Princess Alice*," Vincent replied. "Certainly anything connected with the Irish underworld, until they're cleared of suspicion."

Well, if I were in his position, I would've asked too. Vincent knew something of my past, although I was never quite sure how.

"I was orphaned young and taken in by a family in Whitechapel by the name of Doyle," I said. "At the time, there were Ma, Pat, who was my age, and Colin and Elsie, the twins, who were younger." I cleared my throat. "Colin is nineteen now, and I'm afraid he's mixed up with McCabe's gang. I met with him to ask him to let Colin go."

Vincent's body went rigid. "You made a deal?"

"No! Nothing that affects the Yard's ability to investigate him." Vincent remained silent, and I added stiffly, "I assume Rotherly wants me removed from the *Princess Alice* case."

He raised a hand. "I told him it was out of the question. But don't see McCabe again, Corravan. Not until this is behind us. If you do, and Rotherly discovers it—"

"I understand, sir."

"Did you and McCabe discuss anything else?" Vincent asked.

"Several of his men have been murdered, as you know, and he wanted assurances the Yard wasn't doing it."

His eyes widened. "Good lord, why would he assume that?"

"Eleven years ago, after Clerkenwell, two police killed almost a dozen Irish," I said. "Some were his."

Vincent's expression became chagrined; clearly, he'd never heard this.

"McCabe is worried because guns are being used against his men. Stiles mentioned you've recovered pistols being brought in secretly."

"Yes. One shipment." Vincent closed his eyes briefly. "God knows how many others we've missed."

"McCabe told me the Cobbwallers had nothing to do with the *Princess Alice*. He was disgusted with me for even suggesting it."

"You believe him?"

I hesitated, then shrugged. "He knew people on the boat. And what would he have to gain by it? His interest is in making money. Increased police attention doesn't help."

"So you think it's IRB behind this," he said. "Not the Cobbwallers."

"I'm not certain it's either, sir." I passed Stiles's note across the desk and gave Vincent a moment to read it. "I'm going to see Conway today. As I said before, I'm not assuming he's guilty. For one thing, if he was part of the plot, why would he allow himself to be badly injured? Also, two separate people on the *Princess* said they felt the boat move strangely. Obviously, that has nothing to do with Conway on the *Bywell Castle*, and it makes me wonder if something happened below."

"Below the boat?"

I reminded myself that Vincent was no riverman.

"Belowdecks. The *Princess Alice* is steered at the wheel, of course, but some of these boats have an emergency tiller below, to control the rudder if the mechanism fails."

"You think it could've been tampered with?" he asked.

"If there is one, I want to find out who had access to it."

"Very well." He rose with a relieved air. "Thank you, Corravan. By the way, tomorrow there will be a burial ceremony for the victims at Woolwich Cemetery, beginning at nine o'clock. Quartermain, Rotherly, and I will be there, and I'd like you there as well."

Just then, I loathed Quartermain and Rotherly more than ever, and I despised burials, but I nodded. "Yes, sir."

CHAPTER 21

St. Theresa's Hospital in Turbin Street was a nondescript brown brick building sandwiched between two others exactly like it. The front door was one step below the pavement, and I ducked to be sure I didn't hit my head on the lintel. In a small front room was a desk, where a young woman sat and squinted up at me. "What be ye wantin', then? We don't want trouble. I'll call the police."

"I *am* the police," I said. "Inspector Corravan."

"A Yard man," she said uncertainly.

I didn't bother to correct her. "I'm here to see Mr. Conway. He was injured in the *Princess Alice* disaster, and I have some questions."

"Oh." Her blue eyes became round. "I'll ask the doctor if he can be seen." She vanished, and I studied the two items hanging on the wall. One was a certificate, no more than eight inches by ten, certifying that Dr. Mary Elizabeth Bradford had graduated from the University of Edinburgh. Another framed rectangle named Dr. Michael Bradford as a member of the Royal College of Surgeons. My guess was that he was her father, and this was one of the few hospitals in London where she might find a position. Belinda knew two women physicians, both of whom were only allowed to work as midwives.

"Mr. Corravan? I am the doctor."

I turned and adjusted my gaze downward, to a woman who barely came up to my chest. Her light brown hair was naturally curly, but she had subdued it into a severe style and secured it in a knot at the nape of her neck. She wore a white apron over a striped blouse with sensible sleeves that wouldn't get in the way. She didn't look robust enough for this sort of work. But her brown eyes were clear and inquisitive, her demeanor calm. I imagined she had a great deal of practice keeping it so.

"Dr. Bradford," I said, bowing my head in greeting.

"I understand you wish to see Mr. Conway."

"I won't stay long." She hesitated in a way that caused me to add hurriedly, "Is he still alive?"

"Fortunately, yes," she said, her expression troubled. "He has a head injury, and he's suffered some damage to his larynx and bleeding from his spleen, but we operated, and I believe we've stanched that." She crossed her arms over her chest. "But he mustn't be upset again. One of the other patients foolishly showed him a newspaper last night. It was all I could do to keep him in bed."

"Newspapers don't have the facts. And I won't bring up the rumors."

Relief flooded her features. "Very well, then." She led me through one long narrow ward, with beds jutting toward the center at intervals, then up a staircase. At the top, she paused with her hand on the doorknob, her expression troubled again. "Mr. Corravan, aside from another inspector yesterday, no one has come looking for him. Do you know if he has family in London? When I asked if I could send for someone, he merely shook his head."

"I couldn't say," I said. "If he mentions anyone, I'll let you know."

She nodded, opened the door, and pointed toward a curtain at the far end. "He's our only male patient, and this was the best we could do for privacy." We approached, and she shifted the curtain so I could step inside the improvised room. The man's orange hair was thick and curly except where it had been shaved for a bandage placed near his temple. His body, under a gray blanket, appeared to be of medium height and slight. His gaze caught mine, and I breathed a sigh of relief. He lay flat on his back, but he was conscious.

"Mr. Conway," I said.

"Aye." His voice was a croak.

"I'm Inspector Corravan of the River Police, investigating the *Princess Alice* disaster. Are you all right?"

"I don't know yet," he replied. "The doctor said I was bleeding on my insides, but she's still coming 'round, so I suppose Old Harry isn't snatching me yet." His eyes sparked with indignation. "But I'll have you know I didn't steer the *Bywell* into the steamer, none of us was drunk, and the person you should be looking for is the man who tried to kill me." He touched his throat gingerly.

This wasn't what I'd expected, but at least I didn't have to wonder whether he was willing to talk.

I drew up a chair. "Mr. Conway, I don't conduct my investigations based on what I read in the newspapers."

"Well, you bloody shouldn't," he said, but he appeared somewhat mollified. "Beggin' your pardon, but it is damned hard to read lies about yourself when there's no way of setting 'em straight."

God knows, I understood his frustration.

"Of course," I said. "Could you tell me what happened that night? I came from Wapping and didn't arrive until well after the boat sank."

"How could you? It all happened in minutes." His face settled into unhappy lines. "It was terrible. Those poor people." He gulped, fighting down a cough.

"You were at the wheel of the *Bywell Castle*."

"I was."

"A last-minute substitution," I said.

"Their man didn't arrive. I happened to be at the dockmaster's. At the time, I thought it was lucky for them I was there." His voice dropped. "Unluckiest half hour of my life."

"The captain mentioned there was something wrong with your pay," I said.

"Aye. Usually I'm paid on Monday. But they said the records had gone missing, and my wages weren't ready. So I came on Tuesday and waited for the paymaster."

I felt a prickle of suspicion at yet another peculiar event that resulted in John Conway being on the *Bywell Castle*. "Had that ever happened before?"

"No, never." He looked puzzled. "Does it matter?"

Instead of replying, I asked, "What do you remember of the minutes before the crash and immediately after? Who was near you?"

His right hand came up, unsteadily, and tugged the bedclothes further up on his chest. "I was at the wheel, the captain p'rhaps five steps away. Lookout was up front at the prow."

"Do you know his name?"

"Couldn't say for certain. I think someone called him Dick."

"Was he the man who tried to kill you?" I asked.

"No, no." His fingers fidgeted with the blanket. "He came later."

"All right. Where was the ship at this point?"

"Fairly close to the south shore, but not too close, mind you." He lifted his hand and dropped it back on his chest. "If you know the river, there are shallow spots that change with the tides. The recent rain has brought more sediment into the river just west of Tripcock Point, so we were a hundred yards off the tip." He paused. "I used to work for the Mantel Ironworks, and I've been on the river for twenty-one years. I've seen what the smaller boats do at places like Tripcock, where they hug the shore."

"Where else do they punch the tide?" I asked. His reply would tell me how well he knew the river.

"Ach, half a dozen places downstream," he said. "Bessell's Pier and Shropley Point are two of 'em. Then there's Nine Elms Pier and Saw Mills Timber Yards, upstream."

I nodded in agreement and gestured for him to continue.

"With that in mind, I called to the lookout to keep a sharp eye out for boats."

"How dark was it?"

"Well, the moon was nip and tuck with the clouds, but we could see the running lights of a tugboat and barge nearby, and all the colliers docked near the gasworks. And as we came close to the point, the lookout shouted that there was a ship ahead, and to steer to port—no, to starboard—no, to port! The captain was at his side in a minute, and he shouted, 'Port, man! She ported her helm!' So I turned. But it was too late."

"So the *Princess Alice* changed direction," I said slowly.

"Aye," he replied. "She turned almost broadside to us."

"And what happened after the collision?"

"The captain ordered every hand to launch our lifeboats and lifebuoys—anything we could find—into the water, in the hopes passengers from the *Princess* could stay afloat until we could rescue them. The captain had the whistle going full blast to alert boats passing by, and plenty came to help."

"The captain says he reversed the engines," I said.

"Oh aye, to stop. But not for long. A crewman from the *Princess* climbed up one of the hawsers and shouted at the captain to stop the engines altogether or he'd kill people in the turbines."

"They quarreled?"

He waved that suggestion away. "No. They were just shouting to make themselves heard over the noise. Then he gave the order to stop the engines and ran aft to help."

"Hmph," I said. This didn't quite jibe with what Captain Harrison had said about going aft immediately, but it wasn't far off. I took out my pocketbook to make a note and to suggest a change in the direction of my questions. "Am I right in suspecting you're Irish?"

He gave a crooked grin. "Aye. And you?"

I nodded. "Is your family in Ireland or here?"

The humor faded from his expression, leaving it bleak. "Haven't much family to speak of."

"Anyone in London?"

His eyes lowered. "I live alone."

"Were you married?"

A brief nod, and over his face came a look of such sadness I knew I'd been right to think he wouldn't have left his keepsakes behind.

"Do you have any affiliation with the IRB?" I asked.

His gaze met mine. "I don't hold with their ideas. Not anymore."

That twinged at my nerves. "Did you once?"

He gave a sigh. "I won't pretend I don't know what you're after. I'll admit I have friends in the IRB. I even went to some meetings." After a moment, he muttered, "And I signed their ledger, like that paper said."

I hid my dismay. "How many meetings?"

"Two or three. But then I stopped."

"Why?"

His hands moved restlessly again on the bedclothes. "We *should* have home rule. We need to be able to look after our own. But it's not worth taking the lives of innocents. 'Sides which, bombs just get the English's backs up, causes 'em to dig in harder. To my mind, it comes from years of fighting the French and winning in the end." He peered over at me. "Were you born here or there?"

"There, though I don't remember it. My parents came over in '47 from County Armagh."

He nodded. "We landed in Liverpool in '48. Ma and Da and the four of us. We'd already buried two. That's what finally convinced Ma that we had to leave, and she made Pa see it too." A faint smile curved his mouth. "Lord, she wasn't half his size, but the night we lost Molly, Ma put her hand on his chest, her arm stiff as a broomstick, and told him she was leaving, and he could come or stay as he would. When Ma talked like that, he listened. We all did." I don't know what he saw in my face, but it caused his expression to soften. "You're caught in this, ain't you?"

"The papers are reporting that there was dynamite and the IRB flag at the railway disaster," I said. "And you were at the helm of the *Bywell Castle*. There's plenty who would love to find links between the two accidents."

He blinked in surprise. "Was there any dynamite or flag found on the *Princess*?"

"Not yet. They're still raising parts of the ship," I replied.

"Hmph," he grunted.

"Now, what can you tell me about the man who attacked you?"

His eyes met mine. "Well, I stayed at the wheel, like I was ordered. The captain and lookout started aft, so I was left alone, and somebody came up behind me, threw a line around my neck, dragging me backward." He moved the gown away from his neck, so I could see the raw, red marks from the abrasion. "I wasn't ready for it, so it took a minute to right myself, but I know how to keep my head, and I jabbed a foot backward, caught him in the knee, and he loosened his grip. I fought him with everything I had, him whaling on my stomach the entire time with his fist. I had my knife in my pocket, so I managed to turn and swing it at him. I think it cut his arm, but he hit me hard enough to make my ears ring. I slashed at him again with my knife and I don't know where it struck, but he let out a scream and threw me down on the deck. I don't remember naught else."

"Can you tell me anything more about what he looked like?"

"Light-colored hair, curly, wore a cap."

The similarity with the man who'd attacked Eyres made me ask, "How light?"

"Pale yellow. Almost white," he said. "He was twenty or twenty-five years old. Shorter than you, but sturdy."

A chill ran along my spine. Could it be a coincidence, a man with such fair hair attacking both men? Was it the same man? But how could he get from one ship to the other so quickly? He would have had to attack Eyres and then dash for the lines to climb up on the *Bywell Castle*. The timing seemed nearly impossible.

"Don't look at me like that! I might've lost my memory, but I'm not crazy," Conway said, his voice indignant and rising to a shout. "I know what I saw!"

Before I could explain that I believed him, the curtain swung aside and a nurse appeared, her expression disapproving. "I'm sorry, we can't have our patients upset, and they can hear you."

"Of course." I laid my hand on Mr. Conway's shoulder. "I do believe you. And don't worry. It'll all get straightened out."

He reached up his other hand to grasp my forearm. "I didn't do anything wrong," he insisted, his eyes earnest. "The *Princess Alice* should never 'a been there, much less changing direction the way she did. Certainly not at that time o' night."

I nodded. "I agree with you, there, Mr. Conway."

His fingers eased.

"Mr. Corravan." The nurse clutched my elbow. "I *must* ask you to leave. It's time for the patients to receive their medicines and rest."

"I hope you mend quickly," I said to Mr. Conway. "Thank you."

The nurse steered me to the top of the stairs and bid me goodbye.

I left, mulling over all Conway had said. I wished he had never been to an IRB meeting; it would have made clearing him of suspicion so much easier. But he had, and there was nothing to be done about it. Still, it didn't alter my feeling that the man was innocent of conspiracy. No doubt some would accuse me of believing Conway's account simply because he was Irish, but I had the uneasy sense that he'd been made a pawn.

CHAPTER 22

It had been several days since I'd been to the site of the disaster, and I headed there now, crossing the river. Standing on the south shore to observe, I was grateful for a mild day, overcast but not raining. These men had enough to contend with, raising the pieces of the *Princess Alice*, without a downpour. I wasn't the only bystander. A dozen enterprising men in small boats were ferrying curious onlookers to the site. They craned their necks and pointed, their expressions an odd mix of horror and excitement.

God help us, I thought in disgust, *when this becomes a spectacle people pay to see.*

It was low tide, and the red-painted rail of the paddle box was just visible. As I watched, three men probed with poles to ascertain its stability. Presently, a diver was sent below. As he rose to the surface, I stepped into a lighter and rowed toward the boat that was being used as a site from which to direct the excavation. As I climbed aboard, a man of approximately my age looked me over wearily and seemed about to object to my presence.

"Inspector Corravan," I said. "From Wapping."

"Ah." He looked relieved. "Mr. Wood. Surveyor of Moorings. I thought you might be another of the commissioner's men."

"Rotherly?" I asked.

He pursed his lips in annoyance. "He's been hovering about, trying to hurry us along. The priority was recovering bodies, of course, so we were only allowed to begin our work yesterday afternoon. We've been assessing the site since then."

"Of course." I peered over the side. "What have you found?"

"The steamer broke into three parts," he began. "The bow pointing downstream, the boilers turned sideways in the middle, and the largest part, the stern, pointing upstream. The roof of the saloon is still missing. I imagine it's floated downstream." He waved in the general direction of Rainham.

"Will you be able to raise all of it?" I asked.

"Eventually, yes. But it's infinitely more complicated than raising an intact ship," he said. "With the hull in parts, it's the work of hours to put chains around the bottom and edges. Having to work from the middle of the river makes another difficulty, with the other ships still trying to use it."

"Not to mention this lot." I waved my hand toward the lighter boats with their gawking passengers.

"Enterprising sorts, charging a shilling each," he said. I grunted in response, and he turned and squinted upstream. "I know we're slowing traffic, but there's really no help for it. We waited until low tide before we attempted to raise the forepart."

"At two in the morning?" I asked dubiously.

"We worked by lanterns and war rockets," he said. I knew the military had been practicing for such an event. "We placed two chains, but it wasn't enough. We added a third, and the diver is just arranging a fourth one. We should be able to raise it now, not having to work against the tide."

"We're waiting for the diver to tell us what he sees below," another man interjected.

Ten minutes later, the diver climbed on board and removed the goggles he'd been wearing. His face was filthy, but I could see his distress. "Seems there were people trying to get out of the cabins below, but they're packed together like bottles standing up in a crate. The doors were like corks, holding them all in place."

My stomach turned. Yet more bodies.

"But can we raise it?" Mr. Wood asked.

The diver nodded. "The fourth chain is secured. But we'll want to make the attempt as soon as we can, before the tide shifts again."

As we watched, the *Metis* steamboat approached, and the band on its deck broke off its cheerful ditty and played a more somber piece until it passed. With a creaking noise, the crane began to draw the chains taut, and the lift was attempted, slowly and carefully. The chains slacked, then grew taut, and Mr. Wood shouted, "Here she comes!" The forepart of the steamer rose and floated, partly submerged, toward the south riverbank.

It was drawn to shallower waters, revealing the crumpled bridge, the mangled rails, and the broken funnel. A body floated to the surface, and Mr. Wood beckoned to one of his lighters, which hastened forward, two men rowing. One held the boat steady while the other reached into the water, dragging the swollen corpse over the gunwale with a large metal hook. Then they turned for shore and brought the body to a hand cart. A sturdy man rolled it up the bank, where a flat wagon, of the sort used for carrying hay, waited. Someone lifted a white cloth, revealing more bodies, and he added the latest to the collection.

"Where are you sending them?" I asked Mr. Wood.

"To the sheds at the gasworks," he answered. "Yesterday it was cleared for us to do that, so their families don't have to visit multiple sites."

I wondered if that was Vincent's doing.

"Is there anyone here who would know whether there was an emergency tiller on the *Princess Alice*?" I asked. "And if it was in working order?"

"We should be able to tell you by the end of the day," Mr. Wood said. "It's going to be at least another ten or twelve hours before we can get the chains placed properly around the middle section. The tide is hindering us now."

"I understand. This is a bloody mess, but you're making good work of it."

"Do me a favor and mention that in your report, would you?" he asked.

I nodded. As I climbed into the lighter, I thought I spotted the chief steward, Frederick Boncy, on shore, hatless and in a dark overcoat. Just the man I wanted. Hurriedly I rowed back to shore, tied up, and made my way through the crowd.

"Mr. Boncy," I said.

He looked at me, his face unshaven and haggard. "This is the worst week of my life."

"I'm very sorry."

He ignored me and continued to watch the process of dragging the hull closer to shore, and at last I said, "You told me you climbed up a line onto the *Bywell Castle*."

"Yes, that's what I told you," Boncy said sourly. "Because that's what I did."

"What was your impression of the captain and the pilot? And the lookout?"

"The captain was blowing his whistle and shouting orders, but he knew what he was about. The pilot looked cool enough, but the lookout was screaming his bloody head off."

"Did any of them appear drunk?"

He gave a snort. "You mean, like the newspapers said? I wouldn't say so, not those three, anyway." He paused. "Although there *was* a man who was drunk. One of the crew, a fireman by the looks of him, with his hands covered in coal dust. I ran to help with the lifeboat, and he was laughing."

"Laughing?" I echoed. *Purcell, perhaps?*

"Well, more like singing and chortling," he said. "He was stumbling a bit, so at first I thought he'd been hurt, but as I reached him, I could smell spirits on his breath. He was fumbling the line for lowering the boat, so I grabbed it away from him."

"Mr. Eyres said the tiller on the *Princess Alice* was handling poorly, jerking oddly. Did you happen to notice anything that would suggest damage to the tiller?"

Boncy drew himself up, his expression outraged. "So you're blaming it on the *Princess Alice*! Well, you're wrong, I tell you! We do a thorough going-over every week, and we check the engine and tiller every evening. I already told you—the *Bywell Castle* was racing down the Thames faster than she should've been!"

"I'm still gathering facts, Boncy," I replied brusquely. "Is there an emergency tiller on the *Princess Alice*—a secondary tiller, I mean, below?"

"Of course," he snapped. "In case the wheel malfunctions."

"Who would be down below? Who would have known about it, known how to work it in case something went wrong?"

That gave him pause, and he considered before replying. "Tom Robson, Jacob Sweeney, and Ned Wilkins. They've been with us for years. They're good crewmen, experienced and loyal."

But people can change, I thought. *And they can conceal their true intentions.* "Have you seen the three men since the accident?"

"I saw Tom Robson and Jacob Sweeney two nights ago," he said, a hint of concern appearing on his face. "Both were above decks when the collision happened. Tom was handing out life buoys and Jacob helped unload the lifeboat."

"And the third man?"

"Ned Wilkins was down below." Boncy looked perplexed. "Has no one heard from him? I know he could swim."

"I don't know," I replied. "We've tried to find all the surviving crew members, but some might be recuperating, or they assume someone else has reported them alive." Still, Wilkins should have known to come forward. Why hadn't he? Was he injured like Conway? "Do you have any idea where I might find Wilkins?"

"No. His mother lives here in London, though."

"Is there a ship's roster with his name and address?"

Boncy looked toward the water gloomily. "Drowned. Like everything else. You'll have to go to the Labor Protection League. He'll be registered there."

"What does he look like?"

"About twenty-five or so, sturdy. Blue eyes, I think. Pale hair."

I turned away to hide my quick leap of heart at his reply. Plenty of people had pale hair, of course. But access to the emergency tiller as well?

We stood together, watching the laborious process of craning the first section of the *Princess Alice* out of the water. The poor old girl was covered in muck; she looked beaten and forlorn. The wooden sides were shredded, the jagged edges like teeth with weeds caught on them. It took two cranes to pull the waterlogged hull to the shore, and it would be the painstaking work of hours to shift the four chains off in preparation for pulling up the next piece. As the first chain was removed, Rotherly arrived, stepping from a lighter onto the observation boat, his tall spare frame stalking from stem to stern and back again. I felt a wave of sympathy for Mr. Wood. Even at a distance, I could tell Rotherly was berating him and getting in the way.

I bid Mr. Boncy goodbye, leaving him to his vigil.

Chapter 23

The newspapers had called the next day "Burial Monday," and it was to take place at Woolwich Cemetery.

I've never liked burials. No one does, I suppose, but I find them unnerving. They make me fidget, and I have often distracted myself by seeking the least uncomfortable way to stand in my stiff best boots. But I understood why Mr. Vincent wanted me to attend. From where I stood unobtrusively behind a group of men clad in dark coats, I saw Mr. Vincent and members of Parliament, suitably subdued and mournful. There was Rotherly standing at Quartermain's side. For the entire service, through prayers and hymns, neither looked in my direction, although I sensed they were aware of my presence. After the final prayer was concluded, I breathed a sigh of relief and left. Outside the cemetery stood about two dozen uniformed Metropolitan Police, their hands on their truncheons. As I came through the gate, I saw why.

Across the road was an angry mob of perhaps fifty or sixty people. Many of them held ripped Irish flags, the orange, green, and white tattered. Four men in ape suits like I'd seen once in a music hall wore the Irish flag like a nappy over their nether regions. Some were chanting, but it took a moment to distinguish the words, as the voices weren't in time with each other yet. At last I heard "Dirty Bogs! Irish brutes!" gaining volume and energy with each round.

I pivoted and walked in the opposite direction. It would take me out of my way, but better an extra half mile in these wretched boots than risk being caught up in that.

"Corravan!" came a shout behind me. It was Rotherly's voice.

Unwillingly, I turned. His ivory-tipped walking stick slicing forward and back, he came toward me, tipping his head toward the mob. "You see what's happening here, don't you?"

"Yes."

"The situation worsens daily." His eyes glared from under his thick gray brows. "You need to find and arrest that man Conway. I know you're reluctant"—he raised a hand—"and the entire commission has been informed why, but he caused hundreds of deaths, whether by accident or deliberately."

"You don't know that," I said. "You haven't spoken to him."

"And you have?" he demanded.

I said nothing, unwilling to lie but angry with myself for having replied at all.

"In protecting that man, you are standing in the way of the law!"

I remained silent.

He leaned in, his head thrusting forward. "The safety of London, her economy, her very reputation as a city of civility and rules is in absolute peril! And you refuse to do what's right, simply to protect one of your own." His eyes narrowed. "Are you IRB?"

"I am not," I said between clenched teeth.

He drew himself up and planted the tip of his cane in the ground. "I suppose to some extent, you can't be blamed, given your upbringing. Eighteen years of thieving and fighting can't be expelled from the blood by any amount of training—certainly not completely. There is part of you that will always be greedy and grasping and lawless. But let me be clear. If even one more person dies because you have allowed this man Conway to remain free, to wreak further havoc in our city, you will be on trial with him, I assure you." He turned on his heel and strode away.

I knew what Rotherly was. I valued his opinion of me not at all. And I knew Conway wasn't up and about, wreaking havoc anywhere. Still, his words unsettled me, and I spent the walk to Wapping playing out in my mind various grimly satisfying scenes of Rotherly's mortification and humiliation—as he was proven wrong in a courtroom, in a parliamentary hearing, in the papers . . .

By the time I arrived at my office, I had beaten Rotherly down to the size of a worm, small enough that I could settle at my desk to review the various lists Stiles had provided for me: the dead on the south shore, with a column for the date they'd been retrieved; a similar list for the north shore dead, held at the gasworks; and a list of the crew of both ships that he'd gathered from various sources. I stepped outside my office. "Andrews, bring me the latest lists from the papers, would you?"

He entered carrying pages of newsprint. "What do you need, sir?" He raised his right hand. "The *Times*?" He raised his left. "Or the *Record*?"

"Both," I said and thanked him.

I was combing through the first column of survivor lists in the *Times* for any mention of the missing Ned Wilkins of the *Princess Alice*, when Stiles knocked on the doorframe. His face looked peaked with fatigue and the end of his nose was red with cold.

His expression was somber, and I stifled a sigh. "What is it?"

As he stepped into my office, he brought the brine and dankness of the river with him. He shut the door with a click that in its muted quality suggested that he longed to tamp down my response to whatever he was about to say.

"They raised the aft section," he said.

"More bodies?"

Stiles nodded. "It's gruesome."

"I was there yesterday."

"But there's something else." His expression was full of regret. "I found dynamite, Corravan."

A chill ran down my arms.

"A box of it." His hands sketched the parcel, two feet on each side, about a foot high. "It was waterlogged, but the sticks were obvious enough."

There was no possible way this disaster was merely an accident, and the dynamite would be taken by the papers as yet another powerful link to the Irish Republican Brotherhood. A curse slipped out.

"I know," he said.

"Were any newspapermen there?" I asked.

"I don't think so," he replied. "It's the advantage of working at two in the morning. No one's watching."

I sat back, relieved. "I'm glad it was you who found it."

"Because I was looking for it." He dabbed at his nose with a white handkerchief. "Mr. Wood understood the need to be discreet. He's the only one I showed."

"Rotherly wasn't still there, was he?"

Stiles shook his head. "He'd left long before."

Thank God.

"And you're certain the dynamite never exploded?" I clarified.

"The box was intact, stuffed underneath a bench."

I blew out my breath. "So it may have been a plan held in reserve. If the timing didn't work to steer the *Princess* into the path of the *Bywell*, the dynamite could be used to blow up the *Princess*. One way or another, it seems someone was determined to sink her."

Stiles had the air of someone who wanted to get something off his chest. "Frankly, Corravan, I've always thought it seems too much of a coincidence that the *Princess* and the *Bywell Castle* met there. The *Bywell* was hours behind schedule, what with the barge mishap and having to find a second pilot. Now I think the dynamite was the better plan, the one more likely to bring about the disaster."

"There were half a dozen places the *Princess* and the *Bywell* could have met with the same result," I reminded him. "The *Princess* hugs the south shore for most of the return."

"True," Stiles conceded.

"But I take your point," I said. "You're wondering, why not just use the dynamite? It's the IRB calling card. Why go to all that trouble, just to implicate the *Bywell Castle*?"

"I've been thinking about that," Stiles said slowly. "It could be the IRB's way of showing they can make anything—even a collier—a weapon."

I nodded. It was a powerful, terrifying message. But I had growing doubts that the IRB was sending it.

"Unless," Stiles added, "they were worried the dynamite wouldn't go off. Like last year at Victoria Station."

I remembered. The timer mechanism attached to the dynamite sticks had failed. And that wasn't the only element prone to error. A fuse could become detached, or the dynamite could go bad.

Stiles raked his hand through his hair. "What if there was someone on board the *Princess* who might have been a particular target for the IRB? There were two MPs with their families. Some bankers and businessmen."

"There are easier ways to murder someone than sinking an entire ship," I said.

"Unless the target was a group of people. There were some Salvation Army members and some police, and there might be others we haven't identified," he offered.

It was time to voice the suspicion that had grown since I spoke with Conway. "Stiles, I don't think the Brotherhood caused either the railway crash or the *Princess Alice*." At his startled expression, I raised a hand. "I know that the Brotherhood has the best access to dynamite. But surely, with enough money and the proper connections, another group could obtain it, somehow, from America."

"Yes," Stiles allowed cautiously.

"I spoke to John Conway," I said. "Thank you for finding him, by the way."

Stiles looked disconcerted. "Good God. I was so preoccupied with the dynamite, I forgot about him. Was he awake? Is he all right?"

"He looked to be in pain, but the doctor said she was hopeful he'd recover."

Stiles blew out a sigh. "What did he say?"

"He's not IRB, Stiles. He's been to some of their meetings, but he doesn't hold with their beliefs anymore."

He cocked his head. "You believe him?"

I nodded. "He says that a fair-haired man on the *Bywell* tried to kill him."

Stiles stared. "That's what Eyres said too—a fair-haired man."

"And that isn't a piece of information that has made it into the papers—at least, not that I've seen," I said. As Stiles shook his head, I continued, "There's a man named Ned Wilkins, with fair hair, who was one of three who had access to the emergency tiller. And from what Boncy says, Wilkins was the only one who was down below during the accident." I paused. "He hasn't come forward, but Boncy says he knows how to swim and doubts he died."

Stiles's gaze shifted to the lists on my desk. "You're looking for his name?"

I nodded. "And I'm wondering if Ned might have placed the dynamite. Perhaps he's the fair-haired man who tried to kill Eyres—and Conway as well."

Stiles unbuttoned his coat. "It's possible he turned the ship into harm's way, but he might also have been trying to fix the tiller, if it wasn't functioning properly."

"It's possible." I nodded. "Before I start racing around London looking for him, I want to be sure he hasn't been reported dead. So far I haven't found his name, but the newspaper lists aren't complete. Where are your most recent ledgers?"

"They're not complete either, I'm afraid, with so many unidentified dead." Stiles retrieved them from his desk. "By the way, regarding the dead man from the stairs—Schmidt. I don't suppose it's relevant anymore, but it seems he had been unfaithful to his wife before she died. His father-in-law had nothing good to say about him."

I grunted. That might explain why the man's wedding band looked unworn.

Stiles sat opposite, opened the first ledger, and ran a finger down the first page.

I picked up the *Times* and continued looking for a mention of Wilkins.

Except for the sound of pages turning, Stiles and I worked in silence for nearly two hours. The newsprint was small, and my eyes strained over it. Several times I had to stop, look away, and blink a few times before I resumed looking.

Once, Stiles drew in a quick breath, and I looked up. "Here's a D. *Wilkens*, with an 'e,'" Stiles said, and trailed his finger across. "But it's a woman."

We finished, finding Ned Wilkins on neither list.

"Would you like me to go to the Labor Protection League for his address?" Stiles offered.

"No." I stood and reached for my coat. "The walk will do me good." I didn't even have to take a step to feel the blisters on my heels. "But first, I'm going to change out of these blasted boots."

★ ★ ★

I knew the Labor Protection League's offices were on the second story of a former warehouse one street away from St. Katharine's docks, but I couldn't remember which one. I asked for directions, but several people just shook their heads and turned up their hands. At last, I caught one of the messenger boys—one who had passed me twice, hurrying, with a sharpish look about him. I offered him a shilling and asked for the Labor Protection League. Obligingly he pointed at a door with a window covered over with wooden boards. "Thar, up the stairs," he said. I followed his directions to the top floor. To the right of the doorframe was a small hand-lettered sign: "LPL."

I entered to find two clerks, both peering through their spectacles at some papers on the desk before them.

"Good afternoon. I'm Inspector Corravan, from Wapping."

The younger of the two looked up. I noticed that although his shoulders were bulky, his left sleeve was empty and pinned above the elbow. "Mickey?"

His face wasn't familiar until he removed his spectacles. From some dark region of my brain surfaced a memory of him, fifteen years younger, on the docks, pushing a rolling cart.

"Francis," I said. "Francis Merton."

His mouth curved in a smile. "You remember!"

"Of course. You worked on the docks."

"With you and Pat," he said. "Pat was a friend."

I felt my smile fade, and I let my eyes drift toward his left side. "Sorry about your arm. An accident?"

He nodded. "One of the cranes caught me. Chain broke. It's how I ended up here. I'm trying to make things safer."

"The docks were a dangerous place. Had to keep your eye out all the time."

He frowned, and his tone sharpened: "Still are." I nodded in agreement, and his expression cleared. "So you're at Wapping now."

"Yes. Looking into the *Princess Alice* disaster."

"What do you need here?"

"I'm looking for a Ned Wilkins," I replied. "He was on the *Princess Alice*, and he isn't on any of the lists of survivors. They're not complete, of course. I was hoping to find an address for him."

Francis rose and lifted a ledger from a shelf, laying it on the table in front of me and running his forefinger down the page. Then he turned it around for me to see and pointed. "Expect this is the man you want."

I took out my pocketbook and recorded the information on the line next to Edward Wilkins: *Care of Mary Wilkins. 36 Dove Street, Lambeth.*

His wife, or mother? I wondered.

"Thank you, Francis. I appreciate it."

"Did you ever think you'd be a policeman?" he asked with a dry chortle as he replaced the ledger on the shelf. "I remember you sparring with a constable or two after a night at the pub."

I grimaced. "Ach, did I? Well, I suppose we all do such things when we're young and stupid."

He grinned. "Good luck to you, Mickey."

I thanked him and was at the door before it occurred to me to ask, "One more thing: a man named John Conway, a river pilot. What can you tell me about him? Any marks on his record?"

Francis consulted a different ledger, and a frown creased his brow. "His license was suspended last year in April. The ship he was driving ran ashore at Goodwin Sands. There was a snowstorm."

"Surely they didn't suspend him for running aground," I objected. That sort of misdemeanor usually resulted in a fine, especially given the reputation of Goodwin Sands. "That area is perilous at the best of times."

"It wasn't for that." Francis's brown eyes behind his spectacles were regretful. "Mr. Conway's license only extends to the smooth water portion of the Thames. Goodwin Sands is a good seventy miles beyond Gravesend, which is well past the limit of his license."

My heart sank because I knew the heavy fine a pilot might need to pay to have his license reinstated. Conway could very well have been bribed to do something against his conscience, if he'd been threatened with losing his livelihood.

"My telling you this won't cause problems for him, will it?" Francis asked worriedly. "The rest of his record is clean—even exemplary—for nearly twenty years. Far better than most."

"Don't worry, it won't." I thanked him again and left.

I'd see Mr. Conway again soon. But first, I needed to find Ned Wilkins.

★　★　★

It had been a decade since I'd been to Dove Street in Lambeth, but I remembered it, anchored on one end by a small church and on the other by a theater that featured young women dressed in feathers and not much else. There were plenty of streets like that in London, and the incongruity of the pairing always made me shake my head in bemusement. The street was barely wide enough for a cab, but it was tidier than I remembered. The cobblestones were well kept, without the detritus one often finds in the poorer areas; the stoops were swept clean, and the windows were whole. Ten years ago, when I walked a beat in Lambeth, it hadn't been the case.

The cab stopped at number 36, and I knocked at the door.

It opened, revealing a stout woman of about forty-five, with hair that had once been dark but was now graying.

"Mrs. Wilkins," I said.

"Yes." She peered at me warily and stood with one hand on the door and one on the frame. "You're looking to board? The room won't be free till t'morrow."

I shook my head. "Mr. Corravan, from Wapping Division."

"You're *police*?" She gave a look of disgust and resentment, and her grip tightened on the door and frame.

But I'd had plenty of practice in ignoring unpleasantness, keeping my voice reasonable, and pressing on. "I'm looking for your son Ned—Edward."

Her reply was curt: "He's not here."

"Have you seen him since the *Princess Alice* disaster?"

Her chin came up. "Nae. He don't live here."

"Surely you've heard from him," I said.

She pursed her mouth.

You haven't seen or heard from your son, and you're not worried? I thought, but kept silent, my suspicions roused. I saw no signs of grieving. Either she was the most heartless mother in London, or she knew he was alive and well, and she was lying to me.

Nothing uncommon about that.

"Where could I find him?"

"Dunno," she said.

Clearly she would not willingly hand me a likeness; she'd claim she didn't have one. I'd have to find it for myself.

"May I have some water, please?" I asked. "I've been working since early this morning."

Her eyes widened with indignation, and she began to shut the door.

I put out my hand and stopped it. "Please," I said.

Muttering, she dropped her hands and stepped back, and I slid inside. She headed to the back of the house, and I heard the slosh of water. I stepped into the small, stuffy parlor and took in the room. No photographs or pictures on the walls or on the mantel or above it.

But on the desk was a framed, tinted photograph of three young men, all with fair hair. Two looked to be around eighteen years of age, and the other was somewhat younger. I took it up and studied it, holding it in my hand as she reentered the room with a tin cup. She thrust it at me ungraciously, and there was a foam on top as if she'd spit in it.

"This is a fine likeness," I said, setting the cup on a nearby table. "Strapping young men."

She had her hand out like a claw for the photograph, but I retained it and asked, "Which is Ned?"

Her mouth tightened, and as her arms crossed over her chest, her chin came up, moving in a jerky arc from left to right. "David, Christopher, Ned." Her eyes narrowed. "If you're looking for the others, David's left London and Christopher's dead."

"I'm sorry, mum."

Her eyes remained hard, and the lines around her mouth deepened, like a drawstring pulled tight. It made me wonder if the police had something to do with her son's death.

"When you do see Ned, ask him to come to Wapping Police Station," I said. "We just need a statement for our files."

She stiffened. "I'll tell him, when I see him." She reached for the picture a second time.

"I'll give it to your son when he comes to see me." I slid it into my pocket.

She made a sound halfway between a grunt and a snarl. "You can take anything, and there's not a word I can say, is there? You lot are all the same."

I bid her goodbye, wondering at her vitriol. What had a policeman done to her, or her family? Worry twanged at me, for policemen made mistakes, God knows.

As I closed the door, I saw her gaze darting about the room in search of anything else I might have taken, as if I were a common thief.

CHAPTER 24

At the hospital, John Conway looked slightly better than he had previously. His cheeks were pale underneath his whiskers, and the bandage on his head was still in place, but he was propped up with some blue-striped cushions. There's always something more hopeful about a man who isn't laid out flat on his back.

I took the photograph with the Wilkins men out of my pocket. "You said someone attacked you and tried to push you overboard. Was it this man?" I pointed to Ned Wilkins.

He cocked his head and studied it. "Might've been. There's a resemblance. But I don't think so. I'd say he was a little thicker about the jaw." His eyes drifted across the picture, and he raised his right hand to point with a finger that trembled slightly. "That man. I'd say it was him."

David Wilkins, Ned's brother.

My breath rasped in my throat.

Had Ned been on one ship and David on the other?

Their mother had said David left London. I gave myself a mental slap for not asking her when, for not pressing her to see if she was lying.

"You're certain?" I asked.

"Aye. The moonlight showed him plain. Even if only for a second, I'm almost certain it was this one, not the other. Who is he?"

"His name is David Wilkins," I replied. "Had you seen him before?"

He shook his head. "As I said, it was my first time on the *Bywell Castle*."

"Very well." Next, there was the matter of Conway's license being suspended, and I needed to ask about it, if only because Vincent would press me about why I hadn't.

"Can you tell me why you were out at Goodwin Sands last year—in a storm, no less?"

"Ah." His face screwed up in protest. "What was I to do? The pilot who was s'posed to meet us at Gravesend didn't come. We waited over an hour, but the boat couldn't stay there. Every minute longer, the water grew rougher. Finally, the captain begged me, so I stayed on. I wasn't about to abandon them."

"Were you fined?" I asked.

"Aye, but not much, seeing as it was my first offense." He shrugged. "And truth be told, I'd do the same again."

"I probably would have too." I rested my hand on his shoulder and smiled down at him reassuringly. "I'm glad to see you mending. What does the doctor say?"

"My throat still hurts some, and my shoulder aches," he said. "But she says I'll go home soon."

I didn't like that idea.

It seemed several steps had been taken to ensure that John Conway would be on the *Bywell Castle*. If Conway was an unwitting accomplice, once he had served his purpose, the Wilkinses might still want him dead. Conway was a witness, after all.

"What, ho." Conway peered up at me suspiciously. "Why do you look so? Has she said different to you?"

I didn't want to raise his fears; there was no point. "Not at all. Just concerned for your health. I don't want you leaving before you're fully recuperated."

"Hmph." He squirmed against the pillow. "Look here, what do you know of this man Wilkins? Do you know where he is?"

"We don't," I admitted. "But I will let you know when we find him."

He scowled. "Well, see that you do. I want to speak to that young scoundrel. What was he thinking? Why would he do such a thing?"

"I'll be sure to ask him."

We bid each other goodbye, and on the way out, I found the doctor. "He seems to be recovering his spirits."

"Yes, and there is no sign of additional hemorrhaging or any complicating fevers or injuries." She smiled to reassure me. "He should make a full recovery."

I let out a breath of relief. "Good, good. But—er, can you stall sending him home? Keep him here for a few days?"

Her smile faded. "Not if we need his bed. We're a small hospital, Mr. Corravan."

"At least don't allow him to leave without telling me first. I want to keep him safe."

She studied me for a moment, registering the implications of my words. "I see." She fidgeted with the stethoscope she held. "Where shall I send to let you know?"

"Wapping Division. And mark it urgent." At her nod, I thanked her and departed.

As I stepped onto the street, a gust lifted my hat, and I pushed it more firmly onto my head. The idea of tracking down the Wilkins brothers was daunting. Glumly, I trudged back toward Wapping, heading straight into a raw wind that threatened rain.

Crossing Dole Street, I came upon a young boy who had shouted himself hoarse hawking papers. His voice came out a rasp. I drew a coin from my pocket and dropped it in his palm. He didn't waste words, just nodded and gave me one of the papers.

Was it too much to hope that the *Princess Alice* had moved off the front page?

But no, there it was, in bold headlines: "Dynamite Found on the 'Princess Alice'!"

Damn, I thought. That was quick. And how the hell did—I flipped the paper over: the *Observer* again—get this piece of information?

I didn't even entertain the thought that Stiles or Wood had told a newspaperman.

The other man who knew was the one who put the dynamite on the boat. It seemed the Wilkins brothers might be using the *Observer* to spread rumors to suit their purposes.

But how were they convincing an editor to trust the word of a riverman?

★ ★ ★

I entered Wapping Station to find Stiles at his desk, poring over his notes. I paused beside him, but he was deeply engrossed and didn't notice. "Stiles."

His head jerked up.

"Come with me," I said.

Stiles rose and followed me into my office. I turned the newspaper toward him and watched as his face blanched.

His eyes rose to mine. "You know I never—"

"Of course not. My guess is Mr. Wood didn't either. But I think Ned Wilkins might. What's more, he didn't act alone." I drew the photograph of the Wilkins brothers out of my pocket.

"This is Ned." I pointed. "And this is David, who according to Mr. Conway was on the *Bywell Castle* and attacked him."

Understanding lit Stiles's face. "One for each boat."

Briefly, I outlined my discussion with Mr. Conway and my conclusions, ending with "One of the Wilkinses tipped the papers to the dynamite."

Stiles sank into his usual chair. He rested his elbow on the arm and pinched his lips between his thumb and forefinger. "Do you think the Wilkins brothers are IRB, and they were angry at Conway for leaving the Brotherhood?"

"Possibly," I said. "Or they wanted to keep him from denying that he *wasn't* IRB because they're working for a different group. Perhaps a group that is trying to frame the IRB. That could be why they're using dynamite."

I watched as Stiles turned this possibility over in his mind. I added, "And I'm wondering if someone at the *Observer* is working with them."

Stiles nodded. "To spread terror."

"But until we find one of the Wilkins brothers, and understand why they're doing this, the clues can be made to point in either direction."

"Do you have any idea where to look?"

I removed my coat. "I found Ned's address. It's his mother's house, and she says she hasn't seen him since the accident. But she didn't seem concerned."

His eyebrows rose. "Because she knows he's alive."

"She gave me a strange feeling. She's a bitter woman . . . but she was angry with me. Hostile, even. At first I assumed it was because I'm police."

"Well, plenty of Londoners are still wary about plainclothesmen," Stiles said.

"But it might also be because I'm Irish," I said.

"Likely, if her sons are part of an anti-Irish group," Stiles allowed.

"Mrs. Wilkins said that David left London, but why don't you see if you can find him. I'm going to lie in wait for Ned. I noticed some rooms to let opposite his mother's house. He'll come home eventually. Or there will be a messenger, or someone."

"I'll go to the LPL for his address."

"Ask for Francis Merton. Tell him I sent you." I took out paper and pen, in preparation for writing my report. "By the way, Conway said he jabbed David with a knife, so he might have an injury of some sort. Might help you identify him."

Stiles rose.

"Oh, and Stiles, don't mention this line of questioning to anyone," I said. "Let's just pretend we're still looking at the IRB." I could hear Quartermain and Rotherly already, accusing me of steering the investigation away from the Irish.

"Of course." Stiles nodded and left.

CHAPTER 25

I walked the streets near Mrs. Wilkins's house, including the mews behind, noting that her dwelling appeared to have only a front door, not a rear one, and that the single window facing the back was on the second floor, with no downspout close enough to be a reasonable way of escape. Across the street from Mrs. Wilkins's front door were several shops and pubs. Four of them had very good views of the house, and though I saw no "Rooms to Let" signs in any of the windows, I inquired. All said they had no rooms available, but the clerk at the chandler volunteered that the pub next door had two rooms upstairs, often used by patrons who were too drunk to find their way home.

I entered the pub and found half a dozen tables occupied and a maid sweeping ashes from the hearth. One hand holding a brush and the other a trowel, she peered up at me.

"Beg pardon," I said. "I was told you let rooms."

"Yah," she said, as she returned to sweeping the ashes. Small clots of ash dust rose into the air, and she dropped the last of the bits into a bucket before she stood and wiped her hands on an apron that testified to a range of duties, including pouring wine, if I read the stain rightly. "Two rooms. Both empty. Three shillin's."

I nodded agreement, and she led me to a door and up a set of stairs. At the landing she turned right, and as her hand touched the doorknob, I asked, "Could I have the one at the front of the house? Facing east?"

"But this one's bigger, with a better bed."

"I like the morning sunlight," I said.

Her forehead screwed up in disbelief. "Beggin' pardon, sir, but you don't look like the sort to care about sunlight."

I stifled a chuckle and reached into my pocket. "I'll pay a week in advance, including meals brought to the room. Can you do that?"

She held out her hand for the coins and nodded. "Breakfast and supper."

"Coffee?" I asked.

She shook her head and drew herself up. "Nae. But we don't dust the tea."

"All right, then."

"I service the rooms in the morning," she said, and shut the door behind her.

The room was small, low-ceilinged, and spare, though decently clean. Along one wall stood a narrow bed; along another stood a washstand with a chipped white ewer and a metal bowl on top and a blue chamber pot underneath. Some nails on the wall served for hooks, and the window had a metal rod above but only a single sagging valance by way of draperies. I removed the sheet from the bed and hung it over the bar, leaving only a sliver through which I peered at Mrs. Wilkins's house as I removed my coat and hung it from a nail. I briefly considered calling back the maid and asking for a chair, but instead I dragged the bed close to the window, and then I settled on the corner to watch.

Most people don't recognize that a good deal of police work is waiting for a rat to come out of its hole, its nose twitching to sense the ratcatcher's net nearby. I knew from experience that although I might look like a fool perching by this window for hours on end, it had worked for me in the past.

I spent the rest of the afternoon watching over Mrs. Wilkins's place; no one came or went. When the maid delivered my supper, her gaze took in the position of the bed and the sheet, which seemed very white against the near darkness outside. Her eyebrows rose. "Sunshine," she muttered, but when I didn't reply, she said only, "You want me to light the lamp?"

"I can do it," I replied, "but could I have a chair, and could you send up a messenger?"

"Aye."

Soon the messenger appeared, a slight boy of about thirteen, huffing, and with his cheeks red from running. I handed him a note. "Take this to Wapping for me, would you? To Sergeant Trent." He looked at the folded page curiously. No matter if he read it; it only gave this address and my initials. I didn't want to leave this window unattended, but I wanted to go home to sleep for a few hours and get fresh clothes.

An hour later, Sergeant Trent appeared, and he handed me a note from Stiles:

> *LPL had an address for D. I've taken a room across the way, but no one has seen D in several days. The one hopeful sign is D's rent was paid ahead.*
> *—S.*

Leaving Sergeant Trent in my place, I went home, slept for six hours, and returned. As I entered, Sergeant Trent shook his head. "Nothing yet, sir." As he left, he pursed his lips doubtfully.

At three o'clock that afternoon, I stood up from the chair and stretched, bending over to loosen the muscles in my aching back before I resumed my seat.

For God's sake, did the woman never leave her house?

I knew I should return to Wapping soon. But my instinct—and stubbornness—was holding me here.

At five o'clock, the street below was still noisy with carriages and pedestrians, and dusk was falling. I heard footsteps on the stairs and a knock at the door. I assumed it was the maid, but when I called, "Yes," Stiles slipped inside.

"Corravan," he murmured. By the dim light, I saw a look of satisfaction on his face, and his mouth curved in a smile.

He wouldn't be here if he hadn't found David, and my heart lifted. "David came home?"

He unbuttoned his coat. "Yes, and left almost straightaway. I'll say one thing—even with a limp, he's slippery as a fish. I was determined not to let him see me, so I kept back. I lost him when he went into a print shop just off Paternoster Row. He never came out, so he must have dodged out the back."

I sniffed and wiped at my nose. "Do you think he knew was being followed?"

"I doubt it," he said. "Can you risk putting on a lamp, do you think?"

I drew my makeshift curtain all the way across and lit the lamp on the floor. "Let's stay below the window."

He knelt and drew a printed page from his pocket. "I found this at the printer. David was there to pick up a sheaf of them, likely to hand out this afternoon on the streets."

I unfolded the rectangular paper. It was a handbill. "'Defending our Character,'" I read aloud. "'A lecture by Dr. Quentin Atwell.'" A drawn portrait of the man occupied the middle of the page. The lecture would be given tonight at eight thirty PM, in Booker Street, number ten. I looked up. "Who's Quentin Atwell?"

"I've no idea," he said, "but keep reading."

I barely heard him, for my eye had already traveled down to the bottom of the page. In small type, it said "Sponsored by the League of Stewards."

My heart beating in swift rhythm, I turned the page toward Stiles, my finger pointing.

His brown eyes were bright, intent. "Are you familiar with them?"

I frowned, thinking hard. "I may have heard the name, but not recently. I've no idea what they stand for."

"Perhaps this is the group Ned and David are part of." Stiles sat all the way down on the floor, the tail of his coat rumpled beneath him. "Not the IRB."

"Clever, going into the printer to find this," I said and passed the handbill back to him with a wry smile. "I think you should attend. Improve yourself, young Stiles."

"Why, yes," he said, with a small laugh. "I believe I will."

He handed me a bottle of ale and a paper sack with a meat pie inside. "I thought you might need some sustenance."

I thanked him.

He offered to stay, but I waved him off and turned out the light. I resumed my position on the chair and ate the meat pie— it was still warm—with relish. The ale slaked my thirst, and I kept watch for another few hours to no end. Clouds slid along the sky, but the moon glowed well enough that I could see the street most of the time, even though the lights from the pubs were mostly gone. Carriages, pedestrians, and bicyclists became fewer in number. Eventually the street was empty, and the clock struck eleven, then half past. I longed to sleep, but I beat down the tiredness and stayed awake.

Ten minutes past midnight, a young woman turned onto the street, and a moment later the light in her lantern was extinguished. I might have thought the wind had gusted it, or the oil had run out, but I was on the lookout for something peculiar, so I noticed she didn't fuss with it, and she didn't break stride as she approached Mrs. Wilkins's door, the unlit lantern in her hand.

I put my face close to the glass, my eyes aching as I studied every detail of her movements. She knocked once, then again, and the door opened. I could see the silhouette of a sturdy figure in skirts, whom I took to be Mrs. Wilkins. The girl vanished into the house, and I took a breath. A sweetheart, perhaps, sent with a message from Ned or even David. Without taking my eyes off the closed door, I pulled my coat off the nail and slid my arms into the sleeves. I watched until half past, when the lights in the house went out, as if everyone were retiring.

Damn. I felt sure the woman was a messenger. From what I gathered, Mrs. Wilkins had no daughters. Was she spending the night?

Another quarter hour passed with no sign of light or movement.

And then she reappeared. The moon, my helpmate tonight, slipped out from behind a cloud just in time to reveal the woman leaving the house in her dark cloak. The lantern she held was still unlit, but the moonlight glinted off the metal casing.

In an instant I was down the stairs and out the side door, racing noiselessly through the alley that met the street. I fell in behind the woman and kept at a safe distance, hoping she'd lead me to Ned directly, not by some roundabout route.

Three turns onto three different streets, but she wasn't being overly careful; she never attempted to backtrack and never turned to see if she was being followed, just hurried along with her head down and the lantern unlit, until she entered a house. All was dark within. But a moment later, she lit a candle or lamp, for a pale, unsteady yellow light shone through a crack between the window and a shutter. I tracked it upstairs to a room with curtains that failed to conceal the silhouette of a man who drew her to him and kissed her.

With grim satisfaction, I tucked myself into a narrow opening between two buildings. I'd be watching that door until he came out.

It was a long, cold night. The moon vanished, and in the bleakest hours just before dawn, I ached for a warm bed and a hot meal. The sun rose, and I moved to an alley farther from the door. I couldn't risk being seen, or this would all be for nothing.

Not twenty minutes on, a fair-haired, burly man emerged, and I slipped from my hiding place to walk behind him. That fair hair was only partially hidden by his cap. Like his brother, Ned was quick. He turned the corner, and I hurried my pace. He climbed into a cab, and I waved frantically to hire another. "Follow that cab," I said to the driver. "But don't be seen."

"Aye, guv'nor."

Staying well back, we followed Wilkins several miles, crossing the Thames at Southwark Bridge and heading east past St. Katherine's Docks and the London Docks. At last, on the far side of Shadwell Basin, the cab slowed and halted, and Wilkins disembarked near one of the warehouses. I leapt out of the cab, motioned it back, and ran to the end of the alley, where I could watch. Wilkins reached the back entrance, slid his hand into a pocket—I saw the glint of a key—and after a moment's pause at the door, it swung open, and Wilkins went inside.

By the early morning light, I could see the wrought iron sign above the door: "Houghton's Metal Works."

Even as I read it, I recalled Tom's voice saying the name "Archibald Houghton" and that he was a wealthy manufacturer, an MP, a candidate to succeed Disraeli as the leader of the conservative party.

I'd only caught a glimpse of Wilkins's approach to the door. My impression was that there had been nothing stealthy about his manner—but perhaps that was simply because he believed no one was watching at this hour. Had Houghton given Wilkins a key? Or had Wilkins counterfeited one?

"You comin' back, guv'nor?" the cab driver called.

My mind still reeling, I hesitated. The cobbled street between the shadowy corner where I stood and the entrance to the warehouse was empty. I saw movement but no light at one of the upper windows. I couldn't risk being seen by Wilkins. But what was he doing in the dark? Something injurious to Houghton, I had to imagine. Or did Wilkins work for him? Wilkins was a riverman, after all, and Houghton's warehouse was on the river. Or was Houghton involved in Wilkins's scheme somehow?

"Stay out of sight," I called back. "I'll pay you for your time."

Five minutes later, a carriage drew up, and a dark-haired man stepped out. From his elegant clothes and bearing, the ivory-handled cane, and the "H" on the carriage, I gathered it was Houghton himself. He drew out a key and entered.

Given the hour, the two men must have arranged to meet and did not want to be seen together.

What the devil was an MP doing with a man like Wilkins?

My heart thudding, I watched as the light of a lamp appeared, vanished, and reappeared on the upper floor. Another quarter of an hour passed, and the two men emerged and entered Houghton's carriage.

I dashed back to mine and climbed in.

"Gov'nor?" the driver queried.

"Give them time to leave," I said. "Then drive on."

"Follow them?"

"No. Go to the *Falcon* offices on Fleet," I said.

I wanted desperately to go home and sleep, even for just a few hours, but I had a feeling the tide was beginning to turn, and I couldn't bear any delays.

CHAPTER 26

Tom Flynn wasn't at the *Falcon* yet, so I went to his room to wait. I must have put my head down on his desk, for when I came to, his hand was on my shoulder shaking me awake. Still in his hat and overcoat, Tom stank of smoke and coal and ash.

"Corravan, it's not even eight o'clock," he said. "What are you doing here?"

"Why do you smell like a fire?" I croaked.

He frowned down at me. "I'm just back from the mine, of course. I must write the piece to make the afternoon paper."

Blearily, I rubbed my fingertips over my skull, clearing my brain of enough fog to notice there were dark shadows under Tom's eyes. "What mine?" I asked.

"The Prince of Wales, in Abercarn." When I didn't reply, he added with a quizzical look, "There was a huge explosion yesterday afternoon."

I shook my head. "I've no bloody idea what you're talking about."

He removed his hat and dropped it on the desk. "There were over three hundred underground when the steam whistle blew to signal the emergency. But the winding gear was damaged, and they were only able to lower it three hundred yards. They retrieved some men that way, and one man—a mason named John Harris—climbed down guide ropes to rescue five more men before he was overcome with smoke. It was the bravest damned thing I've ever witnessed."

"How many dead?"

"Two hundred fifty. They've only taken twelve bodies out. The rest are still in there—or were when they stopped working at three o'clock this morning."

"Oh God," I breathed. "And there's no hope they survived?"

He shook his head. "The fire tore through the place, down four or five cracks separately. Those poor blokes were burned alive."

Cold prickles ran over my scalp at the thought of the blaze of heat, how those men must have suffered during their last minutes alive. "Was it dynamite?" I asked heavily.

"They don't know. It might have been, although it was also possible the firedamp was ignited by a lamp." He removed his coat and hung it on a nail. "The timing is enough to make you wonder if it's connected to Sittingbourne and the *Princess Alice*, isn't it?" I didn't deny it, which made him peer at me. "But if you're not here about the mine explosion, why are you asleep on my desk?"

My hands were still on the wooden edge, and as I leaned back into the chair, I realized they were shaking with a mixture of fatigue and fear. I buried them in the pockets of my coat. "What can you tell me about Houghton?"

"Archibald Houghton?" he asked. "The MP?"

"And manufacturer," I said. "You said he was being considered as a possible candidate for prime minister. Is that still true?"

"I haven't heard otherwise." Tom lowered himself into his chair, a troubled look on his face. "Why?"

Worry forged a weight in my chest. "A man I suspect of bringing dynamite aboard the *Princess Alice* entered Houghton's warehouse early this morning." I paused. "A man named Ned Wilkins. He and Houghton met inside, and then they came out together and got into Houghton's carriage."

He looked dumbfounded. "Was this Wilkins a passenger?"

"No. He's part of the *Princess*'s regular crew, and he was the only man, so far as I can tell, who was in a position to manipulate the rudder, causing the ship to turn broadside to the *Bywell Castle*."

"Giving the *Castle* a larger target." Tom blew out his breath in a soft whistle. "If Wilkins is a riverman, he could be doing something else for Houghton. Something legitimate."

I ran my hands through my hair. "His brother David Wilkins was on the *Bywell Castle*, and the brothers might belong to an organization called the League of Stewards." His face altered, and I added, "You know of it?"

Tom leaned back and folded his hands at his waist. "Yes, though I haven't heard the name in years. Assumed they'd disbanded."

"Who were they?"

"A small group of fanatics in favor of 'splendid isolation.'"

"What is that?"

"It's a policy that began back in the 1820s," Tom replied. "Our foreign minister, a man named Canning, wanted to keep on good terms with other countries, but he was against 'meddling vexatiously in their internal affairs.' That was his famous phrase." He grimaced. "Over the decades, the idea's popularity waxes and wanes, mostly depending on which party is in power." I grunted, and he continued, "The League of Stewards was a conservative group who took splendid isolation as its key position, back in the early 1860s. Support faded after the war, when Prussian soldiers sat there across the channel for three years, potentially ready to invade us." His mouth pursed wryly. "Not surprisingly, we had a renewed interest in the internal affairs of other countries."

"Well, the League is still in existence, although their purpose may have changed. Or at least, a scientific man named Quentin Atwell is giving lectures about defending our character, whatever that means, in their name." I shifted, and the chair creaked under me. "What can you tell me about Houghton?"

"I've never spoken to the man myself," Tom said. "I only know what everyone knows. He was born in Lancashire, schooled at Eton and Trinity College, Cambridge. He spent some time in India and delivered his maiden speech in Parliament in 1852 on tea duties."

"Why would *he* care about tea?"

"His company supplies tins," Tom replied. "He's in favor of limited free trade, with tariffs and subsidies being used strategically to benefit England. He supported a number of laws put forth by Disraeli's government this time around, including the Public Health Act of '75 and the Education Act of '76."

"What about the Factory Act and the Workmen Acts?"

"Well, he's against those, as you'd expect," he replied. "Largely on the grounds that it would require too many small factories to be inspected, which wouldn't be practical. But he recently built a new factory himself here in London because the old one presented poor working conditions. Bad light, poor ventilation, bad sanitation, and the like. He improved the one in Birmingham as well."

"Birmingham," I repeated. "Is he in the gun business?"

"Not guns. Bullets and casings for rifles." He met my look with one of his own. "That's not a crime, Corravan."

"I know that." I frowned. "But how does he feel about the Irish?"

Tom planted his elbows on the desk and rubbed his hand over the stump of his index finger. "As I mentioned, I don't think he feels strongly. He's been absent for several of the recent votes regarding Irish matters."

"Is that usual?"

"MPs often absent themselves on days when there are votes on matters that aren't of particular interest to them or their constituents."

Or if he has a significant interest and doesn't want to tip his hand, I thought.

"What about his family?" I asked.

"He had a wife. She died some years ago."

"Of what?"

His brow furrowed. "Don't recall. As I said, we're not acquainted. It was around the time Gladstone resigned as prime minister—and then was hauled back in, two days later when the conservatives couldn't form a government. Houghton appeared in the House with a black armband, and men of both parties were offering their condolences. That would make her death sometime during the spring of 1873."

So Gladstone's return had pulled Houghton back to public life, perhaps before he would have chosen it. He might feel resentful at the obligation, although I couldn't see how that would shape his feelings about isolation on a national scale.

"In short," Tom concluded, "Houghton is more interested in matters of business than international affairs. That's why I can't imagine he's connected with the League—assuming it retains some of its original purpose."

"He may not be," I said. "But one Wilkins brother has connections to the League and the other to Houghton, so . . ."

"You're trying to assemble your train," he said, and I pulled a face to let him know I remembered a comment he'd once made about how we were both in the business of putting the carriages on the track in the proper order.

"I can look into Houghton, if you think it's important—although not today," Tom added.

"Of course," I said. "The Welsh mine. Just one more question, and I'll let you get to it. What can you tell me about Houghton's? The business, I mean."

Tom scratched the fringe of hair above his right ear. "It's a metalworks factory, begun in the early 1800s by his grandfather, I believe. They provide everything from pots and pans to girders and bridges for London and elsewhere."

"Profitable," I said.

"Immensely."

"All right, I'm going." As I stood, my back cracked audibly, twice. I buttoned my coat. "This mining accident. Do you think the papers will blame it on the Irish Republican Brotherhood too?"

"For now, the reports are inconclusive," he said. "Someone could start a rumor, but the mining people I spoke with suggested they weren't assuming sabotage, and they haven't found dynamite." He shook his head regretfully. "Just one of those things that happens. Terrible luck."

"If some newspapers do say it could be dynamite, will you explain that it might not have been? That it's not necessarily the Irish, at least until the mining company knows for sure?"

He frowned. "I'll write the truth, Corravan, like I always do."

"I mean in a timely fashion," I insisted. "The public needs the truth before a false rumor takes hold. You know what happens. You should have seen the protest at the cemetery on Monday."

"I heard." His face screwed up with distaste. "As you've probably guessed, the private talks are stalling. The English MPs want to be sure it's not the IRB behind the two disasters before they proceed. There'll be no point in proposing home rule to Parliament if they can't get the votes."

My stomach tightened. "That's a shame. I'm leaning toward believing the IRB isn't to blame."

He rolled his pencil between his thumb and forefinger. "I'll make inquiries about Houghton as soon as I can."

I left him then and made my way down the dark stairs and out onto the street. The sun was visible above the rooftops, but there was not a cab to be seen.

On the way home, my fatigue made me stumble as if I'd been drinking. *I'm so damn tired,* I thought. The quickest way home was through the small streets that wound north and west. As I reached the lit thoroughfare of Shaftesbury Avenue, only a few minutes' walk from my house, I hailed the lone cab I saw. I took out my pocketbook and scribbled a note. I tore out the page and handed it to a driver with a few shillings. "Take that to Wapping Division, would you?" I asked.

"Aye, guv'nor." He nicked to his horse, turning her head east, and they started off.

I continued on my way, two streets on, until I reached home and fell into bed.

CHAPTER 27

The sound of knocking at my door dragged me up out of a deep, heavy slumber.

I nearly slipped back into it when I heard the muted click of the lock and the creak of the hinges. In a flash, I was out of bed, my hand on my truncheon. In my underclothes, I crept silently on bare feet toward the top of the stairs.

"Michael?" called Belinda.

I freed my held breath and dropped my truncheon to my side. It hit the wall behind me with a quiet thud.

"Michael?" Fear edged her voice.

"I just woke up, Bel. What time is it?"

"Nearly eleven o'clock."

I'd slept for two hours.

She appeared at the bottom of the stairs, looking up at me from under a fashionable dark blue hat with a curved brim. In her left hand was a satchel that appeared stuffed full. "The sergeant told me you wouldn't be in until later. But this couldn't wait. Put some clothes on and come down, would you? I'll brew your coffee."

I returned to my room and splashed water on my face, drying it with a flannel. I donned new underclothes, took out my last cleaned and pressed shirt, tucking it into my trousers as I started downstairs.

The satchel sat on a chair, and on the table was a short stack of newspapers. "What's all this?" I asked.

"Just wait." She poured coffee into a cup and gave me a quick kiss on my cheek. "Here."

I stood at the foot of the table as she began to unfold the newspapers, laying them out across the surface.

I noticed several different mastheads—the *Sussex Post*, the *Standard*, the *Kent Observer*, and the *Evening Star*. England had nearly a thousand newspapers in circulation, as numerous as the pigeons whirling under the eaves of a railway station, but these were some of the more prominent and well read.

She turned to me. "Have you been reading the papers? About the *Princess Alice*, I mean?"

I snorted. "Not more than I can help." I took a gulp of coffee, set down the cup, and absently started to fasten the buttons on my sleeves. "Even if I had time, I'm sure half of them are full of lies, and anything that's certain, I already know."

Her eyes, bright with excitement, met mine. "That's just it, Michael. Some of them *are* full of lies and half-truths, but there is a progression and a pattern to them, and they fit together very convincingly. If I didn't know better, I'd take it for truth myself."

The certainty in her voice as much as her words caused me to suck in my breath and release it slowly. It certainly wasn't the first time she had presented me with an insight that steered an entire investigation into a channel I hadn't explored. I came around the table to where she stood so I could look over her shoulder at the printed pages.

"Show me," I said. "What did you find?"

"Here." She'd drawn an "X" in the margin of the *Sussex Post*'s front page, and she pointed to the headline: "Violent Group Unleashes Series of Attacks."

"This is the most blatant of them, I think," she said, but as I began to read it silently to myself, she said, "No, read it out loud—this section, here."

I did as she bade:

In hindsight, it becomes obvious that a violent group is intent on instilling terror and destroying public safety in London and beyond. First came the Sittingbourne railway disaster, which was caused not by natural erosion or rot, but by dynamite that was laid in such a way that the explosion would detonate and destabilize the track just prior to the crossing of the train. The customary source for dynamite here in England is the Fenians, the powerful and wealthy American branch of the Irish Republican Brotherhood. Next came the "Princess Alice" disaster, during which the iron-hulled "Bywell Castle," steered by another Irishman, heartlessly and brutally killed hundreds of men, women, and small children. Who can be sure what further violence will ensue?

I glanced up.

"And now this." She tugged the paper sideways a few inches to reveal the masthead of the *Kent Observer*, with another "X" in black ink beside the headline: "Irishmen to Blame for Series of Incidents."

"Out loud," she urged.

I complied and read only the first few sentences before the similarities of descriptions and innuendos became obvious. I met her eyes, and her tension eased, seeing that I understood. Hastily I scanned the other two articles she put in front of me, in the *Standard* and the *Evening Star*.

"Don't you see?" she asked. "They're using some of the same words and phrases, and the points are presented in the same sequence. They never explicitly say that the IRB is causing the accidents, but they mention the railway crash and the *Princess Alice*, allude to the dynamite and the Brotherhood, and then make a prediction that there will be more." She bit her lip. "They're setting a story in a particular light, so the truth is lost in the shadows."

"Who owns the papers, do you know? Could that be the connection?" I asked.

"The *Observer* is owned by a man named Clarence Tomlinson. I don't know about the others. But Tom Flynn might know of a connection among the four."

I reached for the cup of coffee on the table, so clumsily I nearly knocked it over. Belinda caught the cup and placed it in my cold fingers as I tried to order my thoughts.

This couldn't be the work of the Wilkins brothers, two rivermen. It *could* be someone connected with the mysterious League of Stewards; it had to be someone with power and reach.

Could Houghton have done this? I wondered. Certainly it wasn't beyond the realm of possibility that he would count editors among his friends.

If Ned Wilkins—or perhaps both brothers—were acting to terrorize London with physical disasters, the newspapers were seeking to build on that terror, to expand it—

"This is aimed at your average Londoner, Michael," Belinda said, breaking into my thoughts. "As well as MPs and influential policy makers. Whoever is writing this wants to shape public sentiment."

"What are the dates?" I asked. "Is there any chance one paper is printing it, and then the others picking it up?"

"I wondered that myself," she said, shuffling the papers so that the dates showed on all four. "But two of these are evening papers on the same day." She looked at me expectantly. "This is intentional and carefully timed."

"Put in place by someone who has the power to give a story to a newspaper and demand that it be printed."

"Someone whose word is credible," she amended. "These are reputable papers."

"You're right, of course." I sat down on one of the wooden chairs, my mind clearing rapidly, thanks to the coffee and her certainty. "How many papers did you read to find these?"

"Fewer than you'd think," she said with a worried look. "Not even twenty, over a few days. And as you know, there are hundreds of papers in London."

"God knows how many more are carrying this story."

She was already reaching for her satchel. "These are the most obvious examples, but I brought some others with me. They mention the Irish, but the hints about the IRB causing the accidents aren't so brazen." She drew out another armful of newspapers and handed them to me. I placed them side by side, and it wasn't long before I discovered repeated phrases to describe not only the IRB but the Cobbwallers of Whitechapel and the Irish generally: "brutal and reckless" appeared in six papers; "clannish and coarse" in four, and "possessing brains of the lower order and thereby more prone to drunkenness" in three. In my mind I heard Captain Harrison's comment about the *Beacon* article that said Irish were more prone to drunkenness, and that paper wasn't even included in Belinda's stack. I also noticed that three newspapers had brief notices about the Edinburgh bombings placed adjacent to the articles about Sittingbourne and the *Princess Alice*. That placement couldn't have been a coincidence.

Shaken, I sat back in my chair and met Belinda's gaze.

"It's horrifying," she said. "I know."

"But they're not only offering misleading accounts of the disasters, Bel. These papers are lumping all the Irish together, muddying the distinctions between everyday Irishmen, the Cobbwallers, and the IRB."

She gave a mistrustful look at the papers. "Yes, I suppose they are." She leaned forward to rest her elbows on the table. "Someone is being very shrewd about crafting this account and dispersing it." She studied me for a minute before her eyes widened. "Why, you know who it is, don't you? Or you have an idea."

"I believe Ned Wilkins planted dynamite on the *Princess Alice*, and yesterday I saw him going into Houghton's warehouse," I said slowly. "So ever since, I've been trying to work out what Houghton might have to gain by causing these accidents and stoking terror."

"Archibald Houghton? The MP?" she asked, incredulous. "Oh, Michael. This sort of violence? Just because you saw Ned Wilkins with him—"

I gestured toward the papers. "But look at this. Houghton is precisely the sort of man who could hand a story to papers, and they'd accept it, no questions asked."

She looked disconcerted. "He wields political power, of course—but to influence so many papers, spread all over London? And if—as you suspect—he's causing the accidents? Well, it's a good deal for one person to orchestrate and bring about."

"We've discovered a group called the League of Stewards," I said, and gulped at the coffee. "Tom told me they used to be isolationists, averse to meddling with other countries. I don't know what their purpose is now. There was a meeting last night. Stiles planned to go."

"You've talked to Tom about this?"

"I saw him earlier this morning because I wanted to ask him about Houghton," I explained. "He was returning from Wales."

"From the mine accident," she guessed.

I nodded. "He said there was no sign of dynamite, but that doesn't mean there won't be rumors."

"That's an additional difficulty," Belinda said. "When the papers suggest more attacks are coming, and they happen, it shores up the authority of the newspapers."

"They seem prescient—or at least well informed." I scrubbed my hands over my face. "Better informed than the police."

"Because the saboteurs provide them the particulars!" Her chin came up and there was a stubborn set to her mouth. "Not to mention that whoever is putting out these stories is a coward. There's not a single mention of who wrote them."

I managed a smile and leaned forward to lay my palm against her cheek. Her hand came up to rest on top of mine, and as I so often did, I felt a wave of gratitude for her cleverness and good sense and—

A knock at the door made us both jump. Her eyebrows rose, and I went to open it. Stiles stood there, with a book and some newspapers in one hand.

"It seems the day to bring me printed matter," I commented.

"What?" Stiles asked, then shook his head without waiting for an answer. "I'm sorry, I couldn't wait any longer."

"Belinda is here," I said. Stiles had met Belinda months ago, when she had been in danger during our investigation of the river murders.

"Oh!" He made an effort to appear nonchalant, but his cheeks grew pink.

"She only arrived half an hour ago," I said, correcting his assumption. "She brought newspapers as well."

"Oh," he said again, his manner easing. He followed me into the parlor. "Mrs. Gale."

"Mr. Stiles." She smiled warmly. "A pleasure."

As Stiles removed his coat, I explained, "Belinda was just showing me how some of the newspaper accounts seem coordinated. There are similar words and phrases, all pointing toward blaming the Irish—the IRB, mostly—for both disasters."

"Well, the League of Stewards scares me worse than the IRB," Stiles said as he hung his coat and hat. His brown eyes were sober, and he turned to Belinda. "It's a group we've discovered, and I went to their meeting last night."

She nodded. "So Michael said."

"Tom Flynn told me the League of Stewards was originally a group of isolationists," I said. "He thought they'd disbanded years ago. What did you hear?"

Stiles's expression was grim. "Before I went to the lecture, I thought I'd discover what I could about the man giving it. I stopped by a bookseller and found this." He handed it to me, and I read the embossed words on the spine: *The Superior and Inferior Races.*

"Open it."

I turned the first few pages until I found the complete title. "*The Superior and Inferior Races, with particular attention to the Celtic and Irish Vermin, consisting of a series of lectures by the eminent and distinguished pure Englishman Dr. Quentin Atwell,*" I read aloud, my voice sliding toward disbelief as I concluded.

"This man calls himself a doctor and scientist of mankind," Stiles said hurriedly, "and he's as bad as Knox or Beddoes. In fact, when I went to my usual bookseller to ask if he carried any works by Atwell, he looked awfully distressed. Well," he amended, "his exact words were, 'I would not allow that man's malicious treatises to cross my threshold.'"

"Good," Belinda said. "I'm glad someone takes a stand against it."

"When I explained why I wanted it, he sent me on to a different bookseller, who pulled it off a shelf in a back room."

I passed the book to Belinda for her inspection. "Was the lecture along the same lines?"

Stiles nodded. "Atwell began talking about English national character and national manhood, and how the Irish are a different race because they have no judgment beyond the animal variety. His first proof was the Irish rates of pregnancy, which he compared with rats; according to him, they're close to the same, proportionate to their size."

"Rats," I said flatly.

His expression was apologetic.

"Go on. I want to hear," I said.

"A woman's pregnancy lasts nine months, and the average Irish woman waits two months before becoming pregnant again; this compares to rats, which have a pregnancy of nine weeks, then two weeks elapse before they're pregnant again."

I stared in disbelief. "How does he know all this about rats—and Irish women?"

He spread his hands. "God knows! I assume he's inventing it out of whole cloth. He concluded by saying it's the natural order of things and God's will. In his words, 'given the viciousness in Irish blood, they'll slay each other, if we provide the means.' Then he blathered on about Irish inferiority having to do with the shapes of jaws and circumferences of heads and some nonsense about what he called the 'indexes of idiocy' and 'measurable scales of depravity.'"

"That sounds almost like phrenology," Belinda interjected.

Stiles nodded. "But afterward, I remembered something I'd read last week. Look at this." He unfolded the *Daily Journal* to the page with letters and read aloud:

All men of genius are orthognathous (less prominent jaw-bones) while the Irish and the Welsh are prognathous. The Celt is closely related to Cromagnon man, who, in turn, is linked to the "Africanoid." The position of the Celt in Dr. John Beddoe's "Index of Negrescence" is very different from that of the Anglo-Saxon. This is all clearly laid out in Beddoe's scientific treatise "Races of Men."

Belinda drew in her breath.

"He spells 'Nigrescence' incorrectly, by the way," Stiles added. "But it's not signed by Atwell. It's signed Dr. B. Lowell—whoever that is."

"Just a moment." Belinda riffled through her stack of papers until she found a copy of the *London Times*. She turned to the letters section. Hastily she scanned down. "Here," she said and read aloud:

The scientific treatise "The Races of Men" (1862), by Dr. John Beddoe, acknowledges the inescapable genetic faults and flaws endemic to the Irish. All men of genius are orthognathous (with less prominent jawbones), while the Irish and the Welsh were prognathous, and the Celt was closely related to Cromagnon man, who in turn was linked, according to Beddoe, to the "Africanoid." The position of the Celt in Beddoe's "Index of Negrescence" was very different from that of the Anglo-Saxon.

She looked up. "It's signed 'Mr. John Paulson.'"

"They're either the same man or reading the same treatises," I said.

"Beddoe didn't write *The Races of Men*," she said, her voice strained. "Dr. Robert Knox did. Beddoe wrote *The Races of Britain*. What are the chances that two different newspapers on the same day have mismatched the title and author? Not to mention both misspelling 'Nigrescence' with an 'i' instead of an 'e.'"

"It must be Atwell, submitting letters under different names," Stiles said.

Could Atwell be the one responsible for the newspaper articles as well? Or was that someone else entirely?

"Stiles, who was at the meeting?" I asked. "Anyone you recognized?"

"David Wilkins was there, in the back. I stayed out of sight," he assured me. "The room was crowded. About a hundred men, I'd say, mostly well dressed. Looked like City men, bankers, and clerks. It was orderly, with most everyone sitting in neat rows of chairs. I'd have felt better if they were a swarming rabble. It gave me the strangest feeling."

"I'm sure," I said, imagining the scene. "Any mention of a newspaper owner or any newspaper in particular?"

"No. But you'll never guess who the doctor mentioned several times as being a powerful friend to the League." There was a glint in his eye. "An MP no less."

"Archibald Houghton?" I asked.

He looked chagrined. "Were you there?"

"No. But Ned Wilkins entered Houghton's new warehouse early this morning, with a key, and he and Houghton left together and got in his carriage. Was Houghton present last night?"

"I doubt it," Stiles replied. "I imagine if he had been, Atwell would have pointed him out in the crowd. He seems rather enamored of him. How did you know it was Houghton?"

"Dressed like a gentleman, entered the warehouse with a key, and got out of a carriage with a swirling 'H' on the side." Stiles's expression altered, and as he remained silent, I paced around the room with quickening steps, the pieces slipping into place in my mind, like oars clicking into their locks. At last, I halted. Mindful of my promise to Tom, I chose my words carefully. "What if the League of Stewards is against Irish Home Rule specifically? And what if the Sittingbourne disaster and the *Princess Alice* were caused by Houghton and the League, with the dynamite and flags planted, and all of this written up to make it *look* like the IRB is behind the violence, in order to prevent home rule from ever happening?"

Stiles and Belinda both stared at me, their faces aghast.

I rested my hands on the top rail of a wooden chair. Between the coffee and my shock, my head was clear as polished glass. Stiles and Belinda hadn't known about the secret meetings for home rule, but I *had*. I should have been quicker to see how the League would leap to action as soon as they heard of them. "Jaysus, how didn't I see it?"

"To not only write false stories about the accidents but to *cause* them!" Belinda's voice broke. "It's . . . monstrous."

"This is why Timothy Luby hasn't released a statement," Stiles said. "The IRB didn't do it."

"Although the newspapers have slandered them anyway," Belinda said.

The room felt very quiet in contrast to the clamor in my brain.

"What else has the League done?" Belinda asked. "Just how much farther does their influence reach?"

I tallied on my fingers. "The explosion at the mine, possibly. Likely also the guns in Whitechapel, the looting, the Cobbwaller murders." I recalled Ma's comment about the abundance of NINA handbills. "They're fomenting trouble among the Irish any way they can."

"In causing the Whitechapel violence, they followed Edinburgh as a pattern," Belinda said. "To make it seem more likely it was the Brotherhood."

I stood silently for a moment, trying to understand Houghton's motives. Naturally, he would direct a scheme like this from the shadows. But what would cause him to be so opposed to home rule that he'd organize something of this magnitude, killing hundreds of people across England?

James always said murderers were motivated by one of four causes: fear, love, revenge, and greed. I dismissed greed. Yes, Houghton was an industrialist, but this scheme smacked of something beyond mercenary concern that home rule might affect his factories and his profits. Fear of the Irish? That didn't feel likely.

Love felt utterly absent from these calculations. But I knew what revenge could do, how it could fill a cavern carved out brutally by loss. Especially the loss of someone one loved. I had only to reach back to the river murders to find an example of that.

And Houghton had lost his wife.

How had he lost his wife? And when?

"Tom said that when Gladstone was voted out and then returned, Houghton was wearing mourning for his wife," I said, my voice tight. "That was spring of 1873. What month, do you know?"

"It was the middle of March," Belinda replied. "I was in the Lake District with my aunt when I read about Gladstone's return in the papers. She was so pleased."

"The Mayfair bombing was on the ninth," I said hollowly.

Stiles drew in his breath. "Could his wife have been killed in it? But how would it not have been in the papers?"

"It probably was, but the headlines were all about the princesses Helena and Beatrice," Belinda replied. "Don't you remember the picture of them clutching each other on the pavement, the three constables around them? Queen Victoria awarded the men medals."

I pushed back from the table. "I'll see Vincent," I said to Stiles. "But can you do something for me?"

"See Archibald Houghton?" he replied.

I nodded. "At the moment, there is nothing to connect Houghton or the League of Stewards to the *Princess Alice* except for Ned meeting with Houghton, a tenuous link that no one witnessed except me. There's no possibility Vincent will let us go after Houghton without more proof. Even the newspapers have no link to Houghton except tangentially through Atwell, who used a pseudonym." I turned to Belinda, knowing I needed to see the man who could put this information to use. "Where can I find Lord Baynes-Hill?"

"The Inner Temple," she replied as she began to gather up the newspapers.

"Leave them, would you?" I asked. "I'll show them to Vincent. They're solid evidence of a coordinated plan—the best we have."

Her eyes met mine, and her expression softened.

Stiles stepped into the entryway to find his coat, and she handed me hers, so I might help her into it.

"Bel," I said, my voice low, "I'm sorry about not staying on Saturday, and we've had so little time since you—"

"Don't," she said with a shake of her head. She rested her palm on my chest. "I know how this is. Just be careful."

I touched my forehead to hers for a moment, then kissed her cheek before I held open her coat.

Stiles leaned back into the room. "I'll go to Wapping after I see Houghton—assuming he'll see me, of course."

"Mr. Stiles, could I walk out with you?" Belinda asked as she slid her arms into the sleeves.

"Of course." Stiles held the door for her. "I'll fetch you a cab."

The door closed behind them, and I started upstairs to finish dressing.

As I reached the landing, I realized there was someone else I needed to speak with, after Vincent and Lord Baynes-Hill. Rotherly be damned. I needed to ask a favor of James McCabe.

CHAPTER 28

The cab took me to Fleet Street, where an accident involving three carriages had halted traffic in all directions. I paid the driver, loped down to the Victoria Embankment, and hurried west along its dark gray stones. Although it wasn't raining, the clouds hung low, and in the absence of sun, the river was like forged steel, gray and impenetrable. The sturdy tugboats and the crowded steamers ploughed along doggedly, and the ships' pointed masts needled the clouds. At the Charing Cross footbridge, I climbed the shallowly puddled stone steps, making my way to the yard behind Whitehall Place, number four.

It seemed longer than three months since I'd walked under the stone arch onto the cobbles that would glint after a good rain. Today they were a muddy, pale brown.

I swung open the door, and the smell rushed at me, old and musty and familiar.

Nodding to the sergeant at the desk, I made my way through the main room to Vincent's door. It was closed, but when I knocked, he called for me to enter.

Unlike the main room, Vincent's room was altered. A new rug covered the floor and the room smelled of fresh paint. Strangely, it seemed the very dimensions of this room had changed. It appeared somewhat narrower. Perhaps it was because the old, battered bookcases had been replaced with new ones of fine dark-stained cherrywood.

I tipped my head toward the door. "May I?"

He nodded his permission, and I shut the door and unbuttoned my coat.

It was only then that I noticed Vincent's eyes were glassy, and he looked feverish, with sweat on his forehead and a nose that looked red from rubbing.

"You're ill, sir," I said.

"It's no matter. Please tell me you've some news."

"I do," I said. "We have an idea about who is behind the *Princess Alice* disaster—although it's a complicated story and runs against the one the newspapers are telling."

His eyebrows rose slightly. "Not the IRB?"

"No, and not an accident either," I began, and continued with what we'd discovered about Ned Wilkins planting the dynamite, manipulating the tiller, and attacking Eyres, and his brother David attacking Conway.

"At first I wondered if the Wilkins brothers were IRB," I said. "But after following David Wilkins into a print shop, Stiles found this handbill." I drew it from my pocket, unfolded it, and passed it across the desk.

Vincent's brows drew together as he read, and he looked up, puzzled.

"Stiles went to this meeting last night," I said, "and listened for two hours about how the Irish are vermin like rats, complete with what Atwell called scientific evidence. There were about a hundred people there. Clerks and bankers. Not working men."

He fought down a sneeze, using his handkerchief to cover his mouth and nose. "What do you know about this"—he glanced at the handbill again—"League of Stewards? Does it purport to be a scientific society?"

"Its purpose seems to be to stir up anti-Irish sentiment, to make it seem as though the Irish present an enormous threat to England."

"To what end?"

"Among other things, to forestall the possibility of home rule being introduced when Gladstone returns."

Understanding dawned in his eyes. "Who is directing the League? Radicals in Parliament? Businessmen with concerns in Ireland?"

"Some of both, I think."

He winced, and it reminded me that as the second son of a baronet, Vincent was on intimate terms with plenty of MPs and businessmen. Being a former correspondent for the *Daily Telegraph*, he could very well know editors here in London, and I added, "It's someone who has influence with the newspapers too." I removed the envelope from my satchel and laid the four newspapers Belinda had first shown me across his desk. "These articles all carry similar stories. More than that—similar words, phrases, the same rhetorical questions pushing the readers toward concluding that not only the IRB are to blame but the Irish generally." I watched him examine each in turn. "What do you think?"

He read slowly, shuffling the papers back and forth to compare them. At last, he shook his head and laid them aside. "Clearly there's duplication. But I know the editor of the *Star*. I can't believe he'd knowingly print something other papers are carrying, particularly something that stirs up distrust and hatred. Someone is abusing the papers."

"We believe we know who is directing it, sir. While Stiles was at the meeting last night, I was searching for Ned Wilkins. I finally found him and followed him. Just after dawn, he entered the MP Archibald Houghton's new warehouse, with a key to the back door. Not a quarter of an . . ."

I halted, for it was clear the name "Houghton" struck Vincent like a blow. After a moment of denial and uncertainty, he regained mastery over himself. He swallowed and tugged at his collar.

"Go on," he said steadily. "After a quarter of an hour . . ."

"Houghton arrived, let himself in with a key, and then he and Wilkins came out and left in Houghton's carriage." I paused. "You know Houghton, then."

"His younger brother Maxwell and I were at university together." Vincent rose from his chair and walked unsteadily to the window to stare out. He took a deep breath that brought forth an involuntary hacking cough that he covered with a white handkerchief.

"Sir, have you seen a doctor?"

"Yes." He continued to look out his window—a window that was clean, providing a proper view to the Thames.

"Was Houghton's wife killed in the Mayfair bombing?" I asked.

He turned. "Not only his beautiful young wife." His mouth tightened briefly. "She was with child."

"I—see," I managed. He remained silent, and at last I asked, "Do you believe him capable of such a scheme?"

"By God, I hope not," he said softly. "But let me think about how to best handle this. Can you leave these papers with me?"

I nodded. "I'm wondering about the League's reach. If it extends to the *Princess Alice* and possibly the railway and the Welsh mine and the newspapers, my guess is—"

"They've enabled the violence here in Whitechapel, yes," he said heavily. When I didn't reply, he added, "Houghton not only makes the casings for bullets; he sits on the board of one of the gun works in Birmingham." He paused. "With my father."

"Which one?"

"Webley and Son."

I stilled. The gun I took from Colin had been a Webley. "What was the make of the guns found in the crate at Liverpool Station?"

He bent over his desk, riffled through a small stack of folders, opened one, and ran his eyes down a page until he gave a ragged exhale that told me my guess had been correct.

He looked up. "They were Webleys. Single-shot pistols."

A small muscle near his eye twitched spasmodically. It was twisting him to pieces, the thought that people he knew were involved in this.

"I'm bloody sorry, sir," I said.

He was silent for a long minute. At last, he dropped into his chair, rubbing a hand tiredly over his forehead. "Is there anything else, Corravan?"

"Do you know of any connection between Houghton and these papers?"

"I don't. But I will look into the matter." He paused. "Don't approach Houghton. Not yet."

"No, sir."

I bid him goodbye, and as I closed the door behind me, a guttural groan of pain and regret and frustration burst from him.

It was the closest I'd ever heard him come to cursing. Meanwhile, my thoughts leapt from point to point. Colin had likely obtained that Webley from Finn Riley, who probably received guns through an intermediary, or a chain of them, one of whom had been paid by Houghton. I couldn't prove it yet, but my instinct was shrilling like a gull screaming in the wind.

★ ★ ★

From Whitehall Place, I took a cab to the Inns of Court. After paying the driver, I strode into the quadrangle of red brick buildings, with green grass and gardens inside and the Thames beyond. The last time I'd been here was to visit Mr. Haverling, an important witness in the river murders, and I remembered this series of black doors. Though numbered, none were labeled in any way, and there were dozens of them. A messenger boy hurried past, and I reached a hand to stop him. "Lord Baynes-Hill," I said, holding out a shilling between my thumb and forefinger. "Where are his chambers?"

The boy pocketed the coin and gestured for me to follow, trotting through an arched gate. Rounding a corner, he pointed to a window on the second story.

I thanked him, and he sped off. I entered the building, climbed the steps, and pushed open the door that bore "Lord C. L. Baynes-Hill" on a brass plate beside it. The foyer was large and square, with dark paneling, shelves of books, a frayed rug, and several lamps to light the room. The air held a smell I associated with Belinda's library—old leather volumes, treasured and well kept.

A clerk looked up from his desk. "Sir?"

"Inspector Corravan to see Lord Baynes-Hill. I don't have an appointment," I added, forestalling the question. "But I believe he'll see me. It's a matter that concerns him."

The clerk pushed his dark hair away from his brow, and though polite, his face was skeptical. "Very well. Please sit, and I'll let him know you're here."

Not a minute later, he returned, stepping with some alacrity. "Please come through, sir," he said and led me to an open door, which he closed behind him.

Lord Baynes-Hill stood behind his desk, in an unconscious imitation of the posture of the white-wigged man in the portrait behind him.

He saw the direction of my gaze and moved to the side, so I could see the image fully. "My grandfather. Also a barrister," he said.

There was an awkward silence, during which he stepped to the side of his desk, so nothing stood between us. "What can I do for you, Inspector?"

"I have something to tell you in confidence," I said. "It may be useful to you. But I ask that you don't reveal where you heard it."

"Of course. Please." He gestured toward two chairs near the window and sank into one, crossing one leg over the other.

The other chair creaked underneath me as I sat, the tawny leather giving way. I began, "We believe that the group behind the *Princess Alice* disaster is called the League of Stewards."

"The League of Stewards?" He gave an incredulous look. "Good lord."

"Do you know of them?" I asked.

He rested his elbows on the chair arms and drew his fingertips together. "The last I heard of their activities, it was—oh, before the Prussian War. I had no idea they were extant."

"They are stirring anti-Irish sentiment," I said. His eyebrows rose, and I continued: "We believe one of their members brought dynamite onboard the *Princess Alice*, and it's likely they caused the Sittingbourne disaster as well. More than that, we believe they're planting stories in various newspapers to blame the IRB. The stories are worded in such a way that they reinforce one another, to give the appearance of verified truth."

His expression grew wary. "Which papers, specifically?"

"The *Kent Observer*, the *Sussex Post*, the *Standard*, and the *Evening Star*. Possibly others as well."

He frowned. "I can tell you that the *Post* and the *Standard* are both owned by Clarence Tomlinson. I don't know about the others."

It wasn't proof of Tomlinson's involvement, but two more papers owned by him, in addition to the *Observer*, seemed a strong coincidence.

"Did the League cause the Welsh mine explosion as well?" Lord Baynes-Hill asked.

"We don't know about that yet. It's a long way from London," I acknowledged. "But that doesn't mean they won't urge the newspapers to suggest it."

His narrow head bobbed slightly as he took this in. "And you're here because you think all this has been done to derail our home rule talks?"

"Aside from stirring up public suspicion out of malice, can you think of another reason?" I asked. "There seems to be a particular urgency at the moment."

His hands dropped onto the chair arms with a deliberateness that suggested the effort he was making to conceal his inner turmoil. "It's a very small group who knows about the talks," he said at last. "Only eight of us, chosen carefully. I suppose there is no way of knowing who spoke out of turn." The skin around his eyes puckered with worry and dismay. "Could you tell me how *you* heard of the talks? It might allow me to trace it back."

I wouldn't give him Tom Flynn's name, but I asked, "Is Archibald Houghton acquainted with any of the MPs in your group?"

He inhaled audibly, and his eyes widened. "You're certain of his involvement?"

"He may be one of the leaders. His wife and unborn child were killed in the Mayfair Theatre bombing."

He rubbed his large, blue-veined hand over his face for a long moment before his hand fell away and he met my gaze. "Two members of the group belong to his club. It likely wouldn't have occurred to them to be wary." He looked pained. "His conservative political positions would have assimilated with those of the League as it was fifteen years ago. If he was a member then, it's only natural that he'd resuscitate the group for a different purpose."

"Tell me what is meant by 'splendid isolation,'" I said.

"It's the theory that it is better to shore up our national boundaries and not meddle in the business of others. Of course, as with any theory, it can be refitted to another purpose. It seems this version shores up our national English identity with the Irish fixed outside of it." He shook his head. "It disgusts me to think governmental policy has been influenced by the League and the press. But thank you for telling me, Mr. Corravan. I only wish I knew who spoke out of turn. It worries me."

"Of course."

"I cannot tell you how it grieves me to abandon the effort, but perhaps now isn't the time for home rule." The lines around his mouth deepened, and his eyes met mine. "It's most unfortunate. We had come within sight of land, Mr. Corravan. We could see the dock."

"That's why they had to work so energetically to turn the tide," I replied.

"But you realize what this means, of course. If we hadn't begun those talks, those passengers would still be alive." He raised a hand to forestall my objection. "I know—the blame lies with the League. The disaster was an unforeseen consequence of our endeavors. But I deeply, deeply regret . . ."

"I know," I said quietly.

He heaved himself out of his chair and stepped to the window, the fingertips of his left hand groping for the sash, as if in search of something solid. His back was to me, and uncertain of whether I was being dismissed, I stood as well.

"Regret is a most unfortunate feeling, is it not?" he asked. "It poisons all satisfaction, all joy, and accomplishes nothing." His voice broke, and I didn't reply. "A friend and I were speaking of our regrets only last week. Perhaps you are too young to understand, but we are at an age when we consider them in wretched detail. The road behind me seems strewn with them. But there is no help for it." He turned. "My friend is a noted wit with an apt turn of phrase. Do you know what he said?"

I shook my head.

"He said a blackguard may find relief from regret in one of three ways: rotgut, rage, or revenge. But a decent man can do very little with it other than carry it to his grave. I'm afraid that I am going to take this regret to mine, and it is a heavy burden." He laid a hand on his chest as if he felt a physical pain. "Upon my heart."

We stood in silence for a long moment. At last, he said, "Good luck to you, Mr. Corravan."

"And you," I said.

Regret, I thought as I closed the door. I was beginning to feel as though it were rising like a tide, lapping insistently at my boots.

CHAPTER 29

It was time to find McCabe. He was the only one I could think of who could help me find Timothy Luby.

I returned to the pub where I'd met McCabe before, but he wasn't there. I went to the Goose and Gander to find O'Hagan, but he wasn't there or at the Waterman. *Damn it,* I thought as I stood shivering on the street outside. How the hell was I going to find Luby if I couldn't even find McCabe?

Reluctantly I acknowledged the Doyles should be my next stop. Even if Colin was no longer working for McCabe, he'd know someone who might know where to find him, or at least know someone who could get a message to him.

I headed toward the Doyles's, and as I reached the foot of the stairs, I heard a cry of alarm from above.

Elsie.

I froze, my hand on the wooden rail, recalling the men who'd followed her into the house.

Pat and I had once spent an entire afternoon training ourselves to creep up and down the stairs so they wouldn't squeak, so Ma wouldn't hear our comings and goings. Of their own accord, my feet flew up the stairs in silence: on that shaky first step, I set my boot far to the left, skipped the second, leapt far to the right on the third—and then I was at the top step, turning the knob and bursting through the door, my truncheon in one hand, and my other hand closed in a fist drawn back.

There were three of them ranged in a semicircle facing Ma and Elsie. The one closest spun to face me and I wheeled my truncheon into his belly, and as he bent forward, I sliced the side of my hand down across the back of his neck, dropping him motionless on the floor as the other two came at me from either side. One shouted a protest, but my boot slammed into the side of his knee, throwing him sideways, and he dropped, howling. The other leapt toward me to shove me to the floor, but my hand reached for my knife even as I fell, and I rolled to my feet, wrapped my arm around him and laid the blade to his throat. He froze, and my eyes sought Ma. "Did they hurt you?"

She shook her head. "Not at all."

"I heard you cry out," I said to Elsie. My eye dropped to her right hand, which held the kitchen cleaver she had snatched from the shelf.

"I was just startled," she said, her chest heaving with quick breaths. "I came into the room and saw them here."

"They're looking for Colin," Ma said. "We don't know where he is."

"Who are you?" I snarled into the ear of the man I was holding.

"You're a feckin' eejit, Corravan. We weren't goin' to hurt 'em. Now le' me go!"

I came around to the front of him, keeping the knife tip at the man's throat. I thrust him down into the chair. By the light of the hanging lamp, I recognized him.

"I saw you with McCabe last week," I said. "What's your name?"

"Keefe." His eyes were black and glittering and fixed on mine. "We're meaning no harm to Colin or them." He jerked his head sideways. "But McCabe wants Colin brought in."

"Why?"

"For his own good," he snapped back.

Slowly I straightened and dropped the knife by my side. "What do you mean for his own good?"

"Hell if I know," he spat. He looked at the two men on the floor. "Go on, get up."

My gaze shifted to Ma. "When's the last time you saw him?"

"Three days ago. He stopped in for something to eat. We haven't seen him since." Her hands were motionless, her voice calm. Ma had that sort of steely courage, and I knew she was more afraid for Colin than for herself.

"McCabe is going to want to know we searched the place," Keefe said, his voice a growl. "Just le' us do that, and we'll go."

I wanted to talk to him, away from Ma and Elsie. "You come with me."

After a moment's hesitation, Keefe nodded to the other two men to stay where they were, and we left the room. A quick glance through the three upstairs rooms and two cupboards revealed no sign of Colin, although his clothes and a few of his choice possessions were still in his room.

He hasn't fled, I thought, worry carving a hollow in my chest. *Where has he been for three days?*

As we started down the staircase that led to the shop storeroom, I kept Keefe in front of me. To his credit, he seemed to bear no grudge that I'd attacked him and his men; he knew I had just wanted to protect Ma and Elsie. I swung the lamp high as we went through the store, and as I expected, we found no sign of Colin. The room was still, silent, peculiar without the usual chatter and liveliness of the daytime. The glass jars behind the counter reflected the lamplight. The wooden barrels stood stolid, with the shadows on the floor between them.

At last, we stood in the middle of the storeroom, eyeing one another.

"What did you mean, 'for Colin's own good'?" I asked.

He pursed his mouth in disgust. "Col's gone over to Finn Riley," Keefe replied. "But the word is he's really a mole for McCabe, so it's only a matter of time before he's a dead man. And McCabe doesn't want to get on the wrong side of you."

My stomach lurched. "Bring me to McCabe." At his first headshake, I added impatiently, "Put me in the damned hood if you want. I don't care. I need to talk to McCabe."

"Don't be an eejit," he said as he started for the steps. "He didn't like you barging in on him last time."

"I have something he needs to know," I said to his back. It was almost the truth. I couldn't with absolute certainty trace the guns that killed McCabe's men directly to Finn and to Houghton. But it was the only thing I had that I could trade for Colin. I was willing to give McCabe what I had and bank on my instinct that I was right.

Keefe paused on the step two above me and turned around. "He'll kill you if he finds you're trickin' 'im."

"I'm not."

He shook his head. "He'll kill *me* if I bring you to him where he is."

"I'll bring down the entire bloody Yard on him if you don't. And I'll tell him I said that to you."

The man's jaw worked, and he studied me for a moment. At last he shrugged resignedly. "It's on your head, not mine." Keefe climbed the rest of the steps, and I pulled the door shut behind us.

"Don't worry, Ma," I said as we reentered the kitchen. "I'll talk to McCabe."

Her right forefinger sketched a tiny, unconscious sign of the cross. "Mickey."

I heard the tremor in her voice, and I turned to the three men. "Wait outside, bottom of the stairs. I'll be down in a minute."

They looked among themselves, and Keefe herded the other two out the door and closed it behind him.

Ma's fear pinched her face the moment they were gone. "Mickey." She swallowed. "He's stayed away for a night or two before, but—"

I pulled her close. Her head came only as high as my chest, and it struck me that it had not always been so. Her entire body quivered, like that of a terrified bird.

"Is McCabe going to kill him?" she whispered.

I drew back and met her gaze. Held it and didn't let it drop. "I made a deal with McCabe, Ma. He won't touch Colin."

"A deal," she repeated.

"What did he mean McCabe wants him brought in?" Elsie demanded over Ma's shoulder. "Isn't he with McCabe?"

I hesitated. "Not anymore."

"Who has he taken up with, then?" Elsie asked.

"Finn Riley," I said reluctantly.

Elsie's eyes were like saucers, and Ma's hand came to her mouth and fell away. "*Finn Riley?* Why would he do such a thing?"

"I think he saw it as a chance to be more important, make more money," I said.

"But Finn Riley is a rat." Elsie's breath was coming unevenly. "And Cooper will never accept Colin. It's always been just the two of them."

That gave me a good idea of who was spreading the rumor that Colin was a mole.

Elsie came close, laid her right arm on my arm. "What can I do?"

"I'll be back as soon as I can." *Take care of Ma,* my eyes telegraphed, and she nodded.

I turned to Ma. Her face had gone white, though her eyes were tearless.

"I will find him," I said, my voice hoarse. "I swear to you, I will."

Ma nodded, and I pulled the pair of them into my arms, against my chest, for a quick, fierce embrace. Then I closed the door behind me and hurried down to the bottom of the stairs, where the three men waited, one smoking what smelled like a French cigarette, its end a pinprick of light flaring and fading in the Whitechapel darkness.

CHAPTER 30

I wasn't put in a hood for the cab ride, and I understood what that meant. I'd either convince McCabe that the information I brought him was worthwhile, or I wouldn't be leaving his presence alive.

We reached an abandoned warehouse north of the London Docks and disembarked. As a man marched on either side of me, Keefe strode ahead down a set of broken stairs and used a key to open a door. It squeaked as if warning of trouble, and we headed toward a lantern at the end of the hallway. Keefe knocked on the door four times, then opened it so I could enter. "Your hangin'," he muttered as I passed him, one of the men still holding my arm.

A stove in the corner threw off heat. The room was lit with lamps and smelled of smoke and sweat, taut nerves and trouble. McCabe sat at a rectangular table with one empty wooden chair opposite, and his jaw slackened as he saw me among the three men.

"What the hell?" he asked quietly, his eyes flashing from one man to the next. "What the devil are you thinking? Where's Colin?"

I shook loose of the man's grip.

"I made them bring me," I said. "I went to the Doyles's myself, looking for Colin, hoping he could tell me where I might find you."

McCabe turned his head and spat a yellowish stream of tobacco sideways onto the dusty wood-plank floor. It could have been a gesture of nonchalance, but I sensed it was disgust with his men. Or with me. Or both. The only thing he respected was dead honesty, and I'd give him that. But I'd demand it of him first.

"I need to talk to you alone," I said. I withdrew my truncheon and knife and laid them on the table.

He nodded at the men, and they left.

I stood behind the single chair. "You lied to me," I said. "Last time we spoke, you let me think I had to do something for you to let Colin out, when you knew all along he'd broken with you and gone with Finn Riley."

He sat back in his chair, his gaze unwavering.

I set my hands on the chair's top slat and leaned over it. "If Finn Riley believes Colin is your mole, he's dead."

"Why the hell do you think I sent my men out to bring him in?" He jabbed a finger at me. "You said so long as he stays alive, you'd stay away from my concerns. Colin ain't important enough for me to get on the wrong side of the Yard."

"My guess is Cooper put that rumor out there."

McCabe gazed at me from under hooded lids. "I'd say so."

"You swear you don't know where he is?" I asked.

He put two fingers to his lips, then raised them toward heaven.

I nodded acceptance of what passed for his oath, pulled out the chair, and sat. "I have two favors to ask you, but first I'll tell you who is putting guns and money into Whitechapel and why."

We studied each other for a long minute.

From the other side of the wall came the muted sounds of a series of shouts, the clunk of a bottle or glass on a table, a cough. But across the rough table, I saw only McCabe, and he saw only me. It was as if our very souls knew each other, spoke some silent language of loyalty and perfect attunement to the worth of what passed for valuable tokens in Whitechapel, like aces in a high-stakes game: information, work, food, loyalty. Loving someone like Colin, who gave himself more bloody trouble than anyone else caused him, gave an adversary an ace he could keep up his sleeve. But I was past caring. I was willing to lay down any card in my hand, so long as I could find him. Although McCabe could lie and deceive, even he'd acknowledged the truth: Colin wasn't safe with Finn Riley.

McCabe set his forearms on the table, one fist cupped inside the other. I put my own hands on the table, one wrapped inside the other, in imitation of his, and I kept my voice low. "Have you heard of a group called the League of Stewards?"

"Nae."

"What about Archibald Houghton?" I asked. A flicker of recognition lit his eyes, and I continued, "He's rich and powerful. A member of parliament and a manufacturer. Has a metal works down by the river and another factory that makes gun casings in Birmingham. You know him?"

He gave an incredulous look. "Oh yah, I had dinner at his club last night."

I ignored the sally. "There's a group of moderate MPs—Irish and English—who have been meeting secretly to talk about a peaceful path to home rule for Ireland," I said, my eyes never leaving McCabe. "Houghton's against it, and he's assembled this League to keep it from happening. They're not just against home rule, McCabe. They loathe the Irish—all of us." I paused. "He has powerful, influential partners. One's a doctor who spouts shite about how we Irish are an inferior race that look like apes and breed like rats. Another is a man who's arranging to have stories printed in the newspapers, like the one blaming the Irish for the *Princess Alice*. And it's Houghton who's buying guns and funneling them into London to try to get the Irish to kill each other."

There was a long silence as he took this in.

"Three of them, you say?" McCabe said, his voice toneless.

"There's near a hundred in the League, but so far as I know, they're the leaders."

He rubbed one hand over the knuckles of the other and eyed me warily. "And they're backing Finn Riley against me?"

"It isn't against *you*," I corrected him. "They don't care whether you or Finn Riley wins this war. They just want you to fight, so we Irish look like ungovernable louts who must be kept in our place. That's why he's funneling guns and money to Riley. It has nothing to do with you."

"This man, Houghton," he said. "You're certain about him?"

"His wife and their unborn child were killed in the Mayfair bombing," I said.

Understanding lit his eyes, and he shook his head, shoving back from the table to pace to and fro before coming back to the chair, wrapping his hands around the top rail, and rocking the chair onto its back legs.

"There's another matter," I said. "The *Princess Alice* wasn't an accident. The League caused it."

"You have proof?" McCabe asked huskily.

"We found two brothers, one on each ship, both members," I said.

Two angry red splotches appeared on his cheeks. "And they call *us* barbaric ratbags. The English bastards! So Houghton's done all this, and now he's playing us for patsies, i'n't he?"

"Both you and Finn Riley," I reminded him.

"Not the same," he said, dropping the chair onto all four legs with a bang. "Finn Riley's been taking guns from them and laughing up his sleeve at me. And now"—his voice dropped to a hiss—"I know why, don't I?" He studied me silently for a moment before pointing at me with his chin. "What do you want?"

"Two things. First, I need to get word to Timothy Luby, tell him he needs to write up a statement denying that he made these attacks. Can you help me do that?"

"I can," he said, dragging out the word. "But no one'll believe him."

"I won't ask him to make it public yet—not until we have confessions and proof that'll back what he says," I said. "Tell him I know—the Yard knows—he had nothing to do with them, and we're gathering proof. Perhaps it's enough to save the home rule talks. Can you get that message to him?"

He gave a slow nod.

"Ask him to send a message to Wapping if he wants to talk. I'll meet him."

"Anything else?"

"Help me find Colin." My voice thickened. "Where would Finn Riley take him?"

He stepped back, rocking the chair onto two legs again, tapping the thumb of his left hand on the wooden rung.

"Colin's been missing three days," I said. "I just want him back alive."

He tipped his head slightly to the side and peered down his nose at me. "You care mightily for someone who had naught good to say of you."

That stung, but I shoved my hands into my coat pockets and answered. "Doesn't matter. I owe Ma Doyle more than I could ever repay. He's a good lad at heart." My voice flattened. "Once I find him and know he's safe, I'll hunt Finn Riley, and I'll find him. If he's committed murder, like I think he has, killing your men, he'll hang for it."

"If he's convicted," McCabe said.

"If he's guilty, I won't rest until he is."

Perhaps something in my tone convinced him, for McCabe nodded, the last measure of resistance dissipating like beer soaking into a sawdust floor. For the time being, we wanted the same things, and it was enough.

"Where does he live?" I asked.

McCabe drew himself up to his full height. "Has a sister in Malone Street, lives with her husband. His ma is around the corner on Yarrow. It's all the family he has, so far as I know. But I've had men watching both places, and he hasn't been seen."

Of course you would, I thought. "Where else?"

He shook his head.

"Where does he drink?" I asked. "Did he ever work on the docks?"

That made him pause and consider. "You know the Half-Moon pub?" He tugged his coat closed over his chest and did up the three buttons.

I rose. "No."

"Used to be a bakery on Locust, near Glamis and Redcastle, south of Cable Street."

"Are you sending me on a wild goose chase?" I asked. He looked at me narrowly and didn't answer. "McCabe, I want your word that you won't kill Finn Riley. He may be the witness I need to convict Houghton and the League."

His chin came up. "Don't give me orders."

"If you kill Finn, I will have to come for you," I said. "I don't want to do that."

He waved one hand dismissively. "I've somethin' to see to. I'll be in Lambeth until tomorrow night. Finn and Whitechapel are all yours." He held the door open and waved me through, no doubt an old habit, keeping an adversary where he could see him. "Until then."

CHAPTER 31

The intersection of Glamis and Redcastle was well east of Whitechapel, not an area I knew well. Locust ran roughly northwest–southeast, and the intersection was one of many in this part of the city not set at right angles. As I stood before the door, I had an unsettled feeling. Not the prickle that helped me anticipate danger, nor the sense that I'd been here before, but a need to orient myself. I backed away from the door and walked the short distance south until I reached the wharf, then I put my back to the river and surveyed the buildings nearby.

The moon cast its pale light on two old warehouses and two in the process of being built. The two old ones were so close together that I might have assumed they were connected if I were standing in a different place. I peered up at their eaves. One was bare; the other had a faded sign, and I came closer to read it. Seeing "HOUG" in faded paint against white, my heart tripped inside my ribs. The rest of the sign had been torn off, but I'd put money on this being Houghton's old warehouse, and it was just south of the pub. What if they were connected? Tunnels were common in these buildings by the river, especially those built when tea was taxed at such high rates that most was brought in by smugglers.

This deserted warehouse was just the sort of place Finn would take Colin. I needed a way in. I circled the building, finding every lower-floor window boarded and every door bolted.

I ran back to the Half-Moon pub and pushed open the door to find an oblong room filled with acrid smoke from an ill-tended fire. A group of four men played a lackadaisical game of cards at a table wedged into a corner against a canted wall. Along another wall stood a table where a prostitute, whose loose gown suggested she'd once been better fed, stroked the hair of a man who sat sullenly at a table, his beer in front of him.

I approached the bar, where a young man with greasy hair falling over his face looked up from a pot he was mending. He eyed me warily, quick to discern I was police.

"I'm looking for Finn Riley. Is he here tonight?"

"Naw." His gaze remained steady.

I kept my voice low. "I need to get to Houghton's old warehouse. Is there a tunnel from here?"

He rocked back on his heel, and this time his eyes darted around the room before he replied. "There was," he muttered as he bent over the screwdriver and the broken handle. "Houghton's men came in and bricked it up last month. Go through the kitchen, take the stairs. You can see for yourself."

I believed him. "I need a lantern," I said.

"Back there." He nodded sideways toward a narrow doorway. I strode through it into the kitchen and found a young girl peeling potatoes, one strip at a time, into a bucket. Her jaw was moving, and guilt registered on her face as she stopped. She was probably chewing a piece of raw potato, or perhaps the peel. Peels were more filling, had a way of sitting in your stomach for longer.

I gave her a smile as I lifted the lantern off the nail and fumbled in my pocket for my matches.

"There, sir," the girl said, and I followed the direction of her finger to a box on a shelf.

I thanked her, lit the wick, and went out the back door into the alley.

Lantern in hand, I walked around the old warehouse once more, side-stepping down the narrow alley between this warehouse and the one beside it, circling the back, and coming around to the front, finding three doors in all. One was down a set of stone stairs, a huge metal door with two padlocks. The other doors' knobs had been removed, so they could only be opened from inside, and my set of picks was as useless as birdshot against a bulwark. The lower windows were all boarded up securely, with no loose boards. The sides of the building were smooth, with no handholds. The very impregnability of the place gave me a growing sense of urgency. Circling again, I looked for a drainpipe and saw that the two that had previously been at the corners were gone.

Perhaps they'd been reused for Houghton's new warehouse, but this struck me as odd. If the building was empty, why go to such lengths?

Because it would be a bloody good place to store guns.

I circled the building a third time. By moonlight, I saw the glint of a window above a slanted one-story roof. I could get in through the glass. But how to get up to it? The walls were too smooth, too well maintained for climbing.

However, the warehouse next door was in worse repair. I hurried back to it and peered up. The brickwork was crumbling and gone altogether in parts, but it could provide toeholds. I could get high enough up this wall to turn and jump for the low roof, then climb in through the window. But I'd have to leave the lantern below or I'd likely set myself on fire. I doused it and lowered it to the ground.

Thank God for the moonlight.

I'd climbed this sort of wall plenty in my early thieving days, when I weighed seven stone, but of course it was harder now, weighing five or six more. It took four tries, but I found that by jabbing the toes of my boots in the wall, and finding crevices with my fingers, I could scramble up ten or twelve feet. At last, I was high enough to turn and leap for the canted roof. I landed sprawled on my belly, slipping down the metal shingles, my hands scrabbling for a hold. My fingertips snagged on a rough edge, and a shingle creaked under my weight, but it held. I pulled myself forward, stood, drew my knife from my boot, and ran it along the edge of the glass to pop out the lower center pane. I set it aside, put my hand through, flicked the hasp, and pushed up the lower sash, so I could drop in. I landed with a soft *thunk* and made my way across the wooden floor that creaked with each step. The moonlight came through two windows, enough for me to see a pair of fire doors at the side with bolts across them and stairs at the far end.

I headed down to the ground floor, feeling my way in the darkness. At the bottom, my hand inched along the wall to the right and found a nail where a lantern might once have hung. Muttering a curse, I slid my hand along the opposite wall and, to my relief, found a lantern, withdrew my box of matches, and lit it. I made a quick circuit of this floor but found no signs of Colin. I continued down to the cellar. The fourth step teetered, and from then on, I stayed close to the wall, testing each tread and holding the banister with one hand as I descended. At the bottom was a door, locked. I took out my small cylinder of picks, unscrewed the metal cap, and drew out the two I usually found most useful.

Crouching down, I slipped them inside the keyhole and began to work away. It took no more than two minutes before I heard the soft, satisfying click. I replaced the picks in my pocket, opened the door, and stepped inside.

CHAPTER 32

The cellar smelled of rat droppings and metal that had rusted in the damp.

It had been partitioned, with a brick wall and a door twenty feet away. This side was empty except for some shards of wood that looked like they once belonged to a crate. The wind whistled at a low pitch through a grate in the ceiling near the outer wall.

I headed toward the door. It was composed of vertical wooden boards, partly rotted, but barred on the other side, and I put my eye to one of the cracks. It seemed all darkness over there, but I pounded my fist against the wood. If anyone was down here with Colin, guarding him, I wanted him to come through that door.

From the other side I heard a sound.

It was almost inhuman. But not quite.

I shouted Colin's name and put my ear to the widest crack. All was silent. Yet I hadn't imagined the noise.

I took out my knife and pushed it between two boards to force the bar up, to no avail. It was too heavy for the blade.

The wood was rotted—but not so rotted I could tear it apart without working at it first. I found one board that was loose and drew my knife repeatedly down the side, shearing pieces off until I could get my fingers around it and pull it away. I reached through the gap and lifted the bar out of its brackets.

As the door opened, I grabbed the lamp and swung it around the room.

As I expected, I was in the other side of the cellar, this part slightly larger than the one I just left. The walls were wetter, the floor was muddier—and there were wooden pillars and some walls, making separate areas for sorting and storing goods.

"Colin?" I cried out. "Are you here?"

My shout returned from the brick walls thin and hollow.

Only silence.

I hurried toward the entrance to the first alcove and then the next.

My lamp threw a misshapen shadow onto the wall, a grotesque of a figure bound to a chair, his head fallen on his chest.

Oh, dear God, I thought.

I dropped the lamp on the uneven dirt floor and bent over him, raising his head, which offered no resistance to my touch. Gently I lifted his arm away from his belly, where a dark red stain spread across his shirt.

"Colin," rasped from the back of my throat. I went down on my knees, laid my fingers at his neck, at his wrist. If there was a pulse, it was too faint for me feel it, though the skin was still warm. My forehead fell against his shoulder, and tears filled my eyes, blurring my vision. I pulled his sleeve away from his wrist and up his arm. It was as I feared. Burn marks up and down. And his fingers. His poor broken fingers. Three of them. He'd held out against making a confession for longer than most would have.

With a sob rising in my throat, I sent a silent, thankful prayer that Ma would never see him like this.

With my knife, I cut the ropes that fastened Colin's arms and legs to the chair. His bulk slumped forward, and I caught him before he hit the floor. I laid him out, gently as I could, and placed my thumb and forefinger across his eyelids to close them all the way.

And they fluttered.

"Jaysus," I hissed under my breath, and hastily raised the boy's head out of the dirt with one hand and ripped off my coat with the other. The buttons popped and flew. I drew the coat around Colin, clumsily, holding it close and settling behind him so he rested against my chest instead of that cold floor, and wrapped both my arms around him. "Colin," I murmured. "It's Mickey. Colin. Colin, can you hear me?"

His eyelids fluttered again, then closed. But his lips parted.

At last, he opened his eyes. I saw the glint of them in the light from the lamp. "I thought you were gone," I said.

"Will be," he managed.

I wouldn't lie, not to a dying man. But I tightened my grip.

An incoherent noise and blood came from his mouth.

"Who did this? Was it Finn's men?" I asked.

A faint nod. "Finn and Coo . . ."

"Finn and who else, Col?"

"Cooper."

"Finn and Cooper," I repeated. Just as Elsie said.

"Tell Ma I love her." His voice slurred. "And Elsie."

Blood was dropping from his mouth and nose now, and a gurgle rose from the back of his throat. I shifted to keep him as close to me as I could.

"Mickey." Weak as his voice was, I heard the brokenness, a note of regret, of something that might have been an apology.

"Shh," I said and rocked him side to side, just once. "It's all right. I know."

I don't know how long we sat there, in that hellhole of a place where the water dripped down the walls and the rats lurked just beyond the circle of light given off by the lamp. Perhaps it was five minutes, perhaps ten.

I'd lain beside this boy many nights, as Ma told us stories about giants and monsters, the fairies and Johnny Freel. Often the tales were violent, and Colin was only five or six, but he would stoutly declare he wasn't scared if he saw Pat and I weren't. Perhaps if he'd been able to admit he was frightened, if he hadn't felt ashamed of his fear, he wouldn't have ended up here. God knows.

He drew in a breath, as if to speak or sigh.

But the breath ended there, and he became a dead weight on my chest.

I wrapped my arms more tightly around him. One throat-searing cry broke from me and then another. The brick walls threw the howls back at me, as if in sympathy, and the tears burned out of my eyes onto my cheeks for this boy I loved.

★　★　★

At last, my tears were spent, and the cold of the place had sheared its way into my hands and legs. My back grew too cramped to sit any longer. A long, low, mournful horn droned from a steamship, then a bell tolled from a church, every sound an insistent summons from the world outside. A world where I had responsibilities.

Gently, I shifted Colin off me, stood, put on my coat; then, hoisting him over my shoulder, I went out to the street. There were no cabs at this hour, of course, but I walked a furlong or so upstream to a new warehouse with a sturdy pier and a boathouse. I bashed the lock with my truncheon and manhandled a lighter off one hook and then the other, dropping it into the water. I put Colin in the prow of the boat. The moon, pale and spare and curved as a shard of oak from a planed plank, shone above, dodging clouds. By its light and the glimmerings from the gas lamps along the embankment, I saw Colin's face. It was beaten and bloody, yes. But in the drift of dark curls over the brow and the softness that clung to his mouth and chin, I saw the boy. Who he was and all he might have been. And the only thing I could do now was deliver his body to his mother and hope I could find a way to live with what I'd done years ago and what I'd failed to do in recent days.

I climbed in and took up the oars, feeling like some terrible spirit of the underworld, ferrying this boy home.

The river traffic was light, with only a few tugboats and barges in sight, and they kept to the middle where the ebb tide would help them. The margin of the river was hushed, quiet enough that I heard the squeak of the oars turning in the locks. It crossed my mind that here was another dead body in a boat—not one of the innocent young women in the case last spring, but still a young person who deserved this death no more than any of them did.

For the next hour, I wasn't a policeman. The tide was running against me, but it made no difference. I rowed as if twin devils powered my strokes, the oars feathering out of the water, dropping to just below the surface, shredding the moonlight on the water again and again. Gritting my teeth against the burning in my arms and back, I wished terrible things from the bitterest, vilest part of my heart. I wished that Finn Riley was shot, murdered in cold blood, by a pistol he'd once used himself. I wished that he was lying dead in an alley. Tortured first, if not by McCabe, someone else—anyone else—I didn't care. I wished his head was held under water, with his body thrashing, his arms and legs pumping in a silent, desperate plea, until they stopped, and he was gone. Dead. Dead. Dead. *Dead.*

The hour on the river worked the worst of the rage out of me, and when I reached Wapping, my chest heaved, and my hands tingled fiercely as I released the oars. The boat drifted the last few feet to the pier's end. I reached for the post and held it, resting my damp forehead on my shirted forearm. The wind from the river chilled the sweat on the back of my neck. As I tied up the lighter, wrapping the line around the cleat, I drowned my fury and regret and grief, sank them deep to cope with later, and trod up the damp wooden planks. At the door, I put my hand on the metal handle, the cold a welcome relief to my hot palm. I heaved the door toward me, the effort familiar, restoring me to something like myself.

The clock on the wall said it was half past nine. Sergeant Trent took one look at me and said, "Sir, are you all right? There's blood—"

"It's not mine," I said. "Colin Doyle's body is in the boat. Fetch the stretcher and bring him inside, please."

Dismay flooded his face. "Oh Jaysus, Corravan. I'm sorry."

I nodded.

From his desk, Sergeant Trent took the key for the shed where the pole-and-canvas stretcher was stored. "Philips," he said, and tipped his head sideways to tell him to come along.

Stiles was standing beside his desk, his eyes on me as I approached.

"I found Colin. Finn Riley's men tortured him. Left him for dead in Houghton's old warehouse."

"Good God, Corravan." His face was full of sympathy, and his hands twitched at his side, as if he longed to do something. "I'm so bloody sorry." I began to turn away when he added, "Elsie Doyle is in your office."

I pivoted back in surprise. "What?"

"She arrived hours ago," he said. "She insisted on waiting for you."

A hoarse groan slipped out from between my lips.

Stiles winced. "What can I do?"

"Find Finn Riley," I said. My voice didn't sound like my own, and I choked out the rest: "I tried to make McCabe promise not to kill him, but he might do it anyway."

"Don't give him another thought," he said. "You look after Elsie and Mrs. Doyle. I'll set up a house-to-house search, working in circles—"

"Start at the Half-Moon pub," I said. "Near Shadwell Basin."

"And I'll send his picture to the train stations and docks. He won't get far." He paused. "Houghton won't protect him; he'll only be a detriment to the League now."

The League.

I added, "Look into a man named Clarence Tomlinson. He owns the *Observer*, the *Post*, and the *Standard*. Perhaps others."

"Tomlinson," Stiles repeated.

I nodded. "And send a message to Belinda for me." I gave him her address in Belgravia. "Tell her what's happened, and that I'll be with the Doyles."

"Of course."

At my office door, I took a breath so deep it hurt my lungs, then turned the handle.

Elsie looked up at me. Her hands were knotted in her skirts, her face full of hope. "Mickey?"

I couldn't answer, and her face crumpled. I closed the door and held out my hand. Wordlessly Elsie took it, clinging so hard her nails bit into the flesh near my thumb, and let out one broken little moan. I knelt beside her as she let go of me, dropping her head into her hands as if she could no longer hold it up.

Some moments passed during which we said not a word, and she uttered not another sound. There came a soft knock at the door.

I pulled it open to find Stiles holding two cups of hot tea, the steam and the smell of bergamot rising from them. As always, it was kindness that undid me. I blinked to stop the burning sensation at the corners of my eyes and held out my two hands.

"Thank you, Stiles."

His eyes flickered to Elsie, tearless and ashen and immobile in her chair. "I'll fetch you a cab," he said. "Whenever you're ready."

I nodded and pressed one hot cup into her cold hands. Mostly she clung to it, but she managed to gulp down a few sips. I leaned against the wall with mine.

At last, she broke the silence with a whisper: "We have to tell Ma."

"She'll want to see him, I imagine," I said. "I can bring her. Better here than the morgue."

She shook her head, her head down, her eyes on her cup. "I don't know, Mickey."

"Why?"

"When she went to see Pat, she took to her bed. Didn't get out of it for days."

I hadn't known that.

She raised her eyes to me. "Was it Finn Riley?"

I nodded, and I saw by her expression that she understood what that meant.

"Then there's no reason for Ma to see him dead, is there? If it's a blood relation you're needing, I can sign any papers." Her chest rose and fell, and her brow was creased with worry. "It'll hurt her worse than him dying, Mickey. Seeing his body, how he suffered."

I put my hand on her shoulder. "She doesn't have to see him," I said. "And I'll come tonight and stay until . . ."

My voice faded. Until what? Until Ma stopped weeping? Until her heart didn't ache anymore? In every Irish story Ma ever told, it seemed the monster was slain or the maiden won or the gold dug out of the ground on the third try. Perhaps our hearts aren't meant to withstand more than three breakings, in life as well as in a story. I knew Elsie was right. After Francis's and Pat's deaths, Colin's might break Ma, break her in a way that couldn't be undone. I could have sat in my office forever that night, putting off the moment when we would have to tell her.

But eventually, we finished our tea, and the cups were cold. Elsie set hers on my desk and stood. Then, fumblingly, she came close and dropped her forehead onto my chest. Her entire body heaved with wordless, splintering pain, and as she sobbed, I held her close, like I had once—I don't remember why—when she was a child.

When we both were.

CHAPTER 33

With Elsie trailing me, I climbed the stairs to the Doyles's and took out my key.

But Ma had the door open before I could use it. She held a lantern, and by its light, I saw her eyes, twin dark pools of fear. "Mickey? Elsie?" She peered around us. "Where's Colin?"

"Ma," I said gently.

Her face went slack and her shoulders sagged, and the lantern she held would have smashed to the floor, if I hadn't caught the metal handle with one hand, and thrown my other arm around her waist. I eased us over the threshold and helped her to a chair.

Words can't describe that night, with the three of us all mired in our pain. Every sound from outdoors—dogs and carts and shouts that we'd heard a hundred times, sitting in this room with Colin—thrashed at our hearts like a lash, but the silence was worse. The tea Elsie made, her hands moving by instinct, went undrunk. Ma clung to my hand with both of hers until my fingers went numb. Grief knifed its way through all of us until well past midnight, and at last Ma closed her eyes. "Elsie, love, help me to bed."

Elsie looked at me questioningly, and I nodded. Of course I was staying. I was so damn bone weary, I could have slept in the wooden chair with my head on the table, but I dragged myself to the couch near the fading fire.

Still, as I lay there, the light fixed my eyes open. I listened to Elsie helping her mother undress, the rustle of the tick and the covers, and the soft puff as she blew out the candle by the bed. She came out and handed me a blanket.

"She'll be all right, Elsie," I said, more to reassure myself than her. After a moment, she nodded and went to her own bed. I listened as she prepared for sleep. I thought back to how we had all once been in Ma's bed, together. Pat and Colin, Elsie and I. Four children.

Dear God, how I longed to go back, back before all of it, before I'd left home, before O'Hagan had thrown me out of the boxing hall, before he'd come to the docks to hire me, before the night I'd watched Elsie mending a skirt with her single precious needle, making me long to earn extra money for this family who had taken me in. How could it all go so bloody wrong? With the best intentions, how could it go so damned bloody wrong?

★ ★ ★

I woke to the hard tap of metal on metal, Elsie setting the kettle on the stove. A dim light came in the window, and the coals were cold. I pushed myself to sitting and set about scraping the ash on the hearth and setting the fire for the day.

The noise drew Elsie to the threshold. Her hair was down around her shoulders, a mane of reddish gold framing her pale face. I couldn't remember ever seeing it down, not since I'd left Whitechapel. It made her look younger than her nineteen years.

"Is Ma awake?" I asked.

She nodded. "I'll set the fire. Go sit with her, would you, while I make the tea?"

I entered Ma's room to find her sitting in the bed, her rosary between her fingers, the long strand of coral beads lying across the bedclothes. I hadn't known her to use it often, and I didn't think she was praying with it. Her lips were still, and she was merely rolling the beads between her thumb and fingertips, back and forth.

"Ma." I sat on the edge of the bed and touched her arm.

"He wasn't a bad boy, Mickey."

"No. Of course not." I took a breath, bracing for the questions I imagined she'd ask. I had my replies ready. But instead of asking how and where I found him, how he died, how badly he was hurt, whether he'd spoken at all, she did what she often does. She surprised me.

"Do you remember the first night you came?" she asked. "When you saved Pat from being beat in the alley?"

I nodded.

"I slept with a knife under my pillow for a fortnight," she said. "Thinkin' on what you could do to us with the one you kept under yours."

My eyebrows rose. "You knew I had one?"

"O' course. Pat told me that's how you saved him, coming up behind that lad, putting your knife to his throat, makin' 'em all stop and run off. He was full o' admiration for you, and God knows I was grateful for what you'd done, but . . ." She gave a shake of her head. "I'll own it frightened me to know ye had that sort of fierceness in you."

I drew in a slow breath. "I didn't know you were afraid, Ma. You never let me see." I paused. "I was so bloody grateful for being taken in. I'd never have hurt you."

"I know that now," she said, patting my arm. "Didn't take long for me to know it then, either. Pat was happier than he'd been since Francis died. And Colin and Elsie . . . well, you were kindness itself to both of 'em."

I couldn't reply to that.

"Ach." Ma sighed, understanding. "P'rhaps Colin didn't remember, but you were. Always givin' 'em summat or helpin' somehow. He was mistaken, blamin' you for Pat's death."

Something twisted inside me at her kindness. Instead of grieving herself, Ma was doing what she could to make me feel less guilty. I should've seen it coming, her unselfish worrying about my feelings. I opened my mouth—but she raised a hand.

"Nae," Ma continued. "Saying you're to blame is like saying if I woke Pat five minutes later that mornin', he might still be alive because his entire day could'a gone different. No one can say so. And Pat warn't careful. Colin was much the same, stubborn as mules, the pair of 'em." A note of sorrow crept into her voice. "Stuff and nonsense, blamin' you."

"Ma, it's all right. I think—" I hesitated. "I think that's just the shape Colin's hurt took. And Pat and I . . . we weren't careful about including him when we could've."

"You and Pat did plenty." Her hands smoothed the bedclothes. "And you talked to him about leavin' McCabe."

"I did," I said. "I just wish I'd known what to say to convince him he could start over, start fresh somewhere else."

"You can't blame yourself," she replied. "Blame is a useless thing. Folks take it up because they think it's easier than grief."

"Easier?"

"Blame gives you the notion somethin' can be done to heal the hole dug like a well into your heart. But it can't." She paused. "The only thing that can fill that well are tears, Mickey. Grief must be borne, unhappy though it makes us for a while." Her head tipped sideways. "Do you understand what I'm saying to you?"

"I do, Ma."

She sat back as if relieved.

Ma was right, of course. Blame wouldn't keep the hurt at bay. Although that didn't mean I wasn't going to find Finn Riley, extract every piece of evidence against Houghton that I could, and then bring him and Cooper to justice. It wouldn't fill the well in my heart. But I wanted it anyway.

"Can I plan the funeral?" Ma asked. "I was hoping for three days from now."

The police didn't need to hold Colin's body. "There's no reason why not. Would you like me to see Father Owens?"

"Nae. I'll go. It'll be a comfort." Her fingers rolled the rosary beads absently. "Mickey, do you despise God, for letting such things happen?"

"Sometimes," I admitted. "Do you?"

She didn't answer at first. When she did, her voice was musing. "My ma birthed seven children. Did I ever tell you?"

"No."

"There was one before me, who died. So I was the oldest. Then came four more. All died their first year of sickness. She didn't even name the last two. She got so she wouldn't until they passed their first birthday. They were just 'baby' until then."

I could understand that.

"Then came Aileen."

"Harry's mother," I said.

"Aye. Mum might'a become bitter, but she didn't," she said softly. "I watched her. Watched how each loss, each trial, each trouble steadied her for the next, taught her what she could survive.

I didn't understand it at the time, but later I saw how it was, how she gathered her strength, piece by piece."

I listened in silence.

"When she lay dyin', I asked her if she believed God was right to send her so much grief. Do you know what she said?"

I reached for her hand and pressed her fingers.

"She said God had sent her both grief and gifts. Aileen and me. We were her gifts. And we should count ourselves lucky to have lived at all. So I've tried to remember that, how any bit of love or joy that has come to me afterward . . . well, it's by the grace of God." She sighed. "Not to say my heart isn't broken today." Tears filled her eyes and her lower lip trembled, and she turned her head away, toward the light coming through the window.

Following her gaze, my own fell on a framed picture on the shelf beside her bed, a portrait of her late husband, Francis. The sight of it reminded me that despite her children and me, and her dozens of friends, Ma had been alone all these years. With no husband, she had run her shop, managed her household, coped with the small, daily trials and the greater losses of her children.

Her eyes were closed, and by the dim light I studied her face, careworn and kind.

Had she ever thought of remarrying after her husband died? And what would happen when Elsie left home to marry? Perhaps she would be reluctant, now that Colin was gone, and I wondered what Eaman would think of that.

From the other room came the sound of water pouring from one vessel to another, and a moment later, Elsie entered with Ma's tea on a tray.

"Good morning, love," Ma said. Her eyes were open, her gaze steady and affectionate. "Did you sleep at all?"

It came to me, with no small measure of relief, that I had been wrong. Three times or no, Ma would grieve, but she wouldn't break. She had gathered her pieces, too, one by one, and she wouldn't be found wanting.

CHAPTER 34

At Wapping Division, I found both Stiles and Vincent waiting for me. They both looked exhausted, and though Vincent looked marginally less ill, he still had his white handkerchief, discreetly folded, at the ready in his hand.

The clock said it was nearly half past ten, and I opened my mouth to apologize for my late arrival, but the words I intended to speak went unsaid at the grim expression on their faces.

With foreboding, I said, "Finn Riley's dead?"

They both shook their heads.

"No word about him yet," Stiles said. "We've distributed handbills all over London, north and south of the river and east to the West India Docks. Train stations, piers—even the pubs down by the Fleet River, in case he tries to escape through the underground sewers." He paused. "Same with the Wilkins brothers. We've circulated copies of their photograph as well, and we've just sent a sergeant to fetch their mother."

My visit to her had no doubt warned her sons to flee. And it wasn't as if they'd have to leave London alone, with nothing; they had each other. If I could have taken Pat with me, I might have gone farther than Lambeth.

"There are forty Yard and Wapping men out looking, in addition to hundreds of uniformed men in the divisions," Vincent said.

I drew a deep breath. "What is it, then? What's happened?"

"Lord Baynes-Hill has been murdered," Vincent said.

A wave of heat ran from my scalp down my back. "When?"

"At around eleven o'clock last night on Grove End Road, just where it crosses St. John's Wood," Vincent replied. "He and his wife were returning home after hearing a performance at St. James's. As they slowed to cross the street, a lone man leapt onto the side of his carriage, threw open the door, and fired a shot at his head."

A cold feeling clutched around my heart, and I swore softly. "He was a good man. What about his wife?"

"Her husband's blood was all over her, but she's alive."

Houghton ordered the murder of another MP, in front of his wife? I reeled at the thought. *Was the man mad?*

"Was it made to look like the IRB was responsible?" I asked.

"No," Stiles said. "They didn't bother."

"Lady Baynes-Hill is all but insensible with grief, naturally," Vincent said. "The only things she could tell us was that the man had dark hair and light skin. He wore a covering over his face, but he didn't wear gloves, so she saw his hands."

"For God's sake," I managed, "what more can these people do?"

"It sickens me to think Houghton could have ordered such brutality," Vincent said heavily. "I don't know how we are going to put an end to this."

"I think it's time to put out in the newspapers that home rule is out of the question," I said. "That might halt the League's activities, at least for a time. And we could bring in Houghton, take away the leader."

"But it won't stop them for long," Stiles said. "Houghton didn't do this alone, and there are always those willing to step into vacated positions of power."

"And we haven't enough proof to arrest him," Vincent said. He raised a hand before I could object. "Think about it, Corravan. Houghton has held himself at just the right amount of distance."

"Quentin Atwell mentioned him explicitly at the League meeting," Stiles said.

"Being a member of a group isn't a crime, as you both well know," Vincent said. "No matter how disgusting their ideas."

"More's the pity," I said, and looked at Stiles. "Were you able to see him?"

He shook his head. "But I did ascertain that Clarence Tomlinson is a League member, and he owns or sits on the board of nine newspapers, including the *Evening Star*, the *Observer*, the *Sussex Post*, and the *Standard*."

"Well, that's something," I replied. "What about the *Sentinel* or the *Beacon*? They're the two that carried the drunken crew rumor, courtesy of Purcell, that steered the story away from blaming the IRB."

Stiles consulted his notebook. "No. Neither of those."

So those articles were likely just a product of general anti-Irish preju-dice, I thought. *Nothing to do with the League.*

Vincent rocked back and forth on his heels. "Houghton was working with both Finn Riley and the Wilkinses—the Irish and the anti-Irish, both. I wonder if they knew."

"That Houghton was playing both sides of the table, you mean," Stiles said. "The Wilkins brothers might have known the League was using Finn Riley for their own ends. I'm sure Riley didn't have any idea."

I sighed. "Well, we need to find Finn Riley. He's the one who can link Houghton with the guns."

"Begging your pardon." Sergeant Trent stood at the door, his eyes looking at Stiles. "We found Mrs. Wilkins. Not that she came willin', I'll say that."

"You've put her in an interview room?" Stiles asked, and Sergeant Cole nodded.

"I'll talk to her," I said.

Stiles and Vincent exchanged glances. "Very well," Vincent said. "Stiles, would you fetch her some tea, or whatever she'd like? She's not a conspirator—at least not yet. I'd like a word with Corravan."

"Of course." Stiles left, shutting the door.

I anticipated Vincent cautioning me not to take my frustration out on a woman who might bear no responsibility for any of this, aside from raising two hateful sons.

But instead, his entire demeanor changed, and he came close enough to lay a hand on my arm, tentatively at first, and then he settled it there. "I'm so bloody sorry, Corravan," he said. "About Colin Doyle."

"Thank you, sir."

He dropped his hand but remained facing me. "I wanted to tell you that—well, I lost my cousin Andrew when I was seventeen. We were riding horses together, you see, and he took a jump. His horse slipped in the mud on the far side, and Andrew's neck was broken." He shifted his weight from one foot to the other. "I blamed myself for years, which didn't do a whit of good. I stayed away from his family, imagining they hated me for it. It was only later I realized my absence hurt them."

I appreciated what Vincent was trying to do, the guidance he was offering, and I thanked him again. But I was more concerned with putting an end to the bloodshed.

"Sir," I said. "I may have a way to reach Luby." His eyebrows rose in astonishment, and I hurried on: "The IRB isn't responsible for these attacks. But Luby needs to declare it publicly, or the violence that the League has set in motion will continue."

"How—" Vincent began but halted himself. "I shall not ask."

We had struck this sort of quiet bargain once before, and I nodded in agreement. "Do we know where Houghton might be?"

"He is visiting his wife's family in Hertfordshire for the day."

My voice sharpened. "How do you know?"

"I assigned a plainclothesman to trail him," he replied levelly. "We won't lose him, never fear."

"What about Tomlinson?"

Vincent grimaced. "He claims he was unaware that newspapers were collaborating on stories, hadn't the faintest idea where those stories originated, and says he has never heard of the League of Stewards. I have a plainclothesman watching him as well." He took a breath. "Are you concerned that McCabe has killed Finn Riley?"

"No," I said. "He knows we need Finn Riley as a witness against the others, and he wants them to pay too." I paused. "You needn't worry. I won't kill him either."

"I'm not sure many men would have that degree of restraint."

"You weren't in the boat as I rowed Colin back to Wapping."

"I can only imagine your state of mind," he said. "But we are defined not by our thoughts and feelings, Corravan, but by our actions."

I didn't admit, even to myself, that the reason I wanted to find Finn Riley wasn't honorable. I wanted to look him in the eye and make certain he knew just what he'd done. I wanted to turn him inside out with fear, to have him feel his bones go soft with it. I wanted him so terrified, he couldn't think or speak or even breathe.

"It's probably time I spoke with Mrs. Wilkins," I said.

* * *

I entered the interview room where Mrs. Wilkins sat in a chair, the tea untouched on the table.

She was wrapped in a shapeless gray coat with coal-colored smudges on the sleeve. Her hands clutched a reticule in her lap, and her eyes were cold, her mouth thin.

"Good morning," I said. "Thank you for coming."

"I had no choice," she replied, her lips barely moving. "I don't expect you'll be returning my photograph, will you?"

"I can, once we find your sons."

She gave a disdainful sniff and turned away, her eyes fixing on a spot halfway up the wall.

"Mrs. Wilkins, are you aware that they helped to murder six hundred people? Six hundred Londoners—men, women, and children all thrown into that river to drown."

"You've no proof of it," she said.

"We do, actually," I corrected her. "We have witnesses."

Her eyes veered to me, and I saw the slight sag in her jaw. But then her bitterness reasserted itself.

"If you know where they are, you could be tried as an accomplice." I paused. "Where are they hiding, Mrs. Wilkins?"

"I don't know."

I leaned back in my chair. "They purposefully didn't tell you where they were going. So you wouldn't be able to tell anyone, should you be brought in for questioning."

She merely looked back at me.

But her lips were in a peculiar shape, as if there were words being held in the back of her mouth—angry words, words of explanation, words that she longed to utter, though she knew she shouldn't.

Words that would help me, if I could get her to speak them.

"Mrs. Wilkins." I stood and leaned against the wall opposite, to give her space. I kept my voice soft, curious. "Why do you and your sons hate the Irish so?" I spread my hands. "I know the usual objections—the Irish take work and housing and food out of the mouths of true Englishmen and women. But you have a pleasant house, and your sons have work. So what of value have the Irish taken from your family?"

Her hard mask fell away. Her eyes flashed with anger, and blood suffused her face, turning it an unnatural, florid shade of pink. "How dare you," she spat. Her chest was heaving, and the words came at me like a torrent: "How dare you ask! How dare you!" Her voice rose to a shriek. "My son, their brother! Our blood, our flesh, our beautiful Christopher—and you monsters burned him alive! His poor body was so charred I had hardly anything left to hold. I almost didn't recognize him! His own mother!"

The third boy in the photograph. The youngest of them, the one in the middle.

I made a quick calculation. The boy looked to be no more than ten. He wouldn't have been alive for Clerkenwell in 1867.

"The Mayfair bombing," I said.

"He was a child! A wee little child!" Her voice broke, and her gasps seemed to stoke her anger. "If every Irish man, woman, and child could be drowned in their own bloody sea, I'd be *glad* of it! All of you!" Her hands clutched her reticule so tightly the knuckles whitened, and she pounded the small bag against her lap. "*Why* did you come here? Why couldn't you have just stayed in your godforsaken huts, living like swine as God intended? We don't want you! We all hate you! We despise you!" The vehemence caused shining spittle to appear at the corners of her mouth. "You must know it, and yet still you come with your diseases and contagions and your mealy mouths and your stink! Why can't you all bloody go back?"

I must confess I could offer no answer. Indeed, there was nothing I could have said that would have stood up to her hatred. And so I said nothing, and she calmed herself, dabbing her mouth with her handkerchief. And just as suddenly, the fury faded from her face, and she rose to leave.

At the door, she cast one final bitter look at me. "This is *their* home. England. Not yours. They're safe here. You'll never find them."

She banged the door behind her.

I let her go because she had just reminded me of an important truth. When in danger, we go home, if we can.

But it isn't a physical home, a house, that makes us feel safe. Even Mrs. Wilkins knew that. It was the people. People who would look out for you, who would hide you and bring you food, who would tell you when to stay put and when it was safe to get away.

The question was, did Finn Riley have someone he trusted? And who would that be?

CHAPTER 35

I stepped out of the interview room to find Stiles at his desk. A large map of London, extending from Battersea in the west to the Isle of Dogs in the east, was spread out before him. As I approached, he raised an eyebrow. "She gave you an earful, didn't she?"

"You heard?" I asked.

"People across the river might have heard."

I grunted. "Show me where our men have been so far."

Stiles had divided Whitechapel and Shadwell into ten sections, marking them off with blue chalk at the corners. As I expected, Stiles was managing the search methodically. The pointed end of his pencil touched the blue area that represented St. Katharine's Docks. "We've had a few men here, just in case. And we have men in each section, beginning in the bottom left and working clockwise."

"And you've heard nothing at all—no rumors, not even absurd ones?"

He shook his head.

That decided me.

"I think he's still close, in Whitechapel," I said. "He grew up there. He can move from place to place if he has to."

"I know." Stiles's face screwed up in frustration. "That's the difficulty, isn't it? If we've searched one place, he might go there and feel safe about staying. We don't have enough men to keep circling back, although I've stationed a plainclothesman at his sister's and mother's houses, just in case."

The smell of coffee came at me, and I saw Sergeant Trent approaching with a cup. He held it well in front of himself, and his nose was wrinkled in distaste. I took it gratefully, finishing it in several gulps.

"Let's take a walk," I said. "I need some air."

"Front or back?" Stiles asked.

"River," I said.

I went to my office, picked up my coat and hat, and met Stiles at the back door. We walked to the end of the pier, gazing out at the midday traffic together. The sky was a cornflower blue, with white clouds, and the sun fell intermittently on the water. The wind blew from the east, causing our coats to flap.

"Do you remember last autumn, when we were looking for those smuggled guns," Stiles said, "and you had me look for boats riding low in the water?"

I knew where his thoughts were headed. "The guns are the proof we need to link Houghton to Finn and the violence."

"And Houghton's new warehouse would be the ideal place, on the water, with locked rooms and all. But we can't search it," he said.

I shrugged. "Houghton is too cautious to store guns there. My guess is he has an intermediary or two passing them along. If the guns ever *were* in either of his warehouses, he'll have moved them out."

"But he'd want to keep control over them, wouldn't he? And he must own other properties throughout the city," Stiles said.

"True. But I think he'll keep the guns away from anything bearing his name."

"I suppose," Stiles admitted.

I turned, and we started back toward the embankment that connected one pier to the next.

"Do you think Finn's still alive?" Stiles asked.

"I've no idea. He's a rat. Canny."

Stiles stepped over an uneven plank. "Where else can we look? We've been combing the city, from basements to attics."

I didn't reply because I was busy remembering. When I fled O'Hagan, I hid in a basement. But before that, in the weeks after my mother left, I found places in Whitechapel to sleep, in doorways and nooks under stairs—

The bells of a church tolled the hour, interrupting this train of thought.

And then another church bell tolled, and I halted.

It took Stiles several steps to realize I no longer paced beside him, and he turned back. His hands were shoved deep in his coat pockets, as if he were groping for answers in them.

"What is it?" he asked.

"Churches," I said. "Some of them have priest holes, like some of the old Catholic estates. St. Patrick's in Whitechapel, where the Doyles go, has one." I didn't explain that I'd once taken refuge in them myself. Some nights there would be half a dozen of us boys sleeping inside a priest hole, which was more of a passage than a nook, with the advantage of two exits rather than only one.

Stiles's face lit with understanding. "For the Romans, during Queen Elizabeth's reign. So we need to look for churches built before the Catholic Relief Act."

"The holes usually led to an underground passage, though most are probably closed up now," I said. "But he could be hiding in one, waiting until we stop looking. Then he'll come out and try to get away."

"Blimey." He whistled under his breath. "But there must be dozens of Catholic churches in London."

"Not so many around Whitechapel built before 1791," I said. "Four or five at most. And Ma might know which the Rileys attended."

★ ★ ★

We climbed into a cab and headed for Whitechapel, disembarking at Leman Street.

Stiles had been to the Doyles's once before, but he followed my irregular journey to the shop. I peered through the repaired windowpane. All looked as usual except that Elsie was dressed in black mourning behind the counter. We stepped inside, where sympathy hung thick in the air, and people spoke in hushed tones.

I approached Elsie and touched her arm. "You remember Mr. Stiles."

"Of course." She nodded a welcome.

"How is Ma?" I asked.

"She's managing. Mrs. Reed's upstairs with her. All her friends have rallied around. She hasn't been alone since it happened."

I drew her away from the counter and lowered my voice. "Have you heard anything about Finn Riley? Anyone seen him?"

She shook her head, a flash of anger lighting her eyes. "We all know what he did. Not just killing Colin but stirring up trouble for everyone here in the Chapel. Finn Riley is a dead man if he ever comes out o' hiding."

I should have realized McCabe would have spread the word. He deployed information as shrewdly as any newspaper. "Riley may have left London, but—"

"Where would he go? What does he know but this?" She spread her hands.

"That's what I think, too. I'm wondering if he might have hidden in a church—a priest hole."

Her eyes grew round. "He might."

"I can't talk to his family, but is there anyone else who'd know where he went to church—or where he didn't?"

"What if he didn't go to church?"

"What Irish boy doesn't go to church with his family on Sunday? Leastwise when he's young."

"Ach, Mickey, I don't know." Her brow furrowed. "We always went to St. Patrick's, and I never saw him there, so I'd try somewhere else first. I don't think Ma would know. But Mrs. Reed might. You could ask her."

I left Stiles in the shop and climbed the inside stairs. In the kitchen, I found Ma and Mrs. Reed at the table with cups of tea. Ma rose and put her arms around me, and I bent to rest my chin briefly on top of her head, my eyes telegraphing a greeting and thanks to Mrs. Reed.

Ma's eyes searched my face. "Have you found him yet?"

I shook my head. "But we will. Every division, train station, and dockyard in London has his picture, and we have forty men dedicated to the task. But I got to thinking, Ma. What about a priest hole?"

"You're speakin' o' Finn Riley?" Mrs. Reed asked.

I nodded. "Do you know his family?"

Mrs. Reed tipped her head. "I know his older sister Sally, and—sure, Mary," she added, turning to Ma, "you know Sarah McDonaugh. 'Twas her son Patrick wot married 'er."

"Sally Riley," I clarified. "She married Patrick McDonaugh."

"Aye." She nodded, setting her graying curls bobbing. "Ages ago."

"Where?"

"Why, Sacred Heart, just south of Spitalfields. Father O'Shay's church."

One of the oldest in the city. Fifteenth century or thereabouts. And it had a priest hole.

I rested a light hand on Ma's shoulder and took my leave.

CHAPTER 36

The sun rode low in the sky, casting the streets in shadow as we reached Sacred Heart. The church was small and plain, the sort I happen to like, without flying buttresses and furbelows. There was a single large stained-glass window as its only ornament, and narrow alleys separated it from two newer, uglier buildings on either side. I hadn't been here in years, but my memory of it was keen. I stood at the entrance with my hand on the door handle, realizing I'd never entered through this door. I'd either gone in the side door near the altar or the secret entrance in the small yard behind.

I dropped my hand from the knob. "Stiles, go in here, would you, and keep watch. One entrance to the priest hole is in the loft. The other is in the back. I'll go there. And there's a side door to the left of the altar."

"He won't get by me." Stiles pulled at the heavy wooden door and entered.

I made my way along the narrow alley to the yard behind, with a stone arch that gave out to the street. A sour, briny smell from a nearby fish shop dragged an old memory from the recesses of my brain, and I approached the hidden door, whose hinges were craftily disguised where two walls came together in a "V."

The wooden panel met the corner of the building as perfectly as I remembered, but the loose board that concealed the metal ring handle was nailed shut. I inserted my knife along the edge but felt no give. Withdrawing the blade, I looked down at the ground by my feet. I might have expected an inch or more of dirt and detritus along the bottom of the door had it not been used recently. But there was none.

If Finn Riley had come in this way, he'd pulled it closed and fastened it from inside. I knew where this passageway connected inside the church, in the loft. But if he was inside and had heard my knife, he wouldn't come out this way. He might try to get out the front or wait until he thought I'd left.

The skin on the back of my neck prickled with sudden heat. I'd have bet money on him being inside, that's how certain I felt. But how could I flush him out?

I went through the arch to the street and peered about for a messenger or a cab. Finding neither, I waved to a young man exiting a pub. "Find me someone who can carry a message, would you, and send him to me?" I drew a coin from my pocket and passed it to him. "A pint for your trouble." He was none too steady on his pins, but a few minutes later, a lanky boy loped toward me, his face expectant.

I scribbled a note for the desk sergeant at Wapping to come and bring a crowbar, with the line at the bottom: *Give the boy 2 shillings.* The boy galloped off on his long legs.

An hour later, night had fallen. Sergeant Trent appeared at the archway, carrying a crowbar and a lit bullseye lantern. Quietly, I explained that Finn Riley was likely inside. "I need you to stay here. Be ready for him to come out this door." With my forefinger, I traced the outline, and the sergeant hefted the crowbar to signal his readiness.

I went around to the front of the church and entered. It was dark, and the light from a single gas lamp on the street made the stained glass glow a lurid red. Out of the corner of my eye, I saw a movement by one of the pillars.

"Corravan," came a hoarse whisper, and as I made my way over to Stiles, I realized why he'd chosen this spot, from where he could see both the side and front doors as well as the stairs leading down from the loft.

In the dim light, I saw him shake his head. No sign of Finn yet. I put my mouth close to his ear. "Stay here. Sergeant's out back. I'm going upstairs."

Soundlessly I climbed to the loft, where the poor crowded on Sundays. Behind a curtain was a latch that I lifted slowly, so as not to make a sound. Praying the hinges were oiled, I pulled at the door, peered into the near darkness, and slid inside, letting the curtain fall back into place. It was warmer here than in the church, and I closed the door behind me so no cool descending air would give me away. There were slits in the outer wall of the passage, I remembered, to let in light. I paused to allow my eyes to adjust to the dimness, and then I started along the passageway.

It had been easier when I was young, with more room to maneuver. The passage felt narrower, and I had to crouch to avoid the ceiling. But it wasn't long before I reached the spiral staircase down. I slid my fingertips along the wall and felt the stone angle away from me. I inched the toe of my boot forward to the edge, then set my foot on the first stair.

The back of my large boot scraped the riser. *Damn,* I thought, and held very still, hoping that Finn wouldn't have heard.

But I knew he had. He'd be listening for my approach.

My only hope was to surprise him with my timing. To hold back long enough, perhaps, that he'd move first. I had to believe his nerves were already frayed after days in here.

I stood utterly still. I could swear I felt him holding his breath, straining to hear mine.

The room at the bottom of these stairs was small, close. I remembered it well. A packed dirt floor. Uneven stone walls. Smaller than any ring I'd ever boxed in. Not much space to maneuver, even when I was a child.

These first steps were stone, solid under my feet, but after half a dozen of these, the treads became wooden. Slowly, I padded down, keeping close to the curved inner wall, my breath silent, the fingertips of my left hand light on the plaster, my feet soundless. Around the wall shone a faint light, as if from a single candle held beyond the passage, leaking the dimmest glow onto the bottom stairs.

A gunshot came from below, and only by the purest luck did the bullet ricochet off the wall and miss my head.

There was no help for it. Praying the gun was a single-shot Webley, I launched myself down the stairs into the room toward Finn, and my hands found him, a dark figure in the murk of candlelight, his emptied gun thrown to the floor, replaced by his knife. We dropped onto the floor, he on his back and me on top of him, but my boot slipped in the dirt, and he threw me to the side. My shoulder hit the wall, but I was already scrambling back toward him.

He fought hard, knowing what was at stake, but I was half a head taller and two stones heavier, and by the flickering light of the candle, my fist found his cheek, then his nose. His right hand with the knife slashed at my arm before I slammed his hand against the stone wall, and it fell from his fist. I planted my knee on his chest and drew my knife from my boot in one motion. The blade glinted where it lay against his throat, and he glowered up at me. His forehead was bloody, as was his nose, and one eye was squinting.

The sergeant's crowbar was hammering the back door. "Corravan! Corravan!"

But it barely penetrated my consciousness. Every bit of me was taken up by Finn Riley, who had gone still at the point of my knife.

"You're going to kill me? Do it," he snarled between gritted teeth. "Better than sitting in this bloody hole, waiting for McCabe."

"You should be glad I found you first. He'd torture you and leave you to die, like you did to Colin," I spat.

"He was a rat, sent by McCabe!"

"It's a lie, you damned fool!" I retorted. "Colin was never spying for McCabe. Cooper didn't want to share his earnings, that's all!"

"He admitted it!" Finn fired back.

"He didn't!"

"He did!" Finn insisted, his eyes blazing.

"He'd have said anything to make you stopping breaking his fingers!"

"He warned McCabe we were coming!" Finn Riley's voice was thick with scorn. And it carried the ring of truth.

I fell silent, and Finn's expression twisted. "Colin was nothin' better'n a two-faced coward."

I gave him a shake that knocked his head once against the floor. "The only reason you had the spine to take on McCabe is you had Houghton backing you. You know what that makes you? A patsy!"

He barked a laugh. "I'm no patsy! And I don't know any Houghton."

"Where do you get the guns, then?" I shook him harder this time.

"Man named Morgan, John Morgan."

Morgan was the name of the man who was supposed to pick up the guns Stiles found at the train station.

"He works for Houghton," I said. "Who's a rich politician who's trying to stir up Irish violence because he wants to show us all for savages!" I shook my head. "You're just a stupid pawn, Riley. A stupid bloody pawn for a man who wouldn't let you lick his shoes."

That was the shot that told. A flush of shame suffused his face, and he was immobile for a moment. Then he swore. "Git off me, you bugger!"

I put the knife back to his throat. "When did it start? When did Morgan contact you?"

"Three months ago," he mumbled.

"Who is he? How did he find you?"

"I dunno. Works for one of the bloody papers. Was in the Waterman one night."

I could imagine Finn after a few pints, bragging about some fight he'd won, or flashing his money about. That would be all it took for Morgan to find his mark.

"Which paper?" I asked.

"Don't remember."

"The *Observer*? The *Evening Star*? The—"

He squirmed. "Yah, the *Star*."

"What did Morgan want?"

"Told me he knew somebody who wanted to get McCabe out of the Chapel. He'd give me as many guns as I wanted and pay me. I could have whatever McCabe left behind."

A bark of disbelief escaped me. "McCabe would never leave. You know that!"

His eyes glittered. "He would if his men knew they could be dead tomorrow. Loyalty only goes so far."

"So you shot those four men, including his nephew?"

Finn sniffed. "Had to make McCabe listen."

"Are the guns Webleys?"

A shrug that I took as an assent.

"How do you get them?"

"Morgan brought 'em to my ma's house." He turned his head to wipe his bloody nose on his shoulder. "Hid 'em under the stairs. They're gone now."

I shifted my weight off my knee. "Did you kill Lord Baynes-Hill?"

"What?"

"Last night. Did you kill him?"

"Nah. I been holed up here."

I wrapped my fingers around the front of his shirt, stepped back, and pulled him to his feet.

"How did you find me?" he demanded, wiping his bloody nose on his sleeve this time.

"How do you think? Every boy in the Chapel knew about this bolt hole. You should've remembered, Riley. I grew up here, same as you. Where is Cooper?"

He spat, and I gave him another hard shake.

A fresh gust of air came from above.

"Corravan?" Stiles's voice came from above. "All right?"

"I've got him," I called back.

Stiles's boots sounded on the stairs, and he appeared, his face relieved. "Took me a while to find that door in the loft. It's well hidden."

He crossed immediately to the outer door and dragged it open. Sergeant Trent entered, red-faced and with the crowbar at his shoulder, ready to swing. He took in the scene before him, and he lowered the crowbar and lantern. "I heard the shot and then nothing else. Didn't want him to get away." His eyes darted to my arm. "You're bleeding."

"I'm all right," I replied.

Stiles reached for his pair of metal cuffs and clasped them around Finn Riley's wrists, and the four of us all walked out into the empty yard. The air was foggy and damp but a relief after the warm, stale air in that room.

Stiles had his hand on the chain between the cuffs, and I kept a firm hand around Finn Riley's upper arm. "You said Morgan would give you as many guns as you wanted. Where are the rest of them?"

Riley gave me a sullen look.

I sighed, as if to suggest it didn't matter to me one way or the other. "You'll hang for Morgan's and Houghton's crimes. The question is, do you want them to hang with you, or do they get away scot-free because Houghton's rich and clever, and you're poor and stupid?" I paused. "You took the risks for him. But he's not going to step up to save you."

His eyes skidded away. "They're in a shed behind a house in Ropemaker's Alley," he muttered. "Overheard him say so."

"Does Houghton own it?"

"Dunno."

I turned to the sergeant. "Take him to Wapping, would you? Use a closed carriage. I'll take the lantern."

"I'll be sure no one sees him." The sergeant gripped the metal chain between the cuffs and led Finn around the corner.

Stiles nodded toward my arm. "Let's get that bandaged. It'll only be a minute." I hated to own it, but my arm was throbbing, and I let Stiles take me across the way to a pub, where he worked his usual charm on a maid, who smilingly provided a basin of water and a cloth that appeared to be mostly clean. He tipped his head toward a door. "She says we can use the storeroom."

It was a narrow room with a single window. Dried herbs hung in tied bunches from the ceiling. Sacks of potatoes and tins of dry goods filled a set of rough shelves. By the light of the lantern, I removed a sack from the top of a barrel and sat down on the wooden end. "Help me with the shirt."

Stiles undid the buttons at the neck and eased my arm out of the sleeve, which already bore a wide stain of blood.

"Finn said Colin was a mole for McCabe," I said. "That he confessed it at the end."

Stiles tore the cloth in two, folding half of it into a rectangle. He dipped it into water, wiped the blood, and pressed it against the cut, which was deeper than I'd thought it would be. "Do you think it's true?"

I had to think about that, and Stiles let me. After a few minutes, the worst of the bleeding had stopped, and while I held the cloth in place, he folded the remainder into a long strip.

"They got what they wanted out of him," I said. "They wouldn't have left him if they didn't. Doesn't mean it was true."

"I know," Stiles said and began to wrap my arm.

I watched as he tied the ends in a secure knot. I wanted to comb back through every moment I'd spent with Colin the past few weeks, to examine them with this new possibility in mind. But I needed quiet for that, and time. It would have to be later.

★ ★ ★

By the light of the sergeant's lantern, Stiles and I made our way to Ropemaker's Alley.

Behind number four, which appeared unoccupied, we found a shed with wooden boards covering the windows and a solid lock on the door. I had to use my heaviest picks, and as we entered, I heard the scurry of rats. Stiles swung the lantern high, but it was hardly necessary. It was obvious the place was empty. However, there were fresh, pale shards of wood that had sheared off a heavy crate as it was moved. The guns had been here.

"Damn," I said.

"They may be out of London by now," Stiles said.

"Could be in Hertfordshire," I said. "That's where Houghton was today, visiting his wife's family."

"What's her name?" Stiles asked.

"I don't know," I replied. But I understood what he meant. Houghton could use her name to conceal his ownership of the property. "We need a list of all of Houghton's taxed properties—and his wife's, if there are any." The Public Records Office in Chancery Lane would be closed now. We'd have to wait until tomorrow.

We stepped outside, and I pushed the doors shut.

At the Yard, we found Vincent—still looking ill and tired—and reported that Finn Riley was caught, that we sought a man named Morgan who wrote for the *Evening Star*, and that our suspicions about the guns had been confirmed. Vincent accepted everything we said without question, but his entire demeanor was despondent as he gave us Houghton's wife's name: Dorothea, née Henley.

CHAPTER 37

The first thing in the morning, Stiles and I were at the Public Records Office, where a clerk found what we needed in less than an hour. There were hundreds of Houghtons in London, but there was only one property owned by Mrs. Dorothea H. Houghton—a small house in Clerkenwell, in Rose Mews, number 31. It had been bequeathed to her on January 13, 1874. When I explained that the woman had been dead ten months by that date, the clerk had shrugged. So long as the title was clear and the taxes paid promptly—which they were, he assured us—no one would care that a man registered property in the name of his wife, dead or alive.

Dark clouds hung low in the sky, and a cold rain fell as Stiles and I arrived at the house, with three sergeants in tow. I wasn't taking any chances in case it was guarded, and we'd need help retrieving the guns and putting them into a wagon, if indeed the firearms were here.

The house was modest, with two stories and a door that opened onto the pavement, without steps. Although it appeared in good repair—the windows were whole, the paint on the door wasn't peeling—it had the air of not having been lived in for some time. No one answered our knock, so we descended the cellar stairs, and I opened the door with my picks.

The dim entryway smelled musty and dank. Ahead of me was another door with a glass pane. Behind me, Stiles shook open his box of matches and scraped one against the stone foundation. The smell of sulfur stung my nostrils in the close space, but I saw a lamp hanging from a hook and took it down, passing it to Stiles as I surveyed the shelves on either side. Empty for the most part except for dust, an old hat box, and a broken wooden crate of the sort used to deliver produce. Stiles lit the lamp, and we filed through a second door.

In a room that had once served as a kitchen and scullery, most of the floor was taken up by three stout wooden crates, standing about waist-high, all closed with nails.

Sergeant Trent put the toe of his boot to one and pushed to no avail. "It's full up o' something."

A shelf nearby held another lantern, so we had enough light to work by. Sergeant Trent hefted the crowbar he'd brought. "This should do it," he said as he forced the forked end underneath the top edge of the crate, wedging it open with a screech from the nails. Together we pushed it up and shifted some burlap sacks on top. By the light from the lantern Stiles held high, we saw ten shining pistols, laid out in two rows of five. I estimated at least fifty guns in this crate—one hundred and fifty guns among the three—which was enough to stir up trouble not just for London, but for all of England.

"Thar you have 'em," Sergeant Trent muttered. "Blimey."

"I'll fetch a wagon," one of the other sergeants said.

"Bring two," Sergeant Trent said. "It's too much for one animal."

Within half an hour, we had a pair of wagons, and between the five of us and the wagon drivers, we loaded the crates and brought them through the streets to the cobbled stone quadrangle of the Yard.

With the wagon drivers at the horses' heads, the sergeants and I remained with the cargo while Stiles went inside. He returned with Vincent, who hadn't taken the time to button his coat, and the wind blew it open as he strode toward the cart. We had left the wooden top of one of the crates loose, and I lifted it so he could see.

The deep breath he took brought on a spasm of coughing. At last, his handkerchief over his mouth, he managed, "Stiles, take this into the storage bay."

"Yes, sir." He led the way across the cobbles as I explained to Vincent how we had found them.

As I concluded, he nodded. "Mr. Houghton is in my office."

I felt a jolt of surprise. Vincent had already brought him in, without me furnishing the guns as proof?

He wrapped his arms across his chest to keep his coat closed, but he made no move toward the back door. "I thought it for the best. And now that we have the guns, we can keep him here. I received word last night that my plainclothesman lost Tomlinson, who boarded a boat to America, but don't worry. We've someone at Pinkerton's who will meet him at the dock. I telegraphed this morning. He'll be brought back for questioning."

"And when Tomlinson returns, he can give us Morgan, the intermediary, if we haven't found him by then," I said.

"Of course." He nodded. "McPherson's body was found last night, washed up on shore."

I stared blankly.

"The Irishman who was to be blamed for Sittingbourne," Vincent reminded me. "The one who shunted the carts onto the primary line."

"Another murder, then." I glanced toward the vanishing wagons. "We certainly have enough evidence to confront Houghton."

"No, Corravan." Vincent's voice was decisive. "Not you. He'll talk more freely to me alone. We have no proof whatsoever that he ordered the murder of Lord Baynes-Hill, and I—I want that."

"But you'll need a witness," I objected. "Can't you put him in one of the interview rooms, so I can listen from next door?"

"It's not necessary," he said. "Last month I installed a *cabinet d'écouté*—a listening cabinet—along the side of my office, behind the bookshelves. There was one in frequent use at the office of the *Préfet de police* in Paris."

"Ah," I said. "That's why your office looked narrower to me."

He stared at me and gave a bemused shake of his head. "Trust you to notice six bloody inches. We took space from the cupboard." He started toward the back door, pulled it open, and waved me inside.

The sudden warmth of the Yard made me open my coat. "Where's the door?"

He pointed down the hallway. "The second one." He dabbed at his nose one last time with his handkerchief and stowed it in his pocket, his expression betraying how much he dreaded this interview.

"I'm sorry, sir. I know he was your friend," I said.

"But I didn't know him, did I? What sort of friend is that?" His mouth tightened as he turned away.

I found the door and slipped inside the cabinet. It was narrow but serviceable, and I could hear Vincent's door open and close as clearly as if I were in the room.

"This is an error, Howard," Houghton said. "An inexcusable one, dragging me in here as if I were a criminal. Your father will be appalled to hear of it."

"I daresay he will be appalled," Vincent said quietly, but I heard the ironic note in his voice.

Houghton continued: "You know, none of us really understands this eccentricity of yours, serving as the director here. You're a baronet's son. What are you doing mucking about with all of this? You ought to be at home, looking after your wife." There was a pause, and then, in a dry tone: "Perhaps then she wouldn't have cuckolded you."

I held my breath, my insides shriveling for Vincent. In the next moment, it occurred to me that he likely knew this revelation was coming and had me listen anyway. I had never esteemed him as much as I did at that moment.

Vincent said, "I would like to ask you for some particulars about the Mayfair bombing."

Houghton's voice was sharp. "Why the devil would you ask me to relive such a painful event?"

I bit my lower lip. Vincent wasn't approaching the matter sideways. He was leading Houghton straight to his motive.

"Did your wife attend the theater alone that day?" Vincent asked.

"No," he snapped. "She went with her friend Mrs. Robeson."

"Had the two tickets been purchased with that intent?"

There was a long silence.

"I was supposed to go with her," Houghton said. "But there was a meeting I needed to attend." He paused. "I knew she wouldn't be able to venture out much longer without her . . . condition becoming apparent, so I urged her to go." His voice dropped low over the last words.

"You can't blame yourself," Vincent said.

"Of course not!" he retorted, his voice rising. "It wasn't I who set those bombs to murder everyone. It was the bloody Irish! But it is to be expected. Soulless, godless creatures, with no respect for life. As rotten as their damned potatoes." An audible exhale, and he continued dismissively, "Oh, I know about the papers you wrote for the Royal United Services, where you defended them, but I put that down to your youth and inexperience. You didn't take into account the Irish national character. Why, God himself deplored it. He sent famines upon them, like he sent the plagues upon the pharaoh and the Egyptians. One year after the next, to punish them for their wantonness and depravity. Still, they didn't learn. They can't. Instead of remaining where they belonged, they came to Liverpool in droves, like locusts." His voice was heavy with disgust.

"And if they hadn't, you would still have your wife, and your child would be nearly three years old," Vincent replied. "It's a tragedy. A terrible thing."

There was a noise, something between a snort and a cough.

"They're not like us, Howard." A chair creaked, and I could imagine Houghton leaning forward. "If we don't keep them in check, they'll ruin this country. They will breed and multiply and sap us and drain us of everything that makes us English. They will rob us of all we own and kill us wantonly and without regret."

The irony of that last accusation seemed lost on him.

"But it is *you* who have wantonly killed hundreds of innocent people," Vincent replied. "You have become the very thing that you hate. Surely you see the parallels between the *Princess Alice* and Mayfair Theatre."

"How *dare* you?" His voice shook with outrage.

"How dare I?" The words were clipped short, Vincent's fury held in check. "Brutal and heartless as it is to murder hundreds of nameless, faceless people whom you did not know, killing Lord Baynes-Hill is something else altogether. How could you do it, Archibald? A fellow MP? You've been to his house, eaten at his table. He was our *friend*."

"He was *once* our friend! No longer! Once he took up their cause, he was dead to me."

"And so you made him dead to everyone—including Marjorie. For God's sake, Archibald! In front of his wife!"

"At least I left her alive!" he burst out.

Good lord, I thought. Even I hadn't expected Houghton to admit to committing the murder by his own hand.

I eased the breath out of my chest silently and took another in, ever so slowly, through a dry mouth. Vincent may never have worn a uniform, but his instincts for drawing out a confession were as fine as those of any inspector I knew.

"Yes, you did," Vincent said. More silence, and then came the sound of paper unfolding. "How do your views, or the beliefs espoused by this League of Stewards, align with the theory of 'splendid isolation?'"

There was a pause before Houghton replied. Perhaps he was surprised that Vincent had a copy of the handbill. "I should think it would be fairly obvious. We are isolated because we are alone, by the very nature of our superiority. We alone have dominated people and countries on every inhabited continent because our way of life transcends theirs. Our economy is stronger; our navy and our soldiers are better trained; our very way of governing is more evolved—and in their hearts, these people understand that. Otherwise, they would not have bowed their heads to our rule. It is our right and our duty to oversee all of those within the borders of our empire."

For God's sake, I thought. *It's not only the newspapers who can set a story in a particular light.*

"Was it Tomlinson who helped you place the stories in the papers?" Vincent asked.

"I will not answer for another man's actions," Houghton replied.

"We're bringing him back, you know," Vincent said. "Pinkerton's men will be waiting at the dock in New York."

There was another silence, followed by a sigh. "Archibald, it gives me no pleasure to accuse you," Vincent said. "But we have ample cause, including witnesses and physical evidence. It is enough to convince a judge that you must be accused and put on trial."

"On the contrary. You have no direct evidence against me. And if you accuse me based on what circumstantial evidence you have, you will look like a fool at trial, and I shall have you removed from your post." A chair creaked and heavy cloth rustled, as if Houghton stood up. "You know I can do that. And the reputation of the Yard hasn't been so rehabilitated that it can't be swept away again. This is the sort of scandal the Yard can't survive."

"Archibald," Vincent said, and his voice was almost gentle, "you, of all people, know my reputation for prudence. Would I risk the Yard, after all the work I've done this past year?"

There was an audible puff of breath. "You will be sorry," Houghton said.

"I am only sorry that you are not the man I thought you were," Vincent replied.

"I shall contact my barrister. Richard Lowell, Inner Court."

"You're not returning home, after what I have heard."

A short laugh. "You know full well you can't introduce this conversation into evidence. It would be your word against mine."

Vincent rose and went to the door. "Sergeant. Please take Mr. Houghton to one of the rooms and remain with him."

There was the shuffle of footsteps and the ping of a cane against a chair leg, and then the door closed. I remained where I was. From Vincent's office came only silence. I didn't have to see him to imagine how he felt after such a conversation.

Finally came the words "You heard, Corravan?" Vincent's voice was weary, dejected.

Had we been in the same room, I might have tried to convey my fellow feeling by a gesture—one small enough that he could ignore it, if he chose. But I replied, "I heard," and hoped he understood.

"Please write up your account while it is still fresh in your mind," he said.

"Yes, sir."

Emerging into the hallway, I found Stiles hurrying toward me with a look of relief. "The Wilkins brothers have been found. They're in custody, on their way here, arriving at Euston in an hour. All those handbills and advertisements worked. A railway servant spotted them on a train leaving Manchester, and telegraphed ahead, and the police were waiting at the next station."

UNDER A VEILED MOON

An hour would give me time to write up my notes of Vincent's meeting with Houghton.

"Was anyone hurt?" I asked.

"No, although the brothers led them on quite a chase. They knocked over half a dozen people and ran a luggage cart onto one of the tracks, smashing it up, before they were caught." His face sobered. "One of the brothers drew a gun, but his shot went wild."

"Thank God," I said. I could only imagine the scene on a crowded platform. "That railway man deserves a reward."

"I'll ask for his name. Shall I meet the train?" he asked.

I nodded. "Take a constable with you. May I use your desk while you're gone? I need paper and pen."

"Of course," Stiles replied. "Top drawer."

It had been years since I'd sat in the main room at the Yard and composed a report. But the whole exchange was fresh in my mind, blazingly fresh, and I recorded it faithfully. Then I blotted the three pages and set them to dry.

Next, I began a message to Dr. Bradford to let her know that John Conway could be released safely. But on second thought, I tore the paper in quarters and deposited the scraps in Stiles's rubbish bin. Conway was owed an explanation about why his name had been dragged through the mud, and he deserved to hear the truth firsthand, from me, as quickly as I was able to deliver it.

I put away Stiles's pen and sat quietly, waiting for him to return with the brothers.

I didn't have to wait long. With Houghton still in one of the interview rooms, the two Wilkinses were brought into another, and the constable remained with them while I gave Stiles the three pages of Houghton's confession to review. He read them through and looked up. "There isn't much we don't know, is there?" he asked.

"No," I replied. "I'd like you to question the Wilkins brothers."

Stiles looked at me in some perplexity.

"I'm bloody tired, Stiles," I said. "At this point we're mostly looking for confirmation."

"Of course," he replied.

"The only thing we still don't know is whether they murdered Schmidt," I said.

"The first murder," Stiles said.

The one that began everything, though we didn't know it at the time, I thought.

"I'll be back in an hour or so," I said. "I've someone to see."

★   ★   ★

I entered the hospital and asked for Dr. Bradford. She emerged from her office, and when she saw me, her expression betrayed relief.

"Is Mr. Conway still here?" I asked.

She grimaced. "I'm glad you've come at last. I don't know how much longer I could have kept him. Is everything all right?"

"He's in no danger anymore," I said. "Is he still in the same bed?"

"Yes." She pointed to the stairs, and I headed up them.

Conway was sitting up, with an open book in his lap. He greeted me with surprise. "Why, Inspector! What brings you back?"

"I've come to let you know the inquiry is finished," I said, "and you can go home."

He peered up at me. "I'll have you know, I didn't appreciate being kept here helpless."

"We've just arrested the Wilkins brothers."

"Ah." He sank back against the pillows.

"I wanted to tell you all that's happened." I paused. "And I have to confess, I broke into your house."

He choked a bit. "Well, I s'pose it's all right. I've nothing to hide."

"You were never a suspect," I said. "Not in my mind." With that, I launched into an explanation, beginning with Mr. Schmidt's murder.

He marveled at parts and swore at others. At the end of it, he stuck out his hand to pat mine. "Don't think I don't know what you did for me," he said. "It might be one time in my life I thank God I'm Irish."

"You're also innocent," I said.

He allowed that was true.

I rose. "I must ask that you not leave London, as there will be a formal inquest in a month. You'll need to appear in court."

"Of course."

"Good luck to you, Mr. Conway."

"And to you, sir." With that, he pushed aside the bedclothes. "Nurse! Where are my proper clothes?"

★ ★ ★

The main room at the Yard was nearly deserted as I entered. Even Vincent's doorway was dark.

But Stiles was still there, his fair head bent over his desk, writing. I approached, and he looked up.

"I went to tell Conway," I said.

"Ah." Stiles's expression changed to understanding. "He must have been relieved."

I dragged over a chair and sat. "He was."

Stiles laid aside his pen. "I told the Wilkins brothers that Houghton has confessed and explained that by turning queen's evidence they'd have a chance to avoid hanging. They confirmed everything. Their actions were all at Houghton's direction, of course."

"Sittingbourne?"

Stiles nodded. "But not the mine. The next incident was to be at St. James Hall next week."

The famous theater could hold hundreds of people. I let out a sigh. "At least we prevented that."

"And," he said with the air of concluding, "the Wilkinses killed Schmidt upstream, as you guessed, and rowed him to the steps at around two o'clock in the morning, during the ebb tide. They did it so the newspaper could report that he'd been murdered by the IRB to bring Conway on board."

"Did they say why he stank of gin?"

"That was a mistake. They borrowed a lighter and didn't realize there was a bottle of gin under a thwart. It broke and soaked Schmidt during the journey."

"Ah." I gestured toward the pages Stiles had been writing. "Anything else in there I need to know?"

He gave a flicker of a smile. "Nothing important. You should go home, get some rest. I'm nearly finished."

I set my hands on my knees and pushed myself to standing.

"Oh—I nearly forgot," Stiles said. "This came from Wapping just after you left." He handed me a sealed letter, and I unfolded it to find this:

I am prepared to state publicly that the IRB had nothing to do with any of the recent attacks. Shall wait for your sign. Place an advert in the Falcon.
—*T. Luby*

With an exhale of relief, I handed it toward Stiles.
The public's terror could be over, I thought. *For now.*

CHAPTER 38

At the Doyles's, I climbed the stairs from the street, my feet beating the treads all the way to the top, until I faced the black wreath on the door. Its frayed pieces flagged in the breeze.

Elsie must have heard my steps, for she opened the door before I had a chance to knock.

I embraced her and looked over at Ma, sitting at the table with a cup of tea. Her eyes were red-rimmed but dry, and her hand clutched a handkerchief. She managed a wan smile. "Why, Mickey. Come in. Have a cup o'."

I pulled out a chair other than the one I'd chosen before. But the chairs must have been moved around, for I was in that chair again, the one whose very wobbliness seemed to suggest all of Colin's failings, all his poor decisions, all his failures to mend what so easily could have been mended. I felt sorry as hell at having chosen it, and my eyes darted to Ma.

Ma's chest rose and fell with a pained breath, but her hazel eyes met mine, and her expression softened. "It's all right, Mickey."

"I can fix it," I offered. "It won't take but a minute."

"Not yet," she said gently. "P'rhaps another time."

"Whenever you like," I said.

Ma reached across the table, slid her fingers around my hand, and squeezed.

This was what her grief looked like, soft rather than sharp-edged.

A weak, watery beam of sunlight dropped in through the window, and we all looked over at once, as if someone had stepped over the threshold.

But of course he hadn't.

Elsie fetched a third cup and saucer and poured the tea, placing it on the table before me.

"We heard you found Finn Riley in the church," Elsie said. "In the priest hole, like you said."

Despite myself, I let out a short laugh at the way nothing stays secret in the Chapel. "Jaysus, Elsie. We took him to Wapping at dusk, out of a deserted alley, in a closed carriage."

Elsie shrugged by way of reply. "Did Finn tell you what you needed to know?"

I nodded. "Once he realized it was the only way of saving his neck, he told me enough that we could charge Houghton—and some others too."

"What will happen to them?"

"They'll rot in jail, or they'll hang," I replied.

"Even the MP?" Ma wanted to know.

"Perhaps." After a moment, I added, "His wife was with child, killed in the Mayfair bombing."

Her face slackened. "Ach."

"He still had no right," Elsie muttered, her eyes flashing. "To make hundreds of people pay for what none of 'em did."

"I know."

Silence fell over us again.

At last Elsie broke it. "James McCabe came to see us." She lifted her chin toward the door. "'Twas he who brought the wreath."

I leaned my weight back into the chair. "Did he?"

"He gave us money he said he owed Colin," Ma added.

"Money he owed Colin," I echoed in disbelief.

Elsie and Ma exchanged a look.

"He said that Colin had been loyal to him," Elsie said.

"Did he tell you he put Colin in with Finn Riley as a mole?" It came out harsher than I'd intended, and Ma winced.

Elsie and Ma looked at each other again, and Elsie replied, "He told us Colin offered."

"Why would he do that?" It wasn't a facetious question. I truly wanted to understand what Colin had been thinking.

"McCabe saved his life once," Ma said.

"Saved him? How?"

"Colin got in a fight with someone at the docks," said Elsie. Her eyes telegraphed a warning, and remembering that Ma hadn't been told about the incident, I merely nodded. "Colin cut one of Shapley's gang. McCabe went to Shapley and told him to leave Colin alone. That he'd vouch for him never touching another of his men again."

So McCabe had saved Colin from Shapley. And Colin had proven his allegiance and paid his debt. That made a certain kind of sense. But despite Elsie's explanation, I suspected it was more than loyalty to McCabe that had driven Colin to be his mole. Ever since Finn Riley told me that Colin had taken on that role, I'd been turning over the possibility in my mind, and I'd come to believe it was true. Being McCabe's mole, held close by a secret only the two of them shared, would have made Colin feel important. More important even than being chosen by someone like Finn Riley.

I only wished it had been enough for Colin to be important to his family, the three people he left behind. What made it so he didn't know how deeply we loved him? Why couldn't he see it?

I let out a long sigh.

Elsie rose and fetched a tightly folded letter from a shelf. "McCabe asked me to give you this."

Not long ago, I'd have opened it instantly, hoping for answers. But I had a feeling I knew what the letter would say: that he'd done what he could to protect Colin, whose death wasn't his fault, and that he'd kept up his end of our bargain. But I didn't need or want to hear anything from McCabe anymore. I wanted him back in the shadows, at a distance, out of sight, where he'd been before all this started. I took the letter from Elsie and slid it into my pocket for later.

"Will anything happen to McCabe?" Ma asked.

I shook my head. "He had nothing to do with the *Princess Alice* or any of the violence here. So long as he keeps to his businesses and stays out of the way of the Yard and Wapping, we've no reason to come for him."

"It's a sorry world," Ma said. "When what he does counts as business."

We conversed quietly for some time, the clattering and banging and shouts from outside grating less on my nerves than before, until the sun had slipped away and Elsie lit a lamp. At the sound of three raps at the door, I rose to admit young Eaman. Sticking out of the pocket of his coat was the head of a hammer, and he carried a covered dish and a sack that looked as if it might contain items for supper.

He greeted Elsie first, then Ma, and then he turned to me. "Hullo," he said.

"Call me Mickey," I said, and took the sack from him so I might shake his hand. It was my way of telling him that I understood and appreciated both of his reasons for being here: human decency and love. He gave a nod of acknowledgment in reply.

I set the sack on the table, hugged Ma goodbye, kissed Elsie on the cheek, told them I'd be back on Sunday for tea, and shut the door behind me. I paused partway down, listening for whether Elsie pushed a chair up against the door.

She did not.

I inhaled deeply, taking in the smell of onions and hops from the Irish pub across the way, and descended to the street. The tread at the bottom of the stairs was no longer loose. I bent to examine it and found the shining heads of three new nails along the edge.

Something about those nails pained my heart, but underneath the sadness was a feeling of relief. Eaman was a good man.

CHAPTER 39

I went to Belinda's, but even before I knocked, I sensed she wasn't home. The entire place was dark. No one answered the door, and wearily I climbed back into the hansom cab, directing it to drive on to my street.

My house was cold, but I was too tired to make a fire.

With my coat still on, I collapsed into my most comfortable chair. I dropped my hands limply over the cushioned arms, tipped my head back, and closed my eyes.

I must have slept, for the room was dark as pitch when I heard a key scrape in the front door lock. My eyes flew open.

"I wonder where he is," came Belinda's voice.

"I'll light a lamp," said Harry. I heard his two suitcases *thunk* to the floor in the entryway, and then came the scratch of a match and the squeak of the lamp key.

I didn't want to startle them, but there was no help for it. "I'm here."

By the light of the lamp, I could see Belinda. One of her hands held a sack with a loaf of bread sticking out of the top; her other hand was just below her throat, and her eyes were wide and peering at me. "What are you doing sitting in the dark? Are you all right?"

"Just arrived home," I said, rising from the chair. Every muscle in my back and legs ached. "I went to your house first, but no one answered."

"I gave the servants the evening off. We must have just missed you. Harry had to stop at the hospital first." Belinda came toward me. "Is it finished?"

I nodded. I didn't have it in me to explain everything. Not now. And she understood, for she rested her open hand on my chest and said only, "I'm glad."

Harry came toward me. He looked taller, somehow, though it had only been three weeks.

"Mrs. Gale told me about Colin," he said awkwardly. "I'm very sorry, truly."

"You didn't know him well, did you?" I asked.

Harry hesitated. "I was only with the Doyles for a few days, back when I first arrived in London. Colin was gone a good deal. Busy with work, I expect," he added hastily, as if to excuse him.

I smiled my thanks at his kindness.

"How are Aunt Mary and Elsie?" he asked.

"Grieving, but they'll manage," I said.

"Have you had supper?" Belinda asked, and when I shook my head, she set the sack on the table and removed the loaf of bread. "Harry and I haven't either. I'll make some tea."

"I'll lay the fire," Harry said. "After I put my cases away."

I heard his boots clomping up the wooden stairs, and I followed Belinda into the kitchen. "How did you happen to arrive together?"

"Oh, he stopped at my house first," she said as she set the kettle to boil. "I'd forgotten some things at my sister's, so I asked him to bring them down for me."

"Ah."

She emptied the sack, set it aside, and turned, so she could look me full in the face. "Are you all right, truly?"

"Just tired. And hungry." I swallowed. "The food will do me good."

She wrapped one arm around my shoulder and laid her palm against my cheek. I took her into my arms and kissed her deeply, feeling some of the hard ache of the past two weeks soften.

At last, she broke away, and her eyes, dark and somber, met mine.

"I've been so sad for you about Colin. And so worried," she murmured. "Ever since I heard about Lord Baynes-Hill. His poor wife. It's just wretched, all of it. Do you know who killed him?"

"Houghton did, by his own hand."

"Dear lord." She shivered. "How could a man be so . . . depraved?"

"Fanatical," I said. "With hate. He's had years to let it fester inside him." I remembered what she didn't know and added, "His wife was with child when she died."

Her mouth formed an O.

Together we listened as Harry came down the stairs, opened the coal hod, and scraped out the ash. The mundane sound was surprisingly pleasant to my ear. I kissed her again and drew her close.

Her breath was warm on my cheek. "Now, go talk to him. I'm certain he wants to tell you about it, but he won't unless you ask."

I went in and sat. "How was Edinburgh? Was it worthwhile?"

Harry hung the poker back on its hook before he sank into the chair opposite. He pushed his hair out of his eyes, studying me for a moment as if to assure himself of my interest. "It was astonishing," he said fervently. "The most exciting, marvelous three weeks I've ever had."

"Oh?" I settled back. "What did you do?"

"I was allowed to watch everything," he said, his eyes bright with enthusiasm. "Surgery began each morning at eight o'clock, and I could sit in the amphitheater all day, until they finished at half past six. No one minded at all. There were nine different surgeons who came and went, but there were three that I followed particularly. They were more careful, more studied in their approach, and none of their patients became infected or died afterward. I saw them operate on lungs, hearts, legs, arms—even an appendix."

"That sounds interesting," I said, trying to add enthusiasm into my voice.

"It was *brilliant*. Yesterday, Dr. Finley operated on a woman with boils, here." He tapped the back of his neck. "She'd begun to have tremors and was losing her sight. He removed the boils, and when she woke from the chloroform, her vision was wholly restored, and her tremors were completely gone!"

"That's remarkable," I said. "When does James think you'll be able to attend?"

His excitement diminished. "Eighteen months," he said philosophically. "They don't take students any younger. But Dr. Everett says he'll help me learn as much as I can before I go. And I brought home some of the books they assign in the first year. That's why I needed a second case."

Belinda entered, carrying a tray with some bread and cheese and ham, and three cups of tea.

"Mrs. Gale told me some of what happened," Harry said. "The *Princess Alice* and all. How that League stirred up trouble for the Irish." He tore a piece of bread and buttered it generously. "There was a man at the hospital who refused to be treated by Dr. McWynn because his name is Irish—although it was just stupid because he was born in Liverpool. He was one of the best surgeons there, too." He grimaced. "It made me grateful Father's last name is English, and I was born in Leeds."

Yes, it was probably for the best that his Irish half could remain safely tucked away, at least for the foreseeable future.

Belinda curled herself up in one of the chairs, drawing her shawl closely around her. "Do you think home rule talks will move forward again, now that people understand it wasn't the IRB behind the railway crash or the *Princess Alice*? It would seem the best way to honor Lord Baynes-Hill's legacy."

"Perhaps." I took up the poker and nudged some of the coals toward the center of the fire. "I hope the newspapers do what they can to disseminate the truth."

"Not everyone reads the papers," Harry said. "Besides, they get it wrong sometimes."

"True enough," I acknowledged.

"Will the League of Stewards be shut down?" Belinda asked.

"I doubt it," I said, "as most of the members aren't directly linked to the disasters or the murder of Lord Baynes-Hill."

"That doesn't seem right." Harry frowned. "They only exist to cause trouble."

"It isn't against the law," I said. "But the police will certainly be aware of their movements now, and that's something."

The warm food, the fire, and Harry and Belinda's easy conversation lulled me to tranquility and then to drowsiness. I woke to Belinda's hand on my shoulder. I squinted up at her.

"You should go to bed," she said. "My carriage is here."

I looked around the room. "Where's Harry?"

"Upstairs, just now."

I fumbled my way to standing. "I'll call tomorrow, love, when I'm awake," I said as I helped her into her coat.

She gazed up at me, her mouth curving in a smile. Just knowing she only looks at me with that much love in her eyes slays me nearly every time. With Harry upstairs, I took the opportunity to take her beautiful face in my hands and kiss her goodbye fiercely, for a long moment, hoping she would take from it everything I wished to convey—gratitude, admiration, love—and regret that I was so damned tired that I had nothing left for her tonight. Eventually I let her go, and her face was tender. "Sleep well," she whispered. I nodded, opened the door, escorted her to her carriage, and helped her in. I kept hold of her hand for an extra moment, anticipating the cold feeling when I let her go. I never liked it.

Inside, I started upstairs to my bedroom, my feet heavy. Harry waited on the landing, at the threshold of his bedroom, with the lantern, and I bid him goodnight.

"Will you be going to the Doyles's for tea on Sunday?" he asked.

My hand on the doorknob, I turned. Again, it struck me that he looked taller than when he'd left. But perhaps my memory was of him when he first came, not as he was a few weeks ago. Memory could be deceitful that way.

"I plan to," I replied.

"I'd like to come," he said.

"I'm sure they'd like that. Only, I wouldn't share too many of the details about the surgeries, if I were you," I added. "The boils and all."

His grin flashed and then faded. "You couldn't have kept *me* from going, you know," he said hesitantly. "To Edinburgh."

I frowned, not understanding. "Why would I have wanted to?"

"Well, you wouldn't," he said. "But if you *had* wanted to, you couldn't have. I'd have gone anyway." A strained, apologetic look came over his face. "I was thinking of Colin."

Now I understood. He meant to take some of the blame off my shoulders. "Your aunt Mary said the same, but it's hard not to feel that if I'd only said something different . . ."

"I know, but . . ." He swallowed. "I want you to know you did right by me." His face was earnest. "Taking me in and bringing me to the hospital that first day. I behaved like an ungrateful, sulky brat, and you were still good to me. Better than I deserved."

His gratitude twisted something inside my chest, but I managed a smile. "It's good to have you home, Harry."

I opened the door and realized with surprise that the room lacked its usual chill. The stove was throwing off heat. Harry must have lit this one as well as the one in his own room. I turned back to him. "Thank you."

He nodded. "Good night."

I shut the door, thinking that Harry would be a good doctor someday. He understood what it was to be considerate, to care for people. I should remember to tell him so.

His door closed in a soft echo of my own.

The burning coals cast a golden light, but not so much that I couldn't see outside my window. I peered out in one direction and then the other, down my long street, with gas lamps at regular intervals and half a dozen roads crossing it, one small section in London's large web. I watched a lone carriage roll along the cobbles and around the corner. Across the way were windows, some lit but most darkened. A gray, skirted shadow moved behind a curtain. The glow of a lamp moved from one room to another.

At that moment, I felt myself connected to every denizen in the entire, sprawling city. All of us across London, across England and beyond, striving and managing, losing and learning. The work of life was as varied as grieving a death and sweeping the ash from the hearth, plying a trade and putting on the water for tea, forgiving one's own worst mistakes and remembering to thank someone for a kindness.

From Harry's room came a loud sneeze. *Bless you,* I thought. Another sneeze followed by what sounded like the cutting of a book's pages with a paper knife. Harry would probably read late into the night.

The thought reminded me of McCabe's note, unread in my pocket.

My stomach tightened.

I'll read it tomorrow, I thought as I undressed. I drew on my nightshirt and climbed into bed. The sheets were cool on my skin, although the stove had done its work and warmed the room. I closed my eyes. But a moment later I opened them.

I couldn't sleep until I knew what McCabe had written.

Barefoot, I felt my way downstairs in the dark, slid my hand into my coat pocket, and drew the missive out. Then I climbed the stairs to my room, relit my lamp, and opened it. There were only two lines:

You told me the truth. I owe you. My grandfather told me what happened to your mother.

The paper shook in my hands, and the words blurred and came into focus as I read them once more and then yet again. I shivered, chilled down to my bones, as if I'd been thrown into the Thames in the middle of winter.

Dear God. My breath came in shallow, jagged gasps. *After all this time.*

As the first shock subsided, my mind began to work properly again, and I realized it wasn't impossible that McCabe knew something about her. McCabe's grandfather's reach and influence extended into Whitechapel in the 1860s, and he could have passed anything he knew down to his grandson. But what had my mother been or done that McCabe's grandfather would know of her?

Next came a wave of anger at McCabe for keeping this secret—a secret that mattered terribly to me—for God knows how long.

Fast on the heels of anger came uncertainty. Did I want to know? If my mother was still alive, of course I did. But what if she'd died a gruesome death? I gulped and stared up at my ceiling. There was a crack in it that seemed to have widened of late.

I lay the paper on the washstand and turned down the lamp. I stood again at the window. There were fewer lights in the windows opposite now. Most of them were dark, like mine would appear to anyone looking. Perhaps someone else was awake and troubled and alone.

Whatever McCabe could tell me about my mother could bring me any amount of fresh pain.

I sank down onto the bed and dropped my head into my hands, already feeling a weight gathering in my chest. Lord Baynes-Hill had spoken of regret being a heavy weight. But the thought of my mother brought more than regret. It brought grief and despair that had once nearly broken me.

The thought recalled Ma's words about her own mother. How every grief showed her what she could bear.

I knew what Ma would say if she was here.

I lifted my head and took one deep breath. And then another. *This weight,* I thought. *My pieces.*

These pieces had a heft that did not ever wholly evaporate into the air of everyday life. My despair over the loss of my mother, my grief over the deaths of Pat and Colin, my regret for my ignorance, my shame for my mistakes, my pain over hurting the people I love—these were ugly, rough-edged shards that cut me sometimes when I touched them. But each shard was also a piece of ballast that lodged inside my heart. Lumped together, perhaps they could guard me from steering once more into the rocks and steady me in the face of the next storm.

They were—if nothing else—my own.

My hand crept up to land on my chest, as if the ballast were a physical thing that I could hold in place.

Let me not lose this, I thought, and my plea was as desperate as any I'd ever made. *For I have earned it honestly, and it is mine.*

I had a feeling I would need it soon.

Author's Note

In writing historical mysteries, I often find myself addressing issues that persist in our world today. The first Inspector Corravan mystery, *Down a Dark River*, was inspired by a contemporary article about race, law, and injustice in the United States. In *Under a Veiled Moon*, I explore the anti-Irish sentiment and the persecution experienced by the Irish in London in the 1870s, and distortions and manipulations in the press, which resonate with present-day events.

But as many authors do, I suspect, I have also incorporated some personal concerns. One evening, about halfway through writing this book, as I was still identifying Michael Corravan's personal stakes, my husband and I were talking and reflecting on various mistakes and missteps we've made. With his usual ability to pierce straight to the heart of the matter, he commented wryly, "Sometimes I wonder how we all live with the stupid shit we've done." We are both in our fifties, and perhaps this is a natural time for looking back, evaluating our past actions, and—at times—confronting our regrets. Then, as it sometimes happens, the universe called my attention to this train of thought twice more in the same week, when friends made comments about their own regrets over mistakes they'd made or situations they might have handled better. And I thought, *This is a valid, significant, and compelling concern.* How *do* we all live with our regret? What do we do with it?

And, perhaps more importantly, is there anything it can do for us? These became some of the governing questions in this book.

As with all my other novels, I have taken a true event or aspect of Victorian England for the kernel of my story. I discovered the tragic, true story of the collision on the Thames when I was down the proverbial rabbit hole of research for *Down a Dark River*. As I was researching Michael Corravan's backstory, including the dockyards, Whitechapel, and the Metropolitan Police, I came upon a mention of the *Princess Alice* disaster. Naturally, I googled it and found the fascinating history not only of the disaster itself but also of the aftermath, when navigation laws on the river were amended and newly codified, with implications for the Wapping River Police.

Much as I have described it, the *Princess Alice* disaster occurred on Tuesday, September 3, 1878, and it was a horrifying tragedy. It was ruled an accident, with no sabotage, foul play, or blame cast on the crew of either the paddle steamer (the *Princess Alice*) or the collier (the *Bywell Castle*). In my book, the crimes perpetrated by Houghton and his League are purely my invention. Some of the characters on the ships were real people—for example, Captain Harrison, Captain Grinstead (who went down with the *Princess Alice*), Mr. Boncy, and Mr. Purcell. Other members of the crew are fictional.

While the Edinburgh and Mayfair Theater bombings are invented for this novel, the Clerkenwell Outrage of 1867 was an historical event, during which a bomb set in London by the Irish Republican Brotherhood killed 12 and injured 120. Some historians have called it the first act of modern terrorism. The IRB developed cells in every major city in England and began a steady campaign of violence, in an attempt to gain home rule, in the 1880s. As I depict here, the IRB did have ties to the Fenians in America, who supplied them with guns and dynamite and trained the Irish in their use. My character Timothy Luby is based on the historical figure Thomas Clark Luby (1822–1901), an Irish revolutionary and journalist who was one of the founding members of the Irish Republican Brotherhood in the 1850s.

Fiction and fact blend together elsewhere in the novel as well. As in *Down a Dark River*, Mr. C. E. Howard Vincent is a real, historical person, though all conversations he holds are the work of my imagination. Truncheon pockets were not in existence until 1887, but I moved them a decade earlier because they're so convenient for Corravan. (Until 1887, truncheons were carried using a spring-loaded mechanism on the belt.) Although tea was the more common beverage, Londoners did drink coffee, as Corravan does. The League of Stewards is my invention; "splendid isolation," however, was a real policy that evolved in the 1820s and was resuscitated periodically. I have altered some of the specifics of the Sittingbourne crash, although it did occur on the date noted, just prior to the *Princess Alice* disaster. The explosion at the Prince of Wales mine in Abercarn occurred on September 11, 1878, killing 268 men and boys and injuring countless others. Surgeons were routinely asked to perform examinations of dead bodies, and craniotomies were performed in the 1870s. When the police divisions were originally formed, there were seventeen divisions (A through S, minus a few letters). Later, more divisions were added, and in 1869 they were reorganized into districts. District 1 comprised G, H, K, and N (Finsbury, Whitechapel, Stepney, and Islington) and, significantly, the Thames River Police. Although it is true that there were hundreds of newspapers in London, only a few I mention here are real; many are not.

For those interested in true history, I want to share some of the resources I consulted, which provided the historical basis for much of this novel. All errors are my own. These include Haia Shpayer-Makov's essential and brilliant book *The Ascent of the Detective: Police Sleuths in Victorian and Edwardian England*; Joan Lock, *The Princess Alice Disaster*; Simon Webb, *Dynamite, Treason & Plot: Terrorism in Victorian and Edwardian England*; Olivia Campbell, *Women in White Coats: How the First Women Doctors Changed the World of Medicine*; Gilda O'Neill, *The Good Old Days: Crime, Murder and Mayhem in Victorian London*, full of primary source material from the *Times* and other publications; "The Medical Evidence of Crime," *Cornhill* 7 (March 1863): 338–318; Henry Mayhew, *London Labour and the London Poor*; Peter Ackroyd, *Thames: The Biography*; Lara Maiklem, *Mudlark: In Search of London's Past Along the River Thames*; Charles Dickens, "Down with the Tide," *Household Words*, 1853; Brian McDonald, *Gangs of London* and *Alice Diamond and the Forty Elephants*; *The Official Encyclopedia of Scotland Yard*, edited by Martin Fido and Keith Skinner; and Judith R.

Walkowitz, *City of Dreadful Delight: Narratives of Sexual Danger in Late-Victorian London* and *Prostitution and Victorian Society: Women, Class and the State.*

My profound thanks to Melissa Rechter, Madeline Rathle, and the entire team at Crooked Lane Books, who loved Michael Corravan and helped me shape this series. Special thanks to Melanie Sun for two spectacular book covers, and to Martin Biro for his immensely helpful editing of both this book and *Down a Dark River*. Thanks to Priyanka Krishnan, my first editor, who took a risk on a new author, and profound gratitude to Josh Getzler and everyone at HG Literary for their unflagging support over the years.

One of the (largely) unsung rewards of being an author is meeting people from all over the world who love books the way I do. My gratitude overflows toward all those who responded warmly to the publication of my previous books, *A Lady in the Smoke*, *A Dangerous Duet*, *A Trace of Deceit*, and *Down a Dark River*. These include innumerable readers, authors (mystery and otherwise), publishers, booksellers, book clubs, librarians, bloggers, bookstagrammers, reviewers, conference organizers and attendees, and members of professional groups, including Mystery Writers of America and Sisters in Crime. A special thanks to Barbara Peters and her entire staff at the Poisoned Pen Bookstore in Old Town Scottsdale, which I think of as my literary home. Thanks also to Phillip Payne and KT Tierney at Anticus Gallery for their warm, constant support. Gratitude to all those who have graciously facilitated signings, podcasts, book tours, blogposts, book clubs, and events in support of *Down a Dark River*, especially Fred Andersen, Natalie Atri, Amy Bruno, Jules Catania, Maria Ceferatti, Peggy Chamberlain, Donna Cleinman, Eva Eldridge, Amanda Goosen, G. P. Gottlieb, Nancy Guggedahl, Nancy Gutfreund, Julie Hennrikus, John Hoda, Nicolette Lemmon, Vanessa Lillie, Jess Montgomery, Libby Patterson, Phyllis Payne, Rebel Rice, Dolores Salisz, Lori Stipp, Susan Van Kirk, and Marshal Zeringue, and to the amazing Tucson Festival of Books. Thanks to all the bloggers who have welcomed me, with special thanks to Dayna Linton, Melissa Makarewicz, and Cindy L. Spear for championing my books. Thanks also to my fellow authors who have supported this new series, especially Shannon Baker, Susanna Calkins, Donis

Casey, Anna Lee Huber, Susan Elia MacNeal, Laura Joh Rowland, Charles Todd, and Gabriel Valjan.

As with all my books, they start as one thing and shift shape, depending in great part on the feedback from my beta readers and experts I consult along the way. A special thanks to all who read drafts of this book: Kate Fink Cheeseman, Mame Cudd, Julianne Douglas (Sister Witch no. 1), Mariah Fredericks (Sister Witch no. 2), Edwin Hill, Syrie James, Barry Milligan, Tina Miles, Anne Morgan, and Stefanie Pintoff. A special thanks to my web designer, Amanda Stefansson, for creating a beautiful website and helping me navigate it. A heartfelt thanks to my sisters, Kristin Griffin and Jennifer Lootens; my mother, Dottie Lootens; and my mother-in-law, Nancy Odden, for their loving support.

Lastly, as always, my deepest gratitude to my husband, George; my daughter and always first reader, Julia; my son, Kyle; and my aged beagle-muse, Rosy, who naps in my office chair. You are the ebb tide under my lighter.

READING GROUP QUESTIONS

1. The collision of the wooden passenger steamer the *Princess Alice* with the steel-hulled coal carrier the *Bywell Castle* could be seen as a metaphor for two different aspects or ways of life that coexisted, sometimes uneasily, in Victorian London—pleasure versus work, an agrarian economy versus an industrial one, and the crowds of people on the steamship deck versus the faceless prow. How do you see these and other various dualities playing out in the novel?

2. By the mid–1800s, London was a bustling, industrialized city. One of the fears people had about modernity was that individuals would become anonymous cogs in the wheel. The passengers on the *Princess Alice* are anonymous because there is no manifest, and the corpses pulled out of the Thames have no names until they are claimed by family members. Similarly, the dead man on the stairs is anonymous until Corravan and Stiles discover his identity. Aside from the practical concerns, does the act of recovering names have symbolic meaning within the larger context of the novel?

3. As in *Down a Dark River*, the newspapers have a significant role in this story. In the 1720s, there were only twelve London newspapers and twenty-four provincial ones. In the early 1800s, there were fifty-two London papers and a hundred elsewhere. In 1846, when Charles Dickens became editor of the *Daily News*, there were 355 papers in London. By 1870, when he died, there were nearly a thousand papers. This was due in part to the removal of

a tax on newspapers (in the 1850s) and in part to rising literacy rates. How do the newspapers function in this novel? What role do they play with respect to the public and to the police? Do you see any similarities with situations in the media today?

4. As a financially independent woman and an author, Belinda Gale is an outlier for her time, although she takes her place in a tradition of women authors extending back to Aphra Behn in the 1600s. Belinda has a significant personal life aside from Corravan, with family and friends, her writing, travel, and social commitments. What traits do you see in her that come into play in her relationship with him? Where do you see her challenging Corravan, and how does that help or hinder him?

5. The letter that Tom Flynn quotes in Chapter 6 was in fact written by Benjamin Disraeli under a pseudonym. Here is a more complete passage from it:

> The Irish hate our order, our civilization, our enterprising industry, our pure religion. This wild, reckless, indolent, uncertain, and superstitious race have no sympathy with the English character. Their ideal of human felicity is an alternation of clannish broils and coarse idolatry. Their history describes an unbroken circle of bigotry and blood.

Were you aware that there was such virulent anti-Irish sentiment in England? In what ways does racism today draw on similar tropes and misinformation?

6. Readers are introduced to Harry Lish, in *Down a Dark River*, as a young man who has come to London to find a place to live after his father dies. He doesn't appear as frequently in *Under a Veiled Moon*, but he has found his place as an apprentice to Dr. James Everett, with aspirations to study medicine. For readers of *Down a Dark River*, how has Harry grown and changed? In this book, what similarities and/or differences are revealed in the early scene between Harry and Corravan that enable Harry to reassure Corravan in the final chapter, in a way that Corravan needs to hear? Do you see Harry, Colin, and Corravan as foils for each other? Why or why not?

7. At the end of the novel, Corravan is told that he may be able to find out what happened to his mother, who vanished when he was young. In some ways, her vanishing with no explanation has shaped his psyche; for example, in *Down a Dark River*, he admits that "missing people claw at him worse than murdered ones." But her vanishing is not the sole defining event in his life. His years with the Doyles presented an alternative to a relationship that ended in uncertainty and abandonment. How do the scenes with Elsie and Ma Doyle and even Colin reflect that? Do you have early experiences that offer two or more models for the ways families function or that provide a variety of beliefs or ways of behaving that conflict?

8. In the second novel in my previous series, *A Trace of Deceit* (2019), my heroine, Annabel Rowe, delves into her brother's history and realizes that perhaps all her memories from their shared childhood carry a trace of deceit in them; memory is by its very nature problematic and flawed and incomplete. Corravan's memory of his time with the Doyle family is similarly imperfect. Why does he not remember young Colin the way Elsie describes him, until she reminds him? Does he have some emotional stakes in not remembering, or are his memories simply limited by what he understood at age nineteen? How do our memories change as we grow and find new ways to interpret past events?

9. The second epigraph for this novel is a quote from a novel by Disraeli: "Youth is a blunder; manhood a struggle; old age a regret." Corravan isn't "old," but at the end of the novel, Corravan comes to the realization that while regret might bring shame, it can also be of some use. Indeed, our memories, heavy with regret, might be a powerful guide. Do you agree?

10. In this novel, Corravan and the reader "read" the newspapers simultaneously and discover the mix of truth and falsehood. Does that make you, the reader, feel more sympathetic with Corravan, as he tries to solve the case? Where in the novel do you feel most sympathetic? Least sympathetic?